The Flower Bed

First Published in 2024 by Echo Books

Echo Books is an imprint of Superscript Publishing Pty Ltd
ABN 76 644 812 395

Registered Office: PO Box 669, Woodend, Victoria, 3442

www.echobooks.com.au

Copyright © Jon Michael Springer

National Library of Australia Cataloguing-in-Publication entry.

Creator: Jon Michael Springer, author.

Title: The Flower Bed

ISBN: 978-1-922603-29-6 (paperback)

A catalogue record for this
book is available from the
National Library of Australia

Book and cover design by Andrew Davies.
Cover image: Shutterstock
Title page: Original artwork, 'An Encircled Life' by Emilie Springer

MICHAEL SPRINGER

The Flower Bed

PART 1

"Flowers"

CHAPTER 1

The afternoon sun lit up the fields, and a soft haze rose from the grass as the light beams rolled gently down the hill, illuminating the landscape in a soft, inviting, and comforting haze as light and land peacefully embraced one another. Gazing into the distance through this classical waltz of the sun and land, the splendour of the fields is abruptly interrupted by the dense forest, much darker in appearance than the fields at that time of day, but even so there is enough soft light falling between the timbers of the trees to reveal it too posed no harm to the body and mind. Although the light in the forest was faint it is nevertheless bristling with the sounds of wildlife happily singing in the forest woodlands. These sounds seemed to float in the air, creating a cacophony within that landscape of open fields and forest, a symphony that only nature could play in such a luxurious manner to the senses. The grass of the fields was a beautiful emerald green; more like a carpet woven by the finest Middle Eastern weavers than fields of grass. To the eyes and ears of a newcomer, this setting would only portray some form of heavenly vision and sound. It was as though nature had selected its finest work of the arts to be displayed and played at this comforting country location; this truly was a work of nature that mankind could never replicate.

In the distance of the fields two people were making a slow path through them; their stride was more that of a mournful march than that of any trepidation. One of them is a tall but elderly man in his seventies; his manner of tired walking suggests that he had carried the burden of life on his shoulders for a very long time. Impeccably dressed, one would think the old man may have been too wealthy to allow life to get the better of him, but the cloth on his back could not hide a demeanour that emanated the scars of life. Despite his sartorial elegance, the expression on the man's face depicted a lifetime of mental struggle, an indelible expression that could only be the product of the mind. The old man looked around him, not to gain his bearings; rather, he looked around like an old soul who was coming back to a known location. Walking next to him was a petite girl, who was perhaps five years of age. She had all the bounce in her step of someone who was innocent and had not known the cruel vicissitudes of life. She had lovely blond hair with a slight wave in it which made it seem as though she had spent a good day at a hairdresser's salon when in fact that was just the natural way her hair sat. A pink bow had been tied into her hair to hold the fringe in place, and she was otherwise dressed as though she was going to a party. The little girl's appearance seemed to be inconsistent with just a mere stroll in the field; like the old man, her appearance displayed there was a purpose for interrupting the wonderful display of nature.

As they walked over a slight hill, the little girl gasped. She said out loud enough to otherwise disturb the tranquil sounds of wildlife coming from the forest, "Look, Grandpa, the flowers! The flowers are so pretty!" The old man stopped to take in the sight of the flowers, and what a sight they were. At the end of the field, but before the thick timber of the forest consumed the landscape, under a large oak tree, there was a beautiful bed of flowers consisting of flowering plants of various colours in full bloom and whilst the area where the flowers were growing was not vast, the array of colour seemed to stretch much further when one approached them. The little girl could not contain herself any longer; she broke free of the old man's hand and ran towards the flowers with a spring of excitement that only the innocence of childhood could produce. She was overwhelmed by joy and excitement, and her desire to be amongst those flowers seemed to drive her little legs faster as she ran towards them. As she approached the flowers, she heard the old man's voice boom out across the fields, "Do not run on those flowers, do not stand on those flowers, not one step closer!" Almost as though a gun had gone off, the little girl immediately stopped in her path at the sound of her grandfather's voice, and even though she desperately wished to hold some of those flowers, she did not dare disobey his command. She froze still and stood in her spot metres from the flowers, silently and patiently waiting as he walked up next to her. He held out his hand, and she gently put her hand in his, "Sorry, Grandpa", she said as she looked at the ground, and she realised there was an importance of the moment that should not invite the folly of childhood wonderment. After a short period, she slowly looked up, and to her surprise, she saw a slight tear in the corner of his eye. That tear began to turn into a single torrent rolling down his face, a sight she had never seen before, and her innocence invited her curiosity. "What is wrong, Grandpa?" she asked in a troubled voice. Her words did not interrupt his mind at that instant; he just looked ahead, lost in his deepest thoughts, which otherwise seemed to take over his conscious state.

PART 2

"A Dark World"

CHAPTER 2

The streets of the five districts of Manhattan are always dark and dirty, but from the last month of the fall and into winter, those streets seemed to take on an even gloomier feel. In the back alleyways, garbage overflowed from the bins, even in the more affluent sections of the borough. Although Manhattan was a remarkable metropolis of commerce, entertainment, and culture, it nevertheless hid its sinister side from people who were not otherwise acquainted with its meaner streets. There are two sides to life in those five districts of Manhattan. There is the life of those people who embark upon a journey into the various districts and neighbourhoods of the city every day to work, and not-withstanding the garbage, smog, and traffic, they otherwise remain oblivious to their environment. Then, at night, the glitz and glamour of the nightlife sections of Manhattan seemed to transform the daytime drudgery of working life into a world of hedonism; sights and sounds that seem to reach for the stars. Life never stopped in these commercial and entertainment districts of the borough, and its cycle of life each day and night was almost like a cinema in which the same reel of film kept on turning around from one projector to the next, playing to an empty theatre. There is also an opposite side to that cinema screen; it's the life behind that screen; it's the life of those people to whom the darker precincts of Midtown West in Manhattan may shape their destiny; it is a destiny of despair and fear. Two different worlds seemingly collide during the day and night to bring these people together in Manhattan, but when the sun goes down, it is only those people who bravely live all their lives in this harsh environment of Midtown West who remain. It is a life of concrete, bitumen, garbage, and most importantly, a life that seems to be free of the wonders of nature. Perhaps, just perhaps, an occasional flower may grow in Midtown West; however, chances are that a flower is an incarnation rather than a new life.

It is in this world of Midtown West that a young boy named Louis O'Brien lives, or perhaps better described, survives. At ten years of age, Louis was not only a veteran of these tough streets of Midtown West, but he was also a veteran of life itself. He was a good-looking boy, but if you looked into his eyes, you would see that this good-looking young boy lived in a tormented world.

Louis' father, Joseph, was a hardened portside worker, a man with little tolerance for anything fancy or fine in life. Joseph only believed in two things in life, namely the unspoken fraternity of the wharves of Manhattan and the so-called 'friends' whom he ruled and associated himself with each day. Joseph was brought up in a hardened household of poor Irish Catholic wharf workers. For Joseph, identifying as Catholic had nothing to do with spiritual belief; it was just a means to band together with his peers from Midtown West, an opportunity to use religion as an excuse to inflict harm on Protestants, or anyone else who crossed his path. Joseph was a thug, a bully, and a bad seed who did not care about anything else other than alcohol and bad women. Louis' mother had left the family a long time ago, when Louis was only two years of age. A woman Joseph referred to as his 'cousin', Mary, apparently lived in their apartment to assist with raising Louis. However, as far as Louis had known since his earliest memories, an older lady across the hall from his apartment named Mavis Fitzgerald or, as Louis knew her, Ms Fitzgerald, had been looking after him, and if it were not for her, he probably would have been left to his own devices to fend for himself at a very young age. Ms Fitzgerald would feed Louis most nights since he could remember, and she would always give him some form of new clothing. Indeed, at Christmas time the only person who ever given Louis any gifts since his earliest memories was Ms Fitzgerald. Ms Fitzgerald was a spinster; accordingly with no children or family of her own she showed an interest in Louis as though he was the child that she should always have had. There was a historical relationship between Louis' estranged mother and Ms Fitzgerald, but she refrained from telling Louis about that connection even though she sometimes felt she should do so. Ms Fitzgerald refrained from telling Louis what she knew about his mother for her safety and Louis'.

Louis had called Mary 'Aunt Mary' from a young age, but nobody, including Mary, had explained to him how they were related. More importantly, Louis detected from an early age that 'Aunt Mary' did not care for him as one would expect a blood relative should care for one of their own. It was a tough life for anyone, let alone a young boy. She hardly displayed the time of day for Louis, and Mary's only focus was to obey what Joseph told her to do. Mary was the cousin of William O'Leary or, as he was known in Midtown West, O'Leary, of one of Joseph's 'union' friends.

When he was six years of age, Mary revealed to Louis for the first time a supposed story about his mother. It was an evening that Louis would never forget. As far as she was aware, Louis' mother was a working-class woman of some beauty who had mistakenly fallen pregnant to Joseph. She told Louis his mother was a young singer and loved all things classical; hence, Louis's name was chosen by her upon his birth. According to Mary, Louis' mother had been singing one night at Joseph's favourite bar when they met. Whether it was true or not, Louis did not know but Mary told him that his mother had too much to drink that night. Louis' young mind did not need to have too much explained to him about how he was conceived, other than Mary telling him that the occurrence of his conception was a mistake that neither parent planned for nor wanted. A mistake! Those words did not sound pleasant to Louis that evening, and they had haunted him ever since. Mary told him that evening people "are who they are" and that his mother was never meant to be a family person. Accordingly, even though she tried hard to be a mother, it became too much for her, and she ran away from the family so that she could sing with a band. Nobody had heard from her since then. Aunt Mary did not explain to Louis why his name, 'Louis', had been chosen and more importantly, the Frankish meaning of that name. It was not until this evening of this discussion that his Aunt Mary told Louis his mother's name; it was Adele. The sound of that name struck a chord in his little heart, and it was a melody like no other he felt before. Louis did not know the meaning of Adele but years later, he would find out through his studies at school that the name in French meant 'noble'. This was a discussion that occupied Louis' mind from that time onwards. He never felt inclined to ask Mary again because, by the tone of her voice, it was apparent she did not like his mother. He could not understand why his mother could not love him enough to stay with him. More importantly, Louis could not understand why his mother did not take him with her. His young heart ached because of these questions and Louis could not turn to his father for comfort. Although Louis was hurt by the fact that his mother had left him, he nevertheless spent every day hoping that one day his mother would come back to him.

Louis had one photo of his mother which Ms Fitzgerald had given to him and neither Joseph nor Mary knew about the existence of the photo. Ms Fitzgerald never told Louis how she came to have in her possession a photo of his mother. He would ask Ms Fitzgerald but Louis could never get a proper response from her; all Ms Fitzgerald would say to Louis was that he should eat his meal, be quiet, and listen to the radio. It wasn't as though Ms Fitzgerald was being rude;

rather Louis seemed to detect that Ms Fitzgerald appeared to be nervous when he asked her this question. "Some things are best not being talked about, and don't, for heaven's sake, tell your father about that photo." Louis would often look at the photo. His mother was classically beautiful but seemed to portray nothing but sorrow in her eyes. Any other photos of her had been destroyed by Joseph.

Joseph's apartment was a large late 19th-century design. The architecture of the building displayed all the wonderful influences of late 19th-century architecture, wood-lined walls, and master plasterer work in the entryway, but the building had been neglected. Joseph's apartment had four bedrooms, a separate drawing room, a separate lounge room, and a dining room. The apartment was more like a large home, but it, too, was neglected. In the late 19th century, this type of large apartment would have been occupied by respectable people due to its large size and finishes. By the early 1970s the area and buildings were considered to represent the downtrodden side of living in Manhattan. Yet the classical design of that apartment seemed to portray that there once was a respectable voice to life that had existed within those walls. Louis' world in Midtown West was a hot pot of hatred and violence. Louis knew that living in this apartment meant something; namely, he was not from the poorest side of life, but the antics of Joseph and Mary suggested they were inclined to be unsettled, nefarious, and even promiscuous. Louis' early evenings were spent in the safe surroundings of Ms Fitzgerald's apartment, eating dinner, and listening to the radio play her songs of the swing era, music such as Glen Miller, before he went back across the hallway to his so-called home where Joseph would usually be entertaining all sorts of unsavoury characters. By the time he was ten years of age Louis had been exposed to Mary as Joseph's lover rather than a relative, and such were the antics that went on within Joseph's apartment. It was against this backdrop of a tough but sheltered life that Louis grew up generally fending for himself during the daytime on the streets of Manhattan.

Louis was enrolled as a student at Midtown West Elementary. Every child at the school came from a marginalised background of some description. The children's views towards each other seemed to mirror the attitudes that they were exposed to at home: white children hating African Americans and Hispanics; African Americans hating whites and Hispanics; Hispanics hated African Americans and whites; nobody in this melting pot of intolerance liked the Asians. Whilst certain words were not allowed to be spoken in the playground, the children nevertheless said words to one another that were indicative of the racial hatred they were being exposed to at home. Bullying at school was common, and it was as though the misery of the children's lives could only be relieved by tormenting each other. Louis could not fit in with any child at school, and he could not stoop to bullying another for the sake of being popular or escaping his misery. More importantly, Louis by the age of ten found himself to be the target of some older bullies. Jose Henriquez and his friends were already a hardened little gang of Hispanic louts. Jose had already been before a juvenile court on several occasions, and his bullying was vicious. Louis could not work out why he was being targeted by Jose, but what he did know was that as each day went by Jose's bullying got worse. Initially, it was just some name-calling, and when Louis did not react to these taunts, Jose interpreted that as being arrogant. The behaviour then escalated into pushing or taking Louis' property. It had now been two months since Jose had started targeting Louis, and there was no end in sight.

To seek respite from the torment of the playground Louis would either stay in his classroom to read or he would seek out books in the school library. The school library did not hold a vast catalogue of books. However, there were enough books there that after two months, Louis had still not read even a quarter of the collection. Louis read fiction and educational books. He would read anything so that he could avoid the playground and Jose. Louis was more intelligent than the other students in his grade, and by the age of 10, he was, in fact, at the top of the academic stream for the school. He would bring home his school reports recording his academic prowess, but his father never had any interest whatsoever in his son's grades, nor did he ever bother looking at the piece of paper. Since he commenced school, it was only Ms Fitzgerald who took any interest in his school grades, and she was the only person with whom Louis could find the comfort of acknowledging his academic success. When he was about eight years of age, Louis had brought home a report card which his father had naturally displayed no interest in, but as usual, Ms Fitzgerald always displayed nothing but devoted pride in the young boy's academic achievements. On this occasion, his eight-year-old mind was just as inquisitive as it was delighted because he had seen recorded on the top left corner of his report the typed words 'Next of Kin', which were then followed by a handwritten notation of the words 'private', and although those typed and handwritten words had appeared on his previous report cards, his young mind now felt inclined to examine every detail of this document. The conversation he had with the old woman that afternoon would be forever etched thereafter in his young mind. The merriment of celebrating his straight 'A' marks was followed by a more sober moment of contemplation, and after a noticeable change in his demeanour, he asked the question: "What does next of kin mean? And why does it say private next to it?" Ms Fitzgerald felt a lead weight drop in her heart; she did not know what to say. The pregnant pause was like an eternity as she searched for an explanation. "Well, let me see, you know what the word relative means?" He nodded his head, and because of the word relative, there was a glimmer of hope in his heart that the 'next of kin' may be his mother. "Of course you do. So, a next of kin can be a person like a relative." She hoped the inquisition would conclude on that note, but his young mind was firing like the engine of a Corvette. "Yes, but who is it? And why does it say private?" Ms Fitzgerald then decided it was best she lied to the boy because she knew that person did not want their identity to be revealed. "It is me, Louis." The lie disappointed the young boy, not because Ms Fitzgerald said she was the next of kin, it disappointed him because he hoped she would say it was his mother. One last question, as the old woman had not entirely satisfied his curiosity: "Why does it say private?" Although she did not display it on her face, she nevertheless felt another lead weight drop in her heart as the young boy's earnest eyes looked into hers. "Louis, oh, ah, look I don't know why the word private is written there, but one thing is certain, I do not want you telling your father. Please, will you promise me you won't tell him?" Her explanation had shot down a glimmer of hope in his heart about his mother; however, Ms Fitzgerald's wishes must be obeyed. Louis nodded his head, and he would never ask her again about his 'next of kin'. Later that night, Ms Fitzgerald penned a letter; her opening words after the customary paragraph of greetings illuminated the importance of the subject matter. "He asked me today about his next of kin, and I did not say anything other than it was me, but his little eyes displayed such a look of disappointment I felt it was necessary to write you." While she continued writing the letter, little did she realise Louis was lying on his bed in Joseph's apartment, pondering what he had been told that afternoon as he looked at the ceiling and wondered why his world felt so empty.

Life in Midtown West continued to grind onwards. Towards the end of his fifth year of elementary school, Louis managed to find a job, but not because of his deliberate endeavour to find work. After school each day, Louis would do a few hours of work for a local grocer delivering people's grocery orders to their homes. The grocery store was owned by an elderly Italian American, Pietro Ricci, or Peter as the Irish called him. Peter had emigrated from Italy after World War 2 when he was already in his mid-forties. Peter never married, nor did he have any family in America. Despite trying to keep to himself, Joseph and the other thugs of Midtown West would lean on Peter for favours, including the current favour of Louis delivering groceries for an hour or two after school. Despite Peter telling Joseph that Louis was too young to walk the streets Joseph demanded that Peter agree to take Louis on. Joseph's response displayed his feelings about Louis. "It will keep him out of my apartment, and we can do with the extra money". Peter reluctantly agreed. Louis' pay was 50 cents per hour, a rate which had been set by Joseph rather than Peter. That money would have to be handed over to Joseph by Louis. Louis never knew what happened to the money, but considering he seemed to always eat dinner at Ms Fitzgerald's apartment it appeared it was not spent by Joseph on food. As far as Louis could comprehend, it was always a struggle to put enough food on the table for him in Joseph's apartment. Joseph on the other hand always seemed to have plenty to eat, and, for that matter, to drink. Whatever money was handed over by Louis, Joseph would spend on alcohol, as well as a never-ending parade of unknown women who would come to the apartment after Louis was ordered to bed by Joseph. Louis could hear the sounds of the strange women's voices, and even to his innocent ears, the sounds these women would make and the words that came from their foul mouths suggested they were being paid by Joseph for his pleasure. What concerned Louis more was that most of the time, Aunt Mary was present with Joseph and these women. Louis wished for a normal, stable, and happy life but in return, he would be exposed on a nightly basis to a den of iniquity.

So, by the evening of 15 November 1971, when Louis was ten years of age he was a hardened little soul living in the harsh landscape of Manhattan. He had finished work at the grocery store later than usual that evening, and Peter gave him an extra quarter for his efforts. A coin was useful for Louis, as he could hide it in his shoe from Joseph as long as the one-dollar note was produced for him. As he walked along the footpath on the way home that winter evening, Louis thought about his mother. He imagined her singing with a band and everyone adoring each word that came out of her mouth. He did not notice the shadows that were creeping up behind him as he walked along the footpath one block away from the supposed safety of Joseph's home. As Louis went to walk around the corner into his street, he felt a sharp blow across the top of his head. The pain was immense, and he immediately fell to the ground, clutching his head in pain. Tears rolled down his cheeks as Louis lay on the ground, and as he looked through those tears, he could see Jose and his gang standing over him. Then the verbal taunts began to fly from Jose's mouth, like daggers, and the words entered Louis' young ears. "Hey fag, we've been watching you. Do you fuckin' think you can walk these streets and not hand your dough over to us, fag?" Louis clutched his pocket. "It's mine; I earned it". With those words being spoken, one of the other members of Jose's gang, Julian, kicked Louis in the stomach like he was kicking a football. "Shut up, fag, and give us your money." Julian's rough Hispanic accent and kick were not persuasive enough for Louis to give up his hard-earned money. "No." Without delay, Jose's fist launched itself into Louis' face while he was still on the ground, the force of his fist smashing the other side of Louis' little head against the pavement. The pain was now immense, and Louis cried in agony. All his tormentors just stood back and laughed. Jose maintained the verbal torment. "Look at the little fag cry, cry like a girl." Louis was now humiliated to such an extent that he reached into his pocket and pulled out the $1.00 bill. Jose snatched it from his hand, and he continued humiliating Louis. "Good, you're learning quickly, little fag. Tomorrow, bring the money to me so that I do not have to chase after you". The gang of boys then left, leaving Louis in a bruised and bloody mess on the ground.

CHAPTER 3

After the violent attack, Louis walked down his street in tears, and he was still holding his sore belly in one hand as he opened the front door to the small lobby of the building he lived in. He walked up the stairs, still crying from his ordeal, and the ignominy of the mugging exceeded the physical pain. Louis opened the door to Joseph's apartment, and his father stood there before him. Joseph stared the boy in the eyes in an unsympathetic and uncompromising manner. "Where is the money, boy?" The words were spoken in a slow, deliberate, and threatening manner. Through his tears, Louis tried to explain to his father the mugging and theft that he had experienced only moments beforehand. He may as well have told his father he was a stuffed Irish pig as the thug of a man punched the young boy in the jaw, knocking him out almost immediately. Mary screamed in the background, not that she wanted to in any way dare to assist Louis or further enrage Joseph. No, Mary screamed because Joseph becoming violent was a startling sight for any person to witness, and she had witnessed enough of his violence to know when he was in that mood he could hurt, indeed even kill, any person. Joseph walked back into the apartment, grabbing Mary by the arm as he slammed the front door behind him. The boy had fallen to the floor outside of the apartment, and that is where his father wanted him to stay. Upon hearing the door to Joseph's apartment slamming, Ms Fitzgerald came racing out of her apartment. In front of her, she saw Louis lying knocked out on the hallway floor. "How can any person possibly subject such an angel to hell?!" She had mumbled her words because she was too afraid of Joseph.

Ms Fitzgerald tapped Louis on the cheek a few times and within about a minute, he was fully awake, groggy but awake. She helped Louis to his feet and took him into her apartment for a meal as well as some medical attention to his swelling jaw. While treating his sore jaw, Ms Fitzgerald finally lost control of her tongue and she spoke freely. "You cannot let him do that to you, boy, you are much better than that, as was your mother." Louis' ears pricked up at the sound of Ms Fitzgerald mentioning his mother. "What about my mother?" Realising she had revealed more than she should have, Ms Fitzgerald looked away as she could not discuss anything more with Louis about his mother for fear of her safety and his. Instead, Ms Fitzgerald very quickly changed the topic and pointed toward the kitchen table. "Come over here; I have cooked your favourite stew for you tonight." Even eating the gruel-like consistency of an Irish stew was too painful for his jaw, but it was Louis' first proper meal for the day, so he persisted. After dinner, they listened to some Jack Benny records. At about 11.00pm, Louis left Ms Fitzgerald's apartment and quietly opened the door to his father's apartment. As he crept down the hallway, he could hear the sound of Mary's voice coming from Joseph's bedroom; the door to the bedroom was ajar, and the sound appeared to be as though she was in pain as she was groaning and moaning. Louis did not stop to listen. He crept into his bedroom, quietly shut the door, and wondered to himself what was happening in his father's bedroom. Louis' young mind was not sophisticated enough to realise the sound of Mary's voice moaning was a contrived sound of pleasure, not pain. Louis took off his right shoe first and felt inside it. To his relief, the quarter Peter had given him was still inside his shoe, hidden under the inner sole where he had placed it earlier that evening. Louis placed the coin inside a rip in the side of his mattress. He decided that from here-on-in any additional money which he ever earned or found would be hidden away from Joseph. Louis lay on his bed, thinking about the treatment he had encountered that day, and a tear developed in the corner of his left eye. Before the tear could fall down his cheek Louis was asleep. Hopefully, his subconscious would be released from the torment of this day.

The next morning, Louis woke up in his bed at approximately 7.00am, his little jaw was sore as he sat up. To Louis' immense surprise, Joseph sat at the end of his bed. He did not know how long his father had been sitting there. Joseph's eyes displayed not one shred of compassion or sympathy for the boy. Louis was initially fearful that Joseph may have found the hidden quarter in the mattress, but Joseph's first words dispelled that fear. "I never wanted you when you were born, and I don't want you now. What use are you to anyone if you cannot even bring home a dollar? Beaten up by a Guinea? You should be ashamed of yourself." There was no sign of remorse in his voice or demeanour for striking the boy the previous evening; rather, the tone of Joseph's voice echoed tones of disappointment with a son he did not love. Joseph got up off the end of the bed and left the room to the sound of the telephone beginning to ring down the hall. Louis heard his father answer the telephone with a sharp tone of "what", "where", and "I'll be there" echoing down the hallway, a succession of words spoken with an increasingly ruthless intent. Like on so many prior occasions his father did not trouble himself with saying goodbye when he subsequently walked out of the apartment shortly after the telephone conversation; instead, there was just the echo of the front door slamming behind him after Joseph stormed out of the apartment. Louis remained in bed, his young mind a toxic mix of hatred for his father but, at the same time, living in fear of him. About a quarter of an hour later, he heard the telephone ring again, and this time Mary was speaking to the caller. He heard his name mentioned. After Mary hung up the telephone Louis remained in his room, contemplating his life; his little heart was wilting from Joseph's harsh words, just like a tiny flower wilts from the sun's harsh rays. It was now 7.00am, and school would start in two hours. Then, a moment of slight hope entered his mind; at least the hidden quarter appeared to be undiscovered because if it had his father would not have spoken to him; instead, he would still be beating him. It was on this glimmer of delight he then proceeded to get up out of bed, put on his school clothes, and face the day. Nevertheless, in that apartment, delight was an ephemeral emotion. To add to his misery, when Louis came out of his room hoping that he might find some breakfast in the kitchen, he instead found Mary. Her eyes narrowed when she saw him, and her subsequent words spoken in a passive-aggressive manner shattered his slightly upbeat mood. "Do not ever make your father upset like again." She stared into his eyes, then she turned her disapproving gaze away from him to stare out the kitchen window as though Louis no longer existed. He was intrigued by her comment. "How did I upset him?" he thought to himself. However, he did not say anything back to Mary because he knew she was likely to tell his father, and this would result in his father beating him again. Louis found some stale bread in the fridge, and he made himself a peanut butter sandwich for breakfast, which he ate at the kitchen table in silence while Mary smoked a never-ending chain of cigarettes and slurped on her coffee. He then excused himself from the kitchen table, picked up his schoolbag from the floor of his bedroom, and proceeded to run towards the front door of the apartment. Even though his childhood tormentor waited for him at school, that environment seemed to be more welcoming for Louis than his home environment. He opened the front door to leave, but standing in his way was Joseph. "Where do you think you're going?" he said in his usual brutal manner as he grabbed his son by the shirt collar. Louis screamed in fright, which caused the door to Ms Fitzgerald's apartment to open slightly, revealing her inquisitive eye. Joseph glared back at her. "What do you want!" Ms Fitzgerald's door closed as quickly as it opened, and Joseph proceeded to drag the boy down the stairs and out of the building; he continued to do so for what seemed like an eternity as he frog-marched his son down the maze of alleyways that morning, parting his way through an occasional passerby looking stunned to see a young boy, bag on shoulder, being marched down an alleyway in this manner. Eventually, Louis was dragged to an abandoned building a few blocks away from his apartment building, and Joseph took him into a room where four men who appeared to be acquainted with his father stood in a line like they were waiting for them both. Their faces bore the same brutal and harsh looks as those of his father, and as he was dragged into the room, the men separated, revealing the horrifying sight of a dead man lying on the floor; blood which had been previously oozing from a substantial wound to his head was now congealing on the floor next to his head, and a blood-stained iron bar was also on the floor not too far away from the dead man's body. The dead man's head must have been struck on many occasions because his skull looked like it had caved in. The dead man was a former member of Joseph's gang at the wharves, and he had gone missing after stealing some of the gang's money earned from their dirty deeds. He had a name, Bill, and it was ironic stealing some dollar 'bills' would lead to his untimely demise. Louis recognised one of the men as O'Leary, who was Aunt Mary's cousin, and he had blood all over the front of his shirt. Louis did not know why it had happened nor did the young boy know why he had been dragged by his father to this place to witness this gruesome sight. "Meet Bill. He stole money from us. This is what happens to people who don't pay me the money I am owed!" His father's words were spat out in a fit of hostile rage. Louis' heart froze; not just from the fear he was experiencing because of his father, but also because he had never seen a dead body before, let alone a body that displayed the head had been bludgeoned open. His father dragged him so that their eyes were only inches apart. "Get the fuck out of here, and don't tell anyone about this because I will do the same thing to you. Now, get to school." With those words, he was pushed to the door, and somehow Louis managed to find his way to school. The rest of the day seemed like a blur; he managed to do schoolwork, but his mind was heavily overflowing with the sight of that dead body. Then, just before the school bell rang his mind had thoughts he had not experienced before as it dawned upon him that one day he would die. This was a different fear, a different terror, and a different world his mind now lived in. The sight of that dead man and this new fear seemed to chill his mind as he went to sleep that night. His mind was preoccupied again that next day at school about death, but then its morbid preoccupation with the topic was broken by the immediate existential threat confronting him as he walked out of the school gate; there was Jose and his gang waiting for him and he was subjected to another beating before making his way to Peter's store. Peter noticed the injuries on Louis' face, but he did not ask the boy how it happened, as asking questions could only lead to trouble in Midtown West.

That evening, when Louis returned home from working at the grocery store his father was drinking alcohol with a group of men in the apartment. Louis had carefully made his way home, keeping to the shadows so that Jose and his gang would not find him again. The images of the dead man were still in Louis' mind, as was the new tormentor called mortality, but these demons of the boy's mind became insignificant to Louis' paranoia about Jose and his gang mugging him again. When he entered the apartment, he could hear the drunken voice of his father, along with the intoxicated voices of other men. When Louis entered the shabby dining room he saw five men sitting at the table with rough cups in front of them as well as at least four empty bourbon bottles on the table, a clear sign there would not be any dinner for him that night. O'Leary was sitting to Joseph's right at the table, and his narrow eyes had not as yet fixed themselves upon the boy. Sitting to Joseph's left appeared to be an older man with a wiry frame but undoubtedly a villain's heart. Louis did not recognise the other two men as he cautiously approached the dining table. He placed the one dollar bill on the dining table next to his father's hand, and he now attracted the attention of the men seated at the table. Joseph glared at him, and the other men's eyes turned his way, which sent a cold shiver down his spine. It was quite apparent to him they had eaten food, as there were some bare scraps on the table. Joseph was very drunk, and the sight of Louis seemed to enrage him in his drunken state. "Ah, the little shit is home! The little shit who gets beaten up by a Guinea lads!" The group of men all laughed out loud in unison. Mary giggled under her breath, which attracted Louis' attention to her presence and he turned to see her still giggling and shaking her head at him as she did so. He had not noticed Mary when he entered that room as she was sitting in a dirty rocking chair in the far back corner; she was allowed in the room but she was not allowed to sit at the table, such was the vile misogyny that accompanied the men's villainous natures. Louis stopped dead in his tracks as fear, and the ignominy of being shamed by his father took over his heart and his mind. With that laughter now tailing off, Joseph picked up a plate that contained the bare remains of one of the group's meals. He then stood up, pulled out his penis from his pants, and started urinating on the plate. "There you go, my little lad. All the nutrients a growing lad needs." The rest of the gang broke out laughing again, including Mary on top note, who was perched further back into the rocking chair and she resembled a parrot as her coarse mouth shrieked out laughter towards the ceiling. Indeed, on this occasion, Mary's laugh rang out louder than anybody else's laugh. Louis could not and did not take his so-called plate of food, and it was too late for him to ask Ms Fitzgerald for dinner. He went to his bedroom; he was hungry, depressed, and traumatised. Louis turned on the old secondhand radio Ms Fitzgerald had given to him as a Christmas present the previous year, and he listened to his favourite songs as he did his school homework on his bed; his bed was the place where he mainly did so because even a desk was too much generosity for his father to extend his way. As he listened to the music while completing his schoolwork, Louis began to cry as he could not understand why his father treated him this manner, why he had been exposed to the brutality and horror of Bill's lifeless body, an image which was prominent in his mind again after seeing O'Leary at the dining room table. Eventually, he cried himself to sleep, but the pain in his heart did not go away. The last thought that went through his young mind before he fell asleep loomed as an ominous warning for his future. "One day, I will be the richest person on earth; one day, I will be free." Just like the process of nature of a stigma being pollinated from the anther within the same flower, the young boy's final wish that night was perhaps too much like his father's primitive greed.

The next morning, Louis had arrived early at school to avoid Jose, and he was greeted outside of his usual classroom by another member of the teaching faculty named Mrs Washington and the school principal, Mr Denning. Delores Washington was a woman of African American background, and she had lived through the horrible years of segregation and poverty in the southern states of America. Notwithstanding the abject poverty she grew up in, she had managed to obtain a scholarship as a mature-age student to study science at the Georgia Institute of Technology in the early 1960s. After receiving her undergraduate degree from Georgia Tech, Delores Washington did not see many career opportunities available to her as a scientist, so she instead decided to pursue a career in teaching. She was accepted into the scholarship program at the University of Buffalo to study teaching. Her graduation from the University of Buffalo led to her securing a teaching role at Midtown West Elementary in 1967.

She was a devoted educator for the less privileged children of Midtown West, and because of her academic achievements to overcome the marginalisation in her early life Mrs Washington was of the firm belief that education could change an underprivileged child's life, and that remained her ethos to the present day. The school principal, Howard Denning, became an elementary school teacher after serving with the American Army as a private towards the end of World War 2. He was spared being exposed to actual conflict by the dropping of Little Boy on Hiroshima, and he decided the best way he could use his good fortune to avoid such conflict during that war was to teach at elementary school. He had worked his way up through the education system in New York State during the late 1950s, and he was appointed to the role of the principal of Louis' school by the time John Fitzgerald Kennedy was sworn in as President of the United States. Mr Denning usually displayed all the signs of dissatisfaction with teaching, and he did not possess Mrs Washington's devotion to his career. These two different lives and different commitments would play pivotal roles in Louis' young life. As Louis walked towards Mrs Washington and Mr Denning, he noticed they both displayed a demeanour of pride. "Am I in trouble?" His question emanated from Louis' own marginalised life. "Far from it, Louis, I, we, are most proud to speak to you today." Mr Denning's words were a relief, but Louis still stood there nervously before Mrs Washington and Mr Denning. "Yes, Louis we are very proud of you at this school. Based on your grade point average, you will be placed into a special learning group to be taught by Mrs Washington. The purpose of this special class is to ensure the best intermediate students have every opportunity to be the best junior high and high school students. With your entry to this class, you can access scholarships to better high schools and, eventually, universities. Yes, Louis, for all we know, you may end up being a Harvard or other Ivy League graduate. We are all very proud of you, Louis, very proud indeed. No students from this school have ever ended up studying at those Ivy League universities; perhaps you will be the first!" With those words being spoken, it was as though Mr Denning's role in this unexpected turn of events for Louis' academic life had ended for the day, so he smiled at Louis and then he left with an air of pride about him delivering this news. Louis turned to face Mrs Washington, and she, too, was exuding pride in him. She had been appointed to this teaching role after the summer break of 1971, and her appointment to teach this class was a promotion for her. Louis did not display a sense of pride about this news. Mrs Washington immediately detected this problem within Louis, as he appeared to her to be somewhat subdued and, to a worrying degree, displaying the warning signs of perhaps being abused. She looked him in the eye. "Are you okay, Louis?" Louis so desperately wanted to scream out his despair and reveal all his pain and suffering. However, Aunt Mary had always impressed upon Louis the importance of not revealing to anyone a person's personal life, an indoctrination to hide from the world the cruel existence of his life. Louis shook his head, and then Mrs Washington asked him to follow her to his 'new classroom'. This news was an unexpected turn of events in what was otherwise his morose existence. It was hard for him to feel too excited about this good fortune in his academic life, as the torment in his home life was too entrenched in his psyche. The first bell rang to alert the other children that school starts at 8.30am as Louis arrived with Mrs Washington at his new classroom. There were only ten other students in the class, as it was a Socrates-style experiment of focused education. For Louis, it was a surreal day that had dispelled from his mind for the present moment the torment he had been exposed to two days ago. Perhaps this young shoot might grow from his uncertain root to one day blossom in the sun after all?

Later that same day, the school bell rang at 3.00pm to notify the students and staff that it was the end of the school day. The doors of the classrooms exploded, with children seeking to go back to their other lives of growing up on the streets of this neighbourhood and the reaction to the end-of-day school bell was not different in Louis' new classroom environment. However, Louis waited, and he took his time as he wanted to make sure Jose and his friends were far away from the school. He had managed to avoid Jose and his friends all day. As far as his persecutors were concerned it appeared that Louis had not managed to go to school that day. Louis did not have to work for Peter that afternoon and he was in no rush to leave the classroom. Mrs Washington looked at Louis as she went to leave the classroom. Her concern about Louis' behaviour could not be contained. "Louis?" Louis briefly looked up at her from his book. "I am always here if you wish to talk to me, child." Louis looked at her again, but he was resolute in his mind that he must not reveal any matter of his life. His eyes returned to the book he was reading; the tales of human history contained within the schoolbook would seal his lips. Mrs Washington left the classroom although she was concerned that all was not well in Louis' world. Louis continued to read his history book. He read about King Louis the XIV of France and the Frankish meaning of the name Louis to be 'ferocious in battle'. Eventually, when he felt that he was safe to leave that afternoon, Louis got up out of his chair and slowly packed his school bag as he was naturally not keen to go to Joseph's home; so unwelcome did Louis feel there that he never in his mind classified it as 'his home'. When he arrived at the school gate, Louis turned around and took one last longing look at the sanctuary of the school building. He then turned back around and made his way carefully home for fear of coming across Jose and his gang.

After carefully taking his time to travel home, he did not stumble across Jose, and upon his arrival back at the apartment building, Louis immediately ran up the stairs to Ms Fitzgerald's apartment. He knocked on her door. She opened the door but, on this occasion, something was different; Ms Fitzgerald seemed to be quite upset. Little did Louis know that Joseph had paid her visit that day and warned her to keep her silence about what went on in his apartment, otherwise he would "break her neck!" After a short pause, Ms Fitzgerald fully opened her front door. "Come in, Louis." Her voice was weak, and as he walked in, Louis could not help to be concerned. "What is wrong?" Ms Fitzgerald initially paused; she dearly wanted to tell him to get away from Joseph and to leave Midtown West, but then her fear took the better of her. "Nothing, nothing is wrong." Her demeanour changed as soon as Louis told her the wonderful news about his new classroom. When Ms Fitzgerald heard that Louis had an opportunity placed before him to escape the nightmare, she started crying with delight. To celebrate the occasion, Ms Fitzgerald made a fresh pot of Irish stew for Louis, a meal that he devoured in a celebratory mood. Later that night, when he made that dreaded walk across the hallway to Joseph's apartment Louis tried to tell his father what he had achieved at school, but Joseph's response was devastating for the young boy to hear. "What? I suppose this means I have to keep on supporting you, you little bastard." Louis felt like screaming at his father. In his mind, he asked the question: "Why don't you love me?" However, Louis was too fearful of Joseph to allow these words to escape his lips. Instead, he took himself off to his bedroom, and the disappointment of his father's reaction was tearing his young heart apart. Louis lay on his bed in his school clothes. He once again longed for his mother to return to his life, as life with his father was sheer torment.

Day two of the new academic regime in Louis' life was similar to what a religious epiphany must have been like for true believers. He arrived at school early in a depressed mood, but as his new class commenced for the day, he felt more at ease about being included in this classroom of students, and it was not a dream anymore. Essentially, what was a curriculum for the end of junior high school was being taught in a combined classroom of only eleven students. Louis was the youngest member of this group of students, who were an equal mix of boys and girls in whom the New York State Education Department had decided to appropriate the additional resources and benefits of this specialised classroom setting. On that second day of Louis' new elementary school environment, he had found his escape from reality; advanced education was an intellectual escape for his troubled mind. A higher level of learning brought sense to Louis' world, which was otherwise a miserable existence. English, math, history, and science were his escape mechanisms, and he could not get enough of it.

When school had finished for that second day, Louis raced to the grocery store to "earn his keep", as Joseph would always tell him. He told Peter his news, and the old man nodded his head in approval, although deep down, Peter had his doubts. His thoughts epitomised the mood of Midtown West. "This kid doesn't stand a chance of getting out of Midtown West." Later that evening, after he had finished work, Louis snuck along the streets from the grocery store to avoid Jose and his gang. Rather than going to Ms Fitzgerald's apartment for dinner, Louis instead went straight to his room to study. As usual, when Louis arrived at his father's apartment, nobody was there but he left the dollar note in its usual place on the dining table. He was hungry and so wanted to knock on Mrs Fitzgerald's apartment to eat dinner but his schoolwork had to come first. After about two hours, he could not contain his hunger, and when he saw the fridge was empty, Louis had no choice; even though it was after 9.00pm, he had to go to Ms Fitzgerald's apartment to be fed. He knocked on the door, and eventually, he heard the security lock being disengaged. Ms Fitzgerald felt sorrowful for the helpless sight of a hungry little boy who was desperate for love and food, and as usual, he was also desperate to tell the story of his day. She let Louis into her apartment and fed him the remaining stew from the fresh pot she had made the previous day. They talked about music and, more importantly, about his new academic life. He explained with unbridled enthusiasm what he had learned that day at school in his new class. For a moment, Ms Fitzgerald thought she had detected the look of hope in the little boy's eyes.

At the end of the first week of his new academic life, Mrs Washington played a movie on the projector for the children in her class. The movie reel and its projector had been donated to the school by the National Catholic Education Association. It was an exciting afternoon for Louis and his class, as a movie being played on a projector in the classroom was a treat. The title of the movie was simple, "Number 1". For the next 20 minutes, Louis watched a short film about a man who married number 1, but when they became older, he then looked at a younger woman named number 2 and married her. The movie continued with another number of wives for the man until he was too old for anybody to want to be married to him, except for the original number 1. When the movie finished, Mrs Washington explained to the class that marriage was special, and no matter what they saw happening in their families or their neighbourhood, they should always remember that marriage was sacrosanct. Louis watched and listened, but in his mind, he only had one question. "What about families like mine? What happens when your father doesn't love you and your mother doesn't want to be with you? Death do us part? I do not want to die!" The thoughts in his mind turned over and over that weekend, but by Sunday night they were dispelled by the accustomed violence and drunkenness of his father; nothing like an unhealthy dose of Sunday reality!

It was during the middle of the second week in his new classroom environment that Louis found inner strength in his intelligence for the first time, and perhaps it was also because he found it to be untenable to listen to Mrs Washington's hypothesis about the outcome of recent modern American history. Mrs Washington had taught the class for her modern history lesson that Wednesday afternoon about the protest years of the 1960s. Mrs Washington had concluded the lesson before taking questions from her students with a statement Louis could not accept. "This is just a further reason why we are the land of the free and the brave." Immediately, his hand shot up to ask a question. Mrs Washington acknowledged Louis' prompt response. "Yes, Louis?" His next words were exceptionally intuitive for a child to say. "Mrs Washington, if this is the land of the free and the brave, then how come so many brave people are not free?" Mrs Washington was immediately taken aback. "Why do you say that, Louis?" Her earnest tone of voice was underscored by surprise. Louis paused briefly, then looked her in the eye and spoke frankly, without any fear in his conviction. "Well, I watch you walk into this school each day and you do not display any fear about dealing with us or Mr Denning." Mrs Washington's inquisitive tone was still underscored by a nervous quiver. "Yes, go on, Louis." He then stood up, like a politician in Congress. "So, I wonder to myself why there are so many brave people like you who deal with their everyday lives so bravely, but they have to put up with people in better jobs telling them what to do, yet those people telling them what to do are not nearly as intelligent?"

By now, Mrs Washington was becoming increasingly nervous, and never had a student strum a chord in her heart, which was the subdued feeling of how she perceived her world. Yes, to Mrs Washington, the principal of the school, Mr Denning, was nothing less than a typical clumsy, reasonably intelligent white male person who had somehow risen through the ranks in priority to more talented people like herself. Mrs Washington previously surmised in her mind on two grounds why this was so. First, because she was black, this was a reason that had been bonding African Americans for several decades now. The other reason was that she was a woman, and women's liberation had such a long way to go, particularly in the education department of the elementary school system in which she was employed. Regarding Louis' probing question, Mrs Washington was inclined to shut down this discussion immediately, particularly because if she agreed with anything Louis was saying about her boss at the school being less intelligent than her, she was then essentially writing her pink slip. "Louis, why on earth would you make such a statement about our great nation, but in particular, if I understand you correctly, about our principal?" Louis challenged her meek response. "Because, Mrs Washington, I watch people like you and others in this neighbourhood every day doing something brave, but that seems to mean nothing to the white people who seem to run things in this neighbourhood." Mrs Washington found herself in a conundrum; here was a student challenging the American way of life. Yet Mrs Washington found deep within herself that this 10-year-old boy had struck a chord in her heart and soul about her struggle, as well as the struggle of African Americans and, particularly, black women. Louis continued his observation without any fear. "You see, Mrs Washington, I cannot understand that if you are smart enough to be in charge of this class, then how come there are others to whom you must answer? Why aren't you the principal? I also cannot also understand why a person born in Africa has the name Washington, as that surname was given to you without you being asked, wasn't it?" Mrs Washington was now left speechless, not because she was offended by what was being said by this child, but rather she was speechless because this young boy had essentially described her inner torment. The school bell rang for the day, fortunately releasing Mrs Washington from this confronting discussion. Mrs Washington quickly gathered her lesson books together and just as quickly departed the classroom with the other students; however, Louis did not leave because he knew that he was marooned there for at least another 20 minutes, long enough to ensure that Jose and his friends had left the school area before Louis dared show his face outside of the school grounds.

CHAPTER 4

Another two years progressed for Louis in the usual manner: He received no love from home, and his mind was a battleground of torment, but at least thoughts about his mortality subsided as he thrived in his academic world. Ms Fitzgerald, as always, continued to feed and clothe him; he was still being bullied by Jose and he still had not spoken to Mrs Washington about his problems. He would tell her about his job with Peter after school, and on one occasion, he took her to Peter's shop when she told him she needed to take some groceries home that night, although it was perhaps a ruse for the teacher to make sure her student was not being subjected to unbearable working conditions. Mrs Washington was satisfied the young man was being treated well by Peter, and she would occasionally from to time drop into the store to purchase groceries before she took the train home.

Nevertheless, there was a feature of Louis' life that did not remain the same. His intellect, knowledge, and comprehension as an academic have placed him at the top of his class for the last 18 months. He had received the Student of the Year award a year before he was meant to graduate from middle school. Such an achievement had not occurred at the school before. He was also in line to win Student of the Year again in his final year. A scholarship was on offer and if Louis' school results continued, he would be eligible to attend a private junior high school on a boarding basis. This news pleased Joseph, as he knew he would be relieved of having to keep Louis in his apartment. However, still, Louis' father and Mary displayed no other interest in his life, and they were just doing the minimum necessary to avoid Joseph being charged with failing to provide care to his child.

One winter evening, Louis was walking home after completing the same mundane duties of delivering groceries for Peter, which had been providing an additional source of income for his father. By now, his nemesis Jose was attending the local junior high school, but that did not mean that Jose was not on the lookout for his usual easy score in the neighbourhood. As Louis turned the corner to walk into his street, he heard the familiar tones of Jose and his gang scream out. "Hey, faggot!" Louis did not hesitate, and he commenced running towards his building as fast as he could. By now twelve years of age, he was much faster, and Louis' entire strength was channelled this evening into getting him home before this group of cowardly bullies could lay one finger on him. "Hey!" This was the further scream Louis heard behind him, but he ran with all his might. Louis bounded up the stairs to the entryway to his building; breathless, he reached out with his key and unlocked the door to his building. As he quickly entered and shut the front door, Louis saw through the glass of that door Jose and his gang arrive at the bottom stairwell of the entrance of the building. Jose and the gang of thugs upturned a rubbish bin, which was located near the front stairs, and they immediately armed themselves with projectiles and commenced throwing them at the building. Jose was the first voice to be heard calling out into the air that night. "Hey, little faggot, you can fucking run but we know where you fucking are." Louis so wanted to go back outside to finally confront his tormentors, but his inner fear locked his feet into place within the foyer of his apartment building. The projectiles continued to bang against the front wall of the building. The taunts of the voices of Jose and his gang continued to ring out with the bombardment of projectiles being thrown. Louis stood in the foyer of the building, and the hatred and anger within him was reaching dangerous levels, but he knew from his classes that displays of violence had no meaning. Rather, violence can result in disastrous consequences for the perpetrator of it. Nevertheless, the final taunt that echoed from Jose's lips ignited the fire in Louis' heart to avenge the bullying. "Hey, fag, I will be waiting by your school fence all of tomorrow until you fucking come out, you fucking little fag."

Louis' antagonists left shortly after the last taunt was uttered from their lips. Louis knew that tomorrow was his D-Day, and as he walked upstairs to the second floor of the building where his apartment was located, he knew there was a confrontation the following day that he could not avoid. As Louis reached the top of the stairs, he looked down the hallway towards the front door of his father's apartment. Joseph was standing at the front door of the apartment. The hallway lights leading to the apartment illuminated the expression on Joseph's face; it was a look of nothing more than sheer disappointment with overtones of mocking display. Louis froze in his spot at the top of the stairs as he looked into his father's eyes. Joseph spoke in the coldest of voices. "I never fucking wanted you, but I have never been so ashamed in my life until now. If you have any fucking balls, you little girly boy, you will confront that asshole tomorrow". Ms Fitzgerald opened her front door slightly, and when she heard the words spoken by Joseph that was the final straw for her; she could no longer hold her tongue. She flung open her front door in anger, which startled Louis, but Joseph did not blink. "Why don't you say something to support your son, you rotten man? He does not deserve to have you in his life." With those words being spoken, Joseph returned a deathly stare towards her. He maintained that death glare for what seemed like an eternity, and then he turned on his heels and walked back into his apartment. Louis was hungry, but he knew now was not the time to go into Ms Fitzgerald's apartment. Instead, Louis walked slowly towards the front door of Joseph's apartment, hoping that Joseph would not leap out from a room to strike him down. As Louis entered the apartment, he noticed Mary looking at him from the doorway of the main living room, which was located at the end of the entry hallway. Mary displayed nothing but disdain for Louis, and it was undeserved, but the expression on Mary's face summed up the injustice of Louis' existence within those walls. Louis initially waited for Joseph to come in and hit him, but after half an hour went by, it appeared he was spared from that torture. Later that night, Louis tossed and turned in bed. There was a full moon that appeared through the murky night sky he could see from his window, bidding misfortune rather than hope. There was also the glow from Wall Street in the far distance, in particular, a golden glow which emphasised for Louis a fortune may await him if he could just escape Midtown West. He knew that he could not avoid the confrontation which Jose was planning. He also tossed and turned because he was worried about Ms Fitzgerald. As Louis went off to sleep, he resolved in his heart that he would speak to Mrs Washington, but only about Jose and his gang bullying him. Later that evening, while he was deep asleep, Louis did not hear the scream that came from Ms Fitzgerald's apartment.

After Louis had gone inside his apartment that evening, Ms Fitzgerald decided enough was enough, she had to write another letter to the mysterious addressee whom the State of New York had recorded as being 'private' as Louis' next of kin. She described the events that had occurred that evening and she made no equivocation about the urgency of the matter of protecting the boy's life. "He needs your help. Please rescue him from his father". With these final words, Ms Fitzgerald signed off on her letter, and she quietly left her apartment and proceeded to find the nearest mailbox to ensure the letter was mailed that night. She crept up the stairs and quietly opened the front door to her apartment, believing she had disturbed nobody that evening, but as she turned around, she saw the terrifying sight of Joseph standing over her, one foot into her door jamb to ensure the door could not be closed. Ms Fitzgerald did not have enough time to properly scream as Joseph barged into her apartment and seized her by the throat. The first blow of his fist to her face knocked her out, but his hands tightly fastened around her neck, ensuring she would never breathe air again.

The next morning, Louis arrived at class 20 minutes earlier than usual. Notwithstanding how hungry Louis was, he had not gone to Ms Fitzgerald's apartment for breakfast, so eager was he to speak to Mrs Washington. The janitor had only just finished his morning duties when Louis arrived at school. He had not stumbled across the path of Jose, or his gang. Mrs Washington arrived 15 minutes later, and she had come to class 20 minutes earlier than she would normally arrive as she was planning a special film lesson relating to the field of science. Accordingly, she wanted to ensure there were no technical faults. As Mrs Washington walked into the classroom, she saw Louis sitting at his desk, and she immediately came to a halt despite being in full stride. Without even a moment's thought, she spoke. "Child, what in God's name are you doing here at this hour?" Louis did not hesitate to get out of his chair. He looked Mrs Washington in the eye and tried to speak his sorrow of the bullying being carried out upon him by Jose and the group of followers, the abuse which he was also suffering at home, but Louis once again froze before opening his mouth. Louis looked sideways in despair and Mrs Washington finally saw an opening. "Louis honey, do not be afraid, child, tell me, please tell me what is causing your sorrow." Louis looked back towards Mrs Washington and found his inner strength, day one of standing up for himself and voicing his despair. "Ms." He spoke with a degree of comfort and conviction. "For about two years now, I have been from time to time assaulted by a bully and his gang of cowards. There are also some other things about my life I need to tell you. However, the bullying is most urgent as last night, the kid bullying me told me that today he and his gang are going to attack me with even greater force than they ever have before. I have two choices, either fight and be severely beaten up or instead speak to you to try and avoid this confrontation. That is why I am here so early." Mrs Washington wanted to ask Louis why he had not spoken to a member of his family; however, she knew the explanation would be typical of so many in this precinct of the city; "could not give a damn" entered her mind. She then asked Louis whether he wanted the Education Department to intervene. Louis nodded his head, and by now, the corner of his eyes were filled with tears as he felt the overwhelming relief of at least revealing one harrowing side of his life. Mrs Washington was not done; she knew there was a story to tell. "What is the other problem in your life, Louis?" Louis' lips otherwise remained sealed about the life that played out at home every day of his life, and he so wanted to tell her, but then the image of Joseph entered his mind. Mrs Washington told Louis to immediately go to Mr Denning's office and she would be there, within five minutes.

Louis sat in the school principal's office for five minutes, waiting patiently; however, Mrs Washington had not arrived. The tenth minute passed by, and Mrs Washington had still not arrived. Mr Denning arrived at the office at this time, and he was somewhat unsettled in the manner of his stride as he walked into the entryway outside of his office. There, he saw Louis, sitting alone on a chair. "Louis, what are you doing here at this time of the day?" He had spoken in a rather stentorian and abrupt manner. Louis was immediately perturbed by Mr Denning's manner, and he replied with the bare facts: "Mrs Washington told me to come and speak to you when she got here, but she is late." Without any consideration of the circumstances, Mr Denning peremptorily dismissed Louis from his presence as he was too busy and when Mrs Washington was ready to speak to him, then they should both return. Mr Denning then entered his office and slammed the door behind him.

After experiencing Mr Denning's reaction, Louis did not know what he should do; however, one thing appeared to be certain in his mind: Mrs Washington had not come down to the principal's office like she had promised. Louis walked out of the administration section and into the schoolyard. His mind was consumed with dark thoughts. He could not understand why Mrs Washington had not come down to the office. Indeed, Louis felt he had been betrayed by Mrs Washington. He was dismayed by Mr Denning's conduct; it was like being at home. He looked at the gates to the schoolyard and he saw Jose and Julian peering through the fence. The look on their faces was provocative in manner, and Louis knew that he would have to now go down that unknown path of standing up to Jose or forever he would be the subject of his bullying taunts, with the haunting tones of his father's derisive voice from the night before still echoing in his mind. He walked towards the gates and Jose and Julian took their positions on either side of the gate; all that was needed was one of the other members of the gang to make it a good old turkey shoot. When he was about one foot from the gate, Louis suddenly sprung into an instant running stride, bounding through the gate like a champion racehorse. Jose and Julian were caught by surprise, and clumsily, they both jumped far too late, their hands only barely touched Louis' hair. Louis turned around to watch Julian fall over, but Jose managed to remain on his feet. Jose looked Louis in the eye, the look on Jose's face displayed that he was now going to fight with even greater ferocity. Jose charged at Louis, ferociously yelling as he ran towards him. Just as Jose was about to strike Louis' face, Louis swayed sideways. The movement caused Louis to fall over, and Jose was tripped up by Louis' right leg. Within one foot of Louis was a piece of timber that had probably been used in the framework of the walls of a building, but it had now been discarded amongst the other rubbish on the street. About a metre in length and two and a half inches thick, the piece of timber appeared to be both a shield and sword for Louis. Louis reached out and took hold of the piece of timber. Jose was back up on his feet again, and he brought his right arm down towards Louis, who by this stage was back up again on his knees. Jose had not seen Louis pick up the piece of timber and therefore he struck out without any thought. Louis raised the timber like a shield and caught Jose on his right forearm. The collision between a solid object and Jose's forearm brought a look of immediate pain to Jose's face as he had fractured his forearm. Jose recoiled backwards in pain and Louis immediately spotted his opportunity. Louis jumped to his feet and in one almighty strike, he smashed the timber onto the top of Jose's head. Blood immediately started to stream from the crown area of Jose's head, and he stumbled like a punch-drunk boxer. Louis had won the fight, it seemed, but he wanted to prove to himself he was ferocious in battle. In a moment of sheer hatred Louis raised the timber and swung it in a baseball bat-like fashion into Jose's left cheek, the blow instantly breaking the true skin. Jose clutched his left cheek with his left hand, but the blood immediately streamed through his fingers like a river of blood. Jose stumbled away up the street, crying out for help. Louis swung around to face Julian. It only took Louis taking one step forward for Julian to turn around and run away in fear for his safety. Peering out through the windows of buildings adjoining the school area were six witnesses to Louis' actions in striking Jose in the face. None of these people had seen the start of the fight.

After the incident, Louis walked back into his school grounds. He entered the school building and walked back down the hall to his classroom. He opened the door to his classroom, and by now the first lesson of the day had commenced for about ten minutes. Mrs Washington was about to switch on the film she had set up that morning on the film projector. She did not ask Louis what Mr Denning had said, she only assumed there had been an in-depth discussion for Louis to be walking in the classroom at this time. She switched on the film and turned out the lights. Thirty minutes after the film commenced, Mr Denning walked into the classroom with a police officer, the officer's hat could be easily seen by everyone in the class as a silhouette in the glass window of the classroom door. Mr Denning switched on the light to the classroom and in a commanding voice, he said, "Louis O'Brien, come with me." Louis got up and left the room. Mrs Washington held her hand up to her mouth in shock. However, after the initial shock, she came to the realisation that she had to do something to help the child. Later that afternoon, when classes had finished, Mrs Washington would take some steps to try to mitigate the inevitable court penalty that flowed from such a violent act for which Louis was going to be charged. She went into the staff office to ring Peter and ask that he provide whatever assistance he could. She then retrieved Louis' file held in the school archive room, walked to the desk where she had spoken to Peter beforehand, and sat down to read the file. She opened an envelope marked private. She pulled a piece of paper out of the envelope and read it and, after considering her next step for about a minute, Mrs Washington picked up the receiver of the telephone on the desk in front of her and began to dial the number.

Louis was charged that same day by the police with an offence relating to the wounding of Jose's cheek. The police officers chastised Louis for using a weapon to inflict an injury which they said could have been far more serious. Although he was concerned about his legal position, when Louis heard the police mention the injury he inflicted could have been far worse, he looked at police officers for a moment, raising an eyebrow to suggest he did not accept that striking Jose with the wood could cause a worse injury than that inflicted. One of the police officers was a tough old Irish Catholic plod named Fitzgibbon, but on Louis' visual inspection, he did not suspect Fitzgibbon could fit into too many things due to his age and weight. Fitzgibbon detected the air of arrogance in this boy, and he then proceeded to do something that he thought would be instructive for the young man's future, but instead, its effect would be long-lived. He retrieved from his desk some horrific crime scene photos of a murder case he was assisting the homicide squad on as the officer first on the scene; the death blow had been caused by a person hitting the deceased on the head with an iron bar and the photographs taken of the deceased in situ were gruesome; indeed, they were photographs which a child should not see. When Fitzgibbon handed the photographs to Louis, the young man smiled as if to say, 'What now?' However, the gore, the blood, the horror, and, in particular, the body of a deceased sent a chill down Louis' spine as the images he had buried in his mind of Bill's body came back to the forefront of his thoughts. Louis must have stared at the dead body depicted in the photo for at least five minutes, and the more he looked at the photo of the deceased the more his mind began to focus on his mortality, but it was not like the thoughts he experienced after seeing Bill's dead body, these thoughts went deeper into his mind to harness the power of real fear. Up until this moment, Louis was previously scared of death, but he had not been embraced by its terror to this extent, and now that he had seen this photograph depicting a gruesome homicide that resembled his previous exposure to Bill's horrific dead body, the anxiety, fear, and terror about its certainty for him one day filled his mind and chilled his spine. He could not get the images out of his mind, and whatever words the police were saying to Louis now, he did not process them fully as, for the first time in his life, he was experiencing true death anxiety.

The news was broken to Joseph by the school liaison counsellor about Louis assaulting Jose. Joseph was initially enraged, not because his bastard son had committed a violent assault, but rather because this meant that the escape from having to care for him was now destroyed by this act of violence. Whereas he had a child who was on his way to scholarship and the education system taking Louis under its wing, Joseph realised that he had to now discharge a parental duty he did not previously care about, and it would be for at least another five years. Government departments were on the periphery of Joseph's life for another five years as he ruminated over this news. "Damn, that little bastard" was the thought which radiated around the inner world of his dark mind. He contemplated just doing away with the child; such was the contempt he had for his flesh and blood. It seemed Louis was done for, but then Joseph experienced a moment of inspiration as he tried to focus his mind on a way to divert his parental duties. "Bring him on board at the shed," he thought. He continued to ruminate over the whole situation. He never wanted this child, but at least there was now a use for him; bring him on board at the shed and there would be a financial benefit. He picked up the telephone to call his superiors. Louis did not realise what lay in store for him.

Later that afternoon Louis was released on bail into his father's custody pending the charge being heard. "How ironic," thought Louis, because being released into his father's custody seemed to be a sentence rather than being at liberty. The whole processing procedure distracted his young mind from its morbid preoccupation with his mortality, and when he was released from the police station, Louis was also on guard, waiting for his father to strike him down at any moment. Joseph did not assault Louis during their 20-or-so-minute foot journey home; indeed, he did not even speak to him. As they walked into the apartment building and made their way up the stairs to the floor of Joseph's apartment, Louis noticed the disturbing sight of police tape around the front door of Ms Fitzgerald's apartment. A detective was standing near the front door and Louis' heart sank with a feeling of horror. The detective saw Louis and quickly stopped him and Joseph in their tracks. "Hey, kid, do you know anything about how this old lady was killed last night?"

Louis was stunned, and he could not believe the words he had just heard. There was enough pause for Louis to digest this heartbreaking and dreadful news. He held his composure, even though he wished to cry. "No, I don't." As Louis said these words, he looked towards Joseph, a hint of suspicion only being discernible to his father. The detective did not pick up on Louis' glance at Joseph; instead, he returned to examining his notebook. He asked a few more questions which Joseph answered him bluntly, 'I know nothing reply'. While Joseph answered these questions, Louis was able to look slightly around the corner of Ms Fitzgerald's doorway, just enough to see her brutalised body lying dead cold on the floor. Another traumatic homicide scene within the same day, but this time the body was real as opposed to a photo. The sight of the kind old woman who raised him now being so vulnerably left dead on her floor some time ago shocked him even further. His death anxiety was not just entrenched in his mind; it was there to stay. Beyond Joseph's apparent ignorance as to what had occurred, the detective had already been provided with a version of events and whereabouts by Mary regarding where she, Joseph, and Louis had been the previous evening, which had satisfied the curiosity of a lazy Manhattan police officer; hell, he had at least 20 further homicide files on his desk to investigate, and the old woman's death was consistent with a robbery going wrong. He had no more questions, and a homicide file could be put to one side. Joseph very quickly escorted his son into the apartment and shut the door behind him. He had picked up on the subtle hint Louis was trying to convey to the detective, and his contempt for his child was manifesting itself in the extremities of his body. Oh, how fortunate for the young boy that a police officer was nearby because the father's rage was at the brink of deadly intent. He grabbed the boy by the shirt collar; the cries of protest started to emanate from Louis' mouth as he was dragged down the hallway, but it was not enough sound to alert the potential haven of the detective. Joseph pulled tight on Louis' shirt collar, and with a good hard jab of the right hand, his big fist landed on Louis' jaw, knocking the boy out. When he eventually awoke the next morning, he had a sore head and a traumatised mind to contend with. The physical pain would wear away; the psychological demon would now embed itself like a parasite waiting for its moment of insidious nourishment.

A few weeks later Louis had to meet with an attorney appointed to act for him by the State of New York. The public defence office in William Street was in a district of Manhattan Louis had never visited before; a moment of his life that illustrated the oppressive world he had to endure in Midtown West. His mind was occupied by the myriad of depressing thoughts within it; his academic opportunity seemed to be lost; one day, he would be dead; nobody loves me. The appointment was the day before he had to first appear in court for the serious charge of wounding Jose. Joseph accompanied his son, more out of concern about what his son may say to the attorney about him than his concerns for his child. The attorney was an elderly man in whom the rigours of legal life were imprinted in the wrinkles on his forehead. His name was quickly forgotten by the nervous child, and he told Louis he would not be the attorney attending the court the next morning, a piece of information that consolidated the harsh machinations of the justice system in Louis' mind. The old attorney discussed the prosecution evidence with Louis, and then he asked him for his version of events. Despite all the evidence of the background bullying that Louis was subjected to at the hands of Jose, he was told by the old attorney that he could not defend that final strike to Jose's cheek. The attorney recommended that he plead guilty at court the next morning as a sign of immediate remorse to display to a judge he was capable of being reformed without a period of detention. When Louis received this advice he wondered where the justice was in this world, as a bully had planned a vicious bashing for him, but he was now considered by the law to be the antagonist. As he got out of his chair to leave the office with Joseph, he was then reminded about the initial news he had subsequently forgotten because of being advised by the attorney to plead guilty to the charge; the old attorney would not be appearing at the court the next morning, and Louis had to meet another public defence lawyer acting for every child that day. "Don't worry, kid, he will have my file notes" were his parting words. Justice! The word ate away at him contemporaneously in his mind that night with his other tormentors, and his dismay for how justice had escaped him would regrettably shape his character from there on. Ms Fitzgerald had been murdered by his father, but Louis could not tell anyone this monster was responsible because he feared for his safety now that the old lady was dead. Death, the parasite of his mind, would, from time to time, come to the forefront of his mind that night, and this morbidity was accentuated by the more immediate depressing thoughts of his life. The bright light which had seemingly been shining through Louis' window was now put out. He knew in his heart the scholarship was gone, and his friend Ms Fitzgerald was now dead. Louis tossed and turned in bed all night as the two traumatic experiences of the police photos and then the glimpse of Ms Fitzgerald's dead body gripped his mind with the fear of death; a fear which temporarily went away as the more existential threat of him being sentenced by the court the next day proceeded to consume his mind.

The next morning, Louis had his meeting with his destiny at the New York City Children's Court. East 22nd Street was a bewildering location for the child, not only because he had not previously been there but also because the moving crowds of people dressed in suits was a sight he had never seen before. It was a walk of shame for him as the telling eyes of these adults around the courthouse displayed the telltale looks of 'another wayward child'. As he walked up the stairs inside the Children's Court, Louis realised that he was the odd child out because all the other children he saw that day were either of African or Hispanic heritage, and his shame overwhelmed him as he walked towards the public defence room located on the second floor of the building near the courtroom that would be his date with destiny that day. His father's rough appearance and sartorial inelegance only highlighted to the crowd of youths and parents waiting around the public defence room that Louis was destined for the same gloomy future as the other juveniles appearing at court that day. His father! Why was he even there? Joseph had shown a total lack of sympathy for his son and Louis knew his presence was more to ward off the potential supervision of juvenile social workers entering his seedy world. Louis stood outside of the public defence room, waiting to see the attorney acting for him that day. A young female clerk sat at a desk just outside of the meeting room, and she recorded on her pad that Louis was there, telling him to wait until she called out his name.

It seemed like an eternity, but after 15 minutes the young clerk called for

Louis. He walked into the room with his father, his belly churning about the unfortunate events unfolding before his eyes. The attorney was a young, thin man dressed in a plain grey suit, white shirt, and cheap paisley tie. The desk in front of him was piled high with about 20 files, and it was obvious he was stressed because of the sheer number of children he had to appear for that day. He ushered both of them to sit down in the seats in front of his desk as he shot out his right hand to shake Joseph's. Joseph did not extend the courtesy back to the attorney; instead, he sat down, his fierce eyes looking the poor young man up and down, behaviour which just added to Louis' feelings of shame. The young attorney was fresh out of university, he was just as nervous as Louis, admittedly for a different reason. He was no older than 25 years and he was still a child on the inside. Sure enough, the attorney had the file, which contained the old attorney's notes from the previous day, recording the advice he had given Louis to plead guilty. The advice he received from this young attorney was the same, namely, there were too many witnesses in the neighbouring building and the knockout blow was not justified or excused. He told Louis the judge was a tough sentencer, so he would call Louis' case on first because the other children he was acting for that day were more difficult cases for him to convince the judge they should not go or return to 'juvie'. Their meeting was brief; the attorney asked Louis to sign a piece of paper confirming he would plead guilty, and Joseph also signed the same form confirming the child could reside with him. An hour went by, which was an excruciating waiting period for Louis, and then the young clerk spoke to a gathering crowd of young offenders and adult guardians, telling them to enter the courtroom. Louis entered the room and sat down in the front of the public gallery with his father, and shortly thereafter, the young attorney entered the courtroom and quickly took Louis by the arm to sit with him at the bar table. Sitting at the other end of the table was the District Attorney, a woman in her mid-thirties who was dressed in the stereotypical suit for that office: dark cloth with a light blouse underneath, her hair was done up in a tight bun and she squinted through her glasses at the first young offender for her day. Then the old, portly bailiff quickly entered a side door near the judge's bench, hollering the dreaded words, "All rise for Judge Schwartz, the Children's Court of New York City is now in session." Following behind the bailiff was his Honour Judge Schwartz, a man in his early sixties, bald on top of his head but white fluffy hair poking out from all sides, wearing his judicial robe, which seemed to accentuate the hostility of his face upon which he wore the thickest pair of black plastic spectacles Louis had ever seen. The judge arraigned Louis and then accepted the guilty plea on his behalf from the attorney. The prosecutor fairly read out all versions of the facts relating to the fight, including a statement from Mrs Washington supporting the fact that Louis had told her about the bullying before the actual wounding event. Then the judge heard from the defence attorney, and his nervous tremor underscored his inexperience in appearing in court. The judge's patience wore thin very quickly with the ineptitude of the advocate appearing before him, and after about five torturous minutes for all concerned, his Honour told the young attorney to sit down. Judge Schwartz then extracted a document from the court file to read into the evidence; Peter had provided a short letter that spoke to Louis' dedication to his work, an item of correspondence Mrs Washington had arranged to be provided to the court as a parting gesture of her sorrow for losing a child of such academic promise. His Honour noted that the public education office confirmed Louis had been expelled from the school because the fight occurred within the precinct of the school, and as a result, Louis' promising academic career was now forfeited. Judge Schwartz also noted Joseph was present, but the father's appearance did not instil any hope in the child's future for him.

After considering the sentence he was proposing to impose for a minute, the judge brought down his judgment. Louis was sentenced to a suspended jail sentence; the conviction was to be publicly recorded. He would no longer be in line for a scholarship at a more prominent high school. Instead, he was destined to be another statistic in the sausage factory, which was the ordinary public education system of the United States, a system in which truancy was not noticed, and if the students received a passing grade, it would be a miracle. His Honour noted these sad facts of lost education opportunity as he concluded his sentencing remarks, but he still pointedly spoke to Louis about him now being a juvenile offender and not coming back before the court! After the sentence was passed, Louis and his father left the courtroom, neither of them taking any notice of the dark-haired man who was sitting in the back corner of the courtroom. As they walked outside of the courtroom, Joseph told Louis he had a job for him down at the docks. No emotion was displayed on Joseph's face, and he spoke his words like a businessman talking to another businessman. Neither of them noticed the dark-haired man had followed them out, to be within earshot of Joseph's daunting offer of work. Later that night, Louis watched the news on the television at home, and Joseph, as usual, was not home at that time of night. The television news broadcast a story about police in Texas subduing a small protest by using their batons. In particular, Louis saw a police officer repeatedly striking a young protester when they were curled up on the ground and not fighting back. "Where is the justice?" he thought before he turned off the television.

CHAPTER 5

The walk along the old wharves of Manhattan was an avenue that appeared to be dedicated to the underbelly of the city. If humanity sought to display its lowest common denominators in one area, then the old wharf community of Manhattan was the central display. Every reprobate, criminal, and desperado seemed to inhabit the wharves. Annex No 2 in the old ferry shed off Whitehall Street seemed to accommodate most of that underbelly. The docks off South Street had been depressed for a long period due to a lack of craft servicing it; however, one area still had a semblance of the wharf life of the hay day of Manhattan's South Street precinct.

As Louis walked the wharves towards where his father worked, he knew that he, too, was now destined to be tarred as being part of this environment. In his mind, Louis was still the same academic; however, the recent turn of events about his assaulting Jose meant that his life was now changed forever. As he walked along the wharves, Louis still tried to come to terms with the fact that he was the villain, even though he suffered from the repeated bullying antics of Jose and his gang. From here on in it seemed to Louis that he would have to survive in his father's world. His various mental tormentors still included his death anxiety, but that condition would be subdued at the proper time by the immediate consequences of his violence. Louis arrived at O'Malley's Shed, not far from the Annex 2 area but just far enough away to ensure there was an observable distance between the two sheds. If the South Street Wharf precinct were depressed and essentially redundant, a person would not know that from the life that existed at O'Malley's Shed. Two smaller freight boats were moored at the docks outside of the shed, and a crane was unloading crates onto a small truck as Louis approached. He certainly noticed that there seemed to be a lack of supervision at these wharves, and yes, the general area essentially appeared to be redundant. O'Malley's Shed, on the other hand, was bristling with life as though the clock had continued to run there for the past 50 years without interruption. Standing at the entryway to O'Malley's Shed was a raggedy man; grey whiskers covered his worn face, and his eyes displayed a lifetime of alcohol abuse. His name was Coonan, and, unlike many other Irish in Midtown West, he had only emigrated from Ireland approximately 25 years ago, and accordingly, he carried all the old-world Irish pronunciations of the English language and the generational baggage imprinted on his psyche from the days of British rule. Coonan was short in stature, but he seemed to be tall to Louis.

As Louis walked up to the doorway of the shed, Coonan suspiciously looked at the boy and then stepped in front of him. "What in the fuck of Christ da ye think ye are doing here, kid?" growled Coonan in his thick Irish accent. Louis was slightly startled by the tone of the voice of the old man; at the age of twelve, there was still an innocent young boy within that skin. "I have been sent here by my father, sir." Louis' nervous voice revealed his innocence. The old man stared at Louis; the glare on his face suggested he was a hostile old fellow. "Well, I am not a fuckin' mind reader, kid! Who is ye fuckin father?" His voice was now increasing with hostility. "Sir, my name is Louis O'Brien. My father is Joseph O'Brien". It was almost as though Louis had spoken a magic password, as the old man instantly relaxed in his demeanour. "Well, why didn't ye fuckin' so say, lad? I'm Jim Coonan, a friend of ye father, but ye are to call me Coonan; only my friends call me Jim. Come inside, ye old man is on that boat docked there, he will be out soon, but we already have something planned for you today. Follow me." Coonan turned on his heels and walked into the shed, and Louis followed behind him like a little lamb following an old ewe.

Louis did not know precisely where the path ahead would lead him at O'Malley's Shed, but he knew that path would not be a glorious one. Coonan walked into an office of the shed, picked up a leather carry case, then turned around, stopped, and took a deep, concerned look in Louis' direction. Coonan believed the kid standing before him could not carry out the task he was about to be asked to perform, regardless of whether the kid's father was one of the tougher workers and union representatives on the wharf. Coonan's voice then rang out in the shed in an eerie tone. "So, lad, do ye think yaw can fuckin' walk 300 yards and turn right into Front Street without losing this bag?" Louis was stunned at the condescending tone coming from Coonan's lips about such a mundane task. "Yes, sir." His forthright voice hid his nervous tremor like a seasoned veteran. "Good then," said Coonan through clenched teeth. "In Front Street, there will be parked a silver 1967 Cadillac Sedan Devil." Coonan then paused as he knew that he had mispronounced the name of the car but he was too bog Irish to be bothered correcting himself. "Don't you mean Deville, sir?" Louis' voice was polite but slightly arrogant in manner. Coonan walked briskly up to the boy, grabbing him by the collar of his tattered jumper, and spoke very loudly but pointedly in his manner. "Ye think you're fuckin' smart. Ye father warned me out about ye. Says ye a little fuckin' pussy of a lad. Warning for ye, ye fuckin little cunt, be a smart ass round here, and all of us, including your Dad, we'll kick the fuckin' life out of ye." The tremor in Louis' body grew to a fever pitch, but he still stood in his path and did not reveal his fear. "Hand the fuckin' bag to the man in the front passenger seat of the fuckin' 'Deville', and he will hand back to ye another bag. Think ye fuckin' smart enough to do that?" Louis just nodded back. He was afraid, very afraid, but he knew this fear would not compare to the fear he felt of living under the same roof as his father. Louis turned around and headed in the direction of Front Street, with each step, his heart dropped as he knew the Ivy League had now forever slipped his grasp.

The walk from O'Malley's Shed to Front Street only took Louis about four minutes, yet it was the most challenging walk ever of his young life because it only took Louis a moment from being told his task to complete by Coonan to then realise he was now being asked by his father's associates to perform some sort of nefarious act. When he walked around the corner from Beekman Street into Front Street, he immediately saw a silver Deville parked 30 yards in front of him. As Louis walked up closer to the Deville, the window of the front passenger was wound down. Louis walked up close to the passenger door and a hand came out. He handed the leather bag over to the outstretched hand of the vehicle. Within an instant, the hand and the bag disappeared back into the car. Louis stood there, wondering to himself whether the next stage would be fulfilled by the occupant, or occupants, of the Deville. He looked into the passenger window of the car, and sitting in the front passenger seat was a young man of Italian extraction counting the money. His hair was oiled back, a look that was very quickly going out of fashion in the USA during the 1970s. However, it was the young man's big nose that caught the eye the most as it had a large bump in the middle of the bridge, which was almost like an arch. He was wearing a suit, an attire which also caught Louis' eye, but it was that nose that was now etched in his mind. Antonio Mancini was a young man with a big nose, and he was an intelligent, street-smart, and connected man from the Bronx. His connections were not known to his underworld associates save for the driver of the car; his mother's first cousin was Mayor Sabatini. Louis could not stop staring at Antonio's nose, but then a voice of another person in the Deville boomed out, a noise loud enough to startle the toughest of men. "Hey, Antonio, would you fucking hurry up already and hand the kid the bag." Antonio raised his arms in defiance. "Dominico, you fat bastard, relax. The kid's cool, aren't you, kid?" A nod was returned. "See Dominico, it's cool." Suddenly, another bag was held out the window by Antonio, and Louis, by now very nervous, walked up towards the car and grabbed the bag to quickly depart the scene. Before he walked around the corner into Beekman Street to make his way back to O'Malley's Shed, he heard the engine of the Deville start up and drive off. He still had the image of Antonio's nose in his mind.

The walk back seemed to take twice as long, but four minutes later, he arrived back at the shed, once again being greeted at the entryway by Coonan. Louis handed the bag over to him. He looked inside the bag and then back at Louis. "Thought ye would have shat ye fuckin' pants and run before ye got to Front Street. Did ye look inside any of the fuckin' bags, kid?" Louis turned his head from side to side to indicate that he had not. "Good lad, I didn't tell ye to do that. In the future, check the fuckin' bag ye are given; if there isn't any money in it fuckin' run back, don't fuckin' walk. I'll let ye Dad know that you can do something else other than be a fuckin' smart ass. Now get the fuck outside and wait until I come for ye." Louis walked out of the shed and waited. He wondered what was in the bag he had taken to the Deville, and what were the contents of the bag he brought back. He knew what he just did must be illegal, and he knew he was being used because of his age, as the police officers were unlikely at first instance to take much notice of a kid carrying a bag in this district of Manhattan. Approximately two hours later Coonan emerged from the shed and explained to the boy his next task: Louis was to go immediately go to the corner of Cliff and Fulton Streets and wait for his father.

Louis arrived at the corner of Cliff and Fulton Streets approximately ten minutes after being dispatched by Coonan. On the left-hand side of the corner of the two streets was a nondescript grey-coloured building. Parked approximately 15 yards from the corner on the left side of Cliff Street was a white 1965 Dodge van, which did not have any rear windows. The rear door of the van opened, and a group of four men all dressed in wharf workers' wear got out of the van. Louis could see that his father was one of those four men, and he held in his right hand a baseball bat; O'Leary was also one of the group of men. These rapidly occurring facts were indicative of intended violence. Joseph marched right up to Louis, and just like Coonan had earlier that day, he grabbed him by the collar of his tattered coat and looked into his son's eyes. "Don't mess this up. Wait right outside of here and keep a lookout; if you see any police officers just yell out pig. The police officers may chase you, but it is a sign for us to get out of here." Louis nodded; his day was just getting worse because his father was content to sacrifice him to the police officers to avoid detection. Joseph and the other men walked into the entryway of the grey building, while Louis stood on the corner of the two streets to keep an eye out for the police. After about two minutes, he heard a man's muffled voice scream out from the building where his father had entered. He heard furniture being upturned. The man screamed again, bellowing out aloud in even greater duress. An old lady who was walking down Cliff Street towards Fulton Street heard the muffled screams, and she stopped, looked at the white van, and then she froze still. Then, everything seemed to become eerily quiet. Two of the men who had entered the building with Joseph came outside and walked towards the van. Within three paces, they both spotted the old lady. One of the men walked over to the lady and grabbed her by the neck. Louis watched in horror as the old lady was dragged by her neck over to the rear of the van, which had now been opened by the other man. Louis' father and O'Leary then walked out of the building together. Joseph stopped, looked at Louis, and he pointed in the direction of Fulton Street. "Get the fuck out of here!" His voice was loud and menacing, causing Louis to immediately run towards Fulton Street. He ran down Fulton Street and kept running as he was consumed with fear because of witnessing these violent acts of his father and the other men. He kept running until, eventually, he made his way home. Louis ran into his room and jumped onto his bed, burying his head under his pillow to try and escape from the events he had just witnessed. Later that night Louis was watching the ABC Manhattan news on his father's old and tatty black and white television. Louis did not know where his father was, but the news report gave him no pleasure; a man had been murdered in a suspected baseball bat attack inside a building on Cliff Street, and an old woman's body had been found on the pavement of a street two blocks away. One word was on Louis' mind that night about his father. "Coward."

As Louis laid his head on his pillow that night, he did not know that at O'Malley's Shed, crates were being exchanged for cash with the powers to be which employed the occupants of the Deville. Louis' exchange had been a mutual success, and the exchange of bags that day had brought pleasure to the people who had Joseph on their payroll. In the presence of these men, Joseph, Coonan, and indeed, all of the men working out of O'Malley's Shed were subservient.

Early next morning, Joseph was drinking at the Four-Leaf Clover Inn with the rest of the unholy swill who were known as his 'union' colleagues. All of them were celebrating the success of the previous evening. Having a kid do the dirty work of carrying bags and keeping a watch out proved to be a success. Using his child was Joseph's idea; even Coonan, who had been around the wharves for much longer than most of those men could not remember a stroke of genius like Joseph's idea of using children on the front line; then again, Coonan was not a genius. "No fuckin' coppers will ever turn an eye twice towards that fuckin' kid, Joseph. What a fuckin' stroke of fuckin' genius!" Coonan had bellowed on top note, causing Joseph to respond in kind. "Fucking yes, Coonan, fucking yes!" Joseph drank from his whiskey glass to toast his misconceived notion of genius, while simultaneously grappling with his other hand the breasts of a prostitute. "That little fuckin' prick of a son of mine, born of a French harlot, will finally be of some use for all of us." Coonan, Joseph, and the rest of the gang of union men drank, sang, fought, and then fornicated with the prostitutes who turned up one by one to the bar. Indeed, it seemed as though with every new bottle of whiskey, a new group of prostitutes came into the bar. At some stage during the orgy which ensued, Coonan had an idea, which he expressed to Joseph in the simplest terms. "Let's bring another fuckin' kid on board". Coonan and Joseph discussed the idea, that the kid would have to be older than Louis as it would ensure that an older child was involved in the more dangerous tasks which the proposed children could perform. As Joseph and Coonan discussed the idea of another youth joining Louis on the front line, one of the prostitutes interrupted them. "Excuse me?" Coonan frowned. "What the fuck do ye want?" The prostitute knew she had stepped over the line with these thugs, but she considered it important for her to be heard by them. "I couldn't help but overhear your conversation. I have a son who is looking for work; he is a hard-working boy; he is the one you are looking for." Joseph smiled at the prostitute; however, it was not a friendly smile, rather it was like a predator that was about to eat its prey. He grabbed the prostitute by the arm and dragged her over to a booth. Joseph threw the woman on her back and proceeded to have sex violently with her, for there was no emotion in anything Joseph did; in particular, there was no emotion displayed when he had sex with a woman. Coonan watched on; he was too ugly for even a prostitute to be interested in, but Coonan was a depraved old soul who gained enjoyment from watching the rest of the men mistreat the prostitutes.

CHAPTER 6

Life had changed for Louis. While he was now attending junior high school, the world of the wharves had well and truly invaded Louis' academic world. By the age of 13, Louis was still an above-average student. However, the lure of life down on the wharves was steadily intruding upon the sacred domain of Louis' mind. After many months working on the wharves, Louis had almost slid down into the soulless existence of the other members of O'Malley's Shed, but there was one factor that kept the fire burning in Louis' heart for him to one day experience a better life, as he had done something once beforehand which almost led to his escape from this world. The next time an opportunity arose, Louis had resolved in his mind that he would jump at it. Nevertheless, opportunities to escape this harsh world were rare. He did not want to be like Joseph. Louis hated his father, but he was now stuck with him on Joseph's turf.

In the late summer of 1974, Louis met a young man who was two years his senior. He had heard Coonan for quite a while talking about another 'kid' being on board; however, Louis had not met him, mainly because Louis spent many hours during the day at school. Jack Kelly was short, loud, and seemingly talentless; save for one particular talent, he could be sent out to hustle like an experienced con. Jack's father died when he was five years of age. From there on, Jack's mother worked in a factory by day to feed the household; however, by night, she worked the streets as a prostitute to bring in money to pay the rent. Jack ignored his mother's additional source of income, as, after all, that source of income meant there was a hot meal on the table more times than not. Jack also grew up in Midtown West until his father died, and then he and his mother moved into Harlem, where the rent was cheaper. Being the minority white in a mainly black precinct, albeit in the supposed white sector of Harlem, Jack learned from an early age to hustle, to be street smart, and to always ensure that your skin was saved before you saved another person. Louis and Jack were two different teenagers, but servitude at the shed seemed to instantly bond these two youths. Coonan's introduction of Jack to Louis attracted Jack's mocking traits. "Ye both will be like brothers before too long," Jack would say, imitating

Coonan. The powers-to-be also saw a useful working relationship between these two young men.

There had been many walks for Louis to exchange bags, but Jack was not initially directed by Coonan to assist Louis with this task because Coonan wanted to ensure Jack could be trusted before involving him in assisting Louis with this task. During the times when they were waiting to be dispatched for their individual tasks, the two young men would get up to mischief. Jack mainly would take matters to the next level by pick-pocketing the cash from the pockets of grown men working at the wharves. Not too long afterwards, Louis joined in on the hot-fingered hobby. It was the first time Louis had some money for himself. Louis told Jack about Joseph controlling Louis' money, but he would hide a small amount of change in the hole on the side of his mattress, though the hole was too small to hide all the pick-pocketing loot. Jack vowed he would help Louis devise a plan to hide his money. The plan did not take too long, as Louis told Jack that his father did not come into his room too often. Indeed, his father wished he were not alive. Jack went quiet for a moment, and then his eyes lit up. "Hide the money inside the bottom of your mattress, and he will never look there!" Louis was curious. "What do you mean the bottom? I already hide the change in the tear." Jack shook his head. "No, Louis, cut a hole in the mattress on the side facing down to the floor. He will not look there." Louis knew straight away the plan was a good one; Joseph would never upturn the mattress to look at the underneath side. Jack and Louis had begun to bond, and it was a relationship that would stand Louis in good stead for several years to come to use his secret loot to feed and clothe himself. Louis had a friend, something which he had never experienced before. Coonan noticed the two youths were bonding, and he now trusted Jack.

Subsequently, on a Tuesday evening at around about 5.45pm, Louis attended the shed after he finished junior high school for the day. Louis had homework to do; however, that would have to wait as he was required by Joseph to do a five-hour shift at the shed on a weeknight. Louis' schoolwork was suffering as Joseph expected him to work all the time. "That crap is of no use to you now," Joseph would tell him. When Louis arrived at O'Malley's Shed that Tuesday, he was told to wait outside by Coonan, but Jack had to remain inside. Coonan knew that as the older boy, Jack should be able to convince Louis to do anything, and the job detail was a confronting one. Coonan walked over to an open crate within the shed, stopped just before it and turned to face Jack. "I got a job which

I think a gutless little son of a fuckin' whore like you can't complete." Jack was immediately on the defensive. "Hey, Coonan, there is no job which I am fucking afraid of, man." Coonan grabbed Jack by the throat, his arms may have been thin, but Coonan had a strong grip. "Listen hear, ye fuckin little turd, if ye go around giving smart mouth again I will cut ye fuckin' throat". Coonan's growl bullied Jack into submission so that all he could do was meekly nod his head in response. Coonan reached into the crate and pulled out two long cylinders, both of which had a wick on one end. As Coonan turned around, holding the cylindrical sticks in his hand, Jack was able to catch a glimpse of part of the label of one of the sticks. The letters he saw on the label were d, y, and n. Dynamite! Coonan then growled at Jack through clenched teeth. "Ye to fuckin' go to Cherry Street and walk along under the fuckin' Manhattan Bridge and keep on going to ye get to 232 Cherry Street. There, you'll find a powerhouse. If ye walk around the back, you'll see there are some open glass windows. Light both fuckin' sticks and throw them through the window. The sticks will take about ten seconds to explode. As soon as ye threw them, run." Jack absorbed every word; however, there was an obvious question he had to ask: "What do I do if the windows are not open?" Coonan grinned sarcastically. "Don't fuckin' worry about that; they fuckin' will be open. Take ye friend outside with ye. See if ye can convince that little birdie to throw a stick of dynamite with ye, that way ye have more time to get away." Jack then received the two sticks of dynamite from Coonan. Jack was about to turn around and walk away when Coonan growled out through his teeth. "Take me fuckin' matches, so that you don't get busted buying matches on the way!"

Jack started to walk to the doorway of the shed, and as he reached the door, he decided that he would not tell Louis what their job detail for the evening was. Instead, as Jack walked outside, he merely gesticulated at Louis for him to follow. Louis asked Jack what they had to do, but Jack would not tell him. "Just follow me, and I'll tell you when we get there." With Jack leading them the two boys began the long walk towards their destination. They walked along FDR Drive until they reached Catherine Street, and Jack felt a sense of relief as there were far fewer cop cars around than when walking along the FDR. By the time the boys had reached number 232 Cherry it was 7.00pm, and they had walked one and a half kilometres. As they arrived at 232 both boys noticed that the building was a small power substation with tall wire fences which were erected around its perimeter. Jack then walked around the back of the substation. Louis followed him, wondering what in God's name was going on. When Jack reached the back of the substation, he noticed that two windows were open. The land at the rear of the substation went up an embankment where the access to throw the sticks through the open windows was not restricted by the fence. Jack walked up the embankment, followed by Louis. As they reached the top, Jack turned around to face Louis, and Jack's face expressed the serious nature of their task. "Louis, we got to blow this fucking place up." Louis was stunned, and it took him a short while to speak as he tried to comprehend the plan. "What?" Jack then proceeded to reach into the knapsack and produced the sticks of dynamite which he then handed over to Louis. "We got to blow this substation up, Louis. If we don't do it, well you know what we are threatened with by Coonan if we don't do something." Louis knew full well what would happen. Jack then handed Louis a strike-anywhere match. "On the count of 3, we are going to light the sticks and then throw them through these windows." Jack counted out loud enough for Louis to hear, and on the count of 3, the sticks were lit. Both boys immediately threw their sticks of dynamite, and as fortune would favour both of them, both sticks of dynamite sailed through the windows. "Run!" With Jack's command, both youths did indeed run.

They ran as fast as they could back down Cherry Street, but they would have barely run 60 metres when the sound of the sticks of dynamite exploding within the substation rang out. As lights came on in the neighbouring apartment buildings on Cherry Street, a further loud explosion erupted from the substation as the transformer had now blown up. Immediately, the lights began to shut down in Cherry Street and cries into the night began to filter out of the various apartments, whether in shock or annoyance at the loss of power, the latter of which provided the best cover for the two boys to run down Cherry Street without being identified. As they crossed over into Catherine Street, the boys could hear the siren of a police car coming down the street from the direction of E Broadway, but in the dark, the police were never going to see two boys running down the street so far away. They ran along the FDR in darkness until Jack slowed the pace of their flight from the scene to a quick walk because "more cop cars may come along the FDR, and we may attract their attention." As they passed under the Brooklyn Bridge, Jack looked back over his shoulder and saw two police cars and a fire engine turning off the FDR to head towards Cherry Street. Louis then grabbed Jack by the shirt. "Why didn't you tell me, Jack, beforehand what Coonan had asked us to do?" Jack just shrugged his shoulders and then broke free of Louis' grip, and walked away. "I am not a coward, Jack."

His loud statement caused Jack to stop mid-stride, and he immediately spun around to speak to Louis. He wanted to tell him he was sorry, but those words were not spoken by him. Instead, Jack turned back around and continued to walk back to the shed, with Louis following him. When both boys returned to O'Malley's Shed, they noticed that the lights were not on in that precinct of Manhattan. Coonan was delighted to see the boys return.

Within hours of the substation being blown up, the Mayor of Manhattan, Frank Sabatini, met with the Commissioner of Police. Like old friends meeting up for their usual chat about the state of the city, they were hardly disturbed by the news of the substation explosion. The words of Mayor Sabatini were simple. "Shut down the goddamn investigation immediately." The Commissioner did not need any further instruction; corruption was entrenched in Manhattan. The police were subsequently unable to find any evidence, which gave them a lead to the offenders responsible for the explosion. The newspapers reported the explosion at the substation as being caused by an unknown source. Mayor Sabatini announced on the news the following evening his office would request the police to shut the case down as police resources needed to focus on cases that could be solved. Despite some reporters querying this wisdom, the mayor said directly: "I have been informed by the Commissioner there is no physical evidence to prove who committed this crime; therefore, why would I waste more public resources?" Louis watched the mayor speak on television that evening, and it appeared to him the mayor seemed to be uncomfortable with making this public announcement.

About five days after the substation was blown up Louis and Jack were told by Coonan that they had a bag drop off and bag pick up to perform in Front Street. The two boys arrived at the usual area of Front Street, and this was the first occasion Coonan asked Jack to perform this task with Louis, where, once again, the silver Deville was waiting. On this occasion, Antonio got out of the Deville because Jack was new, and the street-smart Antonio could tell by looking at him that he was trouble. "Who the fuck are you?" Antonio's words were crisp and derisive of Jack, causing the upstart youth to spontaneously respond: "I'm your mother's other son." It only took a second for Antonio's right hand to belt Jack across his half-smart face, causing him to fall to the ground as blood slowly trickled out of his left nostril. "Listen here, you little punk, if you ever speak to me again like that, I will cut you from asshole to breakfast time!" Jack did not respond; Antonio had won that round. Louis was startled not only by Antonio's physical actions but also by the menacing nature of his voice. Leaving Jack on the ground, Antonio spun around on his heels so that he could look Louis in the eyes. He grabbed the startled youth by the front of his shirt and dragged him closer. "I remember you, you little punk. What is your name kid?" Unlike Jack, he was not inclined to be half-smart, and, in any event, Louis was still startled by Antonio's impulsive violence. "Louis. I'm Louis." He could tell Louis was smarter than the other youth, so Antonio slightly released his grip on the front of Louis' shirt. "You look like you're a smart kid, Louis, so listen carefully because I do not repeat myself. We have two bags to hand over to you today, and the same rule applies. Have you opened any of the bags, Louis?" He shook his head from side to side quickly to convey he had not. "Good. I thought you were a smart kid when I first laid eyes on you. These bags have a lot of money in them, a lot of unmarked bills. If you two little scraps steal any sum of money from these bags, you will die. Not quickly, slowly die." There was only silence after Antonio's harsh warning. He handed two bags to Louis, who then handed one of the bags to Jack, who had slowly stood up. "Well, what are you waiting for? Get out of here; do your jobs!" Louis and Jack quickly walked off with the bags and proceeded to walk back down Front Street to head back towards O'Malley's Shed. The sound of the Deville starting up and taking off seemed louder that afternoon, probably because it was a Sunday and there were fewer cars on the Brooklyn Bridge and the FDR, but the sound of the engine of the Deville complimented the threat posed by its occupants. As they got to 217 Front Street, Jack quickly walked into an abandoned entryway to the building, and there was enough shelter from the street so that he could not be readily seen. Louis followed him into the entryway as he knew his accomplice was up to some sort of mischief. Jack opened his bag on the ground, and to Louis' amazement and accompanying concern, Jack started searching through this bag. Jack was already breaking Antonio's command. "Fucking Guinea doesn't scare me." Jack held up some loose bills of money. "What are you doing, Jack?" Louis' voice had that nervous quiver, displaying his inner fear of Jack's contumelious disregard for Antonio's threat. "Look, Louis, they're loose and unmarked notes, which means the chances are some moron has probably not counted it properly." The view expressed by Jack did not make sense to Louis, nor did it allay his fear, but Jack seemed to be adamant, or he was at least caught up in the moment. Jack then plucked a $5.00 note out of the bundle of loose notes he held in his left hand, and he placed that note in his right pant pocket. "Put that back, Jack; you are going to get both of us into a lot of trouble." Louis' nervous voice could not be directive. Jack did not put the note back; instead, he looked at Louis in disbelief. "What's the problem? Nobody will know. Take some money." Louis shook his head to say "No". Jack shrugged his shoulders and proceeded to pluck another $5.00 bill, which he placed in his pocket before zipping up the bag. Without even a moment's thought, Jack then proceeded to walk out of the entryway of the building; Louis followed a few yards behind him, slowly keeping his distance. Whereas Jack walked confidently forward, Louis, on the other hand walked behind cautiously, looking over his shoulder and wondering whether Antonio, Coonan, his father, or anyone may have seen what had just occurred. Louis knew for his own sake that he could never be placed in this position again for fear of his safety. As they arrived back at the shed Louis knew that he would have to find a way to sever the bag collection relationship with Jack. Coonan took the bags without even checking the contents at the time of handover. Louis sighed silently in relief, as in his heart he knew the thugs, like his father, had no direct proof from Coonan that money was missing directly at the time of the handover. Jack silently rejoiced for he considered he had found a new way to pull a street trick. Louis, however, did not feel comfortable working with Jack on the bag drop-off and pickup. He did not express his discomfort to Coonan, nor did he act differently towards Jack that afternoon, but Louis knew he could not collect the bags with Jack again. Subsequently, Jack would be the first one to leave the shed that afternoon. A couple of thick-necked men turned up that afternoon to speak to Coonan before Jack left, and, by 4.00pm, these men had left, and therefore Jack considered the two boys were not required for any further job details that day. Louis also waited until the two heavy-set men had left the shed before he made his next move.

After Jack had left, Louis walked back into the shed to speak to Coonan. He had devised a plan to try to ensure he was not placed in jeopardy again by Jack's sticky fingers. He put to Coonan a proposal that involved him riding a disused bicycle that was up the back of the shed to do the bag drop-offs again by himself. Coonan, forever a cynic, thought he smelt a rat. "Why? Are you and Jack having some little problems, lad?" Louis shook his head, realising his proposal needed to be quickly explained or else Coonan might twig to the bags of money that afternoon, which were a few dollars down. "No, Coonan. The bike is a much quicker method to do the bag drop off and is less likely to attract attention than two young guys like us walking the street. Anyway, with a bike, we can do more bag drop-offs in one day with less chance of being detected. So, what do you say, Coonan?" Coonan liked the idea and agreed with Louis' proposal. Louis had successfully separated himself from Jack's conduct of stealing from the bags of money being exchanged with Antonio and Domenico. Subsequently, for a short while, Jack wondered why he and Louis had been separated from jointly completing the bag exchange task. He had not been accused of anything by any person within the dark world of O'Malley's Shed, so Jack considered he was in the clear. However, there were other tasks for Jack to do. The use of bicycles to drop off and pick up bags was also a success as Louis was able to ride freely to more spots around those seedy districts of Manhattan to perform this task and, of course, more frequently perform the drop-offs and pickups. Rather than performing one or two drop-offs in a day by foot, Louis was sometimes performing up to five drop-offs in a day. Occasionally, Joseph would slightly nod his head at his son in the form of approval, but such displays of emotion were rare. These infrequent acknowledgements did not change Louis' lack of feelings for Joseph. "Pig, the only reason you did that is because you get more money!" Louis' life seemed hopeless the more deeply he was dragged into the life of O'Malley's Shed. He was depressed, and his mental tormentor of death anxiety would come to visit from time to time.

Twelve months had passed since the day Jack had stolen money from the bags. After he initially wondered why he was not working with Louis, he did not ask him why they were not collecting bags together from the silver Deville. Louis using the bicycle dispelled any concerns Jack may have had, and, as always, Jack found a new way of pinching money from Coonan when the old cretin would fall asleep on the job. Antonio seemed to be more at ease with just Louis collecting the bags. The ominous warnings of a slow and brutal death would occasionally be spoken, and this would always unnerve Louis; it wasn't just Antonio's words that unsettled Louis; it was also his intent behind those words. Occasionally, Antonio would mention how things were done in the borough of the Bronx. His stories were not shared in friendship; rather, they were shared to keep the teenage boy in a state of fear and respect. Antonio was intelligent, and he knew fear would keep order in this corrupt world of bag exchanges. He was also intelligent enough never to reveal who he was to Louis, indeed anyone, that Mayor Sabatini was his late mother's cousin. Not even the mayor's closest confidantes in this shady underworld crime outfit knew there was a family connection; that was Antonio's wish, and it was an intelligent move on his behalf.

Louis also continued to attend school. His marks were good, but he was not anywhere near his potential. Louis and Jack were required to attend to many other tasks set for them by Coonan, which did not involve the bags, and they also became close friends, forever getting up to pranks initiated by Jack. On one such occasion, the boys had been made by Coonan to get him some food. "Go get me a fucking Philly steak and cheese!" Jack did not like being Coonan's servant. "I'll show him," he told Louis as they walked to the dirty old diner. Before returning the sandwich to Coonan Jack spat on it in several places as Louis watched on. After bringing it back to the shed, the two youths then sat down and watched Coonan eat the sandwich, spit and all. The more bites he took, the more the two boys laughed. "What is fucking wrong with ye?" Coonan would only cause them to laugh more. On another occasion, when it was a school night for Louis, he was made to stay around late with Jack as the men drank and carried on in the shed. They were made to stay late and wait outside in the cold for no good reason. Once again, Jack initiated the mischief. "I'll show them!" Jack then proceeded to let down the tyres on one of the thug's cars. Eventually, the thug who owned the car left the shed and drove off at a great rate of knots, despite him being drunk. As he drove away, he lost control of his car and drove straight into the water, much to the amusement of Jack and Louis. The thug was able to get out of his car, but the vehicle itself sank into the gloomy, dark waters of the East River. Without Jack's cavalier antics and companionship, Louis' mind would have spiralled further down.

Not long after his 15th birthday, Louis attended his usual weekday shift at O'Malley's Shed on a Friday afternoon. Jack was already there when Louis arrived, and Coonan was leaning against the entryway to the shed. Upon Louis' arrival, both boys were summonsed into the shed by Coonan. It seemed as though time slowed down that late afternoon as Coonan proceeded to tell them the job they had to perform. The details were simple; they were to complete another explosives job but this time at a gas station located at 25 Beekman Street. Louis was the first one to speak. "A gas station?" Coonan looked at the youth as though he was an idiot. "Yes, a fuckin gas station, ye fuckin' little turd." Louis ignored the insult. "That is dangerous. Is it open? Will anyone be working?" Coonan opened his mouth in shock, more condescending than in actual surprise. "Don't fuckin' ask questions, ye little fuckin turd; ye will just do as ye are told. Now, you

two little fuckers are to throw the sticks of dynamite into that gas station. Don't
stick around; just fuckin' run. If ye get caught by anyone, just fuckin' pray they
kill ye before we fuckin' get to ye." Jack was then handed the sticks of dynamite
by Coonan and the matches.

Jack led the way toward Beekman Street, and Louis reluctantly followed him.
The walk to 25 Beekman Street took about 40 minutes that evening but in the
scheme of Louis' mind, it seemed to take all evening. Louis was adamant they
should not blow up the gas station. "Jack, you know this is wrong. Don't do it.
Please, Jack." Jack did not respond, so Louis thought he was not listening to him;
Jack was listening, and he had made a decision about what they should do. Louis
reluctantly followed Jack, but he affirmed in his mind he would try to disabuse
Jack from completing the task at the scene. When they arrived at 25 Beekman
Street, Jack did not wait, nor did he involve Louis in performing this dangerous
job. He immediately removed the sticks of dynamite from his knapsack, lit
both of them off the same match, and threw them into the gas station within
seconds of their arrival. To his horror, Louis saw there was an attendant behind
the counter of the gas station at the time. He ran away first as, in his mind, he
knew this job detail was wrong, and he did not want to be blamed. Jack quickly
followed. Both of them had run about 50 metres away when the explosion of the
dynamite went off. It only seemed to be a split second later that the sound of the
fuel stored below the petrol bowsers went off, and with that explosion, there was
the sound of the collateral damage of windows in nearby buildings exploding,
the shattering of glass and wood and then the secondary sound of glass falling to
the ground. As Louis ran towards the corner of Beekman and Williams Streets,
he heard a scream behind him, and he looked over his shoulder to see that out of
the gas station ran the figure of a person on fire. Louis looked over his shoulder
to his left, and he noticed that Jack had now run the opposite way up William
Street towards Spruce Street.

Louis did not see the car that had followed him and Jack into Beekman
Street; if he had, he might have seen the dark-haired man driving that car. It was
the same man who sat in the back of the court the day Louis had been sentenced
for striking Jose. The driver had attempted to follow Louis as he ran away from
Beekman Street that evening, but he quickly lost Louis, who had now chosen
to run down alleyways to promptly remove himself from the scene. He was
not stopping at any stage to gather his breath, and when Louis was about two
blocks away from Joseph's apartment, he stopped running. His body could not

carry him any further. Louis lurched towards a garbage bin because he could not hold back his stomach, and he vomited all over the outside of the bin and the pavement. Passers-by side stepped into the area and looked down their noses in disdain. Louis gathered himself together, and he walked towards his street.

Jack returned to the shed immediately after the bombing of the gas station. He ran most of the way back to O'Malley's Shed using the darkness of the backstreets to avoid being detected. Jack took his time to catch his breath, and he was worried about Louis; in particular, he was worried about how Joseph would react if he discovered Louis had not participated in the bombing. Jack knew Coonan would interrogate him about where Louis was and whether he had participated in the bombing as directed. As he was catching his breath, Jack devised an explanation, he hoped would satisfy Coonan, and as a consequence, prevent any harm coming Louis' way. When he entered the shed, Coonan was waiting. "Where in the fuck is Louis?" Jack did not hesitate. "I lost him, or he lost me." Coonan's face crumpled with anger. "What do ye fuckin' mean? Did he do the job or not?" Jack realised he had to elaborate on his story, and Coonan's demeanour suggested he would not tolerate half a story. "Yeah, he did, but not the way you wanted. There was a guy, an older black guy, busking outside of the gas station. I told Louis to steal his money to get rid of him. He took the guy's money and was then chased down the street by him. I lost sight of him because he had to run a long way and then go down an alleyway. After all, that busker continued to chase him. So, I threw both sticks of dynamite, but it was only because of Louis that the job was done." Coonan stared into Jack's eyes to determine whether or not he was trying to deceive him. After a painful period of delay for Jack, the old man shrugged his shoulders and commenced to walk away. "Alrighty then, Louis is a fuckin' hero; now fuck off home." Jack turned around to walk back out of the shed, and as he did so, he also sighed to himself in relief; Louis would be spared the wrath of both Joseph and Coonan.

When Louis eventually arrived at his building, he once again threw up out the front of it as the vision of that gas station attendant being on fire haunted his mind. He eventually gathered himself together and entered the building, walking up the two flights of internal stairs to arrive at his father's apartment. Louis' heart was still racing from running and the thought of the person being on fire, and he was suffering from complex feelings of guilt for failing to stop Jack from blowing up the gas station. As he entered the apartment, Louis' thoughts were distracted by the sound of loud voices moaning, and the sound seemed to come from further up the hallway from the lounge room. Louis crept slowly to the doorway, and he peered around the corner of the door and saw the strange sight of Joseph and Mary being naked and sprawled over the dirty couch. Then, within a blink of an eye, another naked woman joined them on the couch to nestle into Joseph's right armpit; she was a red-haired lady, probably in her late 30s. Her eyes lit up in shock when she saw the outline of Louis' head peering from around the corner of the entrance to the lounge room and she then screamed in fright. With that woman screaming, Mary also screamed, and Joseph leapt to his feet to confront Louis, who was frozen still in fear. Joseph growled like a wild animal. "You fucking peeping Tom." As he finished his final word, he swung his right fist into Louis' chin. Like a house of cards being dismantled, Louis collapsed to the ground in the hallway, and he was knocked out for the count by Joseph's vicious attack. Another Friday night in Midtown West.

Some two hours later, Louis woke up on the floor of the hallway. Joseph, Mary, and the other woman were nowhere to be seen. Louis' chin and head were both very sore, and he needed some rest. He took himself down to his bedroom, looked out of his apartment window and hoped that tomorrow would free him of this mental turmoil; however, he also realised at the same time that he was trapped in a personal hell that he could not escape. He had not thrown the sticks of dynamite, but he felt responsible for what had occurred that evening, including the dreadful sight of the gas station attendant running out onto the street covered in flames. He felt isolated and trapped. The distant golden glow of Wall Street symbolised Louis' feelings of his life being marooned in a world he did not belong to; he had wanted to be a part of that golden glow but now it seemed to be a symbol of lost hope.

That next morning, after the bombing of the gas station, the Commissioner of Police met with the mayor. The gas station attendant was dead, and the press gallery was screaming for answers. Mayor Sabatini was equally concerned about the death of the attendant, but his command was the same as it had been on so many previous occasions. "There is no physical evidence so we are not going to waste valuable police resources on a crime that cannot be solved, so tell the media that!" The Commissioner of Police nodded his head. Another crime in Manhattan was about to be buried under the command of Mayor Sabatini.

CHAPTER 7

During the days that followed the bombing, Louis saw numerous news articles about the incident. Every time he saw an article on television, his heart sank with the weight of his sorrow and guilt for being involved in this crime. The fact that his father was the reason for Louis' descending into this miserable and sordid world of criminal activity only intensified the hatred he silently held for Joseph. All the news reported the same facts, namely, the gas station attendant had died, and there were no leads. Once again, the Commissioner made his usual prompt statement of not diverting precious police resources to cases that could not be solved. The newspapers were furious with the lack of police investigation.

The following Monday, Louis had to go to the shed. He had remained in his bedroom for most of the weekend, and he did not go to school that day. However, Joseph had stormed into Louis' bedroom that Monday afternoon, hurled him out of his bed, and told the depressed youth if he did not go to the shed, he and O'Leary would cave in his head with an iron bar. O'Leary was standing in the hallway of the apartment when Louis walked out of his room, and he had an iron bar in his hand. Joseph was serious; he would kill him if the lad did not leave. He had to walk while O'Leary drove himself and Joseph back to O'Malley's Shed. In what was a walk of shame, guilt, and remorse, Louis arrived at the shed on time at 3.30pm. The silver Deville was parked outside, and the sight of this car caused Louis to pull up in his stride. He caught the eye of Coonan, who was perched in his usual spot like a vicious spider. Coonan ushered for Louis to come over and it seemed to Louis that something serious was taking place. Coonan just snarled. "We have fuckin' company, so wait ere." Jack was not present, but by now, Jack was no longer attending school, so he was 'available' all day long to perform his job tasks. An hour went by. Louis was about to say something when he heard the voices of several men who were heading out of the shed. Four men in suits and ties walked outside and headed straight towards the silver Deville. A man in the middle of the group of four looked familiar to Louis, but he could only catch a glimpse of his face. One of the men opened the back door of the Deville, and then Louis could see with his own eyes the right-hand side of the face of the man he had been trying to look at; the face Louis saw was that of Mayor Sabatini. The sight of the mayor ordinarily would have surprised Louis, but he knew from watching the mayor on television only two days ago that he seemed to be guilty of something. The Deville started up and then drove off in the direction of Maiden Lane. Coonan's sinister grin was the first sight Louis caught as he turned around. "Now, ye know who ye work for, lad." Twenty minutes later, Joseph walked out of the shed, and he didn't stop to speak to Louis. Louis detected that his father had a vicious look on his face, which normally meant someone was in for trouble. Joseph jumped into the driver's seat of the old Dodge van and drove off at great speed; O'Leary and another had already jumped into the back of the van. Something was wrong. Louis spent the rest of his shift sitting outside of the shed. He now realised his father was a pawn, not a king. He also pictured the sight in his memory of the man on fire and was overwhelmed with remorse for the harm, which he thought he should have stopped.

The old Dodge van arrived at the destination, which was a large brick apartment building on Monroe Street. The apartment block was cheap accommodation, and its façade matched the cost of rent. Joseph turned to O'Leary and the other man. "Wait here until you see the signal." His riding orders from the mayor were simple. Inside apartment 103 lived a young maverick police officer named Luke Shaw, who had taken it upon himself to commence investigating the gas station bombing. In particular, Shaw was piecing together a path the mayor feared would lead to him. The tipoff about Shaw had come from the Commissioner. Joseph had to kill Shaw and take whatever evidence he may have in his apartment. Killing a copper, nothing gave Joseph greater satisfaction. They waited in the Dodge van until the sun had gone down and nobody was around. O'Leary was Joseph's backup and the other man sat in the driver's seat as the getaway driver. Joseph started to jimmy the lock on Shaw's apartment door with a crowbar. Shaw was sound asleep on his couch after having performed a night shift, which carried through to the late afternoon because of his leads. He was only able to just rise to his feet as Joseph came storming into the apartment. Shaw looked for his gun, but as usual, he had hidden it in his bedroom, and it was not within his reach. Joseph struck the young police officer over the head with the crowbar, instantly cracking his skull and knocking him forever unconscious. Blood began to ooze from Shaw's skull onto his living room floor rug. Joseph then lifted the blind and proceeded to turn the lamp on the side table on and off, the signal for the driver to start the van. Shaw was rolled up in his blood-soaked rug and carried downstairs by Joseph and O'Leary. Joseph hurried back to Shaw's apartment and gathered up all of the investigation materials he could find. Being the type of building which it was, none of the other residents dared to look outside if they heard any noise. Later that evening, the weighted-down rug containing Shaw's lifeless body was thrown into the water at the East River Park. Subsequent internal police investigations into the young police officer's disappearance were shut down by the Commissioner on the basis that it was more than likely Shaw was involved in some form of street drug corruption, and accordingly, it was a street crime that would never be solved. The reputation of an otherwise good police officer was forever tarnished.

CHAPTER 8

A further two years sped by for Louis after the bombing of the gas station. Nothing had changed at Joseph's apartment. Sometimes, Louis could go for weeks without being assaulted. On other occasions, it seemed as though Joseph's fist was crashing into Louis' face several times a week for no good reason. No matter how hard his father hit him, Louis would always bounce back up.

Louis' shifts at the shed brought the usual job details for him to attend to. Bags continued being exchanged, but the car had changed; a black 1975 Cadillac Fleetwood was now the vehicle that turned up for the bag exchange. Antonio was no longer one of the people involved in the bag exchange; he was moving on from the corrupt world of the mayor and was instead going to use the brains he had been blessed with. All Louis was told by Dom was that it wasn't Antonio's job anymore. Louis and Jack still had to perform lookout duties while the men from the wharf carried out their violent assaults on various people in the shady side of the Manhattan area. Over time, Louis forgave Jack for the bombing of the gas station, and he realised his accomplice spared him having to throw one of the sticks of dynamite.

Louis' interests in life were changing. He was still a relatively bright student, and he had matriculated into sub-senior at high school, but his academic record was blemished by the open recording of the conviction, and he knew once he had finished school his options were limited. Despite this depressing thought, Louis still put some effort into his schoolwork when his time at the shed permitted it. He particularly enjoyed Modern History. He studied the settlement of Australia and the development of the city of Sydney. "I would love to live there," he thought to himself one day at school as he looked at the pictures of that city's beachside suburbs and the harbour; it looked like it was a city where people could start afresh. Louis also knew that at the age of 16, the authorities were less concerned with a parent looking after their child in Midtown West. This factor concerned him as he knew his father would 'broom him' when he finished school.

Louis' mental health had also fluctuated. There were times when his mind would be morbidly preoccupied with his mortality, and this was particularly the case when he saw images on television depicting graphic violence. Sometimes, his morbid thoughts could occupy his mind for weeks, only to be disrupted from his consciousness by Joseph's brutality, which he had to endure as part of his miserable life. He also thought about his mother from time to time, and he wondered where she was in the world and whether she would one day return to his life.

Girls his age were also now enticing to Louis, but at 16, he was awkward around the opposite sex. On one occasion, when he finished a Saturday shift at the shed, Louis came across some kids from his school at a diner nearby where he lived. Jack also accompanied Louis on this occasion. To Jack's amusement, he watched on as Louis awkwardly tried to speak to a girl he liked only to be rejected by her. After they left the diner, Jack could not help himself, and he had to say something about Louis' bruised pride. "Crash and burn my friend. Like a virgin. Crash and burn!" Jack knew by Louis' demeanour that he was still disappointed things had not worked out with the girl just before they went their separate ways that night. Jack had an idea. "Hey, come around to my place tomorrow at 4.00pm as my mum won't be home at that time, and I will have a surprise for you." Being a Sunday, they were not required at the shed. Louis was intrigued by the surprise, but he just shrugged his shoulders in his despondent state of mind. "Sure." Louis had not been previously invited to Jack's apartment where he lived with his mom so when he was told the address, it was a surprise. "457 West 125th Street, you can't miss the building. Buzz apartment 8."

The following afternoon, Louis arrived at Jack's apartment building in Harlem. Louis felt uncomfortable in this district of Manhattan because he had never been there before. He had also never been to Grand Central Station before this day, but he did not get to see the majesty of the old building as he only changed subway tracks far underneath it. The rent was cheaper in this area of Harlem in Midtown West, which explained the reason why Jack and his mother lived in this district. It was not Central Harlem, so it was a melting pot of African Americans, Hispanic Americans, and even European Americans. 457 West 125th Street was a rundown building and it had fire escape stairs running down the front of it. Louis rang Jack's apartment number and there was a slight delay of thirty seconds. Louis was about to press the buzzer again when he heard the door disengaging for him to enter the building.

Louis walked into the foyer. On the right-hand side wall was a board that recorded the floor, rooms, and names of the tenants. The name 'Kelly' appeared next to apartment 8, floor 2. Louis walked up the stairs to level 2, and immediately before him was apartment number 8. He knocked on the door and thought he could hear a girl laughing and then a door shutting. The door opened, and Jack stood there with a sly grin. "Come in." Louis entered the apartment; it was a small space. There was a living area and a kitchen in an open-plan setting. In the living room were the telltale signs of where Jack slept as there was a fold-out lounge in front of the old black and white model television set, which was positioned under the window that looked out onto 125th Street. Two doors ran off the wall to the left; the first of these was open to reveal a bathroom; the other undoubtedly led to the only bedroom, but the door was shut. Jack broke the momentary silence. "It is your lucky day, Louis." A puzzled look came across Louis' face. Jack then opened the door to the bedroom. "Meet Maya; she is from next door." A pretty African American girl walked to the doorway of the bedroom. She stood 5' 7" and appeared at the least to be in her very late teens, probably nineteen years of age if not twenty. Maya's hair had a slight wave, and her features were fine, which included her nose, which suggested European blood had mixed with African blood at some stage. Louis looked at Maya and realised there was a tragic story somewhere in her personal life for her to be mixed up with Jack. However, her attractive looks and Louis' 16-year-old hormones quickly took over his conscious state. "Maya is going to teach you how to do it today, my treat." Louis was surprised about the word 'treat'. "What do you mean, my treat?" Jack's face then displayed a condescending smile, which matched his tone of voice. "You don't think Maya does this for free, do you? It's okay; unlike you, the money I earn at the shed goes to me, so I like I said, my treat." Louis stood still; his nerves with the opposite sex began to take over his body. Just as he was about to freeze up, Jack nudged Louis on the shoulder with his hand to push him in the direction of the bedroom.

Louis walked into the room and the décor suggested a woman slept in there. As Louis walked towards the bed the door to the bedroom was shut behind him by Maya. Louis turned around to face her. Maya was dressed in a thin summer dress and flat heels. By her appearance, it seemed that she was dressed to quickly get out of and back into her clothes. She then undid the buttons at the front of her dress, and the mere sight of her doing this caused Louis' pulse to race. Lifting the dress over her head Maya revealed her pretty body; she had firm breasts and beautifully shaped legs. A small voice of shame echoed in Louis' mind as he watched Maya become naked. "A pretty African American girl having to sell her body." Nevertheless, his 16-year-old male urges were stronger than the voices of protest in his conscience, and as Maya crawled onto the bed Louis followed her. She kissed Louis gently on the lips and whispered in his ear. "It is okay, sugar; I am going to look after you." Maya began to undo the buttons on Louis' shirt, and within a short time, he, too, was naked. Louis was about to launch at Maya, such was the excitement that was running through his veins. "Not without a rubber." Maya reached over to the bedside table and pulled out a condom from the drawer. Jack had thought of everything, including making sure there were condoms strategically placed in his mother's room, or at least this is what Louis surmised to be the case. The whole sexual escapade for Louis lasted no longer than ten minutes, but in the scheme of his life to date, this moment seemed to last for hours; such was the delight and unusual comfort he found in Maya's arms once his heart stopped racing.

As Louis was getting dressed, he looked around at Maya, who was still lying naked on the bed. Louis walked towards the door and turned towards her to ask whether she would get dressed. Then he realised that it was Jack's turn. He opened the door and walked back out into the living room. The boy who entered the bedroom was gone, and now a young man stood in that living room. Louis was still coming to terms with the wonder of losing his virginity as Jack walked by him to enter the bedroom. Jack was already unbuttoning his shirt as he closed the door behind him. Louis sat on the fold-out lounge to wait for Jack. His thoughts were consumed with the images of Maya's naked body, and he had an innocent grin on his face, which emphasised just how young he still was.

Time seemed to drag on, but it had only been 15 minutes when Louis heard a key turning in the front door of Jack's apartment. The door swung open, and there stood before him a face he had seen about two years before when he came home that horrible night after the gas station was bombed. The red-headed woman stood at the door with a paper bag of groceries. Louis realised this lady must be Jack's mother. She did not have an opportunity to have a good look at Louis' face two years ago, so accordingly she looked at him as though he was a stranger. "Who are you?" Anne Kelly had been a prostitute for most of her adult life; her tone was coarse and common. Realising that she did not recognise him Louis responded cautiously: "I am a friend of Jack's." Anne became suspicious about what her son was up to. "Where is Jack?" Louis looked towards the closed bedroom door, and instinctively, Anne knew that her bedroom was being used for something other than sleeping. She marched over to the door and swung it open, but in her haste, she had left open the front door to the apartment. There was Jack on top of Maya in the bed and they were both naked. Maya was startled by the sudden intrusion, and she screamed out loudly, the sound of her voice travelling out the open door of the apartment and into the hallway. Jack yelled in fright. "Hey, Mom, what the fuck are you doing?" Anne also screamed, and the noise caused some of the doors of the apartments on level 2 to open, including apartment number 7 across the hallway, where a balding, overweight African American man stood in the doorway, his face displaying concern and a certain level of bewilderment about the noise. Maya continued to scream out loudly, and the man from apartment 7 knew that voice; it was his daughter's voice crying out for help. He raced across the hallway into Jack's apartment, and his arrival on the scene caused further screams to erupt from the vocal cords of Maya and Jack's mother. Seeing his daughter now standing there naked in the bedroom enraged him. He grabbed Maya by the back of her head and dragged her into his apartment, slamming the door behind him. As if the episode had not already created enough drama, the sounds from apartment 7 suggested Maya's father was beating her. Jack's mother slammed the front door to her apartment and put on the safety latch. By now, Jack had put on his pants, and he was quickly grabbing for his shirt and shoes. He turned to Louis, who had not moved since Anne opened the door to the bedroom. "Come on, man, let's go." Jack then opened the bedroom window which then led out to the fire stairs. He exited through the window to the sound of his mother screaming abuse at him. Anne's coarse tones seemed to magnify as the sound carried out through the window. Louis was not far behind him, and both young men fled the building via the fire stairs.

By the time they had reached the bottom of the fire stairs, they could hear Maya's father beating on the front door to Jack's apartment, and the words bellowing from his mouth suggested that Jack would not live too long if he got his hands on him. Louis and Jack ran down 125th Street, just like they ran when they had fled the scene of bombing the substation and gas station, only this time they were fleeing one irate man rather than the metropolitan police force. They ran to Amsterdam Avenue, where Jack was able to find a spot to put on his shoes. Jack started laughing but Louis was thinking about Maya. She did not deserve to be beaten as far as he was concerned, and Louis could not share Jack's lightheartedness at this time. Louis now knew what it was like to be with a woman, but he vowed he would never again in his life have sex with a woman in return for paying money; he could imagine what Ms Fitzgerald would say if she were alive. After Jack put his shoes on, they continued to walk down

Amsterdam Avenue to then double back around to the subway station on St Nicholas Avenue. They both took the subway to return to Midtown West as Jack decided he should sleep at O'Malley's Shed that night. The next morning Jack explained to Coonan why he had to sleep at the shed, to which Coonan rocked with uncontrollable laughter, and eventually, when he could contain himself, he agreed that Jack could sleep there again that night. When Jack eventually returned to his apartment the next day, his mother asked him who the other young man was who was in their apartment that Sunday afternoon. Jack told his mother it was Louis, and that his father had something to do with the shed where Jack worked. Jack's mother's heart froze; she then realised who the young man was and the night when she performed the sex act with Joseph and Mary. Louis was not welcome in her apartment ever again.

Three weeks had passed since the afternoon with Maya. Louis had begun to feel more comfortable with the girls he knew at his school. His newfound confidence started to become noticed, and one girl in particular started to take an interest in Louis. Her name was Molly Anderson, and she was Louis' age; Molly was cute rather than pretty. Her father worked in a decent job in a factory in the Bronx; accordingly, she was reasonably dressed and at least spoke without swearing. Molly's interest in him had not gone unnoticed by Louis. She seemed to be sweet enough; however, that was what concerned Louis. He realised that in his tough life after school, there was a limit to their interaction, no way on this earth would he ever allow this girl to be exposed to Joseph or the seedy life of the shed. Louis could not have a steady girlfriend in his miserable world.

Louis entered his senior year of high school in September of 1977. By remaining at school, he was protecting himself from Joseph; for as long as he was at school, there was a reason for the authorities to monitor Louis' welfare. Joseph wanted Louis to leave school and get a 'real' job. Louis knew what the real job entailed; it would be full-time work at the shed and forever being a prisoner in the cruel world that Joseph had chosen for his son. His seventeenth birthday came and went; the highlight of this birthday was Molly giving Louis his 'special' present. Molly hoped that by giving up her body, they would become closer and become steady, but unfortunately, it was the start of them growing apart. Louis had to tell her he could not go steady with her, and when she asked why not, he had to lie about being interested in other girls. Molly was too nice for Louis' world, and after her initial heartbreak, Molly realised other boys at school were interested in her.

Louis did not know what he wanted to do once he had finished high school. As he entered the final four months of his Senior year he suddenly had an eerie feeling the 'real job' was becoming the likely scenario for his future life. The open recording of his conviction militated against any remote chance of obtaining a student loan. He began to experience another cycle of depression, and his mind once again became overwhelmed with thoughts about his mortality. Molly was a very fortunate young woman to be spared being exposed to Louis' cruel existence; however, there was also a problem emerging within Louis' complex mind regarding how he treated women. He had unwittingly been programmed with Joseph's misogynistic traits, but regrettably, no person could enlighten him about this unfortunate character flaw.

As he walked out of school one afternoon in late February 1978, Louis' mind was preoccupied with his depressive thoughts. He had accepted that he would not be able to afford to go to college, and it appeared he could not avoid a life at the shed. He was under siege in Midtown West. Joseph expected him to remain working at the shed as a repayment for 'having to raise him'. As Louis walked out of school onto 45th Street that afternoon, he noticed a dark-headed man watching him from the opposite side of the street. He was unnerved by this conduct and by the way he was being watched, it was as though this man knew who Louis was. Louis started to walk at a brisk pace in the direction of 11th Avenue. He looked over his shoulder and saw that the man who had been watching him was also walking briskly. The man then walked out onto 45th Street to now cross the road, and after he did so, he was only 30 yards away from Louis. It was clear to Louis he was being followed, so he started to run, and as he turned the corner into 11th Avenue, he looked over his shoulder and saw the dark-headed man had also commenced running. Because he was looking backward, Louis did not see the large lady walking down 11th Avenue; the collision between both of them knocked Louis off his feet, and the large woman stumbled sideways into a parked car. Seconds flew by as Louis got up off the ground to assist this woman, but she was not impressed with him. "You idiot, watch where you are going next time!" Louis tried to apologise to her. "I'm sorry, mam, but..."; Louis did not get to finish his sentence as the dark-headed man was upon him. "Louis. Stop!" Louis was stunned that this man knew his name. "Louis, watch your step next time! Sorry, lady." The large woman shook her head at both of them and walked off.

As Louis returned fully to his feet, he still looked in disbelief at the dark-headed man and how he knew his name. "Who are you?" The man put his hands up to try to calm Louis down. "We have never met Louis, but I have never been too far away. I am your uncle, and I am your mother's brother. I am Philip." Louis stood there in stunned silence. He never knew that he had an uncle and whilst he considered he should be sceptical about the supposed matriarchal relationship, he nevertheless detected a degree of complete honesty in the words that had been spoken by Philip. "Come on, you look like you need a coffee or Coke or something." Philip offered a handshake in friendship to Louis, and after some initial uncertainty, he shook his uncle's hand. Philip and Louis walked down 11th Avenue until they came to the first coffee shop. The coffee meeting was not planned, and it would forever change Louis' life.

When Philip sat down at the table in the café after placing their order, he remained silent for a minute. Louis waited for Philip to talk, but he didn't. Instead of talking, Philip reached into his pocket and produced a beautiful antique necklace. It was not overly adorned with gemstones but there were enough to suggest this was a valuable piece of jewellery. Two oval-shaped diamonds were both individually surrounded and separated by emeralds and sapphires. The band was made of 24-carat gold. Philip looked at Louis and spoke in a discreet voice. "What I am about to tell you, Louis, regarding this necklace and your mother will shock you. This necklace belonged to my mother, your grandmother. I want you to know that both your grandmother and I always wanted to meet you, but she feared your father." Louis looked at Philip and he was puzzled as to the reason why his grandmother would be afraid of Joseph. "Why? Why was she afraid?" Philip looked up at the ceiling of the café, and when his eyes returned down to look at Louis, it was noticeable that Philip's eyes were welling with tears. Philip regained his composure. "My mother moved us two children out here to New York from France at the end of World War 2. My father had died during the war, and the Germans had taken much of the wealth my father had accumulated or, perhaps to be precise, inherited before the war." Louis was spellbound by the whole notion of his grandfather 'inheriting' wealth. "What wealth did my grandfather inherit." Philip had been interrupted, but he mentioned the subject. "My father's noble line was Poitiers, but I will discuss that with you later. So where was I? Yes, I remember; when we emigrated from France to New York, the only valuable item that my mother retained was this necklace that my father had given her after they first got married. It was a family heirloom from the nineteenth century. She had no family here in America, and my mother had to struggle with bringing up your mother and me. This meant that as we grew into teenagers, she could not be around to supervise us all the time. Your mother was two years younger than me. She was always a pretty girl, and she believed that she could escape the poor life we lived here in New York. We lived in the poorer area of Queens, but your mother would look out over the East River to Manhattan and dream. Queens and Manhattan were two different worlds back in the late 1950s, Louis, and your mother was too star-struck by the lights of this island. One evening in 1959, I came home from work, and my mother was wiping tears from her eyes with one hand while holding a letter in her other. When I asked my mother what was wrong, she merely handed me the piece of paper." Philip then reached into his coat pocket and pulled out the said piece; he looked at it for a moment and then handed it to Louis, as if to say, 'Let the note speak for itself'. Louis took the note from Philip and read it; he was mesmerised by what he read. *"Dear mother, I cannot go on in this world with the way we live. I believe I was born for greater things than this life. I do not wish to argue with you. I know that you say there is safety for me here in Queens, but I want to live my life. I have gone to Manhattan, do not try to get me back. It is not you or Philip, my dear mother, I just need to live my life. Love Adele xx."*

As soon as Louis saw the name of the author of the note, he realised that Philip was being honest with him. Louis looked at the note again, and his mind was now filled with more questions than ever before. "What happened to my mother?" Philip was blunt with his honesty. "Your father killed her." Louis was shocked, but it was not because of the suggestion of Joseph killing someone; it was just that this piece of information was contrary to what he had been told by Mary. "But my Aunt Mary told me my mother had run away?" Philip leaned forward on the table and raised his right index finger. "First of all, Louis, that woman is not your aunt. She is just a nasty piece of work with whom your father has always had his way, and he keeps her around to make it look like you are being looked after. Mary is nothing but a common whore." That piece of information made perfect sense to Louis. He was about to ask Philip how his mother died when Philip resumed his story. "Your mother came to Manhattan as an innocent and impressionable 17-year-old girl. She got caught up in the wrong crowd. I tried to look for her for over a year, but I could not find her. Subsequently, in the summer of 1962, I saw a newspaper article that reported the death of a pretty 20-year-old girl. Her body had been found down by the banks of the East River in Manhattan; her neck had been broken. The police were able to trace her back to giving birth to you, but they had no evidence about who killed her. Your father had told the police she had walked out, and that whore you call Aunt Mary backed up your father's version of events. I subsequently asked around this part of the world about you and was told by a woman whom your mother knew well that your father had impregnated your mother one night as an 18-year-old when he took advantage of her after she had been drinking alcohol in a local bar. Initially, she did not have anything further to do with your father, but as the pregnancy entered its fourth month, your mother approached Joseph for help. Help! Your father did not want her or the baby, but this is an Irish Catholic precinct, and the last thing your father needed was an 18-year-old girl telling the local people she had been screwed by him both literally and metaphorically. He took her in, but within days, he started beating her, raping her, and forever mistreating her. Your mother confided all this mistreatment in her only friend. You were born in early 1961, and, twelve months after your birth, your mother disappeared. Two nights before she died, she spoke to her friend and told her she thought Joseph was about to kill her; so severe had been her beatings, so depraved had been the rapes right in front of that bitch of a woman Mary."

Philip's information was very challenging for Louis. He thought about his late kind friend from across the hallway; he wondered whether Ms Fitzgerald was his mother's friend Philip was referring to. "There was an old woman who looked after me since I could first remember. Ms Fitzgerald. Was that my mother's friend?" Philip nodded. "Yes, Mavis Fitzgerald. I even gave her a photograph of your mother after she had died. I remember going to your apartment building and bumping into Mavis as I searched for answers about your mother's death. We discussed her friendship with your mother, but she also warned me about your father."

Now, it all made sense to Louis. Ms Fitzgerald had been looking after him because his mother had befriended her. Louis reached into his pocket and pulled out his wallet and he opened it to retrieve a photograph. "Is this the photo you gave her?" Philip smiled. "Yes, that is it." Louis was dismayed as he considered this news; the anger and hatred he felt for Joseph was boiling in his blood. "Why didn't you take her friend to the police?" Philip threw his hands in the air to display his frustration with the police. "I did, but the police are just as bad as your father and his friends. Who do you think runs this town? Good guys? Manhattan is full of corrupt people, including the police. They turned a blind eye after he and his friends killed Adele. After I had contacted the police, a car would be parked outside our house in Queens. Your grandmother and I could see people looking in. We went to the ground, and I did not stir the water anymore. I wish I had kept on going, Louis, but I obeyed my mother's wish. Your father is an evil man, Louis, and he works for even worse men. Your father is a murderer, a criminal, and a gambler who loves his whores. Have you ever wondered where the money goes in that household?" Louis did not need to answer the rhetorical question that his uncle had just posed; he knew full well the money was spent on alcohol and prostitutes.

Philip was analysing how his nephew was coping with these dreadful facts, but he knew he needed to provide a further explanation for his absence from the boy's life. He then looked at the ceiling again; he was too overwhelmed by anger and emotion; his hatred of Joseph had been obvious in his voice, and his anger was also an internal taunt at himself for allowing almost 17 years to go by without contacting Louis. "I wanted to contact you long ago, Louis. I engaged a private detective to investigate your life and report back to me. Mavis wrote to me. Your former teacher, Mrs Washington, telephoned me after the police had taken you away from the school. I was there in court the day you were sentenced for striking that other boy; I just could not let your father see me speaking to you as he would have killed you, Louis. I was told by the New York education office they were aware of your father enlisting you down at that feral shed but what could they do? He is your father. I so wanted to get you out of that life, but it was not until my mother died last year that I could do anything about it." Louis was upset his grandmother had only died the year before, and he did not accept the failure of his grandmother or uncle to come and save him; however, he understood how the threat of his father and the people Joseph was associated with could scare an old woman. "How did my grandmother die?" Philip paused for a moment as he still grieved his mother's loss. "Her health failed; she was old. I have placed the urn containing her ashes in the same small plot where we placed the urn holding your mother's ashes."

Louis openly displayed his surprise when he heard his uncle say that there was a plot where his mother's ashes were stored. "I want to go there!" Philip felt he should take his nephew to the plot the very next day, for the young man's piece of mind. "You can go there tomorrow. Catch the train over to Queens Village, and I will pick you up outside of the station at 10.00am. Before I leave remind me to write down my telephone number for you. There is more news to tell, Louis. This necklace is yours; it was willed to your mother long ago by my mother, and you are the only surviving heir of your mother." Louis looked at the necklace and then was suddenly overcome with disappointment. "I cannot take it." Philip frowned. "What? Why do you reject your inheritance?" Louis was blunt with his honesty. "My father will eventually find this piece of jewellery; he knows when I have anything of value. Hell, Philip, I even had to hide spare change inside my mattress so that I could buy food for myself. Where can I hide this beautiful piece of jewellery? I can't take it." Philip was amazed by the response, but after pondering what he was told, he understood what his nephew was telling him: the man who had killed his sister was also torturing this young man. "Okay, I will hold onto it, Louis, until you are ready to accept it." The two men talked some more about life generally before they parted ways. Philip wrote down his telephone number for Louis. Both of them confirmed the meeting time and place for tomorrow so that Louis could go to the plots of his mother and grandmother. They stood up from their table and shook hands, then Louis flung his arms around Philip's shoulders. "Help me, please." Philip held him; this gentle little flower needed love.

Louis lay on his bed in the dark that night. Looking out the window, the golden glow of Wall Street seemed to be blood red that evening; his hatred for his father grew stronger and deeper. Louis thought about his uncle and the story he had just been told, but he could not stand thinking about his mother being murdered by Joseph, or the terrible cover-up which followed her death. His mind wandered back to that evening when he was a six-year-old and Mary was telling him about what had happened to his mother. Louis wondered how Mary could look him in the eye and lie like that; then again, as his uncle had told him, she was a common whore. He knew that he had to somehow escape from his father's world as he went off to sleep.

The following day, Louis got up early and immediately left the apartment. He was meant to go to school, but this was far more important. The train trip over to Queens Village seemed to take an eternity. When Louis walked outside of the station, he saw Philip standing next to an old Volkswagen Beetle. Philip drove Louis to a crematorium on Astoria Boulevard in Queens. During the drive, Louis was informed by his uncle that, as yet, he had not been married, nor had he had any children; he had an elderly mother to look after.

When they arrived at the crematorium, they walked past the All-Souls Chapel, and about 50 yards away from there was an area dedicated to plots. Philip walked in the direction of the plot dedicated to his mother and sister.

The plot was a small rock garden plot, and the plaques were simple for both his mother and grandmother. Louis stared at his mother's plot; his mind spoke his words as he closed his eyes. Louis told his mother that he loved her, that he was sorry for being angry at her all these years, but he had been lied to by Mary. "Most of all, my darling mother, if you can hear me, I am sorry that in having me it led to your death." Louis wiped a tear from his eye. He briefly looked at his grandmother's plaque; more tears flowed down his cheeks and he could not contain his sorrow. Philip put a hand on Louis' shoulder, and the young man began to weep and hugged his uncle; his sorrow for his mother and his grandmother was overwhelming. After about one minute, Louis pulled away from Philip. It was not in his veins to be weak for too long, even though this was the most confronting moment of his life. He told Philip that if he did not arrive at the shed that afternoon Joseph would be suspicious; he would know. Louis had already memorised Philip's telephone number, and he told his uncle that before he alighted from his vehicle at the train station, he would call him, and they would stay in touch.

Later that evening, Louis crossed paths with Joseph in the hallway of the apartment. Joseph was leaving, and Louis was coming home from his shift at the shed. He could not bear to look at his father or Mary. Louis knew he had three to four months left in that apartment before he would be expected to fend for himself. Joseph could not wait for him to be out of his apartment, and he was already making plans to use that bedroom to rent it to a lodger because he needed the money.

CHAPTER 9

There were only two weeks to go until his graduation day. Louis had decided that he would move out from the apartment the day of graduation, and he hoped to obtain some work upstate, but he also realised it was likely Joseph would hunt him down and kill him if he did not work at the shed. It was a Monday afternoon, and the summer sun was hidden behind the buildings when Louis arrived at the shed. Jack was waiting outside the shed; he grinned at Louis like an old friend about to embark upon another day of escapades. By now, Jack was working his way up at the shed, and he assisted Coonan when he could not be there. His elevation in the shed meant that Jack was always there, and like Coonan, he was now tied to the world of that shed without much of a life to look forward to. There had been an increase in Jack's pay, but it was an increase that was squandered on alcohol and prostitutes. O'Malley's Shed provided intergenerational funding to bar owners and prostitutes!

Both Jack and Louis took up their usual positions of sitting on an old crate, just like they did as young boys. They chatted. Louis mainly talked about the fact that school would be finishing soon, and he would have to look for a job as he had to move out of Joseph's apartment, but realistically, that job would be down at the wharves. Jack told Louis that he would come to the graduation ceremony as he had never been to one, so he wanted to see what all the commotion was about regarding this event. Jack then heard Coonan call out from the shed for him. Approximately five minutes went by before Jack came back out again. Jack had a smile on his face. "It is your lucky day! They have no use for you. Get out of here before they change their minds!" Louis did not think twice because there were so many days the pair of them had sat around twiddling their thumbs, so this was a well-earned holiday. As Louis walked away, he looked back at Jack, who had now perched himself in the same spot outside the shed that Coonan used to occupy. The similarity between Jack and Coonan was disturbing for Louis.

Approximately one hour had gone by since Louis had left the shed. Jack was sitting inside the shed on an old crate. Coonan walked out of the office, and he looked at Jack with just a hint of disappointment in his eyes. "Alright, lad,

I've got to go soon. In about an hour a small white Hilux truck will turn up. They will bring with them three bags of money, and in return ye are to show them this fuckin' crate you're sitting on for them to take away; don't fuck this up! Get it right and ye move up the line quick with us. Get it wrong and ye will fuckin' wish ye never had been born. Wait here with the bags; eventually one of our guys will come and collect them from you." With those words being spoken, Coonan walked out of the shed. Approximately one hour after Coonan had left, a white 1975 Toyota Hilux truck arrived. Not far behind it was the familiar sight of the black Cadillac. Various persons alighted from either vehicle. Two men got out of the Hilux and three men came out of the Cadillac. The handover on this occasion was very quick, the sealed crate at the front of the shed in return for three bags. Four of the men loaded the crate onto the Hilux. One of the men from the Cadillac unloaded three bags from the boot. He brought the bags over to Jack, and his words were simple: "There is about $250,000.00 in cash in here; don't lose it, or you'll lose them." Jack could not believe his ears. "About $250,000.00?" The man nodded in response. "We have not counted it exactly." Jack was too greedy and stupid to realise he was being lied to; of course, the money had been counted right down to the last dollar bill, and it had been twice-checked, just to ensure there were no arguments about the amount. The job should have been all so easy for Jack, bar that his sticky fingers could not wait to get into the contents of the three bags. After the Hilux left with the crate, and then followed by the Cadillac, Jack waited for 30 minutes. His eyes were fixed on the bags, and the words "about $250,000.00" kept ringing out in his mind. Eventually, Jack succumbed to the temptation of the money, and he opened one of the bags and saw there were some loose notes. Without any hesitation, Jack reached in and grabbed a handful of notes; in total it was only $100.00 in assorted bills. However, on this occasion, each bill had been counted and Coonan was not there. Accordingly, the money could be easily accounted for.

Louis walked the streets of Midtown West, thinking about Philip, his mother and his grandmother. Eventually, he could not resist the temptation to speak to his uncle anymore. He found a quiet street where he knew there was a public telephone hidden from view. He picked up the receiver and dialled his uncle's number. After four rings the telephone was answered by Philip. "Hello?" Philip's voice contained a welcoming and reassuring tone. Initially, Louis could not speak, and it seemed as though an eternity had gone by before Philip spoke again. "Hello?" Eventually, Louis got the courage to speak. "Hello, uncle." There was a tone of delight in Philip's response. "Louis, is that you?" The concern in his voice overtook the previous consternation for no words being spoken. "Yes, uncle, it is." Philip was concerned by the call and the fact that Louis had been reluctant to talk initially. "What is wrong, Louis? Has Joseph hurt you?" Louis smiled on the other end of the telephone as, finally, in his life, he had found a person who seemed to care for his wellbeing. "No, uncle. I am all right. I just wanted to hear your voice. I am finishing school soon and I know what that means. I will end up working at the shed, surrounded by Joseph's 'union' friends for God knows how long. I just need to talk to somebody, that is all." Philip understood the feelings being conveyed down the telephone line to him by Louis, and he immediately tried to assure him that there was a brighter future ahead for him. "I understand, Louis, but it does not have to be this way. Take the necklace, sell it and get out of Manhattan; in fact get out of New York. See the world while you're young. I plan to be here on earth for more time to come." Louis smiled; his uncle's plan made sense in another world, but in the world of the union, O'Malley's Shed, the mayor and Joseph's vice grip of Louis' existence, he did not believe he would be able to escape. "I wish it were that simple, uncle, but you and I both full well know that I am in too deep with my father's world." There was then an unhealthy pause in the conversation, as though both Philip and Louis did not know how to proceed with the discussion. After a few moments, Louis broke the silence; however, his words caused no comfort for Philip; "Anyway, uncle, I just needed to hear your voice. I do hope that I get to see you again soon." With those words Louis hung up the telephone before Philip could speak another word. Louis then set forth again in wandering the streets of Midtown West. Philip took some time to hang up the receiver of his telephone. He so wished that he could race over to Manhattan and rescue his nephew, but in his heart, he knew that could cause more problems in Louis' already desperate life. The moon was high in the sky that night over Queens, but in Philip's heart, the world could not have been any darker.

Two weeks went by since Jack had taken the money from the bag. Life as usual went by at the shed, and once again, Jack believed that he had got away with another swift act. It was a Wednesday evening shift, and Jack and Louis were back together again at the shed, waiting for a job detail to be provided to them. Louis discussed how his graduation was coming up in two days' time, and it was still a moment he looked forward to. Jack again confirmed he would attend the graduation. The black Cadillac pulled up outside of the shed. All the doors to the vehicle swung open, and four men alighted from the car. One of those men was Joseph. The four men walked up to both Jack and Louis, and there was no hint of any friendly intent on their faces. Louis was the first person to be manhandled; one of the men grabbed him by his collar and dragged him into the shed. Another man grabbed Jack and placed him into a headlock; his tight grip pressed very hard around Jack's neck, and he called out in a muffled tone. "Hey, what the fuck!" Both of the young men were dragged into the shed. Coonan was perched on a crate about halfway into the shed, and the floor area around the crate for about a three-metre radius was covered in about five inches of straw, which covered a thick sheet of black plastic underneath. Louis was dragged to a point about three metres away from the crate, and he watched on as Jack was marched up to the crate. He looked on in horror as he saw his father pull out a revolver from his coat pocket. The words that were spoken by Joseph then sent a chill down Louis' spine and signalled greater distress for Jack. "We don't like fucking thieves in our organisation, and you are nothing but a low-life fucking thief!" Jack screamed out in fear as the cold metal of the muzzle pressed against his forehead. "I don't know what you are fucking talking about, man." Joseph became further enraged. "Bullshit, you little fucking bastard, you are nothing but a low-down thief who is the son of a goddamn whore." Louis was now panicking for Jack as he knew how ruthless his father could be; how could he ever forget Bill? "I don't know what you are talking about, man." Joseph became even more enraged. "Fucking crap, we have been watching you, you're a little fucking thief. You have been stealing from us for quite some time, and now you are going to pay!" Joseph pulled back on Jack's hair with his left hand and placed the muzzle of the revolver against Jack's temple, and in the same movement he pressed the trigger and shot Jack dead. Louis watched in horror; it seemed as though time slowed down as he saw Jack's head explode on the opposite side from where he was shot. Jack's body crumpled and fell into a heap on the straw. Joseph stood there quietly for about one minute, and then, as a sign of ultimate power, he shot two further bullets into Jack's head. With that, Joseph then turned to face Louis. "Let that be a fucking lesson for you! Steal from this organisation and we will kill one of our own." The traumatic event enlivened his mental demon again, but Louis' death anxiety was now competing with the other terror he was also experiencing; his father could kill him at any moment.

About 20 minutes later, Jack's lifeless body was wrapped in thick black plastic and was loaded into the rear of the Hilux van. Joseph displayed no sympathy for

Jack, even though he had his way with Anne for no charge on several occasions. "Throw the fuck's body in the Hudson or East River." Jack's lifeless body was subsequently dumped into the shallow, muddy waters of the river. The dumping of the body was performed quickly and without any concern about the body being found. Later that evening, a police boat on a routine patrol of the river made the grisly discovery of Jack's body lying in the river's mud flats. Louis had been let go by Joseph as there was no evidence to suggest that Louis had taken any money. Louis now knew that he had to get away from O'Malley's Shed as soon as he graduated from high school. "Poor Jack", he thought.

Louis left the shed that evening and made his way as quickly as possible back to Joseph's apartment. Louis knew that Joseph always went out to celebrate his thuggery with his band of fellow thugs. As for Mary, she had become so addicted to alcohol and medication that after 7.00pm, she was comatose. If Louis got to the apartment between 8.00pm and 1.00am, he would be left to his own devices. Louis was adamant that the events that had transpired earlier that night at the shed meant he had to escape from Joseph's world. The way he had killed Jack at the shed suggested that Joseph had no concern for whether his actions were discovered. Louis silently entered the apartment at about 10.30pm, and he packed a bag of his meagre collection of clothes. He took from inside his mattress his secret stash of money; his mind felt sorrow for a friend who devised the plan all of those years ago for Louis to hide his cash on the underneath side. He pulled out $20.00 in loose bills and coins. He then silently snuck out of Joseph's apartment; Mary never knew he was there.

Louis walked two blocks until he found a telephone box. He phoned his uncle and told him what had occurred. Philip told Louis to immediately catch the train again to Queens, and he would look after him.

Not long after midnight two police officers attended at the Kelly apartment in Harlem. They rang the intercom at the front entrance. Jack's mother had been drinking heavily that evening, and she was in the grips of a deep alcohol-fuelled sleep. Eventually, she got up off the couch as she heard the intercom for her apartment ring for the third time. Pressing on the intercom, Anne Kelly enquired in a hostile manner. "What do you want?" The voice on the other end of the intercom remained calm but low-key. "Ms Kelly, we are here to talk to you about your son." It was almost as though a sabre from heaven had reached down to smite Jack's mother in the heart. Her voice was faint. "Come in." Her eyes filled with tears in the time it took the police to walk up the stairs. Then

the dreaded knock on her door. She opened the door to her apartment to see
two uniformed officers; she broke down into uncontrollable grief as one of the
officers explained to her that Jack had been found dead in the shallow waters of
the East River. For her part, she tried to tell them who she believed had killed
her son. Both officers confirmed that a detective would stop by in the morning
to take her statement. After they left, a heartbroken mother searched for her
soul. Jack's mother finished her cigarette, and then she dialled the number for
The New York Times. When the voice on the other end asked for the reason for
her call, she responded in a sad but angry tone. "I want to speak to one of the
reporters about the murder of my son! I want to speak to someone so that I
can tell them about everything I know about some of your city's worst people."
A few moments later, a journalist employed by the *Times* got on the telephone.
Jack's mother proceeded to open up to the journalist everything she knew about
O'Malley's Shed, Louis, and a man named Joseph O'Brien, whom she suspected
had killed her son.

CHAPTER 10

Louis eventually arrived at Philip's home. He travelled by train and taxi to spare his uncle the journey of driving to Queens Station. Philip was surprised that Louis had not called him, but he was relieved to see he was safe when he arrived at his door. Louis proceeded to tell Philip everything about the evening's events and about how worried he was that his father's violence was escalating. Philip desperately tried to convince Louis not to show his face in Midwest Town again, but Louis explained to his uncle he wanted to graduate from high school. Philip knew from the news he heard moments ago that Louis' life would be in jeopardy. Despite every effort Philip made to convince Louis not to return to Manhattan, Louis was adamant; he had earned the right to graduate from high school.

Joseph received a telephone call from Mayor Sabatini's office early that morning after Jack's mother had called the newspaper. He was angered by the news of Anne Kelly speaking to the press about the various criminal activities occurring at O'Malley's Shed that her son Jack had told her about. Joseph was told by the mayor's henchman the mayor was very angry about the fact that Jack's body had been so easily discovered. The henchman's voice was difficult to understand because of his thick Italian accent, but his next question was easy to understand. "Why didn't you fuckin' dispose of it properly? But Joseph, most importantly, your bastard kid knows too much, and he has been named for everything. Kill your kid before the FBI gets to him." Joseph understood perfectly well it was a case of kill or be killed. Such a command was not too difficult for Joseph to follow, as he did not ever like or want Louis. "Tell the mayor I will knock the little turd off." Any doubts about the mayor's intentions were dispelled by the henchman. "If he does not die, Joe, then you had better find a fucking priest." Joseph hung the telephone up, and he realised that he was now in a state of self- preservation. He then put in a telephone call to O'Leary. "Round some of the crew and then come and get me straight away. We have to kill that fuckin' son of mine!"

Later that night, the front page of the *Times* was printed. The headline banner was blunt: 'Murder and Corruption on our Wharves.'

Subsequently, Louis returned to Midwest Town from Queens for his graduation. He knew that he had to keep out of sight, and of course, it was undoubtedly reckless of him to consider he could attend his high school graduation. Although he knew the opportunities open to him academically had been lost years ago, this was still a special occasion. Nobody else in his father's world had finished high school. They were all half-smart and street-smart bog Irish in his father's world. Against all the odds Louis had finished his elementary and high school levels of education. As Louis was about to turn the corner to walk towards his school, he saw a discarded copy of *The New York Times* lying on the pavement. The headline on the front-page story of the paper immediately caught his eye; it read 'Murder and Corruption at our Wharves'. Louis picked up the paper and began to nervously read the article. Anne Kelly had totally opened up to the paper her knowledge about O'Malley's Shed. Worse still, she had told the journalist that her son had been working with Louis, and the pair of them had been heavily involved in the criminal acts of those thugs who were associated with the shed, including the fact that the young boys were responsible for the bombing of the gas station which had resulted in the death of an innocent attendant a few years beforehand. "Hell," Louis said to himself as he knew that the powers to be at the shed would undoubtedly have told his father to kill him. As Louis was reading the paper, he did not realise that a team of thugs were already at the Kelly apartment murdering Jack's mother; neither the journalists nor the police had turned their lazy minds to protecting an essential witness.

Louis threw the newspaper into a trash can and turned into the street of his school. His head told him to flee Manhattan, but his heart drew him towards his school. Initially, he did not recognise the black Cadillac parked outside of the school; such was the state of his mind, which had become overwhelmed with grief for his fallen friend and his predicament in life. When he was approximately 50 yards from the Cadillac, the doors suddenly swung open. Louis stopped, and to his absolute dismay, he watched in horror as his father alighted from the car. Louis saw his father was holding the same revolver which he had used to shoot Jack. Louis instinctively turned around and ran away; however, the sound of the revolver discharging was followed by a sharp and sudden burning pain in his right upper arm. The bullet had only grazed his skin, and despite the pain, he kept running. Louis ran as fast he could in the direction of 8th Avenue because he realised his only chance to live was to get to the subway and try to call his uncle. The Cadillac would have to double back around to catch him, and although the pain in his arm was immense, Louis continued to run towards the subway entrance. His breath had long departed him, but he managed to get to the escalators of the 8th Avenue subway station, which was his chance at escaping. As he entered the escalator, Louis heard car tyres screeching, and then, just before Louis disappeared under the maze of escalators, Joseph spotted him. Although he was breathless and bleeding, Louis ran down the escalators to the subway platform. A train that was heading across town had just pulled in, and without any hesitation, Louis jumped on board just in time. He was able to see out the window of the train his father and two other thugs ran onto the platform. Louis had escaped the attempt to kill him, but he knew that he could not run forever. At some stage, he would have to confront his father again. There was now another harsh reality for Louis that he had to accept; there would not be any opportunity for him to attend graduation day. He was bitterly disappointed Joseph had taken his graduation away from him.

Louis eventually made his way back to Queens Village; he had managed to use his singlet on the journey to bandage his wounded arm, but the bleeding could not be totally stopped. People had occasionally cast an eye his way on the subway as they noticed the bleeding; however, this was Manhattan, and a person bleeding on a subway train during the 1970s was not an unusual sight. When he arrived at Queens Village, Louis called his uncle. Philip had not gone to work because he had also read *The New York Times*, and he had feared he would be needed. Philip's worst fears became a reality when he received Louis' telephone call, and he knew Joseph's world of underworld crime would make its way across the East River sooner rather than later to hunt down Louis. The allegations in the newspaper article were serious, and whether wisely or unwisely, Philip surmised even his nephew offering a plea bargain to be a prosecution witness still involved a prison sentence for a young man with a prior conviction for violence. The television and radio news programs were now reporting that Anne Kelly was dead. His nephew had to disappear forever. As Philip parked his car outside of Queens Village station, he saw his nephew standing there, holding his arm in pain. His thoughts were prescient. "Shit! The clock is running out of time." Louis jumped into Philip's car and gave him a relieved smile. Philip looked very concerned, and Louis immediately knew his uncle was alarmed about this turn of events. The car turned onto the road to travel back to Philip's home. Not a word had been spoken, so Louis broke the ice. "He is going to kill me, Uncle Philip. Joseph did this." Philip glanced at his nephew's wounded arm. "I am taking you to my doctor, Louis. I trust him. He will not call the police." Philip's mind settled on the future course of action. "He is going to be incarcerated in jail or be killed unless I get him out of this country." Now was not the time to share his thoughts with his nephew. They drove to a local doctor's surgery, where Philip knew he could trust the doctor. An extra few dollars in treatment fees would ensure there was no report made to the police.

Eventually, at 3.30pm that afternoon, Philip and Louis returned to Philip's townhouse in Woodside. Philip assisted Louis to lie down comfortably on the lounge room couch; his arm was still very painful. Philip went into the kitchen to make a cup of coffee for both of them and he was lost in his thoughts as to how he could best help his nephew. If he took him to the FBI for protective custody, he might still be killed as the underworld thugs were too well connected to allow an important state witness to live. Even if Louis were not killed, he would still be sentenced to jail time. The best way to protect his nephew was to send him abroad. "We have only just met, and now he must go." These thoughts saddened Philip, but his nephew's best chance of survival was to remove him from the jurisdiction of the United States altogether. After having made the coffee, Philip walked back into the living room and he sat down on the couch. He looked earnestly into his nephew's eyes. "Louis, I cannot protect you. Sooner rather than later, the forces whom you have worked with will track you down here, and they will kill you. Anne Kelly's call to the paper has ensured your fate is sealed. It kills me to say this, Louis, but you must leave America. Whatever your name is now will not be the same name in the next 24 hours. I wish there were something else I could do to keep you here, but your father is likely to track you down in the next 24 hours, and if they don't track you down in that time, then the FBI will track you down and you are still dead." Louis absorbed every word spoken by his uncle. "Then what do you suggest we do now, uncle? How do we do what you have suggested?" Philip looked at the photograph of his sister Adele in the photo frame sitting on the coffee table. "I am going to use my contacts to buy you a new life. Then you may well be able to be your true self, the soul, the life, the person your mother wished you to be. Nevertheless, Louis, this is the end of your time in this part of this world."

Louis looked hard and long at his uncle, and he too became saddened about the whole notion of leaving a relative he had only just met, but there were no other good options. "Okay, well, but how do you actually suggest this occurs, uncle?" Philip wanted to cry but he had to remain strong. "In my many years of working for New York State, I too have contacts, Louis. Trust in me, please." Louis looked into his uncle's eyes, searching for any sign of false intentions, but all Louis saw in return was sorrow born out of the truth of someone who finally cared about his life. He also realised the truth meant to him living abroad. A shocking feeling of fear of not seeing his uncle again entered Louis' mind, but at the same time, he began to realise this was inevitable as so many people were out to get him now. Philip could tell his nephew needed some more time to think. "Think about where you would like to live, Louis, for at least the next 20 years while I make some more coffee."

Louis thought long and hard about his situation; he knew his uncle was right as for him to stay in the United States, he would be locked up or, even worse, killed. However, the thought of having to leave his uncle, his own family, whom he had only recently just met, a man who seemed to care about him more than any other, broke Louis' heart. Eventually, he came to terms with having to leave America, but he wondered where on this earth he could go. He thought about Europe, but that was too close to America. He thought about Asia, but he was reluctant to settle somewhere where he would stand out in a crowd. Then he remembered his Modern History class, and Australia suddenly seemed to be such a promised land save for the fact it was on the opposite side of the planet. Nevertheless, he could hide there, he could start again there, and most importantly, Louis knew he would be free of Joseph in Australia. Philip had left Louis alone for some time to come to terms with all his thoughts, but when he returned from the kitchen with more coffee for them, Louis' mind was firmly made up regarding where his future lay. Louis waited for Philip to sit down again. Philip, now seated, looked at Louis' face, and he could tell the young man had made up his mind. "I want to go to Sydney, uncle, to Australia." Philip contemplated Louis' choice, but he was uncertain about Sydney. "Are you sure, Louis?" Louis nodded his head. "Yes, I am sure. I don't want to leave but I know I have to." Philip accepted the destination had been properly considered, but his curiosity had to be satisfied. "Why Australia?" Louis was silent for a short while, and then he looked back at his uncle with the only truthful response. "I remember studying about Australia in school. I remember there were nights I hoped that one day I could leave all this misery behind me and start all over again in a new city. Sydney seemed to be such a logical choice. A big city for Australia but a small, clean town compared to Manhattan. They speak English and university education is free there." Louis looked up at the ceiling as he could feel tears building up in his eyes. "I don't want to leave you, Uncle Philip, but I agree I cannot remain in this country. Everything Joseph has made me do over the last five years means that I am no better than him. I cannot believe my life has ended up this way, but that is my so-called father for you." Philip just wanted to hug his nephew there and then. He could not believe the wisdom which was espoused from the lips of someone so young.

Philip was saddened his nephew had to go, had to leave, had to start all over again. Philip regained his composure and looked towards the lounge room window, through which he could see a young mother pushing a pram along the pavement. Philip thought of his sister and her desire to start a new life all over again. It ended in tragedy. Philip could not let that happen again. He realised he had to act promptly to protect his nephew. "I need to call an old friend, Louis. Please excuse me." Louis overheard the subsequent telephone discussion his uncle had with a man he was calling Alan. There was the mention of the urgent nature and the need for a passport. Intermittently, his uncle apologised on several occasions for the late telephone call. Photographs, money and quick departure were words he heard his uncle say at various moments of his conversation. It finished with him confirming he would call again at 9.00am.

Everything that grows cannot always be protected. Philip finished his telephone call, and he was thinking about what he had been told. "I can do this." His gaze then returned to his nephew. "Give me 24 hours, Louis, as I need to sell your inheritance to make this work, and then I will have to pay the right people. If anyone comes to the door, do not open it. If they try to break in, go to the laundry, as there is a secret compartment behind the wall of the broom closet, so they will not find you there." Philip then retrieved an old black and white Polaroid camera and a sealed film cartridge from his bedroom. Louis put on a clean shirt after taking off the sling and then Philip took an instant photograph of his nephew; it was not the best photograph, but it would have to do. Then Philip left. There was not a second to be wasted.

CHAPTER 11

Philip had been gone for almost a full day. He had taken Louis' inheritance with him as the jewellery would fetch a handsome price if sold at the right places. Philip had eventually sold his mother's necklace for $10,000.00 by 10.00am the next morning, but it had been a frustrating exercise. He had driven to about every pawn shop he could find in Queens, the Bronx and Brooklyn to try to pawn his mother's necklace, but the prices offered were ridiculously low. He had not slept when a pawn shop owner in Brooklyn suggested to him at 6.00am in the morning he should go to William Barthman Jeweler in Manhattan because 'that item is too expensive for me to pay you what it's worth'.

It was 7.00am by the time Philip had driven across the Brooklyn Bridge, parked his car and arrived on foot at the corner of Broadway and Maiden Lane. Barthman's did not open until 9.30am, so Philip used that spare time to telephone Alan Hodge, who was his old friend from the days when Philip first started working for the State of New York. Hodge was now a long-term federal employee who had worked in the public sector all his working life; therefore, he knew how to bend the rules when needed. Philip explained to Hodge the urgency of what needed to be done and what he needed, namely for NYC Health to generate a fake birth certificate in the name of Louis Montgomery, he must arrange for the New York Department of Education to generate a fake Regents diploma for Louis Montgomery and finally, the New York Passport Agency to issue a fake passport for Louis Montgomery. Philip insisted the urgency of protecting his nephew required an immediate turnaround of these documents. Hodge told Philip it was quite a list, but for a premium payment, he could get the job done that day if Philip collected the New York State documentation and then met him at the New York Passport Agency at the Rockefeller Centre by 1.00pm. Hodge also had contacts at the international cargo port, and once again, for a price, he could arrange for Louis to leave America by ship that night. Hodge asked Philip to call him back at the office at 11.00am because by then, he would have made the arrangements for the New York State documents to be issued. Hodge reminded Philip at the end of the telephone conversation, 'It's going to cost you'. Cost is not an issue when you are seeking to protect a rare flower.

Philip was waiting in line outside Barthman's shop when the doors were opened at 9.30am. The antique jeweller examined the necklace; the flawless diamonds alone would fetch $50,000.00 each at an auction; without blinking an eyelid, he told Philip if he wanted the best price to sell it at auction, but if he wanted to sell it now, Barthman's were willing to offer Philip $10,000.00 in cash now to purchase the necklace. Philip needed the money now, but he was told he would have to wait until 10.30am for the cash payment to be obtained from their bank. 11.00am, he had to call Hodge; Philip had time. It was hard for Philip to say goodbye to a piece of family antiquity, but he needed this money urgently; it was enough money to buy a new identity for Louis, enough money to get Louis onto a boat and enough money for Louis to perhaps have American cash in his pocket for a fortnight when he arrived on Australian shores. The jeweller at Barthman's was true to his word, and the sum of $10,000.00 made up of $100.00 bills was handed over to Philip, which he secured in his satchel.

After selling the necklace, Philip then attended to the task of buying Louis a new identity and, with it, a new life. He called Hodge at 11.00am and obtained the details of where he had to go to collect the birth certificate and diploma. Philip had to madly dash in taxis around Manhattan to collect the birth certificate, and the Regent's diploma and then meet Hodge at the Rockefeller Centre by 1.00pm so that he could introduce Philip to the trusted contact regarding the serious security issue of issuing a fake passport, and of course a fee for Hodge's services. He may have been exhausted, but Philip was desperate, and he arrived on time to meet Hodge.

A passport in the name of Louis Montgomery was urgently issued that afternoon by Hodge's contact. The passport recorded Louis' birth year as 1957 because, as Hodge explained to Philip when he had arranged for the birth certificate to be issued, 'nobody is going to accept that a 17-year-old boy is travelling without his parents'. Hodge informed Philip that arising from his speaking to friends of his at the international wharves of Manhattan, there was a commercial shipping company that would be willing to help Louis escape the United States if the right price was paid. The ship was a Japanese-owned freight carrier named the *Tojo*, and Hodge provided Philip with a handwritten note containing the bank details for him to wire the payment to as well as a contact for a telegram to be sent to confirm the payment. It was a remarkable achievement on Philip's behalf to make these arrangements for Louis; however, neither he nor Hodge realised that Hodge's contact at the passport agency had accidentally left a paper trail that could be linked back to Louis' real identity if a person thoroughly examined them.

Fortunately for Philip, a US Post Office was located near the Rockefeller Centre. He wired the money from that US Post Office to the bank account of the owner of the *Tojo*. He then paid for an urgent US Post telegram to be sent to the *Tojo's* owner in Japan as proof of the payment being made. Now all the arrangements were in place, but Philip still had one more task to attend to in his very exhausted state; he had to make sure Louis had boarded the *Tojo* by 3.00am the next morning.

By the time Philip returned to his home, it was already 7.30pm. He had not slept for about 36 hours and he was exhausted. Notwithstanding his exhaustion, he was on a mission to spare his nephew from his father's mess and to keep alive this offshoot of his dear, sweet sister, Adele. There was so much to tell Louis about the arrangements for his new life. When Philip entered his home, he saw that Louis was slightly agitated. "What is wrong, Louis?" Philip had forgotten he had been gone for 24 hours. "What is wrong, uncle? I have been on guard here for 24 hours. I did not know where you were. I thought my father had found you." Louis realised his tone perhaps displayed a lack of appreciation for his uncle's tenacity to create a new life for Louis in the space of the day. Louis' assessment of Philip's exhausted state underscored his remorse. "I'm sorry. You look exhausted and I should have appreciated your efforts." Philip held up both of his hands to gesture he was fine. "When do I leave? Early next week?" Philip's tired eyes opened wide with surprise. "You leave tonight. I have made all the arrangements, Louis." Now Louis was overcome with a sense of surprise. "Tonight? What about a passport? What about arranging some form of school record?" Philip ushered with his hand for Louis to sit down. "I have all the papers. I have some cash for you." Philip then retrieved his satchel which he had placed on the coffee table, and he then extracted the documents. "Here is your birth certificate, which records you were born in 1957 and your surname is Montgomery. 1957 was chosen as your birth year because nobody in Australia will believe a 17-year-old is travelling without his parents. This document here is also important as it's your Regents diploma; congratulations, you can go to university in Australia. This is your passport, Louis; remember your year of birth is 1957. Finally, here is what is left of your cash after I sold the necklace for $10,000.00 and then paid for your new life."

Louis contemplated how many mountains Philip had to move to so promptly to make these arrangements. He was very grateful for his uncle's industriousness, and he was about to thank him when Philip held up his right hand to indicate he had more to say. "Please listen, Louis, time is crucial. You are going to leave from the cargo port at Newark Bay; I have paid for you to be accepted on board as a deckhand. You will have to work but the captain will ensure that your name is entered in the ship's log as having already come to New York as a merchant seaman to avoid any unnecessary attention from the port authorities or the police. The ship is an international cargo ship, and eventually, it will make its way around the globe to Sydney Harbour. We must leave quickly, Louis; pack whatever clothes you do have and here, place all the documents and cash in my satchel; you need it, not me." Louis looked into his uncle's eyes, and his thoughts were overwhelmed by the mixed emotions that were circulating within his mind. Louis' face displayed absolute glee, but his heart contemporaneously began to develop sorrow as he knew he was now saying goodbye to his newfound uncle, perhaps forever. He then tightly hugged his uncle. "Thank you so very, very much, uncle and now you're saying I must immediately say goodbye to you after just meeting you; you're my friend and I will come back to visit you." Louis' voice had projected the sounds of a teenage child breaking down in tears. Philip then held Louis back for a short distance from his body to look him in the eye. "Let me make myself clear, Louis, you can never come back, not for a long time, this is it, Louis, this is...". Philip became quite teary causing Louis to also become emotional. Philip regained his composure. "You do realise, Louis, that we will not see each other again for a very long while, if at all. This is just the way it has to be, but it will be a new start for you, and that is what my sister, your mother, would have hoped for all of us in these circumstances." Louis nodded his head in response. He could not have known what was occurring around the grapevine of the underworld life of New York's dockland life at this time as the name of Louis Montgomery suddenly appeared on the radar.

Notwithstanding the fact that Philip believed he had been discreet in relation to buying a way out of the country for his nephew, there is no such circumstance in the dark world of the Big Apple and its surrounding areas as discreet. Within half an hour of Philip buying the entry fee onto the container ship the *Tojo*, the word had spread through one lone source aligned to Mayor Sabatini's corrupt gang of reprobates. The call came into the mayor's office at 6.40pm, just as he was about to leave. As soon as he received the news, Mayor

Sabatini called Joseph. "We have found Louis, now kill him." Joseph did not display any resistance in his voice. "Consider it done." The mayor explained where Louis would be found. Joseph then immediately wrote down the details; the ship was the *Tojo*, and it was scheduled to depart at 3.00am from Dock 7 at Newark Bay. Within a minute of Joseph concluding the call with the mayor, he was back on the telephone again, this time to Coonan. "We must kill this kid tonight; bring O'Leary and Murphy." Joseph was firm in his mind, namely he should have killed the mother before she gave birth to the child he never wanted. Now, he would ensure this little bastard would be rubbed out finally. There was not even the slightest hint of hesitation in Joseph's mind as he never wanted a child, and tonight was the chance to finally get rid of him.

At 1.30am, Philip woke up Louis so that they could commence the long drive to the docks at Newark Bay. Philip, too, had a nap for about two to three hours, and whilst he needed more sleep, he could not presently do so as he had to ensure Louis made it onboard the *Tojo*. Despite the sorrow of knowing that he was leaving his only true family behind in Philip, Louis nevertheless had a sense of excitement running through his veins. Within the next two hours, he would set sail for a new life. Once he was dressed, Louis sat down at the dining table in Philip's kitchen. His uncle then proceeded to explain to him in greater detail the plan for that morning. Philip explained that the ship was leaving from Dock 7 at 3.00am on the dot, any later, and their plan was foiled. The seamen would already be on the board at that hour, but Louis was going to be loaded aboard right after the harbour master took his last look over the ship. One final present from his uncle before they left; Philip gave Louis a knapsack of clothing that should fit him as 'we are roughly the same body size'.

Philip started up his car at 2.00am to commence the 40-minute drive at that time of day to Newark Bay. Without Louis knowing, Philip already had a backup plan if they encountered trouble. In his coat pocket, Philip was carrying an automatic pistol, which was a weapon he had purchased many years beforehand when he thought Joseph or his men would try to hurt him or his mother. Louis entered the passenger side of the car. His heart was racing with excitement, but still, there was a degree of sorrow; he would miss Philip. As they drove towards Newark Bay, Louis and Philip talked about many life matters; most importantly, they talked about how they would both miss each other. Then Louis remembered an unfinished explanation from their first meeting. "Hey uncle, do you remember when we first met?" Philip, as he watched the road ahead of him, replied, "I do. Why?" Louis just had to find out. "You mentioned your father, well, my grandfather as well, came from a noble line. What did you mean when you said noble line?" He was right; Philip had not explained the family history his nephew should have known. "My father's family line was one of nobility, and it is also your family line, Louis. Our ancestral line is the House of Poitiers, and they were French nobility, but the revolution put an end to that. Our titles were subsequently restored only to then be taken away again. The House of Poitiers may have lost its title, but it did not lose all of its wealth. The fucking Nazis were responsible for stripping the wealth. Now listen, it's in the past; we can't change the past, but yes, you're of noble blood, Louis and you are rare, just like the rare flower of the Poitier which appears on our family crest." Louis thought about that family history for the rest of the drive. "I'm noble. I'm rare."

At about 2.45am, Philip drove onto the outer docks, which were not too far away from the area where Louis could be quietly snuck into the international dock area of Dock 7. Louis was not paying attention, and Philip had not seen the white Dodge van parked next to a storage area leading to the dock. Philip brought his car to a halt and waited momentarily before getting out. Louis was slightly behind him. The pair began to walk towards the side gate area, which would allow Louis to access Dock 7. They had only walked 20 metres when suddenly the Dodge van roared off its spot towards them. Without any hesitation, Philip commanded Louis to run. It was as though Louis had been catapulted forward without any warning, and his legs began to run as fast as they could. He had seen that vehicle many times before. The van came to a screeching halt only 20 metres away from Philip's car, and fortunately, that vehicle acted as a buffer to block the van from driving any further. Philip had already drawn his pistol from his jacket. Murphy was the first person out of the van. Philip aimed and shot him cleanly through his heart, killing him instantly. Philip then shot at the front of the van, and a cry rang out as the windscreen shattered, and out of the driver's seat stumbled Coonan, holding onto the side of his face. Out of the back of the van exploded O'Leary and Joseph, their two guns blazing away in the direction of Philip. A bullet tore into Philip's right leg, causing him to fall to his knee. However, he still fired back at O'Leary and Joseph. Philip aimed at O'Leary, and a bullet struck a fatal blow in O'Leary's head. Joseph kept on coming and firing his pistol repeatedly at Philip. Another bullet ripped into Philip's abdomen, and this injury signalled to him that he had no escape from this firefight; he would have to fight to the death. He lifted himself back onto his knee, and he recognised the evil face of Joseph. So too, Joseph started to recognise a face he had not seen for years; it was the face he saw in newspapers from many years ago of the brother of that French bitch who had given birth to his bastard son. They both aimed and started firing at each other.

Louis, by this stage, was only metres from the side gate to Dock 7. He saw his badly injured uncle firing from a short distance away from Joseph and the same volley of bullets being fired by Joseph back at Philip. The whole episode seemed to drag on forever, but it only took a few seconds. A bullet exploded into Joseph's skull, bringing him instantly to the ground. At the same time, a bullet seemed to blow out the back of Philip's chest. Philip fell face-first into the bitumen of the car park, and all of a sudden, the world became eerily still. Louis stood there, silent, scared, and sad. Philip had done so much for him, and now he was dead. So, too, was Joseph lying motionless on the ground as mixed emotions ran through Louis' heart. Just then, a South African voice called out. "Hey, kid, what the fuck are you doing? Get in here." It was Captain Proctor who had agreed to take Louis onboard his container ship. Louis remained motionless as the sight of his dead uncle seemed to freeze him in his spot. The voice of Captain Proctor boomed out again, "I am telling you, kid, get the fuck in here or we leave without you." Louis turned towards the gate and ran through it. Captain Proctor grabbed Louis by the arm. "Shit, kid, what in the hell was that?" There was no response from Louis. Captain Proctor then dragged Louis towards the safety of the container ship. Louis was shown towards the gangway, and he hurried up on board. He could see in the very far distance the lights on police cars flashing. When those police cars eventually arrived where the shootout occurred, the *Tojo* was being tugged away from Newark Bay.

By the time the police had started taking photographs and examining evidence at the scene the *Tojo* had already been pulled out towards the shipping lane by the harbour master's tugboat. Louis was safe, but he was also overcome by sorrow, anger, and relief. Philip was dead, as was his father. Philip did more for him in his life than Joseph ever did; his sorrow regarding his loss of Philip would never leave him. His arm was a little bit sore, which heightened his hatred of Joseph; he took so much away from Louis, including Philip. The foundation of Louis' relief was that he was free of his father and all the baggage that was attached to him. However, Louis did not have any relatives who were alive and he now knew what it truly meant to be alone. The harbour master's tugboat pulled away about half an hour after they had left the dock, and the sound of the *Tojo*'s engines bellowed out smoke from the smokestack with pride. The journey was now on, but Louis was frightened as he had nobody left in his life. The sun began to rise at 4.30am as the *Tojo* entered the main seaway. Captain Proctor showed Louis towards the bunks of the officer crew. He had a day to sleep, and then that next night, he would commence work. As Louis went off to sleep in his bunk at about 8.00am he heard on the loudspeaker an announcement they would be in international waters in the next hour.

CHAPTER 12

Louis woke up in his bunk that first day at sea at 6.00pm, and his dry mouth signalled that he was now in a new environment. He was due on the deck at 9.00pm for his first shift. He sat at the end of his bunk, thinking about what had occurred in his life that day. Philip had sacrificed his life for Louis, yet Louis hardly knew him. His arm was slightly better but still sore. As he sat on his bunk thinking about Philip, he began to feel overwhelmed with emotions of guilt and grief. It was a strange feeling for Louis to know Philip had cared for him so much; Philip could have sold the necklace, but he kept it to one day give it to his nephew. Perhaps it was his mother's brother displaying the feelings that his mother would have displayed had she lived long enough, but still, there was a pain in his heart; a good man had died for the sake of protecting him.

It was about an hour after he had awoken that Louis could face the crew of the *Tojo*. He got dressed and walked towards the licensed officer's meeting room of the ship, exactly where Captain Proctor had told him to go once he had awoken. The daytime officers, including Captain Proctor, had finished their duties for the day, and the handover occurred between the captain and the first mate. Louis knocked on the door to the licensed officer's meeting room. The door swung open, and Captain Proctor stood in the doorway; he ushered Louis into the meeting room, and upon his entry, Louis was met by the hardened faces of seasoned seafarers sitting around the meeting table. Those faces were of various nationalities: Asian, African, Middle Eastern, and European. Captain Proctor's harsh guttural accent conveyed the reason why he was in charge when he spoke; you could not help but listen. Captain Proctor resumed discussing the meeting agenda. "I want all of you to meet Louis. You can get to know each other personally later. All right, lads, Louis is a paid member of this crew, which means he will work to earn his full ticket, but he has bought his way on board, and he is entitled to be protected from some of the scum who work on the decks of this ship. Louis, these men are your superiors. If you but give them one bit of smart lip, they can knock your fucking teeth out. However, if one of the other crew members tries to do anything to you, yes, even if they grab you by the balls, tell one of us, and we will cut them from their fucking asshole to breakfast time." The rest of the licensed officers laughed as Captain Proctor had a unique way with words. "Seriously though, he is a kid, and you lads need to protect him. Now, Louis, you are needed on the deck tonight and for the next three nights. You finish at break of day, so don't stay up; instead, go to bed again and get your rest as four nights in a row on the deck will wear you out, and you can't afford to get sick." Captain Proctor turned towards Omar, one of the North African men in the room. "Omar, take this kid down to the clothing store and make sure he puts some proper clothes on him. I don't want the kid catching his death when someone has paid such good money to get him on board."

Louis then got up from his chair at the meeting table and was escorted by Omar to a lower deck where a room was being used as a rudimentary uniform store. Omar was a tall Sudanese man, at least 6 feet 4 inches, but there was also an ease about him. Louis sensed that he was in the company of a gentle giant. Deck clothing was provided to him, which he changed into. Omar then escorted Louis to the merchant seamen's mess as he needed food and water. In the mess hall, Louis was able to see with his own eyes the 'scum' the captain had mentioned; several members of the 'scum' stared at Louis, and he felt it would not be an easy life for him while he was travelling on the *Tojo*.

After four nights on deck duty Louis eventually went to bed in his bunk at 4.30am knowing that he had a full two days off before he was due to work the nights again. Then, for another three nights, Louis would start on deck at 6.00pm and work through the night until 3.00am. He had worked under the watchful eye of Omar for those first four nights. Due to his immense size, the men on duty would behave themselves as they knew Omar was physically very powerful. At the start of each night shift, Omar would tell the crewmen that if anything happened to Louis, they would have to answer to him. As Louis went to bed after those first four shifts, the *Tojo* had now almost made its way half the distance across the Atlantic Ocean on the way to its first stop at the Port of Gibraltar. The excitement of seeing a full day of sunlight again for the first time in four days caused Louis to wake at 11.00am. After eating an early lunch, he made his way up onto the deck. As he walked out onto the deck, Louis heard the odd disparaging comment directed at him by some crew members. It did not surprise him. One of the crew was the most vocal agitator. "Girly boy. Don't you look cute? Why don't you come over here and kiss old Hans?" He ignored Hans' comments as he continued to walk towards the bow of the ship. Eventually, Louis made his way to the bow, and he took up a position where he could watch the ocean roll by. There he sat for a good hour pondering his life. He still had vivid memories of the shoot-out between his uncle and his father. He had mixed emotions of sorrow for the loss of Philip and hatred for Joseph. Eventually, the sorrow won out; somewhere in the middle of the Atlantic Ocean, Louis broke down into tears over Philip. Eventually, one hour after he had gone to the bow, Louis felt a wave of exhaustion come over his body. He made his way back towards where his bunk was in the junior officers' compartments of the *Tojo*. Louis went back to bed again and fell into a deep sleep. He had time to rest. For the next two days, Louis tried to keep mainly to himself. However, whenever he had to mix with the crew, it was obvious that Hans had taken an unhealthy interest in Louis. Hans could not touch Louis on the ship as Omar was maintaining a close watchful eye on the young VIP member of the *Tojo*.

Eventually, the *Tojo* docked at the Port of Gibraltar, where some of the crew members got to leave the ship for the half day it was berthed at the port. Louis left the ship on his own, but Omar was keeping a close watchful eye, not allowing the young man to go far out of his gaze into this foreign environment. Hans and some of the other crewmen were also keeping an eye on Louis as he set out to explore Gibraltar, but they were unaware of Omar's watchful eye. Louis walked down N Mole Road, heading towards Waterport Road. He heard some noise behind him, but he did not take too much notice as he started walking down Waterport Road. However, as he walked further down, Louis heard whistles and was followed by the distinctive voice of Hans, who was taunting him. He looked over his shoulder to see Hans and three other men following him; they were about 50 metres away. Louis walked around the corner into Varyl Begg Estate, and as he did so, he could hear Hans and his friends calling out louder. Louis looked over his shoulder again to see Hans and the other men now running around the corner onto Varyl Begg Estate. Louis instinctively ran to try and get away from them. He ran into St Paul's Church, but in doing so, he was met by the dead end of the church's grounds.

When he reached the dead-end, Louis turned to see that Hans and his goons were now only 30 metres away. There was no way out. It did not take too long for Hans to reveal what he had in store for Louis. As Hans started walking towards Louis, he undid the fly on his jeans as the other three men formed a semi-circle ring behind him to ensure Louis could not run away. Hans walked closer towards Louis; he was more broadly built, but being shorter in stature, his reach was not as long. Hans' menacing Germanic tone of voice emphasised his intentions. "I like your tight behind, boy; my Schwanz will have fun with such a tight Arschloch. I'm going to make you my bitch." Louis did not panic about Hans' threat of sodomy. Instead, the ferocious fighter in him, like the day with Jose, came to the fore, and he allowed Hans to creep closer towards him. Hans got to be within two feet of Louis but that was as far as he would get. Louis jabbed hard with his left hand and caught Hans on the point of his chin. Hans was stunned and stumbled backward one step. Louis then swung through with a right hook to Hans' jaw. As his fist connected with the jaw, Louis could feel the bone give way, and Hans fell sideways to the ground; the sound of Hans' skull hitting the hard dirt let out an almighty thud.

One of the other men proceeded to charge at Louis, but he was met with a left jab to the nose. Just then, Omar appeared behind the other men, and his massive frame was overwhelming. Omar grabbed the other two men by the collar, and he smashed their heads together like rags dolls. Louis hit out with another left jab towards the other man's nose again, and this time, his fist connected perfectly with the tip and instantly knocked out his attacker. The two men Omar had smashed together, skull to skull, tried to get up, but Omar smashed one of them in the face with his big right fist, splitting his cheek open and causing the man to fall to the ground unconscious. The other man, whose head had been smashed together with his accomplice, was almost to his feet. Omar grabbed this man by his neck and rammed his head into the stone wall of the cathedral.

Hans and his colleagues were all knocked out, and they were not allowed to reboard the *Tojo*. Omar ushered Louis to walk forward, and his rich African accent brought comfort to Louis' mind. "It is alright; they cannot harm you now." Louis walked with Omar back to the *Tojo*. While they were walking, Louis conveyed his gratitude of sorts. "Thank you for your help, Omar, but I would have taken all of them down." Omar smiled; his admiration for the young man's courage was clear on his face. "I know, lad, I know."

Later that week, the *Tojo* left Gibraltar to head on its way towards Alexandria Port at the entry to the Nile Delta. The departure had been delayed due to the inefficiency of the port hands unloading the containers at this port. After the events of the first day at Gibraltar, Louis did not leave the ship again. The port at Alexandria would be the last stop before the *Tojo* would travel through the Suez Canal. It would be a fascinating journey of almost 2,100 nautical miles.

On the way to Alexandria, Louis worked on the deck again, but this time, for his safety, it was during the day. During his downtime, Louis spent a lot of that time speaking to Omar. Louis revealed scant details about his life in Manhattan to Omar. Omar knew there was a sorry tale to be told by this young man, but he also noticed an immense intelligence dwelling inside Louis' head. Omar was a good and honest man who did not bear any grudges against white skin. 'Strange' was the word that came to his mind about Omar's demeanour, but at the same time, Louis also realised this gentle soul had not been exposed to the tyranny of what was the world of post-segregation American lifestyle for African Americans. They formed a friendship during this leg of the journey. Omar was the finest man Louis had met of those to whom he was not related.

When the *Tojo* arrived at Alexandria, the ship would be in port for a full day. Alexandria was a stopover for the unloading of most of the containers and the reloading of new crates that were destined to be unloaded at Goa. Captain Proctor had decided he would take some of the unlicensed officers to Giza to see the Great Pyramid. Omar suggested that Louis should also go along. If Louis had been enchanted by reading about the Great Pyramid and the Sphinx at school, then the actual sight was even more breathtaking for him. After being processed at the immigration gates of the wharves, the small group of men used several taxi services to transport them from the wharves to Giza and then return them to the ship. Louis was accompanied in the taxi by Omar; the kind man would not allow any harm to come Louis' way.

When the party eventually arrived at the site of the Great Pyramid Louis felt so insignificant. As he began to walk amongst the ancient ruins he found his desire for acquiring knowledge being revived again. Louis was particularly mesmerised by the Sphinx. He wondered why the body was shaped like a lion, yet the head of the structure seemed to be carved in the form of a human face; it was almost as though someone had come along at a later stage and carved their head out of the original sandstone head. He rested near the base of the Sphinx and talked to Omar; during their discussion, Omar enlightened his mind with his simple philosophy. "I have not known you for a long time, Louis, but I feel as though I have got to know you well. Your heart seems to be full of pain; your mind seems to be preoccupied. I don't know why, lad, and I do not need to know. But here is something I want you to remember." Omar looked away towards the skies around Giza, contemplating his next words, but Louis could not wait. "What is it? What should I remember?" Omar indulged Louis' impatience. "My homeland has been a feast and famine for a long time. The last time I was home was seven years ago, lad, right when we were in the middle of a severe drought. My wife and child died during that drought." Omar once again became silent for what seemed to be an eternity for Louis. The silence was broken by the quivering tone of Omar's voice. "I wanted to die with them, lad, but I didn't. I wanted to die, but I didn't. Eventually, lad, I came out the other side to find a new life, and you must do the same. I don't know what happened to you back home, but you are still carrying that world on your shoulders." Omar's speculation was accurate, and Louis did not know what to say. "Lad, you must find a new life, whatever that life will be. The thing about being at sea is that you get to find that new life."

After Omar had spoken about a new life, Louis could only look away; he found this conversation very confronting because his new life had come at a terrible price. He considered Omar's wise words. After a few seconds, Louis looked back towards Omar and nodded his head. Omar's words had resonated with a strange truth in Louis' mind; he thought he was ready to move forward and to leave behind the baggage he had been carrying for the past month since he had left Manhattan. Perhaps Louis O'Brien had finally died, and Louis Montgomery was now alive. Perhaps a rare flower could bloom in fresh soil.

Louis was able to find a shop that was selling copies of *The New York Times* newspaper before the *Tojo* left the port at Alexandria. The main headline on the front page of that newspaper caught his eye. 'Mayor of Manhattan Under Investigation'. To read this headline brought joy to Louis' heart so he purchased a copy of the paper and hurriedly found a bench seat outside of the shop for him to sit down on to read the article. Mayor Sabatini was under investigation for corruption as well as the link to the death of a man from Queens and a teenager whom the police were searching for but now believed to be dead. "I am not dead!" Nevertheless, Louis then realised his demise should at least end the search for him. The article also reported that Coonan was now the District Attorney's chief witness in its investigation of the mayor. Louis always thought Coonan was a rat. The article concluded by stating the police had already made arrests relating to O'Malley's Shed.

After he finished reading the article, Louis then walked back towards the port. Along the way, he thought deeply about the article, and he hoped he might be able to find a subsequent edition of *The New York Times* at some other port the *Tojo* would travel to. "Perhaps there is justice in this world after all." This thought about justice brought him a slender glimmer of hope. That night, as Louis lay in his bunk, he thought about the life he had escaped. He looked at the forged papers Philip had obtained for him. The high school diploma was like a bar of gold in his hands because he may be able to immediately commence studying at an Australian university. He had read some years beforehand about free tertiary education being made available to university students in Australia, and his fake high school diploma should hopefully be a passport for him to blossom as a person and student in that country. He was resolute in his convictions that night; in Australia, he would resume his passion for knowledge as that character trait separated him from Joseph's lawless ways.

The *Tojo* took Louis to many different parts of the world over the next few months as it made its way towards Sydney. Every port seemed to behold a new experience, a new sense of excitement, and new cultures. Louis worked like he was expected to, and each day he finished a shift, he was a step closer to disembarking from the *Tojo* when it reached Sydney Harbour. Then, one October morning in 1978, Louis woke up to an announcement over the intercom that he had been waiting to hear; it was the first mate announcing that in the next 30 minutes, the *Tojo* would be making its way through the heads of Sydney Harbour. Louis jumped out of his bunk and quickly put on his clothes. He was so excited that he did not even bother to shower. He raced up onto the deck, and in the distance, Louis could see two cliffs separated from each other by a seaway. He did not need anyone to tell him because he knew that the *Tojo* was only minutes away from Sydney Harbour. As the ship approached the heads of the harbour, the *Tojo*'s horn blew out loud into the skies of the early morning, and it was the most exhilarating sound Louis had ever heard on the journey. The sights of Sydney Harbour were spectacular, and all the pictures Louis had seen in books did not compare to the actual sight of that beautiful harbour. The Opera House and the Harbour Bridge, indeed the whole city, seemed to beckon an exciting new life whereby Louis could start afresh.

Eventually, the *Tojo* docked at the port of Glebe Island. After what seemed like an eternity for everyone on board, they were told that they could go ashore. Louis had now showered and changed. He had also packed the knapsack Philip had given him. He raced towards the licensed officers' meeting room as he wanted to say goodbye to his friend Omar. The room was empty, and it seemed as though the officers were on deck or had already made their way to leave the ship. Louis ran up ladders to the deck. He looked around to try and find Omar, but all around him was the chaos of many men making their way to the gangway to disembark from the ship. Then Louis spotted through the crowd of seamen the familiar sight of the big Sudanese man striding his way along. Omar stopped when he saw Louis, and the pair looked at each other, knowing full well this may be the last time they saw each other. Louis walked over to Omar and extended his right hand. Omar grabbed Louis' shoulders instead of shaking his hand, and he gave him a reassuring hug of friendship. "You will be okay, Louis; life can only improve." Omar released him from his grip so that Louis could now see Omar's face. "Thank you for being a friend, and thank you for your wise words." With those simple words being spoken, Louis turned away to walk towards the gangway, but then he stopped and called out to Omar. "We all deserve a new start, my friend. You go find yourself a new life and a new wife; you deserve it." Omar's face revealed an appreciative grin. Louis then turned and stepped onto the gangway so that he could disembark from the *Tojo*.

Louis walked down the gangway with a sense of purpose, and when he disembarked from the ship, he turned around for one last look at the ship, which had been his home for so many months. After a brief moment of examining the ship and reflecting on his time aboard her, Louis then immediately made his way towards customs and immigration. He had all the papers to start his new life in Australia as Louis Montgomery, but in his haste to leave the port, he had neglected to thoroughly examine the recorded details. He stopped at a desk with a sign above it informing people entering the immigration gate that they had to fill out the required Australian government paperwork to enter the country. Louis was so excited about his imminent entrance into Australia that he did not check the form he had completed against his passport, and he instead briskly walked towards the immigration gate.

At the gate, Louis handed his passport and the form he had completed to a uniformed Australian Immigration officer. That officer was a slightly portly man who looked to be middle-aged, and he did not even display on his face a hint of a welcoming smile. The immigration officer looked at the form Louis had just filled out and then proceeded to open the passport. At that moment, it was as though the sword of Damocles had fallen onto Louis' head because he realised he had not checked the form against his fake passport. The immigration officer picked up on the obvious error in the forms Louis had completed, namely the wrong year of birth. The immigration officer's eyes immediately flashed up to peer into Louis' eyes; Louis was a mirror of his true soul, and he was doing his best not to reveal the terror that had overcome him because of his mindless mistake. "What's going on with your paperwork, mate?" It was a rhetorical question, but playing stupid was perhaps the best way to work his way through this very delicate and potentially dangerous decisive moment. "What do you mean?" Louis deliberately spoke the worst drawn-out American accent that, by its very nature, made him sound stupid. "I will tell ya what I mean, Yankee doodle, your passport records you being born in 1957, but in your paperwork, you have written 1961. So which one is it?"

He had to think fast and come up with a plausible answer because it was obvious the immigration officer was now extremely suspicious of Louis. It took only seconds for him to respond, but in his mind, it was like hours, and once again, the over-enunciated American accent was used to try and pass himself off as stupid. "Oh, that entry of 1961 was an error, man, because I had just been speaking to one of my good friends on the *Tojo* before I left the ship, and he was telling me his son was born on this day in 1961. He was excited but also sad because his son could not be with him today, and gee, after that, I must have unconsciously been thinking about 1961 when I completed the form." The immigration officer accepted the premise of the mistake, but this did not happen too often. "Wait here." The immigration officer picked up the various documents from his desk and then proceeded to walk about ten metres away to an office.

Louis was very nervous that his false identity may have already been revealed by his own mistake. He tried not to watch what was going on in that office, and he instead did his best to use his peripheral vision. He could see the immigration officer throwing his hands around in the air, whereas the person he was speaking to remained calm. After two minutes of discussions, the immigration officer returned with a fresh form. "Fill this in properly, including the right year." He was unhappy, but it appeared to Louis the officer's manager had accepted the story Louis had told and thereby directed the subordinate officer to permit Louis' entry into Australia. As he completed the new form, Louis displayed no emotions on his face, whereas inside his body, a party was going off like the 4th of July. The immigration officer read the new form and stamped it, along with Louis' passport. Without even a hint of a smile, he then welcomed him to enter the country in a traditional Australian manner. "Yeah, enter, you silly twit, but be more careful when filling out Australian government forms." Louis nodded his head without any verbal response.

Louis quickly walked through the immigration gates, and when he was far enough away from the immigration officer, he felt relieved. His excitement began to build as he was now about to stand on Australian soil. He also had approximately $3,000.00 in American currency, an amount that increased since he left Newark Bay because he had been paid in cash by Captain Proctor for the work he had performed on the *Tojo*. Louis was financially secure for the present moment to start his new life, and he knew that from here on, he would always have to ensure that he had enough money to support himself. Money had been a problem in his life because of his late father's greed, and he affirmed in his mind he would not be anything like that man he detested so much by wasting his money on wine, women, and song. These darker thoughts were, for the time being, restrained in the back of his mind because he was now in a new country; he was now on Australian soil, and the excitement of the opportunity of a new life was boiling away in his veins so much he could not wipe the smile off his face.

PART 3

"Demons Within"

CHAPTER 13

Louis now stood on Australian soil, and he looked around the alien landscape of Australia, a country he had never been to before and where he would now live. Surveying his new surroundings, the excitement within him seemed to overcome his entire physical state, and he could only stand still and take in his new environment. The air smelt cleaner than Manhattan, and the sky seemed to be brighter. The air temperature was warm and inviting. All these new sensations were absorbed as he remained motionless in the spot he had stopped in outside of the port entrance. He was now at his leisure to explore his new world of living in Sydney in late 1978. He also began to realise for the first time since escaping Manhattan just how alone he was; he was an orphan in an alien world. Sydney was not nearly as large as Manhattan, but it was still a big and overpowering city for any outsider to become accustomed to. Louis hailed a taxi near the Glebe Island port. He entered the St George taxi, which had pulled over in response to his hail, and it was at this time he first appreciated the strange sound of the Australian accent. "How are ya, mate? Bonza beauty day in paradise, isn't it?" A statement with a question, Louis was immediately intrigued and perplexed by Australians. "Where ya off to, mate?" Louis quickly processed his memories from his studies at school. "Near Hyde Park, please." Then came the innocent slur. "Ah, you're a yank!" Louis was taken aback for a moment; "Yank?" he thought to himself. "Hyde Park it is mate." The driver's horrible and strange nasal accent had to be endured by Louis for the entire trip. He did not like being referred to as a 'yank' because the nickname seemed to be underwritten by prejudice. He looked out the window of the taxi during the journey, and the flowers blooming on the Jacaranda trees appealed to his mind. Would this new soil help him bloom into adulthood like a beautiful and strong new flower? Only time might tell.

During his first two weeks in Sydney, Louis stayed at the Hyde Park Inn, which was a lovely and quaint little hotel overlooking the beautiful grounds of Hyde Park in the central business district. He had selected the hotel because of its location in the centre of Sydney's business district, an area where Louis believed he could start to integrate into Australian society and become accustomed to the unique proclivities of their daily lives. From this location, Louis was able to commence his journey exploring the sights and sounds of Sydney. He visited the Opera House and took in the majesty of this man-made wonder of the world. He caught a bus for the first time in his life to travel to Bondi Beach, and when he arrived there, he sat on the sand, as he had dreamed of doing years beforehand back in Manhattan. Each spot Louis visited reminded him of the times when he was younger back in Manhattan, and he would be reading about Sydney in the school library books. That first week Louis spent in Sydney was almost like a dream; each new sight stimulated his otherwise hardened heart. Nevertheless, at night, Louis would think about his now-deceased Uncle Philip, and his grief would overcome him. Those nights in his hotel room, Louis felt so alone. If he were not overcome by grief for Philip at night, Louis would otherwise stew in anger about Joseph. He would dream each night about the terrible events that he had witnessed during his life, including the death of his uncle.

Louis knew he had to find alternative accommodation because the cost per night at the hotel was too expensive. Eventually, towards the end of his second week of living in Sydney, Louis found an advertisement in the local newspaper about a good clean room for $25.00 a week in the inner city suburb of Newtown. Sydney University was also nearby. It was shared accommodation in a terrace home, a style of architecture that was foreign to the architecture of Midtown West. The terrace house was owned by an elderly lady named Eunice Smith, a lady who was born and bred in the inner suburbs of Sydney. Though she introduced herself as Eunice Smith, she told Louis she preferred to be called Mrs Smith. It was not luxurious, but the room was clean. During this tour of the home, Mrs Smith asked Louis some questions about his background as his accent reflected that he was not an Australian. Louis divulged very minor details about himself. He told Mrs Smith he was 21 years of age, from New York and he was looking to commence tertiary study in Australia, hence that was why he had moved to Sydney. Louis otherwise remained silent about his personal life back in America.

After she had shown Louis his room, he was then ushered to the kitchen table by Mrs Smith to discuss the terms of the board and lodging. The room itself was $25.00 a week, but for an extra $20.00, she would not only feed Louis but also clean for him. In return, he had to keep a clean lifestyle within her home; there was no drinking or use of drugs. The room was immediately available to be moved into. Louis accepted the terms of his accommodation, and with that, Mrs Smith nodded her head to acknowledge the agreement had been made. She then made Louis a cup of tea and proceeded to explain to him her life story, which was drawn out as Mrs Smith was very fond of a cigarette, and she would take her time drawing back on each one as she told her story, but Louis listened because she seemed to be a very honest person. She told him she was a widower who had lived in Newtown for 40 years after marrying her late husband. She had no children, and she did not have too many close family members; indeed, there were no nieces or nephews, brothers, or sisters to speak of, and accordingly, the house was quiet. Louis was relieved there would not be a parade of family. "Thank goodness for that."

The following day, Louis checked out of the Hyde Park Inn. After he arrived at Mrs Smith's home, he spent some time just sitting in his room to become accustomed to this area of the house being his space. Louis' bedroom satisfied his desire to embark on university study; the room contained a desk for Louis to study at, and the room itself was not located over a street. It was the perfect environment for a 17-year-old young man to live in while he commenced a new life in a foreign city. Within a day of having moved into Mrs Smith's home, Louis thought she was similar to Ms Fitzgerald in the standard of care she provided, but more importantly, there was one distinct difference, namely, the threat of Joseph was no longer an element in Louis' life. Although he would speak to Mrs Smith about America, he was very guarded about his actual life in that country as, after all, he had been a person of interest in the activities of Joseph and his union colleagues at the shed. At night, Louis would lie on his bed and think about many of the cruel circumstances he was subjected to as a child. During these times of reflection, Louis' heart was filled with hatred for his dead father and all of those people whom Joseph was associated with, including Mary, but it was not a healthy exercise for the young man's mind to dwell on these matters.

Louis knew that he had to take many steps to reap the benefits of this new life Philip had created for him. He decided he wanted to study business and commerce at university. He made the necessary enquiry at the University of Sydney, which was a prestigious Australian university. In keeping with the ethos of being a member of the egalitarian academic community of Australia, Sydney University would take in a quota of foreign students each year. He had to apply for a student visa as he was currently residing in Australia as a temporary visitor. That student visa would be granted to him upon proof of his being accepted into a university course. His Regents diploma accompanied his foreign student application to study business at Sydney University. He applied for a learner's permit to learn how to drive a car, and his fake passport facilitated the issuing of a permit recording his birth year as 1957, a local identification document that was easier to carry on his person. He also searched for work opportunities, an endeavour that was not an easy task in the prevailing economic circumstances of the time. He eventually found a very low-paying job stacking shelves at the local supermarket. During his interview, Louis was not asked too many questions by the store manager, other than a fleeting reference to him coming from America. Although it was casual work, Louis could earn approximately $90 a week, enough money to pay for his board. It was a start as he now had a job, but inside his heart, Louis wanted to earn more or, in what was to be an early warning signal about an emerging and ominous character attribute, acquire more money.

It was an unusually cool, wet, and windy day in Sydney on 15 December 1978. Louis had been waiting each day since submitting his application to Sydney University. He had only made an application to Sydney University because that institution was like an Australian version of the Ivy League universities back in America. The postman delivered the mail to Mrs Smith's mailbox at midday that day during a heavy downpour of rain. Louis heard the postman's scooter stop outside Mrs Smith's house and he ran down the internal stairwell and out the front door to quickly retrieve the mail from the increasingly damp mailbox. To his delight, there was an envelope that had marked on the front of it Sydney University's crest, addressed to Mr Louis Montgomery. He was eager to open the envelope, but he took a moment to consider what was a contemporaneous moment in time; he had received his first item of mail bearing his new name, and it was the most important item of correspondence in his life. Louis carefully opened the envelope and removed the neatly folded piece of paper. The anticipation as to what the nature of that correspondence would be was causing Louis' heart to race. He unfolded the letter, and within a few short moments, he smiled as it informed him the Dean of the Business School had granted preliminary approval in response to his application to be a student at the start of the 1979 university year, but he would have to attend at the university for an interview with Dean Moore before the final approval could be granted. Louis could hardly believe how life had changed for him. He had a new start in a new part of the world, and he had been tentatively accepted into one of the top universities in Australia.

Later that afternoon, Louis decided he would take himself into the city to see a motion picture to celebrate the response he received from the university. The inclement weather had subsided, so he walked from Newtown to the cinema complex on George Street within Sydney's central business district, a leisurely walk that took him about an hour to complete. There were no familiar faces he saw on that stroll; this anonymity since arriving in Australia had brought ephemeral feelings of safety and comfort to his mind. He arrived at the cinema complex, and after considering which movies were being screened that night, he decided to watch *A Clockwork Orange*. He was too young to watch this movie, but his stamped permit to learn how to drive a car meant he could prove he was 21 years of age and, therefore, entitled to admission into the cinema. The images of juvenile delinquency, violence, mistreatment in prison, and other graphic depravity disturbed his mind rather than enlightening it. The movie triggered the awakening of the morbid beast that had otherwise been lying dormant within Louis' mind while it had been distracted by the wonders of his new life.

When the picture had finished, Louis walked out of the cinema, and the streets were quieter. The movie he had just watched haunted his mind and heightened his anxiety as it made his mind relive the traumatic life he endured in America. There was nobody he knew to go and visit to distract his mind, and he now felt the despair of isolation. Even though it was only 10.30pm for Louis, it felt like 4.00am, which was the difference between Manhattan and Sydney. As he walked the streets to return to Newtown, Louis experienced an unforeseen feeling of the abyss of despair caused by loneliness, which was not assisted by the strange and unfriendly faces walking by him that night. An unease grew in his heart regarding this new life as he realised he had nobody around him from whom he could seek good counsel. During that dark and lonely walk home, he continued to dwell on his past life, and he started to feel angry and depressed by the time he reached Newtown. The content of the movie and the lonely walk home at night had only revived and empowered the demons within his mind.

When he returned to Mrs Smith's home, Louis was already in despair, anxiety, and depression. At 17 years of age, he was barely a man; he still had the heart and soul of a child. He was carrying inside his heart a lifetime of mistreatment, and on that night, walking home alone, he discovered a new city does not cure that heartbreak; it does not cure the trauma. Mrs Smith was asleep in her lounge chair with the butt of a cigarette still held between her index and pointer fingers where it had burned out long ago after she had fallen asleep watching television. Louis did not disturb her as he quietly crept up the flight of stairs that would take him to his bedroom. As much as he looked at the letter he received from the university that day with a sense of hope, his mind's propensity to embrace depressive thoughts and memories could not be extinguished by a mere letter.

As he sat on his bed, Louis started recalling again the images of all the people he had seen killed or being killed when he lived in Manhattan. He had seen a lot of death occur in his lifetime, and Philip's death haunted him the most because Louis now felt he was responsible. His mind contemplated these macabre memories of these various deceased persons, and these memories took him down a path of then dwelling upon his mortality. He feared death and had struggled with that fear since he was ten years of age, but this was a different fear as suddenly his mind descended deeper into a deeper pit of anxiety and morbidity than he had previously experienced, a feeling in which that fear seemed to overtake every cell in his body and every stream of thought of his consciousness. His morbid preoccupation with his mortality took his level of anxiety to a place of just utter fear, hopelessness, and distress. He wrestled with these acute thoughts of fear and anxiety until Louis' tortured mind went to sleep at about 3.00am. This new level of death anxiety was a paradox of him now living in a safe world; whereas in Manhattan, there was the constant threat of actual violence to interrupt his mind here in Sydney, his mind had found the comfort of safety in which this demon of his mind, this demon of death anxiety, could flourish like an untrammelled noxious weed.

When he awoke later that morning at 7.00am, his conscious mind was not different; the same depth of fear and anxiety engulfed his mind. The skies outside his bedroom were consumed by dark grey clouds, and on the other side of the street, a black Labrador was barking incessantly for no particular reason. The irony of the symbolism of the dark clouds and a black dog barking at his door was lost on Louis.

Christmas came and went in Australia in 1978, and the only person Louis had to celebrate Christmas with was Mrs Smith. She had cooked a roast meal in keeping with the goodwill of the season. Nevertheless, Louis' mind was still overwhelmed that day with his acute death anxiety. While they were eating their Christmas meal, Mrs Smith finally asked Louis a question, she had been wishing to ask him for a long time. "So, Louis, where are your family? Do they know you are in Australia?" Louis stopped eating and tried very hard not to reveal how confronting this line of questioning was for him. "What do you mean?" It was obvious what she meant, and Mrs Smith persisted with her enquiry. "Well, Louis, I have had a lot of young people stay here over the last few years, and they always have family they wish to call or talk about them to me. You do not ever talk about your family, and you certainly do not try to call any of them, including, for that matter, today."

Louis remained silent for a minute; his stare did not depart from the inquisitive eyes of Mrs Smith. The truth may have set his mind free, but he instead skirted around the fringes of the truth. "My family are all dead, and I was raised in an orphanage." Mrs Smith's curiosity had not been satisfied by Louis' response. "An orphan? Are you telling me that you have no family whatsoever?" Louis nodded an affirmative reply to the query. The old woman was not done yet. "So how did someone so young manage to raise enough money to get here then?" Louis decided that part of the truth was best. "My mother left me a little bit of money, which was held on trust. I managed to find work on a merchant ship, which eventually brought me here to Australia." She absorbed this information into her mind, and eventually, Mrs Smith's face changed in expression from inquiry to acceptance, so she shrugged her shoulders and continued eating her meal. The immediate threat of his true identity being revealed under questioning had departed so that his inner demon was left on this empty stage of his mind. His acute death anxiety maintained its dominance in his life, and as he went to sleep on New Year's Eve of 1978, his mind tore itself apart with one final thought, "I don't want to die."

The syllogism of 'All living things die; I am a living thing; therefore I will die' could not be cured by then turning a page of a calendar. Louis' death anxiety did not abate during that summer of 1979, and everything Louis looked at reminded him of death. His morbid preoccupation with his mortality consumed every waking moment of his mind; his acute death anxiety was all-powerful and overwhelming. It had been the season of joy and new hope, but there was no joy or hope in his heart and mind. Louis vowed to himself that he would just remain focused on his opportunity to resume his studies. However, that inner demon remained at the forefront of his mind.

CHAPTER 14

Louis longed for his interview with Dean Moore to occur; anything to relieve his mind from this preoccupation with his eventual demise. Even though he was surrounded by all of the splendour and beauty of Sydney in summer, Louis' mind was stranded in a dark and barren world.

Two weeks after the new year, Louis arrived at Sydney University for his interview with Dean Moore. He was still deeply depressed with thoughts of his mortality, but Louis focused his mind on this day to concentrate on the interview. As Louis walked through the grounds of the university, he could not help but look at the Australian girls walking around the campus. The girls would smile at him, but those mere smiles could not assist Louis' morale. He could only cope with one thought: "Get through this interview." Unlike the Cultural Revolution, which had taken over most other courses at Sydney University, the Business School remained tied to its conservative roots. Dean Moore's secretary showed Louis into the Dean's office, and in keeping with the conservative image, this woman dressed like someone who had never left the 1950s. Her dress came down to well below the knee, and she wore a blouse that buttoned up to her wrist. She spoke with a nasally Australian accent, and when Louis spoke, the irony of the woman's response could not escape him. "Aw, you're American; what a funny little accent you have."

Another five minutes passed by before the Dean entered the reception. Dean Desmond Moore was a clean-cut man in his early fifties. After introducing himself, the Dean asked Louis where he was from in New York State. Louis briefly paused to think about his response; then, he lied by saying "Queens" as he did not feel comfortable telling the Dean that he was from Manhattan. The Dean then proceeded to tell Louis he was very impressed with Louis' academic record. During the discussion, the Dean told Louis there were not many places open for overseas students in this course, but Louis' academic record made him the top candidate for admission as a foreign-based student, and he explained the purpose of the interview process was for him to assess whether the foreign student could cope with the challenges of the curriculum. They discussed basic concepts of business, which displayed Louis' capability to learn more, and it was perhaps ironic that some of his business knowledge had been acquired from the abomination that was his life in Manhattan.

During the interview, Louis did his best to display a calm demeanour, whereas the inward state of his mind was this battleground of insurmountable fear. However, he listened carefully to each question the Dean asked him, and then he chose his words wisely. In what was a decisive moment regarding his being accepted into the course, Louis told the Dean he wanted to remain in Australia after he had finished studying and working for an Australian company. To Louis' surprise, the Dean then told him that he would sign the required documents to facilitate the approval of the student visa and that, subject to his academic performance, he would support him when he eventually applied for a permanent visa as well as 'happily' assisting him with future employment if it was necessary. The inference Louis could distil from Dean Moore informing him he would support any future application he made for a permanent visa, was that he had passed the interview stage. He should have been ecstatic, but the underlying pathology of Louis' mental health could not entertain such an emotion at this time. Before expressly telling Louis he had passed the interview, Dean Moore explained to him a fact that was already known by Louis, namely that tertiary education was free in Australia if he was approved as an acceptable recipient of one of these special foreign student course places. After he had discussed the fees, the Dean then proceeded to inform Louis that he had passed the interview and the formal acceptance documentation would be sent in the post to him. As he subsequently walked Louis out of his office door, he invited Louis to go and inspect the undergraduate library because the Dean was proud to say the resources available included a new system called microfiche, which stored micro imprints of various documents, including newspapers from around the world.

As a result of hearing this news about the microfiche, Louis immediately made his way to the undergraduate library. Louis' relief to have passed his interview could not subdue his curiosity. He desperately wanted to find out what happened to the mayor, Coonan, and any other people involved in the criminal underworld linked to O'Malley's Shed. His journey to Australia on the *Tojo* meant there were long periods out at sea when Louis could not access any stores that might have sold a copy of *The New York Times*, and he could not find a store in Sydney that sold copies of that particular newspaper. He now hoped to find out what had happened in Manhattan regarding the prosecution of the reprobates whose clutches from which he had escaped.

Louis walked into the modern environment of the undergraduate library; a building that had been constructed during the 1960s. A librarian assisted him in accessing microfiche containing copies of *The New York Times* for the past few months. Louis scrolled through the various editions of the newspaper until he came across a report within the 4 October 1978 edition regarding the investigation of the mayor. The article reported the District Attorney's main witness, a man named Coonan, was found dead in his apartment by the police after he hanged himself. The article proceeded to report that because of the death of Coonan, the District Attorney may not continue its prosecution of the charges of criminal corruption the mayor had been indicted for, but the prosecution of the mayor's fraudulent business dealings would still proceed in the civil courts. Louis was stunned as he read this news. "How did the District Attorney allow the mayor to get to Coonan?" Louis scrolled further through the microfiche records, and sure enough, one week after Coonan had died, the District Attorney announced he would not proceed on the indictment he had previously presented in the State of New York's criminal courts, and the federal investigative authorities confirmed that due to a lack of evidence their investigations regarding Mayor Sabatini allegedly breaking federal laws would cease forthwith. At least this subsequent report confirmed the District Attorney would continue his prosecutions of criminal charges against mafia henchmen connected to O'Malley's Shed; however, Louis had suffered enough misery from reading the unfortunate news about the mayor not being prosecuted for criminal charges, so in turning off the light on the microfiche viewfinder, Louis did not read the further news reported in the final paragraph of the article about another unidentified mafia henchman willing to give evidence about his colleagues in return for a lenient plea bargain, nor did he read subsequent editions of *The New York Times* which reported Mayor Sabatini's health was quickly deteriorating.

Subsequently, Louis' heart sank as he walked out the door of the library, and he was overwhelmed by the dismay of the feeling that there truly was no justice in this world. "My uncle is dead; I have to flee the country, and this bastard is going to walk free!" He walked slowly back to Mrs Smith's terrace house from the university that afternoon, trying to reconcile a positive outcome arising out of the facts he had just read, but no such positive outcome could be found. An evil man in Mayor Sabatini was going to walk free in circumstances where that man had been responsible for overseeing, encouraging, and inducing so many murders and other criminal acts in Manhattan. When Louis returned to Mrs Smith's house, he took himself upstairs to his bedroom and closed the door for the day. His mind was preoccupied with the conflicting emotions and thoughts regarding his death anxiety, his anger, and his future studies at Sydney University, a future which now seemed to suggest injustice could prevail as an evil man had escaped prosecution in Manhattan. Louis' young mind, no matter how intelligent, was spinning forever downwards with his thoughts about all his tormentors; the mayor, his father, and his eventual death. At some stage later that evening, Louis fell asleep, but there would be no imminent respite from his mental torment.

When he awoke the next morning at the break of day, Louis took himself to his small bedroom mirror and looked himself in the eye. His mind was a putrid field of fear, anger, and dejection. His sotto voce words described his innermost thoughts. "Bastards, bastards, bastards, get out of my head." He had to get on with his life, and most of all, he had to remain focused on his opportunity to take advantage of his academic good fortune. However, Louis' mind continued to be consumed with depression, anger, and anxiety. His mind was mentally worn by this non-stop torment, by these non-stop thoughts. He did not leave his bedroom that day, and later that evening, at about 7.30pm, Louis fell into a deep sleep. He did not even come down for dinner that night. This was the deadly mental cycle that Louis continued to experience throughout January 1979. He became withdrawn, and when he did not work, Louis otherwise spent a lot of time in his room. Mrs Smith would occasionally enquire whether he was fine, and Louis would say he was, although internally, he so desperately wanted to talk to her about everything.

Louis' mental state was quickly deteriorating, and he had no means of addressing the problems, nor did he have the insight to properly understand them. He took himself down to Circular Quay one afternoon in early February 1979 when he was in a very deeply depressed state. He walked aimlessly around the outside of the Opera House when suddenly his mind snapped as it accepted a dreadful thought. "Perhaps death would not so be bad; end it all and escape this torment." His mind was so tortured that now death itself seemed to be his only means of escape. Louis looked into the waters of Sydney Harbour, and the deep blue water seemed to be inviting him, an invitation to end the torment within him as he had never learned how to swim. Louis stepped up onto the railings which otherwise would prevent a person from falling over into the water below. He balanced himself perfectly still; taking a final breath, Louis steadied himself to jump. He started speaking to himself in a bizarre display of motivation. "Do it, do it. End the pain. You can do this!" Louis then placed a foot on the top rung of the railing; he would push off and plunge into the waters of Sydney Harbour, never to be seen again. He was ready to jump, and as he was about to do so, Louis looked towards the heavens. A ray of sunlight shone through the cloudy sky, and its radiance caused a shot of logic to push through the heavy soil in his mind. "What do you think you are doing?" This voice of logic called out within his mind, and then, almost in unison, the sound of a man's voice called out nearly the same words. "Hey there, you idiot, what do you think you are doing?" Louis turned to see the frame of a large middle-aged man standing 20 metres away from him. The man was a security guard employed at the Opera House, and he did not look happy. His voice called out again, and although his words were spoken through a strained Australian accent, at least, they seemed to bring Louis to his senses. "What in the hell is going on?" The guard's face was stamped with the look of authority. "Go on, get down from there and get the hell out of here, you stupid little wanker!" The harsh Australian tone of the guard had further awoken Louis from the deepest trench of his mental sorrow, and he quickly got down off the railing to obey the command. He turned and walked away from the fence of the Opera House to the sound of the harsh and critical voice of the security guard still ringing out from behind him. As he walked away from the Opera House, Louis only hoped that his tormenting thoughts would soon settle in his mind.

Later that night, Louis was lying on his bed looking at the ceiling, wondering why his morbid thoughts had become so overwhelming when he was seconds away from committing suicide. Louis could hear the Labrador across the street barking. It seemed as though the dog was barking to the same tune that was barking in Louis' mind. Louis lay down on his bed that night, and although his mind was consumed with the same morbid thoughts, at least there was a positive thought entering his mind, which was his university studies were soon to start. He looked out the window of his room from his bed, and the clouds had dissipated, so the night sky looked so beautiful. Louis' eyes then seemed to light up, and his mind started speaking in a different phase of mind. "I want to live! I want to live!" It was a forthright message that rang out in his mind. Louis went to sleep later that night and, although his mind was still preoccupied with his death, at least he had moved one step onwards as he now did not want to kill himself in what had been a misconceived attempt to relieve his mind from its agony. Now, as Louis went to sleep, he promised himself he would eventually find a method to escape his inner despair.

CHAPTER 15

In late February 1979, it would only be a short period until Louis started studying business at university. He remained true to his vow in his mind that he was not going to jeopardise this opportunity which had been presented to him by Uncle Philip, despite his mental anguish, which he could not escape. He had slipped into a deep depression, and therefore, his coping mechanism was to become introverted. As Louis eventually commenced campus life at Sydney University in early March 1979, he should have been basking in the glory of this achievement, but instead, he was anxious, afraid, and lacking in confidence. Amidst all this anxiety, apprehension, self-doubt, and depression, Louis became even more thankful that he was living under Mrs Smith's roof as at least there he found some form of comfort of escape by staying in his room to study.

It was in March of 1979 that Louis found a job that was perfectly suited for his commitments to student life at university. The Union Hotel on King Street in Newtown had advertised on its front doors that the bar required a bar hand most days of the week. Louis had seen the flyer posted on the door of the hotel as he walked past one afternoon, and he immediately enquired whether the job was still available. Bill Jackson, who was the hotel manager, came into the public bar and proceeded to interview Louis on the spot. The job was indeed still available, and Louis could earn enough money working three days a week to pay for his rent without eating into the nest egg that he had brought with him after disembarking from the *Tojo* last year. More importantly, it was better money than the casual work Louis had been performing at the supermarket. Indeed, later that day after Louis accepted the position, he calculated that he could save $25.00 a week after paying for his expenses, which was enough surplus money to build on his nest egg. Unlike his father, Louis was an acquirer of money, but he did not realise there was a common denominator: greed for money.

His work at the Union Hotel commenced a week before Louis was to start his university studies. He had promised Mrs Smith that evening after accepting the position, the life of alcohol would stay at the hotel and not enter her home. The patrons of the hotel were mainly working-class people, and a lot of them were railway employees. Louis' main job was to collect glasses, but some of the older staff were to teach him how to pour beers into a glass, which was a necessary skill if you were going to work in an Australian hotel. During that first week of work, Louis listened to the various patrons talk about their lives. Arising from what he heard at the hotel, one thing was for certain to Louis: he must complete his university studies, or his life would end up as miserable as the lives he was watching being spilled out before him most nights.

Louis commenced his business degree at Sydney University in March of 1979. His life was perfectly set up to commence studying at a tertiary level. He no longer had any tormentors such as Joseph or Coonan in his life, and he was free of the terror that was his life living in Joseph's apartment. Nevertheless, now Louis was a prisoner in his mind. He had suffered so many traumatic experiences, so many moments of mental anguish that just when he should have found his mental relief, a new tormentor entered his mind. Louis could at least find salvation in his study. In his textbooks, Louis tried to escape the dark thoughts that were consuming him. The nights in Sydney began to become darker sooner rather than later. As the last remnants of summer were swept away by the year approaching the Easter break, Louis' mind was no better being back at university. Mrs Smith had detected something was wrong, but she was still getting to know Louis. Accordingly, Mrs Smith kept her tongue, and she did not dare ask her relatively new lodger what thoughts seemed to be occupying him.

Life at university was a struggle for Louis; a young mind with these many internal demons would find it difficult to concentrate, let alone study. But study Louis did, and he somehow compartmentalised his depressing thoughts into one part of his mind as he used the other parts to study. His lecturer was a vision of comic relief, a small balding man; Ian Jenkins was the epitome of a lifelong scholar. Although he was well-book-read, Jenkins lacked life experience. The rest of the students seemed to be oblivious to the comical presentation that Louis saw before him each day; nevertheless, the general lack of intention in his lectures seemed to reflect that Jenkins was lacking in not only stature but also authority. Despite Jenkins' comical presentation, Louis nevertheless eagerly participated in the lectures, so much so that one day Jenkins spoke in frustration. "Why can't the rest of you be like Louis here?" Without fail, a half-smart Australian student named Russell Jones piped up from the back of the class, "What, be like a yank?" Louis immediately turned around and looked into Jones' eyes. Jones was a stocky and cocky little half-smart 18-year-old, but he would now be unnerved by Louis' reaction. Louis' stare was fierce, and his words were even more tormenting for his adversary. "You have a problem with that?" Jones was startled; the subtle degree of hostility in Louis' voice beckoned a fight, and Jones was not a fighter. Louis continued, just like that day with Jose so many years ago, but he did not know when he had won. "If you have a problem with me, we can always step outside." Jones shook his head.

Louis continued staring at Jones, but Dr Jenkins broke the silence. "Settle down, boys; if you want to display your testosterone, there are sporting teams on campus for that." The lecture class let out a relieved giggle at the lecturer's comment. Louis maintained his deathly stare into Jones' eyes and then turned around 30 seconds later. Russell Jones was a defeated young man, perhaps because there was not much of a man within him. However, the cold, hard, and deathly stare he received from Louis broke Russell's spirit. Whereas other people thought he was still a strong-natured person, Russell felt insignificant in the presence of Louis, such was the power of Louis' confrontational nature.

Winters in Sydney were bleak and cold. The books Louis read at school back in Manhattan did not report about life during winter in Sydney. During the height of winter, it became cold, and the trees lost all of their leaves. Louis' mental state had not improved, but his life studying was at least a relief from when his mind had time to think about life itself. However, Louis was also lonely; he had no family and friends, and if it were not for Mrs Smith, he would not have anyone to interact with. His classmates at university all seemed to have their little social circles; they were, after all, from the same part of the world, so, of course, quite a few of them already knew each other from school. Some of them took an interest in Louis' accent as an American, which was a novelty.

As hard as he tried, Louis just found it difficult to interact with Australians. He, in particular, found the amount of discriminatory behaviour troubling because, unlike America, where racially intolerant comments had started to become frowned upon, in Australia, racist comments seemed to be part of everyday life. People from the Mediterranean region of the world were referred to as wogs, Asians were referred to as slopes, and worst of all, the indigenous Australians, the people whose lives had been destroyed by the European invasion, were referred to as coons or Abos. Unlike in America, where the racist comments and names had started to disappear behind closed doors by the time Louis escaped, in Australia, racial intolerance was out in the open. In addition, so many of the population seemed to be subservient to the idea of the British monarchy ruling over them. Louis would concede in his mind that most of the Australian population was of British background, but their devotion to the monarchy of the United Kingdom intrigued him.

These thoughts about Australia's devotion to monarchy then led to him thinking about his pedigree and what he had been told by Philip about his noble bloodline in France. These thoughts about his ancestral background would be quickly displaced by the thoughts of his father belittling him, indeed emasculating him. Jose's bullying would also enter his mind and further compromise his self-confidence. His lack of self-worth could not be cured by escaping to another country, and it was another inner demon that would terrorise his thoughts.

CHAPTER 16

Despite the attitudes of some Australians, there was one Australian who was trying his utmost to win over Louis' friendship. After the confrontation that had occurred in the lecture theatre, Russell Jones was gradually trying his hardest to extend an olive branch of friendship to Louis. Eventually, late in 1979, Louis opened the door of friendship to Russell. For Louis, it was a relief to finally form a friendship with a person who was at least worthy of conversation. For Russell, there was a secret that he held onto as to the reasons why he wanted to befriend Louis. Initially, their friendship commenced by talking increasingly to each other around the campus. Russell began to then introduce Louis to his group of friends. The social interaction with Russell and his friends was a mental relief for Louis, and he found as the final days of August 1979 began to wind down, so did, to a certain extent, his mental torment, which he had been enduring for such a long time.

Towards the end of the winter of 1979, another change occurred in Louis' world. His mind was now up to eight months on non-stop preoccupation with his mortality, and Louis wondered when he would experience respite from these depressing and morbid thoughts. The old couple who owned the terrace house next door to Mrs Smith had moved out in late July and a younger couple in their late twenties had moved in during the middle of August. Louis had caught a glimpse of this couple on the day they had moved. The male was a non-descript type of man, not overly tall, and he was already giving in to aging. The woman, on the other hand, seemed to be far more vital, slim, and tall; she was cute looking. They seemed to be an odd-looking match as far as Louis could ascertain, but then again, he was still too young to understand what made a good relationship.

About a fortnight after the new neighbours had moved in, there was a knock on Mrs Smith's front door one Saturday morning. Mrs Smith opened the door to the woman who had moved in next door. "Hi, sorry to bother you. I am Lyndall from next door, your new neighbour." A slight upward intonation revealed her social background. Mrs Smith looked at the young woman like she was looking at a door-to-door salesman. "Yes, hello." Mrs Smith's response was a no-nonsense reply. Louis was watching from the kitchen bench where he was eating his breakfast. He could see down to the front door, and he caught Lyndall's eyes. "I was wondering if I could borrow a cup of milk because my husband Bob has gone away with his friend for the weekend, and I don't have a car to go to the shop." Mrs Smith nodded her head. "Of course, come in; I am Eunice." Louis heard Mrs Smith refer to herself by her Christian name and was somewhat intrigued. "She always requires me to call her Mrs Smith," he thought to himself. Lyndall entered Mrs Smith's home; Louis kept a close eye on her. Lyndall had a cute but not pretty looking face, but she had a nice long slim body and long, full flowing hair. Lyndall walked into the kitchen; her long legs in her tight jeans caught Louis' immediate attention.

The focus of Louis' attention also caught the attention of Mrs Smith, and unknown to Louis, Lyndall as well. Mrs Smith was quick to speak. "Louis, there is a woman in the room, so stand up and act like a gentleman for once in your life." Mrs Smith's voice was commanding; he leapt to his feet. "Hi, how are you? I am Louis." Lyndall raised an eyebrow in approval. "Hi, I am Lyndall." There was an uncomfortable pause as nobody spoke, and then Lyndall broke the silence by stating the obvious. "So, you're American." Mrs Smith raised her eyebrows in contempt, "can this woman be any more stupid?" she thought to herself. Louis, however, found that there was strange electricity in the room, and a conduit seemed to be running between him and Lyndall. "Yeah, I am." Mrs Smith's eyebrows raised even further; she could not believe the soap opera that was occurring in her kitchen. "I love your accent. Where are you from?"

Louis could detect that Lyndall was not only genuinely interested in talking to him but also, seemed to be flirting with him, particularly by using the 'love' word. "I am from Queens, just across the river from Manhattan." His eyes seemed to be fixed on Lyndall's eyes. Mrs Smith had enough of the soap opera, so she interrupted it. "And I am from Newtown. Now, you want some milk?" Mrs Smith's question finally broke the sexual tension that seemed to have been running out of control between Louis and Lyndall up to that moment. Lyndall turned back towards Mrs Smith. "Yes, please." Lyndall realised she had been too obvious in displaying her interest in the young man who was before her. Mrs Smith poured a glass of milk for Lyndall and in turn, Lyndall thanked her for her generosity. Louis' eyes did not depart from being fixated on Lyndall as he knew that he had just been flirted with by an older and sexually experienced woman. Mrs Smith walked Lyndall back to the front door, nodding her head courteously as Lyndall walked out, Mrs Smith then shut the door. Louis was still looking at the front door as though Lyndall was still standing there. Mrs Smith's voice interrupted Louis' thoughts. "Wake up, lover boy, she is married."

For the next week, Louis' mind was no longer preoccupied with the depressing thoughts about his life, thoughts about his inadequacy, and thoughts about his mortality; his mind instead was now preoccupied with Lyndall. She was not beautiful, but her sexual attraction to him was immense. Louis' self-confidence had diminished so much after the events leading up to his departure from Manhattan, and the state of his mind had only become worse in the last eight months, but the fact that an older woman with some sexual attraction showed interest in him had now consumed his thoughts. During that week, Louis would lay in bed at night thinking about Lyndall, and he pictured her pretty body in those tight jeans; he pictured her body being naked against his.

The following Saturday, Louis heard Lyndall's husband once again call out goodbye as he left in a car; once again, he seemed to be gone for the weekend. Mrs Smith had left to go to the shops by this time, and before she left, she told Louis she would be back after lunch. Approximately one hour after Louis heard Lyndall's husband leave, there was a knock on the door of Mrs Smith's house. Louis initially hesitated; his heart started beating in anticipation. There was a knock on the door again and Louis then opened it. As the door swung open, Louis was met by the sight of Lyndall dressed in hot pants and a singlet top. She was not wearing a bra, and Louis could see the outline of her breasts, and his heart started to beat with lust as he looked at her. "I need to move some furniture, but my husband has gone away again. Can you help me?" Lyndall's request was spoken with a tone of enticement, and she had an alluring slight grin on her face, which could be detected. Louis hesitated; his blood pressure was rising with sexual desire for this woman who was being so obviously flirtatious with him. After what seemed like an eternal pause, Louis agreed to help her. "Yeah, sure." His words were nervous, a reaction which seemed to entice Lyndall. "Great." When she turned around, Louis looked at the back of her body for the first time, and everything was perfectly shaped.

Louis followed Lyndall into her terrace house, which Louis noticed was not as well kept as Mrs Smith's home, but Louis did not care because his mind was preoccupied with Lyndall. He followed her into the dining room, where Lyndall motioned towards a table that seemed to be pushed against one wall. "I want it to be in the middle of the room. Do you think you can move it there for me?" She asked this question in a provocative voice. "Sure." Louis' eyes could not move from the outline of her firm breasts, which he could see through her thin singlet top. Louis moved the table to the centre of the room.

When he had finished moving it, Lyndall smiled, and her provocative tone increased the sexual tension that was rapidly developing between them. "It is so nice to have such a good-looking and strong man move this furniture for me. And your voice, I love your accent. Say something for me". Notwithstanding the corny line, Louis seemed to be tongue-tied due to his sexual desire. Then he spoke; his words were strangely stupid for a person of his intelligence. "What do you want me to say?" Even to Louis, at that moment, he thought he sounded stupid, but Lyndall swooned. "Oh, your voice is so sweet." She now commanded Louis' full attention. It was as though a piece of string between them had been tightened, and they both walked towards each other. Lyndall made the first move by grabbing Louis' hair and pulling his mouth onto hers. Louis was initially awkward; it had been a long time since he had been with the opposite sex. Lyndall kissed Louis even deeper and more passionately, and Louis relaxed and gave in to Lyndall's passion. They undressed each other quickly and Lyndall then laid down back on the same dining table Louis had just moved. They proceeded to make love on that table, and any demons that had been occupying Louis' mind for the past year seemed to disappear; sexual interaction was his remedy, and Lyndall was an extremely willing participant in his treatment.

Later that afternoon, Louis started to get up out of Lyndall's matrimonial bed. They had made love all afternoon, and he thought that she was asleep. As Louis went to put on his underpants, Lyndall reached out and grabbed his arm. "Where are you going? My husband is not back until tomorrow afternoon." Lyndall pulled Louis back into the bed and jumped on top of him. Her sexual aggression was growing, and it was almost as though she had been starved for intimacy for far too long. Lyndall continued to make love to Louis into the early hours of the next morning. Finally, they both fell to sleep in sheer exhaustion. Later that morning, Louis got up as it was about 8.30am. Lyndall was still fast asleep, and her naked body was exposed. Louis looked at her for about two minutes and then kissed her head before leaving. Even though he was in another man's house, Louis was not concerned, and it was almost as though he was meant to be there rather than her husband. His lack of insight into his behaviour failed to recognise he was now following a similar amoral path as Joseph regarding his behaviour towards the opposite sex.

Louis walked out of Lyndall's terrace house, and the day seemed bright and beautiful for him for the first time in a long time. He opened the door to Mrs Smith's home and did so quietly just in case Mrs Smith was still asleep. However, there was no such luck for Louis as Mrs Smith was sitting in the front lounge room sipping a cup of tea, smoking probably her fourth cigarette for the day, and her stare drilled a hole in Louis' head. "Welcome back. I hope you enjoyed your chicken dinner!" Mrs Smith's voice displayed nothing but sheer anger. "What did I do?" It was a confected question and a feeble response. "What did you do? I will tell you what you did. You may well have started World War 3 in my own home by screwing the wife of someone else in the home next door!" Mrs Smith's crude but sharp tone stunned Louis. "If you want to start the World War all over again, that is fine, but don't start it in my house!" Louis felt that what he had done was his own business. "Hey, I have not done anything under your roof. You said no monkey business in here and I have obeyed that." It was an equally terse reply. They both stared daggers at each other for what seemed like hours, but it was only 30 seconds. Mrs Smith then spoke first; her voice displayed some semblance of sorrow. "As long as you know what you are doing, lad. Look, young women like that are evil. Further, she is married, and I do not want some drongo jealous husband to come charging into my home one night wanting to kill you." Louis stood there for a second looking at Mrs Smith, then smiled as he realised she was acting like a protective mother. "I will be okay" was his short response. "I hope so," was Mrs Smith's response as she walked away to go and do the laundry. Later that evening, Louis thought about Lyndall; he thought about her naked body, and he thought about their lengthy moments of passion. Her sexual interest in him had temporarily settled the thoughts he carried in his mind of being an insufficient excuse for a human being, thoughts which had been entrenched in his mind from a young age by his father.

Louis' relationship with Lyndall continued in the secret manner in which it began. Lyndall's husband would go away at least every second weekend; without fail, his friend would pick him up to go fishing for the weekend. Within half an hour of her husband leaving, Lyndall would knock on Mrs Smith's door. Sometimes, Mrs Smith would be home, which in turn would require an explanation from Lyndall; however, a simple response would be that she needed to move some furniture. As the relationship entered its second month, Mrs Smith could stand it no longer as the whole nature of what was taking place, while not necessarily under her roof but, needless to say, too close for comfort, resulting in her speaking her mind. As the fateful sound of Lyndall's husband departed in his friend's car, Mrs Smith decided to go and speak to Louis, not to fight with his relationship but more to plead to him. She knocked on the door to Louis' bedroom. Louis opened the door and saw her standing there, an old lady with a concerned look on her face. "I want to have a chat with you, Louis; I know that you may not want to talk to me." Louis looked at Mrs Smith for a moment; he detected a different look on her face as her anger had been replaced by concern. Louis knew that he could not avoid this conversation, in particular, Louis knew that as he lived under Mrs Smith's roof, he would have to talk to her. "Sure, come on in."

Mrs Smith walked over to Louis' study table chair and took a seat. She did not say anything; rather, she sat on the chair, looking deep into the room's floor. Louis spoke first, but his words were interrupted. "What is it?" Like a wise old leader, Mrs Smith held up her hand to stop any further words being spoken by him. The pause then seemed to go on forever as Louis waited for Mrs Smith to talk. Eventually, the words she spoke were calm. "Louis, I know that I am just some old landlady to you, but I want to say something to you that I hope you will listen to." Louis, by this stage, had sat down on his bed to face Mrs Smith, and he opened his hands in an open and neutral gesture to indicate he would listen, "Sure, talk to me." Mrs Smith remained silent for a further 15 seconds, then she spoke. "Louis, when I was young, it was frowned upon for a young man and young woman to explore their desires. We were taught to wait until marriage. Now, some of my friends could not wait to feel the body of a man, Louis, but I was not one of them. My late husband was a beautiful man. He wasn't greedy, but he knew how to look after a woman." Mrs Smith stopped mid-conversation and looked deep into Louis' eyes to search for a response, but she soon realised that he was not going to be too responsive to this most important conversation. "Yeah, so."

So? That was not a satisfactory response to such a sensitive matter for the old lady. She was abrupt as she instantly stood up to face him eye to eye. "So?" Mrs Smith was now impatient; the obvious sign of her trying to contain her anger did not go unnoticed by Louis. "So, I just wanted you to know that this young lady is the devil incarnate." Louis was amused by Mrs Smith's line of reasoning when he should have been appreciative of her wise counsel. "So, Louis, the point I wish to make is that Lyndall is not right for your head, she will distort the true position for you regarding how men and women are meant to interact." Louis was offended, and his lack of insight into his behaviour was regrettable. "Oh, well, is this your business?" However, Mrs Smith was not going to back down. "It is when you are living under my roof, and I feed you, wash your clothes, and then watch you play around with my neighbours, so sit down and shut up."

Louis was taken aback by Mrs Smith's terse response; however, her commanding voice signalled that he should show respect under her roof no matter how much his upbringing suggested he should fight back. After a brief pause, Louis was calm. "Sure." Mrs Smith took a seat on the chair, and Louis sat on his bed, looking at her, waiting for a word to be said. Mrs Smith stared into space for about 30 seconds, then she spoke in a much calmer voice. "Louis, I was married to my dear late husband George for 30 years before he died. They were 30 great years, not because of the sex; no, they were great years because I had a friend who cared about me as much as I cared about him. Look, I know you are young, and women like Lyndall excite you because she satisfies your urges, but pay attention, young man, women like that are trouble. With her sluttish behaviour you are already forming the wrong impression about us women." Mrs Smith paused; her voice had a slight quiver in it as though her internal grief was about to erupt through her voice for Louis to witness. She looked towards Louis' window, once again lost in deep thought, before turning back to Louis. "Look, Louis, I don't mean to interfere, but that girl is trouble. You are going to a great university, you are doing well with your studies, don't lose sight of what you are doing at school, and most importantly, don't forget there are a lot of Lyndall's types out there who want to distract you, but most importantly, there are a lot of nice young women out there who want to ensure that the best in you shines through."

With those words, Mrs Smith became quiet. She looked into Louis' eyes for a response. There was a most uncomfortable pause. "Sure, I will watch out for myself." Louis' insincere response was underscored by his condescending tone. Mrs Smith didn't say anything in return, instead, she nodded and got up to walk out of the room; however, her mind was speaking loud and clear. "Garbage, he won't change."

Half an hour after their discussion about Lyndall, there was a knock on the door to Mrs Smith's home. This time, Louis answered the door, and when he opened it, there standing before him was Lyndall, dressed in her hot pants and singlet. Mrs Smith's words were still running through his mind, but the sight of Lyndall dressed this way was too overpowering for him. He walked out the door, and as he closed it, he saw Mrs Smith's disapproving stare looking at him from down the hallway. The following morning, Louis returned to Mrs Smith's home, and when he walked into the kitchen, he saw Mrs Smith sitting at the breakfast table, and her silence spoke more than words themselves regarding her disappointment. "Sorry." His apology was again insincere. Mrs Smith moved as though she was going to speak in anger; however, no words came out of her mouth. Louis then turned around to walk towards his room. "You have a lot to learn in life, Louis, a lot to learn!" The old woman was right. He also failed to understand his conduct with women was now not too dissimilar to that of his father, and it was this lack of insight that he would ultimately live to regret.

Two weeks had passed since Louis and Mrs Smith discussed Lyndall. Louis had not seen Lyndall for almost all that time, and he knew that with the weekend approaching, it was likely her husband would disappear again, leaving her and Louis to get up to their usual weekend antics. As Louis returned home from university in the middle of a fine Thursday afternoon, he saw a removal truck outside Lyndall's terrace house. Lyndall's husband was standing near the entryway door to the front of the terrace house, and his back was turned to Louis, as he was keeping an eye on the men removing the furniture from the house. Before Louis had a chance to put his key into the lock, Mrs Smith's front door opened. Mrs Smith was standing in the doorway, and with her hand, she hurriedly ushered for Louis to enter the house. As Louis walked through the door, he tried to speak, but Mrs Smith drowned out his words with a quick hush as she shut the door behind him. Louis was still seeking an answer. "What is going on?" Mrs Smith grabbed Louis by the arm and walked him into the living room.

When they entered the room, Mrs Smith made Louis sit on the couch with her and then spoke to him in a lowered voice, so that nobody outside would hear her speak. "Lyndall's husband told her two nights ago that he has met somebody else. Those weekends away, Louis were a cover-up; he had been secretly seeing another woman for a long, long time. Lyndall came over this morning to tell me the news, she has already left to go back to her parents' farm near Nowra. She wanted me to tell you she is sorry she did not say goodbye. Poor thing, she was so heartbroken about his deceit." Louis could hardly believe it. "His deceit? She has been seeing me for the past six weeks!" Mrs Smith nodded her head, acknowledging Louis' words. "Yes, I know Louis, but he has been having his little secret affair long before she started playing up." Louis sat on the couch; a blank stare was pasted on his face as he thought about the loss of such an easy sexual relationship. "Anyway, this is the reason why I didn't want you mixed up with her." Mrs Smith walked off towards the back of the home. Louis just continued sitting on the lounge chair for at least another 15 minutes ruminating on the sudden departure of Lyndall from his life. "Nobody stays around me for any length of time," he thought to himself. Eventually, he got out of the chair to return to his room. He had to study for three hours before going to work at the hotel for the late afternoon shift and then he would resume studying again after dinner.

Later that night, Louis lay on his bed; his thoughts were consumed by Lyndall and the fact that he was unlikely now to see her again. He thought about her pretty body, those well-shaped legs, thin waist, and perfectly shaped bottom and breasts. The relationship with her was just sexual, and Louis had not felt any emotions beyond sex, but as he lay on his bed, he began to feel alone again. He wondered whether he could go back to a life of solitude; as far as he was concerned, studying and working part-time were no match for those moments of passion. The moon was new that night, and it lit up the skies of Sydney, but inside Louis' heart, it was a dark and confusing night.

CHAPTER 17

The remaining weeks of 1979 seemed to flash by for Louis. Lyndall had boosted his confidence within himself when it came to interacting with the opposite sex, and the young women at Sydney University suddenly did not seem to be so difficult for Louis to talk to, nor did it appear as though they were too difficult for him to sexually conquer. The words spoken by Mrs Smith were disregarded as his appetite for sex was far greater than that for searching for true love. However, Louis always obeyed Mrs Smith's wishes when it came to her home, and his sexual liaisons were never taken back there.

His friendship with Russell had grown stronger. Russell would invite Louis to parties that he knew were being held by university colleagues, but Louis would mainly decline because of his studies as the end of first-year examinations were about to commence soon. Russell would laugh when Louis said no and respond by saying, "If I was a woman, I bet you would not say no." Louis' devotion to his studies all year paid dividends at the end of that first year. He had easily completed each exam, and when the university published his results just before Christmas, it was no surprise to Louis that he had achieved the best marks out of any of the students. Russell, and, for that matter, many others in the class, only just passed. Louis joked with Russell that afternoon about the reason why. "You spend all night at a party, whereas I will spend only a matter of hours with my gals." One matter Russell was certain about Louis, was that he seemed to be a different person.

Subsequently, after Christmas Russell and Louis met up with each other at the university party being thrown by one of the class members from the law school; it was a party to celebrate the turn of the decade. As the clock turned over to 1980 that night, Louis howled at the moon, and naturally, Russell followed suit. Affection was being displayed by all the students towards each other. Louis was dragged into the arms of a willing first-year law school student. Caroline McBride ticked all of Louis' boxes for a casual liaison; she was bright and attractive to look at. Within moments, Louis was dragged away to a bedroom where he would welcome in the new decade with a bang of his own making. Russell was momentarily disappointed to see his new friend disappear with Caroline, but after a few moments, he maintained his enthusiasm for the clock ticking over and continued howling in the middle of the party. Russell's disappointment about Louis leaving the party early was generated from a more meaningful emotion than just mere companionship but he never revealed these emotions to anyone.

Caroline McBride was just a fleeting moment in Louis' life. Two days later, while on duty at the Union Hotel, Louis was eyed off by an attractive blonde-headed woman on the opposite side of the public bar. During his shift, they talked, and just before closing time, she told Louis that she wanted him to come with her that evening. Louis' insatiable sexual appetite could not resist the offer from this stranger, and, in full view of the manager, Bill Jackson, he disappeared arm in arm with the much older woman. The following day, when Louis arrived at the hotel to commence his next shift, he was left in no doubt by Jackson about his conduct. "Do that again, and I will not only sack you, kid, but I will also cut your balls off!" If Louis were not so keen on the money he was receiving, he would have fired back a response at Jackson; however, Louis treasured the money he was receiving for the job that suited his study schedule; accordingly, he kept his mouth shut. During the rest of his shift, Louis constantly scolded himself, "Don't jeopardise the money, don't jeopardise the money", he would say in his mind over and over. For the rest of the time that Louis would work at the Union Hotel, he would obey that command by Jackson and despite being propositioned by many women, he did not dare sexually interact with any female patrons. Money meant more to him than sexual pleasure.

Notwithstanding what had occurred at the hotel, Louis' sexual appetite away from there did not diminish. For the rest of the university holidays that summer, he went out of his way to frequent university parties to seduce women. It did not matter whether those young women were 18 years of age or 30; if they even looked at him, Louis would go out of his way to seduce them. There was Alice from the Arts course, Sylvia from the Science course, Heather, who was studying psychology, and Therese, who was even studying Theology. Some of these women sought more from Louis than just a casual encounter, and he would promise each of these conquests that he would contact them "soon" or "shortly", but he never did. Instead, Louis hunted for his next prey. By the end of February 1980, Louis could not even remember who he had slept with in January. He found the more time he spent concentrating on seducing women, the less his mind focused on his mortality, and he instead somewhat strangely felt immortal. However, when one inner demon subsided, another would rear its head by way of his father's demoralising treatment of him, which not only generated feelings of anger within Louis but also a lack of self-confidence. It was meant to be a fresh start on more certain soil for this rare flower to bloom his independent and individual brilliance. Instead, Louis, who was oblivious to the sign, was a more gentrified version of his father.

CHAPTER 18

The next two years of university life raced by for Louis. His scores placed him at the top of the class and all his lecturers marvelled at his intelligence. Toward the end of his third year, the Dean called Louis into his office and the discussion was simple. Louis was told that he was likely to win the University Medal for his course, "but you have to work". Indeed, the Dean told Louis that it would take a miracle for him not to win the medal. The Dean also told Louis that if he won the University Medal, then he could essentially choose his meal ticket in life in the business world. Louis was delighted to hear this news, and as he left the Dean's office, he subtly looked up towards the heavens and spoke silent words in his mind. "That is for you, Philip. I knew I could make you proud of me."

Life at Mrs Smith's house did not change, and she continued to charge Louis the same amount of money for rent and board. At $45.00 a week, Louis was saving a decent sum of money each year, and towards the end of his third year, his bank balance had just passed $10,0000.00 Australian in savings. Louis' desire to accumulate wealth motivated him to save his money, but that desire emanated from another monster of his personality, which had regrettably been an offshoot of Joseph's greed.

Mrs Smith was still dismayed by Louis' sexual behaviour; she must have pleaded to him on at least another three occasions since their chat in October 1979 to stop being so promiscuous with women. "Fine," said Louis to himself after the second of their discussions in September 1980, but he was more inclined than ever to continue to satiate his sexual promiscuity. Notwithstanding her dismay about Louis' promiscuity, Mrs Smith had otherwise grown quite close to Louis. He was almost like the son she never had, and she enjoyed their time together over a meal talking. Louis, for his part, also felt attached to her and there was a symmetry between Mrs Smith and Ms Fitzgerald, which made Louis comfortable.

Louis' intimate life was attaining even greater heights. Russell continued to seek a friendship with Louis, and he helped Louis to get to know more people on the campus, particularly female members. Their friendship would never extend into the realm of Louis revealing his past life, revealing the demon of his mind, but he had grown to trust Russell and therefore opened the door to friendship. As Russell was a member of the university Rugby Union team, he was well-connected in the university ranks. Any of the parties that Russell would go to he would also invite Louis. In the two years since Lyndall had left, Louis' sexual confidence and prowess had grown enormously; the women now seemed to flock to him on the social nights, and in keeping with the sexual revolution, these younger women were not shy in seeking passion with him. Some of the women were up to 15 years older than Louis, but that did not worry him because as long as their looks were attractive, Louis did not care about their age. Such was Louis' sexual appetite that it was not unusual for him to be with two women on the same day. In his usual style, Russell joked with Louis one Monday morning during the spring of 1981 after Louis had a particularly busy weekend with three young women on campus. "Who are you trying to be, Louis? Warren Beatty?" Louis did not like talking about his personal life, but he indulged in his friend's playful banter with an undertone of displeasure. "What is your problem, you little dweeb?" Russell did not know when to quit with his banter. "Louis, since I have got to know you, you have had more women over the past two years than I have had cooked home dinners, and I have no money to eat out, so I eat at home all of the time." Louis initially laughed at this comment, but then he drew a line in the sand regarding his tolerance of any further discussion about his sexual proclivities. "Okay, that is enough said about my private life." However, what Russell had said was true; to an outsider, there was an element to Louis' seduction of women that was inspired by a desire to attain a reputation as a great lover. Little did Russell know his friend's womanising was part of a larger pathological problem relating to his mental health. His lust or promiscuity was a subconscious distraction from the pathology of his mental health and, more concerningly, a character trait of his father's conduct with women. Louis' sexual prowess had become so renowned around campus that the girls had started calling him the 'American Gigolo', much to the dissatisfaction of the other men on campus.

During these two years, Louis' inner demons would not relent from a torturous cycle within his mind. His mind could be consumed with anger about how Joseph treated him and consumed with the injustice of being bullied by Jose, and then his mind would collapse with feelings of utter hopelessness. These feelings could dissipate when he engaged in his promiscuous sexual proclivities with women. From a more disturbing aspect for him regarding his mental health, his mind would continually focus on his mortality. One inner demon could follow the next. Indeed, his demons within never left him. Sometimes, it was an acute feeling of death anxiety that plagued his mind for weeks, and this occurred particularly during the mid-semester periods of the autumn and winter months when he had to devote more of his time to the solitary and lonely discipline of academic pursuit when the skies outside were dark and grey. There were two common triggers he was ignorant of, which precipitated each event of his mind being overwhelmed by this demon, namely him observing some form of violence, whether it be an actual event, a depicted event, or even a written event. Because he was ashamed of his death anxiety, Louis did not seek psychological treatment, which may have identified the correlation between violence and his inner demon. He was too ashamed to tell any person about his repeated events of death anxiety, for he feared revealing this demon of his mind may make him look weak and it may make him look childish.

The other trigger was one that possibly may not have had a professional remedy to ever address; the great bard's sonnet number 12 was always a conundrum for a mind that counted the clock that counts the time. On some occasions, Louis' mind could quickly expel those thoughts by way of his gratuitous sexual interaction with multiple women. The low point of the uprising of the old demon to consume Louis' thoughts was during August of 1981. He had just finished a lecture for the afternoon and was sitting on the grass overlooking the Victoria Park swimming pool. His thoughts had not been entirely consumed by death anxiety since June of that year, as his sexual frolic during the mid-semester break had imbued his mind with misconceived perceptions of immortality. When the second semester commenced in the middle of July his life from there on was dedicated to studying and work. He looked at the beautiful blue winter sky while he rested on the grass in Victoria Park. "Life will always be like this." However, the serenity of the moment was interrupted by the horrible sound of screeching tyres, followed quickly by the sounds of metal-on-metal colliding with one another at speed at the junction of City Road and Parramatta Road. A car had driven through a red light facing City Road, which caused the flowing outbound traffic on Parramatta Road to pile up in a nasty vehicle collision. One of the vehicles involved was a truck that was carting on its rear tray a wooden electricity pole that had not been properly fastened. The pole dislodged itself from the tray and ploughed through the windscreen of the car colliding with the truck's rear, decapitating the unfortunate driver. Louis raced over to the scene of the accident, and he saw the decapitated body.

After he eventually left the scene of the accident, the traumatic image of the decapitated driver was firmly entrenched in his mind that evening and at 9.00pm that night, while he was trying to study, his inner demon became active in his conscious thoughts like a light switch in his mind. Once again, his mind tortured him for weeks on end, and Louis would look at other people and wonder if their minds were so self-obsessed with thoughts about their eventual death. He studied even harder at this time, but it was a mental marathon as the obsessive side of his mind would try to continually distract him with these morbid thoughts. Russell noticed Louis had become particularly withdrawn and insular, and he asked Louis if something was troubling him. Louis, in his typical manner of shutting people out, would say yes, and it was just his studies consuming his mind. Resorting to sexual relations with women, when he could do so, assisted Louis in gaining respite from his mind's torment. Like it had done in February 1980, eventually, by late September 1981, Louis' morbid preoccupation with his mortality once again subsided.

When Louis was not busy with studies or work he would try socialising with Russell and his campus football friends. Louis did not understand Rugby Union or its crowd of followers. The followers of the game at the university were a force in themselves. While these friends of Russell's were accepting of Louis, it did not take Louis too long to realise Russell himself sought the sanctuary of acceptance amongst the ranks of this novel crowd. They were mainly people who had matriculated from private schools in and around Sydney. Louis was perplexed by the strange behaviour of the male component of this crowd because they participated in bizarre post-game rituals that could only have offended the female component of the crowd.

The female component of the Rugby Union crowd was not offended by the men's misogynistic behaviour, but they very quickly would take the opportunity to escape these post-games rituals by maintaining a roaming eye amidst the madding crowd. Louis always seemed to be the target in the crowd for those roaming female eyes because his mature good looks and American accent excited their uninhibited desire for sexual domination. These young women were predominantly from wealthy families of Anglo-Saxon heritage, and they were instinctively arrogant but also the most lascivious of lovers behind closed doors. Louis was attracted to these young women, but he could not commit to a long-term relationship with them, indeed any woman, because his promiscuity distracted his mind while also feeding his avaricious greed for sexual conquest, and he had been exposed in Manhattan to life without love since a young age. Russell did not seem to display any sexual interest in these young women. Louis would write this off as Russell being precious and waiting for 'Ms Right'.

There was also a consequence for Louis being a university campus lothario, namely, one of his female lovers was bound to publicly condemn him. It was a late October afternoon in 1981 when Louis was furiously accumulating a dossier of doctorate theses from other university business schools which were kept within the catalogue of business documents at the undergraduate library. As the clock turned over to 4.00pm the sound of a person walking up quickly behind him could be heard by Louis. As he turned around in his chair, Louis could see in his peripheral vision the outline of a younger woman with a big mop of curly black hair. It was one of his campus conquests; a young woman named Penny Greenwood who was a final year law student. She was displeased with the notion of being one of Louis' solitary occasion conquests. As Louis turned fully around in his chair to face Penny her right hand slapped his left cheek. Louis was startled by her aggression. "Hey, what the hell are you doing?" Penny then verbally excoriated Louis, and her bark was more ferocious than her bite. "You bastard, you bastard, you pig and whore of a man. Do you think you can just fuck me like that and then not be with me anymore? Not speak to me anymore? Not to even call me?" Penny's voice had attracted the attention of virtually every person present. "Is that a question or a statement?" Louis' half-smart response only generated further public condemnation by this jilted lover. Penny slapped Louis' left cheek twice more while her vitriolic words contemporaneously rang out loud again for everyone present to hear. "You pig of a man. Do you think you can just fuck me then starve me of attention? Do you think I am just some whore for you to casually use?" Louis looked at Penny hard and for a brief moment. Although she had asked a series of rhetorical questions, Louis believed an unequivocal answer was warranted. "Yes. I never said anything to you which suggested there would be another night." Penny was enraged by the response she received, and she briefly looked away to regain her composure before she struck his face once more with her hardest slap, which knocked him off his chair. Penny turned around and walked away from Louis, cursing profanities about him as she walked out of the library.

The rest of the people witnessing this event unfold in the library remained motionless in sheer surprise as Louis got back up off the ground, but as he stood up, he then heard a woman's giggle. He turned around to face another desk approximately four metres away from his. Sitting at that study table was the beautiful woman Louis had not laid eyes on around the campus; she had blonde hair, blue eyes and a beautiful body to match her stunning good looks. She was surprised to have witnessed Penny Greenwood's very public outburst of anger, and while Louis' response to his former paramour may have seemed cold to some, this blonde-haired beauty admired his honesty. "Most Australian men would probably run away after that public display of hostility, but not a virile American boy like you?" Her looks attracted his eye, but it was her immaculate noble English accent that stroked a chord in Louis' heart. Although he was immediately spellbound by this young woman, he tried to remain composed given what had just occurred with Penny. "There are moments to run but now was not one of those times." His calm tone of voice could not hide his gushing eyes for her. "Well then, you had better learn to run because with your reputation on campus, I am certain a few other hands will fly out and strike you on the face." She had raised one of her eyebrows in a provocative manner as she finished her sentence, and Louis wanted to walk over to her desk, but as he did so, she raised her hand to cause him to stop midstride. "Stop there, lover boy. I only wanted to have a friendly chat. I did not plan on, and nor do I want to be, your next conquest for the week." Louis fumbled for the right words to say. "What is your name?" The young English woman displayed an alluring and slight grin on her face. "I am Victoria, Victoria Cumberworth." Louis smiled at the sound of her lovely name, and he commenced trying to introduce himself, only to be interrupted by her. "You don't need to introduce yourself to me, Louis, I know who you are." Victoria then gave Louis the slightest hint of an interested smile, which was then gone again in the blink of an eye.

Just before Victoria left the library, Louis found his heart beating at a great rate of beats, but it was not a primal sexual, physical response. No, this was pure attraction; it was pure, immediate infatuation with a very noble lady sitting at the desk just across from him. Louis stood there still, and his eyes did not depart from the obvious stare he now found himself in as he looked at Victoria. She knew Louis was extremely interested in her, but Victoria was not going to succumb to this well-known lothario on campus. Instead, she looked at her watch as though his time was up. "Oh, is that time? I had better get going."

Victoria gathered her books, stood up and started walking hastily towards the entryway of the undergraduate library. After walking about 15 feet, Victoria turned back towards Louis and his eyes were still fixed on her. She smiled. "Goodbye, Louis; I will see you around on campus sometime?" Louis watched Victoria walk away. This was a very different woman, and she was a trophy he wanted to acquire for good.

When he returned to Mrs Smith's home that night, Louis could not stop thinking of Victoria. As Louis sat at the dining room table eating his dinner, Mrs Smith detected something was up with him, and she suspected the subject of his thoughts was a woman. Even though his exams were approaching, Louis could not study that evening, and instead, he lay on his bed thinking about the beautiful Victoria until he eventually drifted off into a peaceful sleep. It was not just her beauty that attracted Louis; it was something else; it was an undefinable quality of a young woman who had obviously been born into many generations of the English upper class. Louis thought about his own nobility, which Philip had told him about. However, when he thought about his own noble ancestry, thoughts about Joseph's demeaning treatment of him quickly followed.

When Louis woke the next morning, his mind returned to the task ahead of him. He had to sit for the final examinations of his second last year at university, and the lure of winning the University Medal in twelve months' time meant he had to return to that isolated and lonely world of studying. The thoughts of Victoria had to be pigeonholed as Louis set his mind to his focus on achieving the top score in his class. His dark thoughts of his inner demon thrived in this solitary world, but he had to persevere. The University Medal was dipped in gold, and it was that colour of gold which was a symbol of his ultimate goal of achieving immortality by the acquisition of a fortune. Louis was at the top of his class again when his examination results were provided to him in writing as 1981 drew closer to its conclusion. He had frequently thought about Victoria, and he knew she was the woman of his dreams; she was intelligent, beautiful and not easily seduced. The public scene Penny Greenwood perpetrated in the library caused him to exercise greater discretion with the women he met, but her unanticipated attack did not cause him to totally refrain from promiscuous ways, much to the lament of Mrs Smith. Louis did not rest on his laurels for the end-of-year break as he returned to full-time work to continue to accumulate his precious savings; he had an insatiable desire to accumulate wealth.

CHAPTER 19

Russell frequently visited Louis at his home after the university year had concluded at the end of 1981. He planned to return to his parents' cattle station in western New South Wales for Christmas, so he had plenty of time to lead Louis astray. Mrs Smith would not make Russell feel welcome. On the first occasion that they had met, Mrs Smith detected something was not right about Russell, and in particular, she did not like the way he would stare at Louis when Louis wasn't watching.

One evening, over dinner, Louis decided to speak his mind to Mrs Smith about the way she treated Russell. "So, what is your problem with Russell? He is my only friend, and he respects your house. Why don't you like him?" Mrs Smith lifted her head and returned Louis' gaze over the kitchen table. "You are such a child, Louis, that young man isn't who you think he is. There is something which isn't right with him, although you are too naïve to see it." Louis was contemporaneously intrigued and also defensive. "What do you mean?" Mrs Smith was able to detect Louis was oblivious to Russell's intentions, and she had remained quiet, but now she had opened a door she could not close again. She could not vacillate about this topic. "I think he is more interested in you than anything else."

Louis was surprised to hear Mrs Smith's observations about Russell, and he very quickly became annoyed by them. Russell was the only male he had formed a friendship with since Louis arrived in Australia, and he had begun to trust him perhaps more than he had trusted Jack back in Manhattan. He stood up from his dining table chair and forcibly pushed it under the table, causing the old woman to place her cutlery down and defiantly cross her arms. "What do you mean?" He knew what she meant, but he wanted to hear her opinion. "What I mean is that I think that young man is in love with you, Louis." Mrs Smith held her gaze for a moment, and then she resumed eating her meal. Louis could not accept the premise of Mrs Smith's blunt opinion. "He is my friend, my only friend, Ma'am. I would prefer if you did not speak about my friend like that." Mrs Smith looked at Louis for a brief moment, and she then shrugged her shoulders as if to acknowledge her supposed wrongdoing. Louis left the dinner table and went up to his room. Later that evening, Louis was lying on his bed thinking about what Mrs Smith had said to him. His only male friend at university was Russell, and now his friend was being accused by Mrs Smith of having an ulterior motive for being friends with him. Louis did not care about any person's sexuality; he was annoyed Mrs Smith was suggesting there was some form of breach of his trust. Russell had not acted in a manner to suggest he was interested in Louis. Eventually, Louis went off to sleep, and he thought Mrs Smith must be mad.

Two weeks after Mrs Smith had expressed her reservations and thoughts about Russell's true intentions for befriending Louis, the two young men were meeting up for a Saturday night on the town in King Street. Mrs Smith had not raised her thoughts about Russell with Louis again, and Louis did not think about the discussion again. Louis had finished work at the Union Hotel at about 4.00pm. Being summertime, the sun would not set until late and with daylight saving it would not set until 8.00pm. They met at the Bank Hotel, which was not too far from the Union Hotel. The young men entered the public bar at the Bank Hotel at approximately 5.00pm; beer and pool were the order of the day. Initially, the public bar environment at the Bank Hotel was relatively calm.

Louis and Russell continued to play pool without any distractions, but then at about 7.00pm, the first signs of trouble entered the Bank Hotel, as a wayward and unruly group of men of various ages arrived, and their presence was immediately felt by many in the hotel. This unruly group of patrons were not from the inner west of Sydney, and they had travelled into the city from Sydney's far outer suburbs with a larger group of men to watch a game of cricket while drinking in the sun. Because these new patrons were so rowdy, the bar manager decided to come out of his office to pay close attention to the public bar. These rowdy patrons were joined by some more obstreperous colleagues, and by 8.00pm, their numbers had doubled. Two members of the group wanted to take over the pool table for the evening. One of the men wishing to take over the pool table was a large, ugly, and ignorant specimen of a human, and his obnoxious nature could not be restrained. "Alright, you little fuckers, get the fuck off this table and let us have a turn." Louis turned from his position of lining up the cue, and two matters were remarkable to him. Firstly, it was he and Russell who had just commenced playing a new game, and they had inserted their money into the table. Secondly, the drunken man's command of English and grammar suggested he lacked commonsense and brains. He did not like being bullied, but Louis thought diplomacy was the best option. "Hey, pal, when we finish this game, we will play you in a game of doubles, and if we lose, then the table is yours. How does that sound?" The man stood silent for about 20 seconds and then he mocked Louis. "A yank, a fucking yank in our fuckin' pub. Get the fuck out of here, Yankee, before I cut your throat." Louis shrugged his shoulders in defiance; his father's rambunctiousness had been passed onto him. "I will get out of here when a dumb mother fucker like you gets down on his knees and truly proclaims that the only good purpose he has served is to fuck his mother."

Russell stood within a few feet of Louis, watching this confrontation unfold before his eyes; he did not move, but he wanted to be a thousand miles away as this group of men looked like they were very dangerous individuals. The bar became silent, and the other members of the unruly group who had heard Louis' disparaging retort to their colleague gathered around him, and they were not happy. The big man started to move towards Louis, but that was the last movement he would make for quite some time as Louis instantly picked up a jug of beer and smashed it over the top of the man's head. The sickening sound of thick glass and skull bone startled the bar manager before he then hurried back towards his office to call the police because it appeared a bar brawl was now likely. No sooner had Louis smashed the jug on the big man's head than he had also grabbed Russell to escape from the hotel. Louis was a skilled fighter, but 20 or so men on one or two was not going to end well for the young men. Louis and Russell ran across King Street and headed towards the back streets of Newtown.

They continued running as fast as they could back in the direction of Sydney University. They could both initially hear some of the group of men coming after them, but as they ran further into the back streets, it was obvious they had escaped from their pursuers as they could hear those voices becoming fainter and fainter. After ten minutes of breathtaking running, the pair of them had reached the grounds of the university and once they were safely inside and out of view, they both stopped running. Although he was out of breath, the joy of the moment had not escaped Louis. He started laughing and he grabbed Russell by the arms to join in the celebration. Russell was also breathless, but he, too, was overcome by the joy of escaping from a certain and perilous fight. Russell grabbed Louis by the shoulder, took a short and deep breath of air into his lungs, and then he paused as he looked into Louis' eyes. Russell then closed his eyes and instantly tried to kiss Louis on the mouth. In what was an immediate reflex reaction, Louis pushed backwards from Russell and, with a left hook, smashed his fist into Russell's right jaw. Russell screamed out in pain, but Louis was not finished, and he then landed two more furious blows to Russell's face. The final blow of Louis' fist landed on the bridge of Russell's nose; a scream of pain rang out from Russell's lungs as his hands reached up to his nose. Louis stood there long enough to detect the sight of blood leaking out from Russell's hands while he covered his nose.

Louis did not assist Russell and instead, he then turned and walked away. He thought Russell was a friend, but it appeared Mrs Smith was right; he had an ulterior motive. Russell tried calling out through his blood, pain, and tears to apologise to him for the attempted display of his true feelings, but such remorse could not persuade Louis to return. Louis had not let any other person at university into his life, as he had done with Russell, and he felt betrayed by him now. When Louis returned home, Mrs Smith was perched in front of her television. As he entered the house, Mrs Smith immediately detected something was up with Louis. There was no need for Mrs Smith to say anything. "You were right about Russell; he only wanted to be friends with me for all the wrong reasons." Louis headed towards the stairs to go up to his room; however, Mrs Smith jumped out of her chair and started following behind Louis, who was now walking up the stairs. "Louis, what happened? What did that queer do to you?" They were intolerant but concerned words which Mrs Smith spoke at this time. Louis entered his bedroom and slammed his door behind him, a signal for Mrs Smith that Louis did not want to speak to her now about what had occurred with Russell that evening.

Louis slept and slept that following Sunday morning. He did wake up briefly at 7.00am, but the thoughts of Russell trying to kiss him were still upsetting. He also now held feelings of guilt he entertained for his violent actions. He fell back into a deep sleep by 9.00am. Eventually, at 10.00am that morning, Louis was awoken by the sounds of Mrs Smith calling out to him. Louis sat on the edge of the bed for a few moments to think to himself. Mrs Smith called out again for Louis, and the tone of her voice suggested it was urgent. While Louis was sleeping, there was a knock at the door, and when she opened it, Mrs Smith was surprised by the sight of Russell with a shiny nose and two black eyes. After her initial reluctance to let him in, eventually, she begrudgingly allowed Russell into her house. "Nice eye makeup. I shall let your boyfriend know you're here." Mrs Smith's intolerance of Russell's sexual proclivities was a product of the era she grew up in, but she was also protective of Louis.

Louis got dressed and then made his way toward the stairwell to ascertain the reason why Mrs Smith had been hollering at him. As he walked down the stairs towards the front lounge room, Louis caught sight of Russell's face; both of Russell's eyes were black, and his nose shone brightly because of the injury it had sustained from Louis' punches. Louis walked into the living room, and Russell got up out of the chair he was sitting in. Mrs Smith watched on in anticipation as to what would happen next. Russell's swollen eyes were now welling up with tears. "I am sorry Louis. I should not have done what I did last night." Louis did not say anything; instead, he looked at Russell. Louis was displaying no signs of remorse but inside he felt very guilty. Louis felt very remorseful for inflicting these injuries on Russell's face, but his eyes returned a look of nothing more than mistrust. Russell looked towards the ceiling, trying to hold onto his composure, but then he could not hold back his emotions; a mixture of tears and words spurted out of his mouth. "You see, the thing is that as hard as I try to be manly, I can't but help to like men. I tried so hard not to like you, Louis, but when you are attracted to men, it is hard, very hard not to be attracted to someone like you. Last night, the whole drama of the fight and flight overcame me; I could not hold back. I am truly sorry for that, Louis, and I have realised this morning that your friendship means more to me." Russell's emotions were too powerful now to be concealed, and his regret for his actions and fear of losing a friend caused him to cry out loud for forgiveness. "I am so sorry, Louis; all night I have been upset, not because you hit me but because I thought I had lost a true friend. Yes, I do have feelings for you Louis, but those feelings are only of friendship. My desire to kiss you last night will not happen again. I am so sorry, Louis; please forgive me because I don't want to lose your friendship."

Louis stood there in silence, but his face displayed he was assessing every inch of Russell's face for the slightest hint of him being insincere. After examining Russell's display of emotion for at least a minute, Louis then accepted Russell was contrite and sincere. He nodded his head in acceptance of Russell's words. "Okay, I will forget what happened, but don't ever try that again." Russell nodded, but he still looked at Louis, searching for words of further acknowledgment to be spoken. "Yes, of course, I can accept a friend who likes men. Promise me you will not try to do that again." Louis then held out his right hand, and Russell grabbed Louis' hand with his right hand in a shake of trust, and his words were convincing, true, and free of the tears that had consumed him earlier. "I promise." Mrs Smith had seen enough; she got up out of her armchair and muttered on top note, "freaks." Fortuitously for Louis, he had let Russell back into his life.

CHAPTER 20

Christmas day in 1981 was once again a solemn and peaceful affair between Louis and Mrs Smith. A roast meal of lamb and vegetables was cooked, followed by a dessert of sticky date pudding. The discussion was kept to a minimum over lunch, and just when it seemed that all the limited Christmas festivity was over for the day, Louis told Mrs Smith to sit down in the living room as he had a "surprise" for her. Eunice Smith was intrigued to find out what the surprise would be. Louis disappeared upstairs to his room; his excitement could hardly be concealed as he bounded up that stairwell. During his previous life in Manhattan, he never had an opportunity to celebrate Christmas properly. Now that he had Mrs Smith caring for him, albeit for a small amount of board and lodging, Louis did not want the significance of what she had done for him over the past three years to go unnoticed. After a short absence, he walked back into the lounge room carrying a relatively large box that had been professionally wrapped. "Merry Christmas, Mrs Smith".

Eunice Smith was overcome with emotion as Louis placed her large present on the coffee table in front of her. "Oh, Louis, you silly boy, what have you done? Dearie, dearie me, this is too much." Louis smiled; he was glad to see the look of delight on Mrs Smith's face. Suddenly, Mrs Smith's face went ashen grey. "Oh lord! I am so sorry Louis, but I have not got a present for you." Louis smiled; he did not want this moment to be about him, nor did he expect a gift in return. "I have already received my gift; I was a lonely soul from another country when I came here into your home three years ago. This is about you today Mrs Smith. I wanted to buy you something for Christmas which I knew you would enjoy. Go ahead, open it up." She started to carefully unwrap the gift, and as soon as she had removed the paper from the top of the box, the surprise was revealed: a lovely state-of-the-art video recorder. Mrs Smith gasped in shock and her eyes filled with tears. "Oh Louis, this is too much. I could never accept this." Louis rolled his eyes. "It is something you need and deserve." Mrs Smith could not speak, and her face was overwhelmed with emotion.

It must have been his generosity that then caused Louis to open a small window into his soul that Christmas. "Back home in the US I did not have any family to celebrate Christmas with." His revelation to Mrs Smith finished where it began. He regained control of his emotions and returned to being his usual overly dry self. "Anyway, it is top quality, Mrs Smith, and now you can record all of your favourite TV shows. I bought it at Grace Brothers, and it is top of the range." Mrs Smith nodded in approval; however, she was still embarrassed and worried about Louis spending so much money. "Louis, this is too much. What about your money?" Louis shook his head immediately. "Don't worry about my money; I have plenty saved up. I never had my mother on Christmas Day, so consider this to be the way I would treat my mother." Mrs Smith's normally hard exterior had been broken down, and her face softened, and her eyes filled with tears. "Just wait. I have one more present for you." Mrs Smith was about to express her concern at being showered with another gift, but Louis had stepped out of the room too quickly for her to speak.

Louis returned shortly thereafter, and, in his hand, he held a smaller gift, approximately the size of a larger-than-normal book. "And here is something for you to play in your new VCR; it is a video cassette movie." Mrs Smith gasped and held onto her chest as she accepted her further present. She opened the present. To her delight, it was one of her oldest and most favoured pictures. "Seven Brides for Seven Brothers. Oh, thank you, Louis; I don't know what to say." Mrs Smith could speak no more; her emotion overwhelmed her, and tears ran down her face. Louis came over to her and cuddled her like a son would cuddle his mother in what was a new moment in their relationship. "Hey, don't be upset. You deserve it, as you have looked after me more than I have given back to you. Merry Christmas, you deserve it." Later that afternoon, he connected the video recorder to Mrs Smith's television, and then they watched Seven Brides for Seven Brothers, a movie that was as long as it was boring for Louis to watch.

When businesses resumed operating on 27 December 1981, Mrs Smith went to the local video store to hire a videotape, an old movie from the nineteen sixties named Charade. When she returned from the video store, she implored Louis to watch Charade with her, which he reluctantly agreed to do. After the movie had finished, Mrs Smith made a pot of tea as she had not finished with Louis for the night; she wanted to open that window into his life in America, which he had partially opened on Christmas Day. Over their cup of tea, Mrs Smith finally asked Louis the questions she had always wanted to ask about his life in America. "You told me on Christmas Day you did not have any family to celebrate that day with. Why did you say not really?" Her kind manner ever so gently opened that door to Louis' life just a fraction more. "Life was not easy for me." Mrs Smith smiled. "I know, but please tell me what life was actually like for you back home."

Mrs Smith's kind manner opened the floodgates of Louis' mind; finally, he could open up about his life back in America. For the next two hours, Louis opened his heart and told Mrs Smith everything that had occurred in his life back in Manhattan. Mrs Smith listened intently for the two hours, and occasionally, Louis would become tearful, especially when he discussed his mother and uncle. On other occasions, she would become slightly uncomfortable as Louis told her about his life at the shed. He told her about his uncle's efforts to cover up his identity, including all his fake identification documents; however, he could not open up about the demon within his mind because of his shame. When he finally finished his life story, there was an uncomfortable silence. He was concerned he had said too much because she was silent for a moment. Her silence was due to her internal despair that a child could have been exposed to the horror of a man like Joseph.

Eventually, Mrs Smith spoke, and her voice was warm and comforting. "My heart is breaking for you, Louis, so please do not misunderstand my next words. That life is gone now, and you have a new life here." Her words were comforting, but he was alarmed that his candour would now cause him trouble. "Please do not tell anyone, Mrs Smith. I have not told anybody else in this country about my past life in America. I have not even told Russell." The old lady nodded. "You have my word. I will not tell a soul a single word about any of this, Louis. I promise you. Now, it is past my bedtime, so it's time for me to say goodnight." Louis extended his gratitude to Mrs Smith. "I trust you. Thank you, Mrs Smith, thank you for everything you have done for me." She smiled and then opened a door from her heart. "Louis, forget calling me Mrs Smith; we have come too far tonight. Consider me to be like a new family member. Call me Eunice, and you're welcome, child." Eunice lay in bed that night, still accepting the miserable life Louis had endured back in America. She wanted to make a difference in his life, and eventually, she affirmed in her thoughts what she should do. Two weeks later, Eunice met with a lawyer, but Louis would never know she had gone to see this person, nor did he know what she had instructed her lawyer to do.

Subsequently, summer passed by without too many other dramatic moments for Louis. He continued to worry from time to time that he may have revealed too many details to Eunice about his previous life in America, but as the calendar rolled over to the beginning of February 1982, he accepted she would not tell any other person. His job at the Union Hotel kept him busy, and on the nights when he was not working, he would occasionally have sexual encounters with women he met socially. His insatiable sexual appetite had waned as his mind was not preoccupied with his mortality during the early months of 1982; therefore, he did not need to acquire lovers to distract him from such morbid thoughts.

Russell returned from his family property towards the end of January 1982. Louis had missed Russell's company. The pair of them caught up again as though nothing had happened the previous year, except, of course, he would sometimes watch Russell disappear for the night with another man. Russell was free to display his sexual behaviour around Louis. It was an odd friendship for the times, but Louis accepted that his friend was a homosexual and Russell, for his part, accepted there would never be anything other than a platonic relationship with Louis.

CHAPTER 21

The year at university in 1982 was a battle of his mind, a torturous ordeal of academic discipline challenged by his inner demons. He studied and remained focused on achieving the best results in his class. Initially, his mind was only focused on achieving an A score in every aspect of his work. However, as the university year ground into its second month that year, so did his old tormentors commence grinding their axes in Louis' mind. This other state of his mind would plague him, and it was a battle for Louis to concentrate on his studies. He would once again be subjected to the continual torture of his mind's preoccupation with his mortality throughout that year, the triggers for which varied, but it was when he was alone in his room studying that would make him so vulnerable.

That final year of university required so much additional study as Louis' sole focus was being awarded the University Medal and the financial rewards he believed would flow from that achievement. He was tempted to tell Mrs Smith in June of 1982 about his ongoing mental torture of this monster within his mind, but once again he was too ashamed. However, a year of mental adversity was to reward Louis as he achieved the top marks in his class, and he was to be awarded the University Medal. Louis had remained so committed to his studies that year that he even disabused himself of his usual pass time of promiscuity. Therein lay the problem for Louis because previously, he could distract his mind by being promiscuous, but over this final year, when he had to focus on his marks, he could not pursue women; winning the University Medal was his solitary goal for 1982. Russell, on the other hand, had become more wayward. He had given up playing rugby union, and instead, he frequently visited the gay bars of Oxford Street in Darlinghurst to satisfy his insatiable sexual desire. There were occasions when Russell would turn up to lectures with a swollen eye or a bruised face. Louis wanted to ask Russell whether he was fine, but Russell himself had become quite secretive.

Eunice was overly sensitive to Louis' need to study during his final year of university. She knew how important it was for him to be awarded the University

Medal and she rewarded him like a mother. The true extent of her generosity would be revealed in the future, but for the present moment, she had one surprise for him, which she knew Louis would appreciate. One afternoon over tea in late autumn of that year, she told Louis that from here on in, there would be no board and lodging as he would live with her like a child would with their parent. When Louis asked her why she was being so generous, Eunice could only respond by telling him that she did not want him to worry about paying for his board because she, too, wanted him to win the University Medal. She did not wish to reveal the actual reason for her generosity.

Eunice, by this time, knew she was not well. Having lived for almost 75 years, she knew inside of her there was an ailment, a yet-to-be-diagnosed physical problem. The following day, after she told Louis his board payments had been waived, Eunice went to see her doctor. During this medical appointment, she was told to go and have a series of tests done. Two weeks later, Eunice returned to see her doctor. Eventually, she walked outside of the surgery and a look of shock could easily be detected on her face. She would have to bury these emotions before she went home because she did not want to interrupt Louis' study; he was like the son she never had.

Occasionally, during his final year, Louis wondered what had happened to the English woman he had met that fateful day in the library the previous year. He had asked Russell about Victoria Cumberworth, but his response was always in the vein of 'she is out of anyone's league, don't worry about her.' Upon being pressed, Russell would explain to Louis that she was a medical student, and he was a business student, so to forget about it. These comments of Russell's annoyed Louis as he was not one to believe in a class system and Russell's remarks were expressly suggesting Louis lacked the class to be able to be with this woman.

Louis battled through his depressed thoughts that year, and by the time the university had assessed the final examinations, it was beyond doubt that Louis Montgomery was at the top of his class. Louis was awarded the University Medal for his course. With that relief of succeeding with his study, so came the temporary relief for Louis' disturbed mind. Subsequently, the graduation ceremony was a proud moment for him, and he considered that he had repaid his uncle for his sacrifice. Eunice Smith attended the ceremony, as did Russell. Eunice watched on like a proud mother as Louis accepted his University Medal. Eunice had kept secret her health issues to ensure Louis was not distracted, and despite her pain, this moment made her happy. It was a happy moment for Louis as he had previously imagined what this moment would be like when he was a young boy in Mrs Washington's class. Life had not transpired the way Louis had imagined it would back then in elementary school, but here he was now, over a decade later, celebrating not only a university graduate but also the University Medallist for his course.

Another benefit of Louis being the university medallist is that the Dean of the Business School had to keep his promise to find Louis gainful employment. Even though Australia was in the grips of an economic recession, the staff at the university promoted Louis aggressively to ensure he found a good job, befitting his status as being at the top of the class for the 1982 class of Sydney University Business School. Eventually, in March of 1983, Louis was contacted by Dean Moore, and that telephone call forever changed the course of Louis' life. Dean Moore told Louis the university had been contacted by a relatively small and new multi-national company from America that was interested in employing Louis in their Sydney office. This company was Business Machines Incorporated or, as it was known by the abbreviation BMI, and they wanted to employ Louis as a business development manager. Louis knew the title meant that he was an overindulged salesman. However, he also knew that his ability to move ahead in the ranks above junior staff was enhanced by starting at a level that was some form of management. He attended his interview at BMI two days after Dean Moore had contacted him. It only took the interviewer half an hour to offer Louis a job. It was a small step for some, but it was a major step for Louis.

In commercial life, Louis properly found his feet for the first time in his life. His life in New York taught him to be cunning when he needed to be. He had a direct managing superior in Jim Toomey, with whom all the worst aspects of an aggrieved corporate life could be found. Toomey was in his late forties, and he had not attained the upper echelons of commercial life, but he was a person whom Louis could trust because once a junior employee proved themselves to him, they had his unequivocal support. Initially, Toomey was unsettled by the notion of the University Medal working underneath him, but Louis went out of his way to use his cunning strategy of making Toomey's life easier with his job of managing by Louis absorbing the manager's sales work. Another employee in the team Toomey managed was a 30-year-old salesman named Brad Meredith. He was a small and aggressive man, and Meredith had spent the last four years trying to get ahead in this new American company, but to date, he had only attained the position of account manager. Meredith's jealous disposition was felt by Louis the first day he started work at BMI. Louis knew that he was now in a contest. Meredith, for his part, did not like this newcomer. Meredith was intent on ending Louis' career, and he was determined to see an end to Louis in this workplace.

Louis suddenly had a new interest that consumed all his thoughts. His working career was like a drug, and the opportunity to achieve success was intoxicating. Eunice, for her part, admired Louis' enthusiasm, but she was worried about his fanatical devotion to his work. She often thought, "I hope he finds a nice young woman, which will slow him." However, Eunice also had her medical worries, and she had noticed that she had been coughing a lot, more than usual, so upon further examination, her specialist informed her of some grim news. The old woman had been a good spirit guide for Louis, but the clock of Sonnet 12 was counting the time too quickly for her.

Perhaps after a troubling start in new soil, the soil itself may now treat a young and rare flower well, and he will be in good stead after that. While he may be a rare flower, he was also very naive about his DNA. There was too much of his father imbued into his nature, and his desire to accumulate wealth should have been a warning alarm for Louis.

CHAPTER 22

The competitive workplace environment appealed to Louis. Delivering better business outcomes for BMI seemed to flow naturally from his veins, and it was a skill that would result in Meredith being quickly brought down in the battle by pride. The business sector was more optimistic, but money flow and borrowing were tight. Nevertheless, the Australian government had deregulated its banking sector, and Louis had absorbed this event regarding the new utility in lending policy. He quietly worked out a strategy for the company involving the deregulation of the banking sector. For weeks, he worked silently on his strategy, meticulously doing the sums until Louis was satisfied that he had a business proposal that would not be challenged. Eunice would ask him why he was working so late, why he didn't socialise anymore, and why he wasn't catching up with his weird friend Russell. Louis would tell Eunice that he was working on something for his boss and that he didn't want to be disturbed. Fourteen months after Louis had commenced work at BMI, he had drafted a business strategy that was beyond the effectiveness of anything being postulated by more senior executives in the Australian branch of this international company.

Louis had not been in contact with Russell for several months during the latter half of 1984. Russell understood this lack of contact because the last time Louis had spoken to him, he had explained to Russell that he was busy and would be for several months. The lack of contact did not bother Russell as he was now free of university and his football friends. While Russell had found a good job in a Sydney office of an Australian-based company, he had not found what he was truly after; he had not found a man to come up to his standards to fall in love with. The bars of Darlinghurst brought no emotional joy for Russell, and the establishments only fed his promiscuous side about his endless liaisons with other like-minded men. Each man only presented the same problem for Russell; they were not like Louis, and of course, he knew that he could never love Louis in any other way than platonic as a friend. Louis could see an immense opportunity was available to him at BMI, and he just had to wait for the right moment and the right person to deliver his business development theory to the executives. Once again, the accumulation of money was the more dominant purpose in Louis' life.

In July 1985, the sales executives of the American parent company of BMI were in Sydney to address the executive and management staff of the Australian wing of the company. Little did the Australian staff know there was litigation unfolding back in California between BMI's founder and a rival company; the outcome of that litigation would be pivotal for Louis' future career progression. Meredith had been ferociously sniping away at Louis for the past two months. No matter what the nature of the comments coming from Meredith's mouth, which Louis heard, he remained quiet and did not bite. Louis remained patient because he knew a moment like the impending company meeting would be a day for him to shine, so why spoil it by brawling on the battlefield of the office floor?

On 16 July 1985, the Australian executives and account managers met with the senior executives of BMI America. The meeting started at 9.30am in the main conference room of the Wentworth Hotel. Louis was already prepared for this meeting, including the fact that he had in his briefcase 100 copies of a two-page memo summarising his business plan. The American executives provided their overview of the Australian marketplace and how the Australian subsidiary had performed over the past two years. The message being delivered that day was a simple one: the company had been performing poorly in Australia. After the senior executives had spoken, the forum then broke into discussion from all avenues, and all executives were invited to put forward their ideas on how they proposed the company's Australian operations could be improved. The discussion moved tediously around the room; the speaking order began with the more senior Australian executives. However, considering the senior Australian executives were responsible for the poor performance of the company in that country, they did not have anything valuable to say.

The business conference then moved to ideas being put forward from the managerial level, and the more senior managers of this level spoke first. None of the ideas from the senior managers caused any interest from the American executives, that is until Meredith spoke. Meredith suggested an aggressive marketing campaign that would convey to the public and business community a price reduction of 15% to 25% on a range of machines. Initially, the American executives thought about the idea of a price cut, but Louis could tell that as they discussed the idea with Meredith, the lure of price-cutting was not the silver bullet they were after to cure the problems of the Australian company. Within a very short time of open discussion, Meredith's proposal was unequivocally dismissed as being "uncommercial." Then, the most senior of the American executives called out Louis' name, and much to everyone's surprise in the room, Louis reached into his briefcase and produced for distribution around to everyone present a hundred copies of a short 2-page memorandum Louis had prepared. Louis' direct supervisor, Jim Toomey, quickly and nervously explained to the American executives that Louis was the company's prize recruit, being a former university medallist from Sydney University. Meredith scoffed under his voice, audible enough for Louis to hear. Meredith's conduct did not deter Louis; indeed, it just strengthened his resolve. Louis then proceeded to regale the audience with his business plan; he explained every carefully thought through detail and captured the audience's attention. Louis discussed the deregulation of the banking sector in Australia and how this opened the door for competitive terms and rates for business lending. He told the audience how they could market the machines based on the monthly loan repayments, which could attract significant tax deductions for the companies hiring the machines under loan agreements. Most importantly, Louis concluded delivering his business strategy by telling the American executives that by hiring or leasing the machines, the financiers would pay for them at full price, and there would not be any need for a price reduction.

The room remained silent for a short while after Louis had finished talking, and then the most senior member of the American executives stood up from his chair. Gene Foster was the vice-president of sales for the company, and he displayed extreme admiration for the comprehensive business plan. "Congratulations, young man, in my 40 years in business, I have not heard such a comprehensive overview on a national level in any country. I detect from your accent that you are one of us." Louis nodded his head to confirm the American connection. "Tell me this, though, son, do you have any evidence that this method of sale may work?" Louis gave a broad grin back to Foster. "Indubitably Mr Foster. The heavy industrial manufacturer, CAT, has already been utilising the tax deduction scheme, but they have a limited market and are internally loaning the money, which I see as too risky. Based on my proposal, the machines are purchased off us by a financier, and then it becomes an issue of repayment between the finance company and the customer." Foster's greedy capitalist instinct was immediately captured by Louis' well-thought-through proposal. Foster looked at the other executives, and then in unison, the rest of the American executives stood up and started applauding. To Louis' great humble appreciation, the reaction of the American executives resulted in the rest of the conference room standing up and applauding. 80 Australian executives and account managers all started applauding, and even Meredith had to stand up on his unwilling feet and join in the celebration.

When the business conference concluded for the day, Louis decided to stay behind to discuss his idea with both the senior American and Australian executives. As a supposed 26-year-old man fresh out of university, he had just incredibly climbed the corporate ladder. By 23 July 1985, Louis had been promoted to the position of junior executive director on the Australian board of BMI Australia. In the history of the company, none of the older members of the company had ever heard of such a meteoric rise through the ranks of BMI.

Despite his sudden elevation in the company, Louis continued to live at Eunice's home. He was young, and she was like a mother to him; most importantly, her home was very clean, and Louis had been living there for almost six years. However, given his newfound fortune, Louis had now been paying his way more generously. One night in August 1985, after she had finished her usual cigarette and cup of tea, Eunice decided to talk to Louis about a matter of great importance. Louis was watching television when Eunice approached him. The fireplace was burning several old fat logs, and the harsh August winds of a Sydney winter were blowing outside against the front door of the terrace house. "Louis? Louis, I want to talk, to have a chat with you." Louis sat up in his chair, and even though Eunice's tone was neutral, he knew it must have been something important for her to talk to him about at this time. "What is up?" Eunice came and sat down next to him on the sofa, and the concern on her face gained Louis' full attention. "Louis, I have been seeing a doctor for the last two months, an oncologist." Immediately, Louis was concerned, and he realised this discussion was not heading in a positive direction. "What? What is wrong? Why didn't you tell me earlier?" Eunice put her hand up to slow down Louis, as she could tell he was becoming distressed, but she had not even told him the main news. "Louis, I am going to need you to be strong. I..." Eunice suddenly became consumed with emotion, and there was a detectable quiver in her hand. "I am too sick, Louis. The doctors have diagnosed me as being terminally ill with a lung disease, and it is cancer."

Louis could hardly believe his ears; the woman who had taken him in was ill, perhaps not long for this world. All the devils in his mind began to resurface at this time. The news was crushing, as he had become very close to Eunice, and she was like the mother he had never had. "Perhaps I have two years, or perhaps it is only six months; maybe it is longer. I cannot be cured, and I will be in a lot of pain." Eunice stopped for a moment to gather her composure; Louis looked into her eyes with nothing but sheer sorrow for her plight. "Louis, you know that I do not have any family. When I go, there is nobody to leave anything to. I have, therefore, made a decision. I am leaving this house to you in my Will. I have had a lawyer draft up my Will in such a manner that if some mystery relative came along to challenge my Will, you would be safe." Louis sat there motionless; he had been overloaded with information, and his heart was breaking at the same time. Eventually, he spoke, and his voice was overwhelmed with emotion. "Have you sought a second opinion?" Eunice smiled. "I have been examined by many doctors and they all tell me the same thing."

Louis was devastated by Eunice's sad news; this old woman was like a family member to him. He immediately reached out and hugged Eunice, then after a couple of minutes, he wiped his tear-filled eyes and blew his nose with the handkerchief she washed, dried, ironed, and then placed in Louis' suit jacket each day. "Well, why are you still smoking? Eunice, there may be some hope." Eunice smiled back at Louis; by now, her eyes were welling up with tears. "I should have done that at least 25 years ago, Louis, but a cigarette is the only little vice I have, and I like it. I am not worried, Louis, and neither should you be. Death is a part of life."

After talking to Eunice for another ten minutes, Louis took himself upstairs to his room. That night, Louis could not sleep. His mind was working overtime thinking about Eunice; her predicament caused a chain reaction of depressing thoughts and feelings for Louis. The more Louis dwelled on Eunice dying, the more he dwelled on his death, the death of his deceased Mother and his Uncle Philip, whom he had left behind dying on the wharves in America. As he dwelt on his past life in America, his memories of life with Joseph entrenched his depressed mind that night with the images of the deceased people he had seen in his previous life in Manhattan. The sight of Bill's dead body was an image that always haunted his mind. Eventually, Louis fell asleep at about 2.00am. He had only three weeks beforehand thought that his world was becoming brighter; now, his world had been shaken by the terrible news he had been told by Eunice.

When Louis woke up the next morning, his mind was a thick broth of thoughts and emotions. He had hardly slept, and all the depressing thoughts from the night before were pounding away in his head. During the sombre moments of that morning, Louis had resolved in his own heart he would unconditionally look after Eunice, a resolution which included her need for care being his primary consideration in place of the egotistical pursuit of his career. The genesis of his altruism that morning emanated from the dark caverns of his mind where his inner demon resided, but Louis, regrettably, would not be able to establish the nexus in his psyche. His shame in not revealing his inner demon would ultimately shape his life; a shape that would be remarkably different to this altruistic epiphany. He sought approval from Jim Toomey for his unpaid compassionate leave that same morning. The leave was granted so he could spend as much time with Eunice as was needed.

CHAPTER 23

By January 1986, Louis' business plan had already resulted in a significant increase in sales for BMI in Australia. He had remained focused on his work whilst his primary focus was dedicated to Eunice's care. BMI America had already sent him a request to develop a business plan for the American market. Louis was earning more than enough money to move to the more exclusive suburbs located on and around Sydney Harbour, but he wanted to remain with Eunice. His lack of intuition to resolve his mental battle with his inner demon was portrayed by his refusal to accept Eunice's condition, which was terminal; he believed if he looked after her, she would live. Louis prepared for Eunice meals, which consisted mainly of purées, as she could not eat heavy meals anymore. By February of 1986, Eunice was a mere skeleton of a lady who required constant assistance, and she required constant nursing care. His compassionate leave had expired, so Louis made sure that he paid for a private nurse to look after Eunice every moment while he was working.

Russell occasionally came to see Louis, but a leopard cannot change its spots. Eunice was still harsh in her treatment of Russell; her intolerance of his sexual proclivities was the only blemish on her character. Russell would express his disappointment to Louis about Eunice's attitude. Louis would always assure his friend that deep down, Eunice was fond of Russell, but that was a disingenuous assurance. Louis could not understand why she was still so hostile towards Russell.

At night, Louis worked furiously away on a business plan for BMI America while he contemporaneously cared for Eunice. His mind was seized by the morbidity of his current circumstances, and he tried to seek respite in his work. The commercial banking sector was deregulated in America. Louis formulated a plan for an extension of credit terms, which meant a company could even use the equity of one of its encumbered BMI machines to secure the company's hire purchase loan for another BMI machine. The acquisition of computer hardware was now a mandatory feature of commercial enterprises. The American finance companies agreed to extend credit to the purchasers of BMI machines on the terms of Louis' business plan. By March of 1987, Louis' business plan was generating a significant increase in profit for BMI America. Louis was also now earning more money than a senior director of the Australian wing of BMI, and his greed for acquiring wealth had by now buried any streak of further altruism in his veins.

Despite his burgeoning wealth, Louis remained committed to Eunice's care. He continued to pay for a private nurse to look after her every day. His rare spare time continued to be devoted to Eunice at this time, but his belief he could save her life was shattered in June of 1987 when she had to be hospitalised. Her imminent mortality could no longer be denied by him, and his inner demon was again unchained in his mind. Louis paid for Eunice to be cared for at St Vincent's Private Hospital. Eunice protested about Louis spending his money on her this way, but he would not listen, and his wealth was increasing, so money was not his issue. Despite her medical condition, Eunice had a strong heart, and she fought her illness with all her might. It was a harrowing experience for Louis to watch her life rapidly coming to its conclusion, and his mental health was also rapidly declining. Her treating oncologist, Dr Phillips, met with Louis at the hospital one Tuesday evening in June of 1987 to discuss Eunice's future care. "She certainly has a strong heart and will to live." Louis nodded his head, but he waited for the doctor's prognosis. "She has outlived my expectations because when she was admitted to the hospital, I did not expect her to live longer than a few weeks due to the advanced state of her condition." Louis' mind just needed a simple number. "So, how long does she have to live?" Dr Phillips acknowledged Louis' eminently reasonable inquiry. "Louis, she may live for another six months, but then again, she may pass away within the next week. All it will take is one internal infection, and she will very quickly decline in her state of health. Look, she cannot walk anymore, so in my experience, she has only a matter of weeks, but the human spirit is a strange thing, and some people can fight on."

Louis wiped some developing tears from the corner of his eyes as he considered the oncologist's advice. He knew she would fight with all her might to live on, but Louis could not stand the thought of her being in pain. Money! Would money make a difference? "Well, doctor, I don't mind spending the money on her, so do whatever you can do, and I will look after her medical expenses." Dr Phillips acknowledged Louis' words, which he knew had emanated from a place of hope, so he decided now was not the time to be frank. "All right, Louis, we shall maintain the current treatment regime." Louis watched Dr Phillips walk away. The meeting with the specialist had been very confronting for Louis, not only because of Eunice's medical state but also because his preoccupation with his mortality was now a rabid beast within his mind. However, he could not give up on Eunice, and notwithstanding his inner demon flourishing in the melancholy of Eunice's world, he would not give up his hope she would prevail. At about 10.00pm that evening, Louis decided to go home for the evening as he was simply too tired and despondent to stay at the hospital any longer.

As Louis walked through the main foyer of the hospital in his sombre mood, he heard a familiar voice from his past. "You need to ensure that her family does not try to take her home tomorrow morning." He knew that lovely sound of the English tone. Louis immediately turned around, and there to his left, only twenty metres away, was Victoria. She was even more beautiful now than when he last saw her on the day of his public condemnation in the undergraduate library of Sydney University. As Victoria turned to walk away from speaking to the staff at the front desk of the hospital, she caught sight of Louis. Louis smiled whilst his heart skipped a beat. "Louis, Louis Montgomery. I remember you from university." Victoria's sweet English accent rang out like a magnificent orchestral harmony in Louis' ears. He gathered himself together to disguise the sorrow in his heart about Eunice. At the same time, he found an attraction stirring in his soul which he had not felt for many years. "Victoria, fancy meeting you at a hospital. I thought since leaving university, you would already be retired or saving the world by now." Victoria's faint smile hid her own heart's desire. "Louis Montgomery, I hardly recognised you without someone slapping you across the face." Louis laughed as he recalled that infamous day in the library. "So, what are you doing now, Louis?" Louis portrayed his occupation in the best possible light rather than how he looked upon it as a glorified salesman role. "I am an executive director at BMI, the American computer company." Victoria nodded her head in approval; his putative corporate success impressed her. "And you, Victoria, what are you doing here?" Victoria had now walked closer over to Louis as she was now caught in her web of desire. "I am completing my internship in paediatric care." The words 'paediatric care' left her lips with such poetic sound, and her words were music to his ears. Louis could not hide his delight at seeing Victoria again, but then his reality would come to the fore. "Why are you here, Louis?" Eunice's parlous state displaced this giddy moment. "An old friend is very ill." Louis then became silent; he could feel his distress about Eunice beginning to surface, but he did not want to reveal these emotions. "I would like to catch up with you while you're away from the work environment, Victoria. May I have your telephone number, please?"

Victoria looked at the man whom she remembered as being a lothario. She wondered whether he was still that same person. After 20 seconds of cautiously examining him, she then smiled and reached into her jacket to retrieve a pen. Victoria wrote down her telephone number on a piece of paper, but then her cautious mind intervened again. "Why are you here?" Louis remained silent, but then the gravity of Eunice's predicament caused the hint of a tear to appear in his right eye. "A good friend of mine is admitted to the oncology ward. Her doctor believes she does not have long to live, but I am not ready to give up on her." Any concern she had about his intentions was now dispelled by the haunted image of his soul she saw in his eyes; if only she knew the full extent of his inner turmoil, she may have been able to save his mind now. Victoria's sympathy for Louis' distress was an unbridled expression of true compassion. "Oh, I am so sorry Louis. Give me a call; I would be delighted to see you again." Victoria then handed over to Louis a small piece of paper that recorded her telephone number. As she placed it into Louis' hand, Victoria gripped his hand in a comforting, friendly manner. Victoria then placed her hand on Louis' arm for a moment to comfort his obvious distress, and then she turned to walk away. She had gracefully walked approximately 30 metres away when Louis allowed his feelings for her to escape from his lips. "You are even more beautiful now than when I last saw you, Victoria." Victoria smiled, blinked her eyelids at Louis like a silver screen starlet, and then walked away. Louis watched every step of Victoria's as she walked away. His heart was overwhelmed with emotion as there was something different about this lady; the emotion was love.

Over the next two weeks, Louis could not stop thinking about Victoria. The sight of her eyelids blinking had left an indelible image in Louis' mind. Unwittingly, his thoughts for Victoria were an escape mechanism for his mind, but then, towards the end of that second week, self-doubt entered his mind. Is he really up to her standards? Would she see through him and question who he is? Did he know who he was anymore other than being the rejected child of a vicious criminal? How could he be loved by anyone? His mind wandered back to the day in elementary school when he asked the same question of himself after watching the short movie 'Number 1'. However, his inner demon of self-doubt gave way to his greatest demon every time he saw Eunice at the hospital in her deteriorating state; his mind reverted to the darkest corners of his unspoken inner turmoil. On paper, he had turned 30, and even though he was only 26 years of age, the counting of the clock in his mind to his ultimate demise seemed to be set to him being 30. Somehow, he had to also continue delivering his business skill for BMI America, and the so-called founder of the American company was now aware of the fact of there being some 'wonder from down under' delivering an increased profit for the company.

Louis' primary concern was Eunice; her health was rapidly deteriorating, but she was fighting to stay alive. Eunice's health weighed heavily on Louis' mind, and he began to realise that he had to move out of Eunice's home because the environment was too depressing for him. He began searching for an apartment to purchase, and after two weeks, Louis had found an appropriate apartment to purchase at Mosman on the Lower North Shore of Sydney. Unit 1, 61 Prince Street, would eventually become Louis' new address. It was a large art deco-style apartment that he could easily afford to buy for its reasonable price of $70,000.00. Indeed, he had already saved over $70,000.00, but he preferred not to use all his savings as that account represented wealth to him, and it satisfied addressing his inner feelings of self-doubt; a terrible childhood could never be left behind, and the stigma of life in Midtown West was only being covered over by a paper-thin bandage called wealth.

Subsequently, Louis attended an interview with the bank manager of the city branch of the Federation Bank, where he had initially opened an account, when he first arrived in Sydney. After a 15-minute wait, Louis was eventually ushered into the bank manager's office by a bank assistant. The bank manager stood up and held out his hand. "Bruce Cartwright, it's a pleasure to meet you." Louis held out his hand as he also carefully assessed the character of the person he had to do business with. "Nice to meet you, Bruce, Louis Montgomery." Cartwright's handshake was not as firm as Louis', and he knew he would receive the loan before even asking for it. "You sound like you are not from this part of the world originally." Louis could only sarcastically think, "Well done, Holmes", but he smiled without answering the question. They both sat down, and Cartwright then got down to business. "So, Louis, I understand you want to buy a property. However, you seem to be a bit too young for a loan on your own. How much do you earn?" Louis was slightly shocked to hear the reference to his age as he believed he was more mature than any other person who was his fake age. "$80,000.00 a year, but that will increase in the next month." Cartwright was shocked, and he dared not believe that such a young man could be earning such a high salary. "$80,000.00! Do you have any proof?" Louis nodded his head and opened up his leather briefcase. "Sure, I do; here are six months of pay slips. Is that good enough?" Cartwright reached out and took hold of the financial material, and he carefully looked through the pay slips, to eventually smile, in disbelief. "Are you sure you only want to borrow $70,000.00?" Cartwright stammered nervously. "Actually, I only want to borrow about $35,000.00 as I have already saved $70,000.00 in cash, but, well, how do I best explain it? I don't want to put all my eggs in the one basket, if you understand what I mean?" Cartwright did, and now you could cut the air with a knife because he was surprised somebody who was only 30 had such a strong income-earning capacity. Louis would be granted a loan, but even bank managers by now were sniffing the profitable returns of lending money. "Very impressive, Louis, very impressive, but tell me, on your salary, don't you want to buy a more prestigious property? I don't believe there will be any issue in arranging finance for you." Louis shook off the proposition without a moment's thought being given to it. "No sir, I want to own this property outright sooner rather than later."

By the time Louis finished talking to Cartwright, he had managed to negotiate a loan agreement for $35,000.00. Louis would now own, in two short weeks, a stylish little apartment of his own, and due to Eunice's generosity, he would also end up owning at the right time a three-bedroom terrace house in Newtown. As for Eunice's terrace house, Louis decided that he would offer it for rent; the whole idea of selling a home that Eunice had maintained for so many years of her life did not sit well in his mind because she had been loyal to him and not revealed to anyone any details about who Louis Montgomery actually is. There was also one remaining task for Louis to attend to in this strange mix of mental sensations he was experiencing; he had to call Victoria. That telephone call was long overdue, and she began to wonder if she had done something wrong.

At 3.45pm on a Saturday in July 1987, Louis picked up the telephone at Eunice's home and dialled the telephone number that Victoria had given to him that evening some weeks ago at the hospital. Victoria picked up the line at the other end, and her properly spoken hello had already caused Louis to experience a degree of nervousness. "Hi, Victoria?" There was a pause, or perhaps it was better to describe it as an opportunity for Louis to display better telephone manners to say who he was. "Yes, who is this?" Victoria knew it was Louis, but she did not want to reveal her enthusiasm in relation to receiving his call. "It is Louis! Didn't you recognise my voice?" Victoria continued to remain composed; she liked Louis, but a man should be gallant. "Oh, Louis, it must be the telephone line. So nice of you to call; how may I help you?" She was calm, but on her inside, she was delighted to hear from him. Louis, on the other hand, was American and displaying his emotions was not an issue for him. "I have been trying to call you, but with everything going on, hey, it has been crazy for me. Believe me, I have been wanting to speak to you since we last met". Victoria smiled to herself; then she let down her guard. "I am glad you called me, as I was so pleased to have seen you again." Louis picked up on the eager token of Victoria's response. "Victoria, I want to take you out to dinner this coming Saturday. Are you free?" Victoria became quiet for a moment; Australian men just asked her to meet them at the pub or club; this was a proper and polite date invitation. "Of course, Louis; I would be delighted." Louis smiled as he had just secured a date with a beautiful doctor for whom he had held out a bushel since he first met her. Victoria then proceeded to inform Louis about her home address, and they agreed on Saturday evening at 6.00pm. After she hung up the telephone, Victoria smiled. She liked Louis and she had liked him at university, but now, she liked him even more after university. For his part, Louis also smiled after the call, as he was attracted to her more so than any other woman he had ever met. His promiscuous womanising was a misspent time of trying to avoid the dark caverns of his mind. A noble flower meets another noble flower. Perhaps this new soil in Australia may just help him bloom after all.

The next night at the hospital, Louis spoke to Eunice about Victoria. Eunice was relieved to hear Louis talk about a woman he had proper feelings for. On this occasion, his face gave away his emotional state. "So, what in particular do you like about this woman?" Her voice was weak and tired, which was underscored by the state of her health. Louis paused for a while; he had not thought of answering such a question. "Because she has style, yes, I think that is it, she has style." Although she was exhausted, Eunice smiled, and she knew that what Louis was saying also meant physically attractive, but the fact that he had used the word style meant there was something different about this woman. "Style." Then her sick lungs prevailed; she coughed and coughed until she commenced to bring up fluid and blood. Louis looked away in despair. Eunice saw Louis' face, and even though he wasn't crying, Louis' eyes displayed that he was distressed. Eunice waited for a moment until she had regained her composure. "Don't worry about me, Louis; what I am going through is just life, or the lack of it." Eunice looked deep into his eyes. She knew what was occupying his mind. "You fear death, don't you?" His eyes displayed the truth without a word needing to be spoken by him. "Don't fear death, Louis, as life is too wonderful to fear the inevitable."

Eunice's words seemed to resonate briefly in Louis' mind, to comfort him, but that would be an ephemeral circumstance of comfort. Eunice was intrigued by his news about Victoria. "So, Louis, why do you like this young lady?" Eunice's persistence in questioning him about Victoria distracted Louis' mind from the comment she had made. "I don't know Eunice." With all her might, Eunice raised her voice at Louis. "Silly boy! Don't you ever get involved with someone without knowing the reason why you like them! So why do you like this woman so much, Louis?" Eventually, after half a minute's silence, Louis had the right answer. "Because I love her, Eunice; I loved her from the moment I laid my eyes on her." Eunice persisted, and like a trial lawyer, she was determined to extract from Louis the full extent of his emotions. "Why, Louis? Why have you always loved her?" Louis felt compelled to answer. "Because Eunice, because, okay, here is the truth, because I look at her and see someone I want to be with, in my old age, and I see somebody I want to grow old with. Does that answer your question?" Eunice smiled and she was now happy within her own soul. "It took me a while, but it looks like you may have finally learnt something lad". With those words being spoken, Eunice closed her eyes for the evening, and Louis left about ten minutes later. He returned to Newtown, and Eunice's words were still prominent in his mind, like she had only just spoken to them. His mind was ringing with how Eunice had intruded into so many areas of his psyche that night. If only he had opened up more to her about his death anxiety and feelings of inadequacy.

CHAPTER 24

Six nights after Louis had revealed to Eunice how he felt about Victoria, he then took Victoria out for dinner. Louis picked Victoria up in a car he had recently purchased. In keeping with his desire to acquire the finer things in life, Louis had purchased a Mercedes 380SEC Coupe. Victoria walked out the door of her apartment at Double Bay, and to her surprise, she saw the car that Louis had picked her up in. She wore a splendid evening dress and fine feminine coat because it was still winter, and she took Louis' breath away as such was her display of sartorial elegance to accompany her beauty. He was gallant, and he opened the passenger door of his car for Victoria to assist her to sit down comfortably in the seat. His display of gallantry was not lost on her. When he reentered the vehicle, he looked at Victoria, and her beauty was breathtaking. "So where are we going?" Louis hesitated for a moment; hopefully, he had chosen the right restaurant for their first date. "There is a great little restaurant just before the bridge crosses over on Spit Road to Fisher Bay. Have you ever been there?" Victoria was impressed as a restaurant by the Harbour was indeed a special dinner date. "No, but it sounds divine." Louis then drove off down New South Head Road, and for the first two minutes, a word was not spoken in the car. Eventually, Victoria broke the uncomfortable silence, and her direct manner seemed to relax Louis. "So, is the date going to be like this all night? A silent encounter?" Louis smirked because Victoria's very dry English humour was not lost on him. "No, sorry, just trying to make sure I concentrate on the road. I am really happy to see you tonight, Victoria." Victoria smiled as she looked out of the window of Louis' car at the sights of Sydney. "So am I Louis."

The pair then talked casually as Louis drove to the restaurant. The setting of the restaurant was perfect for Louis to impress Victoria. Over dinner, they talked freely, and it was not until dessert that the conversation became more meaningful. "So, Louis, I'm curious, you went after every girl at university. What was the matter with me?" Louis was slightly taken aback by Victoria's direct question. He put down his spoon and thought carefully. "You may recall that day in the library you told me to stay away?" Victoria quickly retorted through her friendly smile. "Why, Louis, I was merely explaining that I did not want to be another one of your one-night stands." Louis realised Victoria was revealing that he may have had an opportunity to be in a relationship back then, and he realised how immature he had been during his university life. "I can only say, Victoria, that I liked you, but I guess I felt as though I was not in your league." Victoria almost spat out her dessert. "Not in my league? Who do you think I am, the goddamn Queen?" Louis smiled, and he then looked into Victoria's eyes and spoke honestly. "There are not many women like you on this planet, yet I am just an everyday guy. I guess I felt back then like I would not be good enough for someone like you." Victoria's eyes raised in surprise. "Someone like me?" Louis found his opportunity to speak about how he felt about Victoria. "Yes, a woman like you with your beauty, your style and your immense intelligence. As far as I was concerned, all of the other women at university lacked your style and class." Louis wanted to tell Victoria how he really felt when he first laid eyes on her that day in the undergraduate library, but he struggled in his mind to find the right words.

As Louis struggled to find his words, Victoria broke the silence because she was interested in him. "So, Louis, tell me more about you. Where in the United States are you from?" Louis carefully searched for an answer which placed some distance between him and his father's world. "Queens. Good old boring Queens." Victoria would not settle for such an insufficient response to her question. "So, what about your family?" Louis again carefully processed an appropriate response. "I am the only one left as far as I am aware. My parents are dead, and I don't have any siblings." The truthfulness in the manner in which he delivered his response seemed to satisfy Victoria's curiosity. "So, what about you? What is your story?" Victoria initially seemed to be slightly uncomfortable about having to tell her story, but then, as she looked at Louis, she decided that she could trust him. "Well, let me put it this way, Louis. Have you ever heard of the saying to the manor born?" Louis nodded his head, although realistically, he did not fully understand. "Well, that is me. My father is an Earl. He is an arrogant old sod, but I love him, and he has come from many generations of the peerage, of old English money." Louis nodded his head as though he understood. "Sure, that sounds fine." His response intrigued Victoria because there was no sign that Louis cared about her coming from money. "What about your mother?" Victoria became quiet for a moment as it was a difficult question for her to answer. "My mother passed away before I came to Australia." Louis could see the topic distressed Victoria. "I am sorry, I should not have asked you." Victoria's eyes returned back to Louis' eyes, and there was a small hint of a smile to reassure him that she was not upset with him.

They continued talking about other topics over dinner, and time just disappeared. After their dinner date, Louis drove Victoria back to Double Bay. He walked her to the front door of her apartment building and kissed her on the cheek. They agreed they would catch up again in the next few days. He would spend another night wrestling with his inner demon of lacking self-worth; he even had Joseph telling him in his mind he was fooling himself if he thought he was the right man for that lady. Guilt also overcame his mind because Victoria was an open book, and she had no secrets, whereas he was hiding another life behind this pseudonymous name, and he could not reveal his real identity for fear of losing her.

Three days later, they met up again, and it was another dinner date at another fine dining venue overlooking Sydney Harbour. During this dinner, Louis felt more at ease in discussing his life in general in Sydney. He told Victoria about how he was so well looked after by Eunice, and what she had done for him. He also explained to her Russell's coming out to acknowledge he was gay and how Russell had even tried to kiss him one evening. The entire evening was far more comfortable than the first dinner meeting, and both of them were far more at ease in each other's company. As he had done after their first dinner date, Louis drove Victoria back to her apartment in Double Bay, and he walked to the door of her building to bid her goodnight before kissing her on the cheek. Victoria told Louis that because of her work at the hospital, they would not be able to see each other again for a week. As he walked away, Louis did not realise that Victoria was staring back at him. It was obvious she liked him.

Victoria and Louis spoke to one another over the telephone during the next week. Notwithstanding where either of them was, time did not matter when they spoke to one another. Eventually, one week after their last dinner date, they met up again. Louis took Victoria out that Saturday afternoon for lunch at another fine restaurant, and this time, the venue was overlooking the beach at Manly. They spoke freely during lunch, and as they were enjoying their dessert, Louis found he could not contain his feelings; he had to tell Victoria how he felt. "When I saw you at the hospital that night, Victoria, my heart started beating again like it did that day in the university library when I first laid eyes on you. No other woman has ever made me feel that way." Louis' eyes then looked into

Victoria's; in his mind he had hoped he had not revealed too many feelings now. Victoria was slightly surprised but also relieved by Louis' honesty. "Well, I guess that makes two of us, Louis. I felt like that when I first saw you at university and then when I saw you again at that hospital all these years later."

Their eyes displayed their affection for one another, and then Victoria reached out across the table and took Louis' hand. Her skin was so soft, and Louis' hand seemed to melt into her hand. It was almost two weeks after their first date, and now that they had expressed their feelings for each other, their desire could take over. After lunch they returned to Victoria's apartment, and they were already kissing each other as they walked through the front door. Unlike his previous sexual liaisons, this sexual encounter was passionate; it was meaningful in his heart, and it was tender. He was lost in her beauty and her fine body was gently handled by him during their passion. Her skin was unblemished from sun damage, or any form of scars and her milky white breasts were perfectly formed as though a great artist had painted their appearance. She liked his tender touch, and she too gently felt his athletic and masculine body, and her hands wandered down to feel his tight buttock muscles. Then, their passion for one another was fully embraced as they repeatedly made love until late that night before falling asleep in each other's arms.

When he awoke that next morning, Louis looked at the splendour of Victoria sleeping, but as he looked at her, his mind commenced that fateful path of questioning his adequacy to be entitled to the privilege to be her lover and companion. Fortuitously, she gently awoke to see his handsome face, and she could not resist him. Victoria's right hand slowly reached out to cup the back of Louis' neck, and she gently pulled his head close to her so she could kiss him. Her kiss put to bed one of his inner demons for the moment as they resumed making love again. Eventually, Louis left late on Sunday afternoon. He felt as though the shackles of his upbringing and mind were being released because, in Victoria, he had found everything he was hoping for in a partner. She was beautiful and intelligent, but most of all, Louis felt love when he was in her arms. So, promiscuity would perhaps be discarded by Louis to be a relic of a bygone age of his existence, but what about his zest for acquiring money? If he was truly going to feel worthy of her hand, then he must continue to amass a fortune of wealth.

Louis returned to Eunice's home that Sunday afternoon after his night with Victoria. This was the final week he would live there, and he looked around at nine years of his life within those walls, remembering how he went from being a scared 17-year-old young man to now a corporate executive. He remembered the nights that he would sit down to dinner, or the mornings he would wake up to breakfast. Christmas meals and Easter solitude. Most of all, Louis remembered that within these modest walls, he sometimes felt like he finally had a stable life, but there was also a history of his mental torment that was held within those four walls. Eunice's little terrace house was also now scarred by the history of death seeking her out between those walls. Louis lay in his bed that night alone and once again feeling isolated. He thought about Victoria as he wrestled with the memories of his childhood in Manhattan and the emasculating abuse by his father, which still laboured on his mind. He thought about Philip and wished he were alive so he could speak to him. He finally thought about Eunice and how scared she must be as he drifted off to sleep just before midnight.

After a rigorous day at the BMI office, Louis was late travelling to the hospital to see Eunice. When he initially walked into her room she was in a deep sleep. Eventually, Eunice woke up after an hour of Louis watching over her; she looked very pale and lost in her mind. Her concentration was poor, and any words that Louis spoke would be interrupted by her repeatedly slipping in and out of an unconscious state. Finally, as the clock neared 10.00pm, there was a lucid moment for Eunice. Louis told her that he and Victoria were now in a relationship, and in her weakened state, Eunice sparked for one moment. "I want to meet her." Within minutes, she slipped back into her drug-induced sleep. The sight of her in this state ignited his death anxiety to such an extent that Louis drove back to the BMI office that night to work rather than returning to Eunice's home. He held at bay the beast within him that night by focusing on his desire to accumulate as much money as he could.

Subsequently, Louis moved out of Eunice's home the following Saturday after the settlement of his purchase of the Mosman property, which had been completed the afternoon before. Louis could not sleep in Eunice's home for that past week, and he had stayed in a hotel close to the BMI office, a hotel room that was more like a changing room for him as he worked around the clock when he was not holding a vigil beside Eunice's hospital bed. He had already taken most of his belongings from the terrace house, so this was one last look through Eunice's home. Although she had bequeathed in her Will her title to pass to him upon her passing, Louis considered it to be Eunice's home. His memories of living within Eunice's four walls were a mixture of pleasant and unpleasant moments of his life. He was still a child when he first walked through those doors, and now he was leaving as a man, but that child was still within him. As he closed the front door of Eunice's home, he was also closing the door on a chapter of his life, and he felt a chill in his spine about how quickly the hands on the clock of his life had just clicked over. Walking through the doors of his new apartment at Mosman should have been an exciting chapter of his life, but it was not. Death's foul atmosphere had followed him to Mosman from Newtown just as it had followed him from Manhattan to Sydney.

A few weeks later, on a cold Wednesday night in late August 1987, Louis finally brought Victoria to the hospital to meet Eunice. He had not been avoiding the occasion as his work schedule was now intruding further into his life, but that intrusion was primarily of his own making as he relentlessly chased the corporate dollar. Work would have to wait, for tonight was the opportunity he had for Eunice to meet Victoria, as the old woman was not expected to live through the next day. He had also convinced Russell to come and say goodbye to Eunice, although Russell was somewhat reluctant considering the history of him enduring Eunice's hostility. Victoria remembered Russell from her days on campus at Sydney University, but what she noticed this evening as he walked towards Louis' car was a lesion on his neck that signified to her that he might not be well. Victoria would keep this opinion to herself as her warm smile through the car window greeted Russell.

When they arrived at St Vincent's Hospital, the cold night air seemed to nip at their heels as they made their way from the car park into the building, and that winter air added to the sorrowful atmosphere of the occasion. Louis asked Russell to see Eunice first, and she was barely conscious when he walked into her room. He stood close to her bed where her head lay, and his presence caused Eunice to turn her head to face him. The old woman barely recognised him as she tried to focus her eyes on the harsh artificial light. "Is that you, Russell?" She held no venom for him anymore, and to say those words had caused her to lose her breath. Russell could see the pain in her face Louis had previously warned him about because she was refusing to receive morphine, and despite his relationship with the old woman, Russell's heart now ached with sympathy for her plight. "Yes, Mrs Smith." The old woman shook her head from side to side as she tried to regain her breath to speak. Russell thought she was upset with him. "I didn't mean to upset you." Eunice once again shook her head, but it was not because she was upset with him. She had realised somewhere within her beleaguered state of mind she had been too harsh for too long, and she wanted the formality of him calling her Mrs Smith to end. She held up her hand as she built up her strength to speak. "Please, just call me Eunice." She once again lost her voice because her brittle lungs were now collapsing, but she took a deep breath as she held back her cough. "Sit down, Russell, please sit." He pulled one of the chairs in her room close to her head as Eunice took another painful breath of air into her lungs. "I'm sorry, Russell, I'm sorry for offending you for all these years."

Russell's eyes displayed his appreciation for her extending an olive branch to him. She tried to speak, but as she tried to breathe in, she instead then commenced to cough uncontrollably. Russell tried to assist her by placing a kidney dish under her mouth as she was expectorating dirty coloured sputum that was mixed with the fresh blood from her lungs. After two minutes of coughing up her lungs, the fit subsided, and to Russell's surprise, her withered left hand reached over to grip his left forearm so that she could bring him closer to her. Eunice's eyes sincerely and earnestly looked into Russell's eyes. She built up her strength to speak as she tried to take air into her lungs. "Russell, please look after that boy. He's my boy, and I worry. He needs a good friend like you and…" Eunice could not finish her sentence as her coughing fit returned, and she unintentionally expectorated her sputum and blood onto her sheet while gripping Russell's forearm. When she stopped coughing again, she looked earnestly into his eyes. "Russell, I'm sorry, I'm sorry for that. Please, Russell, please promise me to look after him when I'm gone?" Russell genuinely felt sorrow in his heart for her, and his emotions began to overwhelm him. "Of course, Eunice, he is just as much my friend as he is your friend." Eunice nodded to acknowledge his promise, but her eyes were closed due to her constant state of exhaustion and pain. Russell's eyes welled up with tears as Eunice's dying words touched his heart. He leant over the bed rail and kissed her on the forehead, and as he did so, a tear dripped out of his eye and fell onto her forehead. "Bye, Eunice, and…" Russell could not finish his sentence because of his sorrow. He walked out of the room, and his emotional state was obvious as he walked by Louis and Victoria to take a seat in the waiting room of the hospital ward.

Louis then gently took Victoria by the hand to lead her into Eunice's room. She gently squeezed his hand as a sign of her support for him. The ghastly sight of splattered sputum and blood Eunice had just expectorated onto the sheets added to the atmosphere of imminent death within that hospital room, and

Victoria found her eyes were already on the verge of filling up with tears, but she did her best not to cry at that time. Eunice had once again drifted into a semiunconscious state, so Louis reached out to gently hold her left hand. "Eunice, I have somebody here I want you to meet." She slowly opened her eyes and looked towards Louis and Victoria. Eunice then focused her eyes on Victoria, and smiled an ever so faint smile of approval. She once again fought to take in a breath of air to her lungs. "Come closer, child; I want to look at you close up." Victoria slowly walked up, and Louis stood aside so that she could be close to Eunice. The old woman looked into Victoria's beautiful but now teary eyes. "I am so pleased to meet you, Louis has..." Victoria could not finish her sentence as Eunice had gently reached out to touch her lips. She drew another painful breath of air into her lungs, and then the faint smile appeared on her face again. "Just as I hoped, you would be my sweet. You look so kind and smart. He needs someone like you."

Louis tried to speak to the dying woman as she looked like she was struggling for her breath, but Eunice held up her hand to silence him before returning her gaze to Victoria. As she drew in another breath, it felt like a knife was being dragged through her lungs, but she held back her cough with all of her might. "He is a nice boy, but you must be patient with him and..." Eunice commenced coughing harshly, but she swallowed the fluid in her mouth to finish her sentence. "Love him as he needs your love." With those words, Eunice commenced the horrible ordeal of expectorating her blood-filled sputum again, and once she had finished, there could be no more words spoken by her as she had lost all her energy. Her monitor started beeping, and the palliative care doctor came into the room. Louis and Victoria walked out of Eunice's room as more hospital staff came racing in. They both walked into the waiting room where Russell sat waiting for them, and it was almost in unison as Victoria and Russell started shedding tears, whereas Louis held back his emotions to display he was not weak, for that had been belted into him as a child. After a torturous wait of one hour, the palliative care doctor walked into the waiting room. His prognosis was not favourable as he told them Eunice's fingernails were starting to turn blue, which meant her body was beginning to shut down. After that distressing news, Louis put Victoria and Russell into a taxi as he was going to stay by Eunice's side until she passed. It was a mentally challenging thought for Louis to remain in that hospital room, but demons and all, he would stay by the side of a lady with whom he had placed his trust to tell his story.

In the taxi, Victoria worried about the ordeal Louis was about to go through; the idle chatter with Russell hardly registered in her brain until the taxi pulled up out the front of her Double Bay apartment. She turned to Russell to say goodbye and to thank him for dropping her home first, but as she finished her words of gratitude, she caught sight of that lesion on his neck, and he detected her medical mind knew what it was. "How long have you had it?" Russell did not expect Victoria to be so blunt, but he also knew he could not fool her, and the taxi driver was oblivious to what 'it' actually meant. "I was diagnosed six months ago, and I do not know how long I have to go before the next stage." Victoria could see the fear in his eyes, and she politely nodded. "Okay, I understand. I will not tell Louis, but when will you do so?" Russell looked away for a moment, and when he turned to face Victoria again, his eyes began to fill with tears again. "I don't know. I just can't tell him now, but I will tell him." He turned away again as tears began to trickle down his cheeks. "Goodnight, Victoria and nice to see you again in all of the circumstances." As quickly as Victoria closed her door, the taxi set off on its journey to Russell's home, and as she watched it drive away, she knew Louis had many months of sorrow to go.

Eunice slipped into a coma at 1.30am that next morning. Louis sat there holding her hand and talked to her, but there was no decipherable response that left Eunice's lips. His inner demon of death anxiety was roaring within him, but he persevered with his bedside vigil. At 5.15am, Eunice took her final breath. Louis was upset but also scared. Watching Eunice take her final breath caused his old demon to rise up in his consciousness as he grieved by her bed. The nursing staff came in because Eunice's heart rate monitor was ringing the fateful tone of the end of a life. One of the nurses led Louis by the arm into a waiting area so that they could attend to dealing with Eunice's remains, to present her in a dignified manner. After a delay of ten minutes, Louis was shown back into her room, and although the sight of her lifeless body worried him immensely, her face displayed that she was no longer in pain. He leant over her body and kissed her on the cheek and tears were welling up in Louis' eyes again. "Goodbye, Mrs Smith, you were very good to me. You were better than most people have been, and I will miss you. I will miss you." With those whispered words being spoken, Louis kissed Eunice on the forehead, and then he left the room. As the sun began rising above the horizon to shed its light on Sydney for the day, Louis left the hospital. It was a new day, but an old dark demon rose again in Louis' mind.

Four days later, Eunice's remains were cremated at the Eastern Suburbs

Memorial in Matraville. Apart from Louis, Victoria, and Russell, there were no other people were present for the occasion. Louis spoke some brief but personal words about a kind old lady who had become his close friend, perhaps even a mother he needed at that time of his life. There was nobody else to speak about her. An important life not celebrated as much as it should have been, Eunice's remains were removed from the chapel at the end of the ceremony to be ever deleted from the face of the Earth in the fiery flames of the crematorium. Two days after Eunice's funeral, Louis went to see her lawyer, and, just like Eunice had told him, her terrace house would now be his. Louis should have been overjoyed about his newfound prosperity, but he could not receive this windfall to only then liquidate in the face of Eunice's death. He would hold on to the property and not even rent it out; it was Eunice's house, so it would remain to be just that. In addition, the passing of Eunice meant that Louis had his own continual battle about his mortality. Once again, it was a mentally arduous time for Louis, and even though he had Victoria in his life, the demons in his mind would either disassemble his self-worth or torture him about his mortality. This time, these morbid thoughts seemed to be even further entrenched in his thoughts, and he could only just keep them at bay by devoting his time to his work. Louis' pain was BMI's gain.

CHAPTER 25

Over the next three years, Louis continued to dedicate his life to his business career. He also dedicated his personal life solely to Victoria. Louis still could not forget the look of approval that he saw in Eunice's dying eyes when she saw Victoria. Louis, for his own part, travelled through a rough ocean of mixed emotions after Eunice's death. The memories of his harsh life in Manhattan returned, the sight of his uncle dying, and most importantly, his preoccupation with his mortality, all returned to occupy a significant proportion of his conscious life. Eventually, by June of 1989, Louis' mind began to settle down again, and perhaps it was the intensely physical relationship he shared with Victoria, or maybe it was his frenetic dedication to his career at BMI, or maybe it was just the cycle of his tortured mind coming to a rare moment of bliss before the damaging cycle resumed in his mind.

Notwithstanding his inner toil, Louis' relationship with Victoria grew closer, and she had moved into his apartment at Mosman by the end of that decade. Victoria's father had come out to Australia early in 1990 as he wished to see his daughter about her continuing to live in Australia and, more importantly, her relationship with this American fellow she had told him about. Victoria met up with her father on her own one morning in the tearoom of the Wentworth Hotel after he had rested the night before to recover from his long journey in the British Airways Boeing 747. Earl Henry Cumberworth presented as a typical member of the British nobility. He was a man of reasonable height, a thin build rather than being solid. The Earl's hair was thinning, but there was still sufficient for him to style it across his head without it being a vulgar comb over. His clothes had been made by the finest English tailors. After their initial warm wishes at seeing each other for the first time in about three years, the Earl spoke first as they sat down in front of a scrumptious brunch of tea, sandwiches, and cakes. Victoria's father wanted nothing to do with Louis on this trip; rather, his mission was to convince his daughter that she should not be involved with an American. Indeed, the Earl was quite specific, and his words were harsh but commanding. "I don't want you being in a relationship with him, Victoria, indeed you are not to marry that fellow, my little girl, no matter how much he may beg for you to do so."

Victoria could hardly believe what her father had just said; her defiant tone was just as harsh as his commanding tone. "Well, Father, that is none of your business. I am going to keep on seeing Louis because I love him and marry him. I shall if that is the way our lives are meant to be, and you will not have a single word to say to interfere with our happiness. Do you understand that?" Her father was a hard, cold, and emotionless Englishman to the core. "Yes, well, you have received my views. If I can't convince you to end this relationship, so may that be. However, that common American will not be welcome in my home in England, so keep his bones in this country." As Victoria got up to leave the tearoom at the Wentworth Hotel, she turned back towards her father with tears in her eyes. "I am happy, Daddy; can't you at least respect that?" The Earl held up his hand in a gesture to silence his daughter, and then he revealed to Victoria why he was so against her marrying Louis. "I have previously asked some friends of mine in MI5 to do some background checks in relation to your Louis. It seems there is very little information in America about Louis Montgomery. They cannot prove that he isn't who he says he is, but I have my concerns. That is why I do not want you having anything further to do with him." Victoria looked at her father in a disapproving manner and shook her head. "Oh, daddy, you will never change." Victoria then turned around and walked away from her father's presence.

The Earl had asked friends in MI5 to do some background checks, but those checks were performed by the CIA in a cursory manner. Had the CIA staff member been engaged by MI5 to do a thorough investigation of Louis' identity, the truth may well have been revealed by this time because all those years ago, when Hodge's contact at the Passport Agency was issuing the fake documentation, he had mistakenly entered the code on their files which signified a name change by deed poll. Because only a rudimentary search was conducted on the file by the CIA, this file code error entered on Louis' file was not identified at this time; however, a special code had been placed on its corresponding electronic file version, which meant Congress' privacy laws protected it. Should Louis' file be accessed without proper approval it was an offence the FBI would investigate.

After the Earl had left the country, Victoria tried to explain to Louis that her father was very protective of her and that this was not the right occasion for him to meet the man. Louis knew better as he had grown up around a man whom he knew they did not have the time of the day for him, and once again, Louis sensed this was the same situation. Victoria did wonder about what her father had told her regarding Louis' background, but she dismissed it because she believed it was just her father being overly protective of her.

Australia was in the grips of a torrid economic recession in March of 1990. Nevertheless, Louis, by this time, was earning more money than ever as the American parent company of BMI had begun to gain a windfall in a changing international business market that began computerising the workplace. That windfall was, in no small part, a result of Louis' carefully thought-through business plan several years before. Louis, in turn, was rewarded by the company as his salary was increased into the six-figure range, and he was now elevated beyond national management. Indeed, he had now entered the ranks of one of the international-level directors within the Sydney office for the company. Louis' duties now entailed him travelling not only to each Australian capital city to confer with the relevant local BMI offices, but he was also required to travel to each of the capital cities of the Pacific region countries, which included China and Japan. The more he worked, the more he earned; the more he earned, the more he worked. Pleonexia had now become a further demon in his mind, and he could not acquire a fortune quickly enough. Victoria's profession as a paediatric surgeon also kept her busy, but she had concerns about Louis' unwavering devotion to his job. She wanted a husband, not a house guest.

Louis had also been rewarded by the company to be given all the technological spoils of someone on their way up the corporate ladder: a carphone installed in his luxury European vehicle and an even more important status symbol of the upwardly mobile executive class of his generation, a mobile telephone although the device was like a brick rather than some sort of practical portable device. Status symbols, physical possessions, and the cynical world of acquiring personal wealth became the dominant focus of Louis' existence. He had now acquired more wealth than many 50-year-old people, but that was not enough money to satisfy him because acquiring wealth was Louis' current life goal, and there were no limitations that he placed on the highest dollar value. The more wealth he acquired, the more his mind would focus on making more money, and his daily sessions to raise his productivity level revolved around his ongoing desire to accumulate increased wealth. The young man who had been so philosophical as a 12-year-old was disappearing into a world in which he had never experienced before but nevertheless wished for back in Manhattan. Sometimes, when wishes do come true, they can be for a wrong purpose, and that was an emerging problem for Louis as his Pleonexia was controlling his life.

While Louis was receiving the benefits of his toil in Australia, somewhere on a ship in the Indian Ocean, an aging Sudanese man wondered how life had transpired for the young American boy he had met many years before. Omar was still a merchant seaman, dealing with the scum of the seas every day of his life. However, he did hope that the young man whom he had taken under his wing on the *Tojo* all those years beforehand had grown into a good man, a man with a strong moral fibre and a man of substance. Omar believed in Louis' good-natured heart. Had Omar engaged Louis to talk about his mind at this time, he may have been able to circuit break his insatiable desire to accumulate wealth; however, regrettably, he was too far away and too removed in a different life to be able to be the much-needed leveller in Louis' world.

CHAPTER 26

By 1990 Louis had become consumed with his work, consumed with earning more money, and consumed by the notion that he would never be good enough in this world unless he acquired a fortune. Had Louis been alive during Socrates' time, the great philosopher would have used Louis' image to depict the embodiment of pleonectic desires. He had paid off the loan on his apartment at Mosman. However, despite being financially free of debt, he then decided he would pay a visit to Bruce Cartwright again, only this time Louis wanted to buy a house overlooking the harbour at O'Connell Street in Greenwich. Cartwright once again spoke in a defeated tone. "So, Louis, you are obviously only borrowing what you need?" Louis nodded his head. "Have you taken over the world since I last saw you?" Louis smirked because he knew it was just small talk. "No, no sir, not yet, but don't worry, you will be the first to know when I do." Cartwright laughed; however, in his mind, he suspected that this young man was an empire builder. "Well, Louis, you are proposing to borrow $300,000.00 this time around. You had better tell me why I should approve this loan." Louis smiled, and then he provided a handful of documents to Cartwright. "See this first group of documents? This is my proof of income. I am now being paid $200,000.00 per annum, and that does not include my other entitlements. My commission payment at the end of this financial year is likely to be the same amount."

Cartwright almost spat out his coffee; a 33-year-old man earning almost three times his salary was more than Cartwright expected or could tolerate. Little did Cartwright realise he was dealing with a person who was only 29-years-of-age. "See this statement, Bruce? This is my shareholding in BMI. I now own $250,000.00 in the company's international shareholding, and it is growing each year by 25% on the previous year's figure. Then there is my property portfolio here in Sydney; I own two unencumbered properties, the combined value of which is probably $300,000.00. So, what can go wrong, Bruce?" Cartwright held up his hand in a manner to convey that he had heard enough and that he had agreed to approve the loan for the Greenwich property. Half an hour later, when the loan documents had been prepared, Cartwright handed them to Louis for him to sign. "Congratulations, Louis; the rest of the country is in the grips of a severe economic recession, but you seem to be your own personal bull market." Louis smiled. His mind was totally fixated on making money, and he knew that he had just purchased a luxury property at a bargain price, which in years to come would make a lot of money for him in a good market.

Four weeks after Louis had signed off on the loan, he drove Victoria around to O'Connell Street. He had not told her that he had bought this large five-bedroom home overlooking Sydney Harbour. When they arrived, Louis decided to keep the surprise on foot for just a few more moments. "So baby, I would like to introduce you to someone you are going to like. " Victoria quizzically raised an eyebrow. "Who would that be, sweetheart? A family member you have discovered in this part of the world?" Louis smiled and then shook his head. "No baby, say hello to your new life overlooking Sydney Harbour." Victoria was breathless for just a moment, then she turned and hugged Louis as he sat in the driver's seat. "Oh, you gorgeous man, I love you." Louis felt at that moment that he was a worthy suitor for her, and he smiled, but his satisfaction would be an ephemeral moment. Victoria became overwhelmed with her excitement. "When can we move in?" Louis now delivered a further surprise for her. "Well, my beautiful angel, now I own it; we can move in today if you want". Victoria reached over and kissed Louis deeply for 20 seconds, and then she alighted from the car in an excited manner and rushed towards the front door of the house. Louis was not too far behind her. He opened the front door and Victoria entered a partially furnished 5-bedroom home.

They walked around the lower floor of their new home. The living room overlooked Sydney Harbour, and a beautiful fireplace was the central feature of the interior of that room. Louis grabbed Victoria by the hand and pulled her close to him. They embraced in a passionate kiss, and then Louis pushed himself away and looked out the window. "What is wrong, Louis?" Louis turned back towards her; his heart was racing, but Victoria would not have known from the calm exterior that Louis displayed to her at this time. "Victoria, I don't want to muck around with words, so I will just be myself, I want, I want you to mar..." Louis' nervousness took over and he could not finish his words. Victoria was initially stunned but also joyful, and then she spoke. "Are you asking me to marry you, Louis?" Louis subdued his nerves and took hold of Victoria's hand. From his left trouser pocket, he produced a ring case and, upon him opening it slowly he revealed a beautiful 3 carat c class diamond. "Yes baby, will you marry me?" Victoria's eyes overflowed with tears of joy then she kissed Louis again deeply on the mouth for a moment before speaking. "Of course, you beautiful man, there is nobody else in this life I have ever wanted to be with other than you." It was a happy moment for them both. Five days later Louis and Victoria moved into their new home at Greenwich. A home such as this one would have been enough of a status symbol for Victoria, but Louis did not know the meaning of 'enough'.

Louis telephoned Russell two days after he and Victoria had moved into O'Connell Street. He wanted to tell Russell in person about his engagement to Victoria, so he invited him to dinner in the new home. Louis had not seen Russell for almost half a year; so busy had he become that he had not had any time for even his only male friend. No sooner had Louis opened the door than he noticed that something was wrong with Russell because he was very thin, and it appeared as though he had some sores on his neck. Victoria already knew Russell had contracted the human immunodeficiency virus, but she had not informed Louis. From her medical training, she could now see the physical progression of Russell's condition was now the acquired immune deficiency syndrome or 'AIDS' as the medical literature so referred to it. Louis was too polite to initially ask Russell what was wrong; rather, he walked his old friend around his new home, doing everything possible to avoid looking at him. When they eventually returned to the kitchen, Russell stood before Louis and Victoria, and his eyes seemed to be teary.

The air could be cut by a knife at this time. "I guess you are both wondering what is wrong with me; well, I am not going to lie and say it is nothing. No, it is not nothing, although I wish it were." Russell's eyes filled with more tears, then he turned back towards Victoria and Louis and paused for a moment. Russell took a handkerchief from his pocket to wipe his eyes and nose, and then he turned around again to face the very concerned faces of his hosts. "I have AIDS. I initially had HIV, but it has now developed into AIDS, and I have had it for the past two years, and because of the virus, I have now developed lymphoma." Louis' mouth opened in surprise. The media in Australia, indeed around the world, had been warning people the epidemic was spreading and it would affect the lives of people they knew. Now, here before his eyes, the epidemic had made its way into his home to smite his friend. Russell courageously ventured forward with his dire news. "I have only months to live." He looked into his friend's eyes and knew Louis needed to be told twice. "I have only months to live, Louis; do you understand me?" Louis fell backwards into the kitchen bench in disbelief; another close friend was now not long for this world. Victoria immediately reached out and cuddled Russell in her arms; as a doctor, she knew that there was no risk in personal contact of this nature. Louis was devastated, and he uncharacteristically wept. He wiped the tears from his eyes with his hand and looked at Russell in a state of utter sorrow.

Eventually, the emotion of that moment subsided, but Louis needed to know more facts about his friend's parlous state of health. He ushered Russell and Victoria into the living room to sit and talk; the otherwise dazzling lights of the city on the harbour now seemed to be dimmed. "How did this happen?" Russell gathered his thoughts so that he could be factual as opposed to emotional in answering Louis' earnest question. "I met a man named David about four years ago; he was young, fit and good-looking, and I thought he was perfect. I loved him, and he loved me. After two months, I knew David was the one, and he even moved into my apartment. I thought this would be my forever blissful life. David did not display any physical signs of ill-health, and I somewhat naively started having unprotected sex with him. What I did not know was that he had been working the streets, so to speak, as a gigolo for quite a while, and he had contracted the disease. Six months into our relationship, he told me he had been diagnosed with HIV. Sure enough, when I went and had a test performed by the doctor, I was told the devastating news. That was three years ago. Now I am in the final stages of AIDS."

Victoria remained silent; she had known about Russell's health since that terrible night when Eunice had died, but she wanted Russell to tell Louis long before tonight, a night that was meant to be a happy occasion. "So, how long do you have?" Louis' question was dripping with despair. Russell paused for a moment, and then he delivered the worst news of all. "Three months at best, but I am told that with the lymphoma that could become even more debilitating in the next month, so perhaps it is only two months. I am so scared, and I am so sorry I did not tell you before tonight." Louis looked at Victoria, and his eyes were filled with tears as he processed this terrible news. Without consulting his fiancée, Louis made a decision. "Well, there is only one thing that needs to be done then." Russell thought an answer was coming, but after 20 seconds, he knew it was more a statement than actual information. "What is that?" Louis looked at Victoria, but even she was oblivious to what plan her fiancée had on his mind. "Well, I did invite you to break the news of us becoming engaged to be married in six months' time. However, Victoria and I will just have to move our wedding plans forward because, you see, my friend, I want you to be my best man, and we can't get married in a hospital."

Victoria was naturally surprised her fiancée had made this unilateral decision, but she nodded in an unequivocal manner, conveying her approval of this change of plans; however, deep down, it meant a lot of work to be done in a very short space of time. Russell broke down in tears, and Louis took him into his arms for a moment of compassionate friendship; however, the thought of Russell's untimely demise was already feeding the demons within Louis' mind, just when he seemed to be in a place of rare mental harmony. Later, the three of them sat down to dinner and talked about the wedding, about Russell's health and about life. Later, after Russell left, Victoria was assured by Louis that he was fine. He was not fine. Louis sat in the living room until the hour of dawn after he had kept mumbling the syllogism about living things dying and so would he. The dark demon of his consciousness had erupted in Louis' mind, and as he fell asleep, he hoped his mind would not slip into the obsessive thoughts of his mortality that had bedevilled him so profoundly in the past.

Two hours later, the alarm on Louis' mobile telephone commenced its ear-shattering melody, signifying the world was waiting for Louis to attend to conquering it. His mind was still engrossed with the news that Russell had informed him about the previous evening, and he was now overwhelmed with death anxiety. Victoria had awoken from her slumber to an empty bed, and she was immediately concerned about Louis. She hurriedly walked out of the master bedroom and found him where she had left him about seven hours before. She noticed he had not even changed his clothes. Victoria tried to engage Louis in conversation about how he felt after hearing Russell's sad news, but Louis would not let the genie out of the bottle for fear that his true thoughts would make him look weak before his princess bride. Weakness may only be found in silence, and it was within those walls of silence Louis would now be vulnerable.

Notwithstanding the apocalypse within his mind, there was much to be done, including rearranging the wedding, and the frantic pace of making the alternative arrangements consumed both Louis' and Victoria's spare time. Three weeks later, Louis and Victoria had a simple but stylish wedding ceremony on the shores of Fisher Bay, where they had first had dinner several years beforehand.

Russell proudly attended as the best man, but he needed to sit during the ceremony as his health was quickly fading. Victoria's father did not attend. The

Earl knew of the wedding, but he would never give his approval to his daughter marrying a common American. It was not a large wedding; Louis invited about five couples from the senior executive corps of the Australian division of BMI. Victoria also kept it simple, and there were about 15 close friends from her medical life in Australia, as well as her best friend from England, Elizabeth Drysdale, who was the head bridesmaid. Elizabeth had spent a few days in Sydney with Victoria before the wedding. She had spoken to Victoria about the merits of marrying outside of their class to a common American. Victoria had told her old school friend that she would choose to ignore remarks of this nature.

Louis found the day of his wedding to be a memorable one, but he could not but be preoccupied with his close friend's deteriorating condition and, as a corollary of the former, the ever-present demons of Louis' mind. Neither his work nor his wedding could disengage his mind's torturous confrontation. During the day, Louis took himself into the male toilets of the restaurant where the reception was being held. He looked into the mirror, and then he closed his eyes. "Please! Please, of all days, don't overtake my thoughts!" His mind would not yield to his request. Louis returned to the wedding table, and he was just in time for the speeches. As the best man, Russell made a memorable speech about the Yankee who conquered the university then Sydney, about a friend whom he had watched assimilate with certain difficulties into Australian society and finally, the woman whom all other men wished to be with but who his friend was able to somehow convince that she would agree to be his wife. "Out of all of your achievements, how did you manage to pull that one off?" The small wedding party all laughed out loud in response to Russell's joke. Louis smiled in response to the joke, but the sight of his sick friend battling so hard to get through this afternoon concerned him, and his inner demons preyed on his mind.

Later that night, in the wedding suite at the Menzies Hotel, he looked back in time to a night in Manhattan when he wished as a young boy that he could be free from the torment which was father's world. He looked upon his life now, and whilst he was free of Joseph, his mind was not freed from that abuse, and his lack of self-worth, the monster of the other torment of his mind, which was a product of his childhood abuse, was now on his wedding night playing in his mind the mocking sound of Joseph's voice and those poisonous barbs of his which were eating away at Louis. The boy had escaped Manhattan, but Manhattan had not escaped the boy's mind. His wedding night passion with his new bride was far more physical than it was passionate, but Victoria was none the wiser as she was engulfed with the thrilling sensation of marital sex that extended well into the early hours of the morning as her husband tried to metaphorically pound his own demons. Victoria would subsequently drift off into a satisfied sleep, whereas her husband remained awake, looking at the ceiling, wondering why he could not be happy and contemplating whether he should open the door of his mind to his wife. The next day, they flew to the Maldives for a short 4-night honeymoon. Louis did not like travelling on an aeroplane at any time as the turbulence scared him, even if it was for his honeymoon.

Four weeks after the wedding, Louis received a telephone call on a Thursday evening from a police officer. The police had been provided Louis' home telephone by the building manager of Russell's apartment building because he was recorded as the next-of-kin. The news was as grim as Louis' state of mind; Russell had been found dead in his unit in Paddington by a police officer after a neighbour had complained about a strange smell in the hallway, which was emanating from under Russell's front door. According to the police officer, Russell had experienced a sudden heart attack due to the combination of his weakened state and an influenza virus he had contracted, and based on the entomology report, he had been deceased for a week. It was a ghastly end to human life, and Louis' despair could not be contained. It took at least half an hour for him to stop sobbing, and in his still vulnerable state, a crack opened in the steel wall of his mind. "I am sorry, honey, that I am so upset, but I just cannot stand losing people in my life anymore." Victoria held Louis' head close to her chest. "That is alright, sweetie. I, too, am upset, but of course, he is your friend." Louis lifted his head away from Victoria's chest, and the pain in his heart radiated through his eyes. "No, you just do not understand. It is me, nothing good comes to people who know me."

Victoria was deeply concerned for her husband, and his equivocal statement required further consideration. "What do you mean, honey? Do not be silly; you did not cause your friend's death; he was an ill man." Louis got up and walked away, shaking his head in torment and frustration. "No! No, you don't understand. I am bad news, I am jinxed. I am nothing but bad news for anyone, for whoever comes into contact with me. I, I...". Louis could not finish his sentence; instead he looked out the living room window of his home, searching for some sense in the deep and dark waters of Sydney Harbour. Victoria stood up and walked over to him, gently placing her hand on his shoulder. "Tell me, Louis, what is wrong? Please tell me what is troubling you so much. I know

Russell is dead, but your words are scaring me. Please tell me what is wrong." Louis walked away from Victoria as her touch was strangely irritating for him at this particular time, and after a few moments of chaotic thought, he turned back towards her, and his face displayed great pain and shame. "Victoria, I don't want to lose you." Victoria smiled, but it was a nervous grin. "And you won't, Louis, so please speak to me. I am your wife, and I love you no matter what it is you wish to tell me."

Louis hesitated, then after some further moments of confused thought he opened a door to his mind to let his wife in. "I am an orphan, but not because of any accident. My father was an underworld criminal in Manhattan, and he murdered my mother." Victoria was naturally surprised by his revelation, but it was not as though he was confessing to infidelity. She tried to reach out to comfort her distressed husband with a hug, but he held up his hand signalling for her to come no further. "I was subjected to horrific acts in my father's household, and save for an old lady across the hall, I probably would have died as a young child. However, I somehow survived, and I was selected by my school to be set on a path to an eventual scholarship at an Ivy League university. Eventually, my father's world became hell on earth for me. I was so full of fear and anger that by the age of twelve, I savagely beat up an older boy who had been bullying me, and I went too far. I was removed from the higher education stream in New York and instead, I was placed into a school from which nobody had ever made anything of their lives."

His confession came to a momentary pause as he then focused his attention back on his wife, but she displayed no sign of animosity, so he ventured further with his life story. "To make matters worse, my father conscripted me to work without pay in his evil world of underworld crime, where I helped him, and others, carry out their criminal activities. Just when I thought my life would always be part of his cruel world, my mother's brother, my Uncle Philip, came to my rescue. He told me my father had murdered my mother. He told me about his father's noble French ancestry and that I was not some bog Irish kid from Manhattan. He helped me escape Manhattan, Victoria, but by doing so, he sacrificed his own life. He helped me because my father was going to kill me. I watched my uncle and father exchange bullets, which took both of their lives the night I escaped Manhattan."

Once again, he paused to ascertain how his wife was receiving his story and it was evident to him that she was concerned for him, but she still displayed no hostility. In her mind she was now shocked listening to her husband's confessions as it partially explained her father's previous comments of 'little information about Louis Montgomery'. Louis then took a deep breath, for he knew what he was about to reveal may have a significant impact on the future of his relationship with his wife. "I am not Louis Montgomery, Victoria; my uncle arranged for a false identity to be used by me anywhere in the world, including false documents, for me to be accepted into Sydney University. All my family are dead because of me. Me Victoria! Now Eunice and Russell are dead, and I fear... I fear..." Tears began to run down Louis' face. He wanted to go further and reveal to Victoria that his mind was continually preoccupied with thoughts of his mortality, that he had no feelings of self-worth, and these inner demons haunted him to the point of torturing his conscious and even subconscious thoughts. However, Louis could now see his wife's face displayed telltale signs of shock and perhaps even disappointment with his deception. "What is it, Louis? What do you fear? Please tell me?" Louis would not open the door to his mind any further.

Victoria was not disappointed with her husband; however, she was also coming to terms with the fact her father was partially right. Louis, for his part, now collapsed into a lounge chair. He felt he had said enough to his wife, and he did not wish to further burden her with his innermost fears. That undoubtedly was a mistake, for had Louis revealed to Victoria his true inner demons, she would have found the appropriate psychiatric treatment and counselling for him; he may have even been cured to live happily ever after. Louis instead kept the vault door closed on these feelings and thoughts, much to his detriment. Victoria was not going to punish a man whom she loved with all her heart. After considering his confession for some moments as she looked out upon the Harbour, she resolved within her heart to keep this news secret and to pretend it had never happened. That reaction was a product of her own vulnerability, the shame that she may be exposed to if her father and her friends ever found out. Victoria slowly walked over to the lounge where her husband was sitting; she gently sat down, and then her hand reached out and took Louis' hand. "Well, I don't care who you are, Louis; I love what you are. You are a man who is much better than his past; I trust you and love you. Let us pretend this never happened." Louis crumpled into Victoria's arms like a lost little boy.

Victoria lay awake next to Louis for at least another hour after he had gone off to sleep. Her mind was filled with mixed feelings about Louis' revelation.

She understood the reasons why her husband did not initially reveal who he really was, but some of the other facts he told her did disturb her. "He assisted his father with his criminal activity. He lied to the university. My new surname is not even Montgomery. Who is this man? Is there anything else that will pop up to surprise me? Should I tell my father?" However, Victoria was as headstrong as she was intelligent. There was no way she would ever allow her father to be right. Accordingly, she vowed never to reveal to the Earl or any other person what Louis had just confided in her that evening. Not long before she fell asleep, Victoria concluded that Louis was a good man exposed to unfortunate circumstances as a child, but that changed the moment he escaped to Australia. Her last thoughts perhaps underscored the future. "Please don't let my father be right."

PART 4

"The Devil's Web"

CHAPTER 27

During July of 1991 the board of BMI America Inc. was given a shake-up by the founder of BMI Incorporated, Lawrence Edward Naylor, otherwise known as Larry. BMI Incorporated was the controlling shareholder of BMI America, but its founder was not welcome within the elite business class of Wall Street. Larry was a secondhand car salesman born and bred in Wisconsin who ventured over to California during the middle of the 1960s in search of the American dream. He commenced operating a small car dealership business in the South Los Angeles suburb of Crenshaw in 1969 when he was only 29 years old, and by virtue of his innate charlatan traits, he had managed by the end of 1972 to transform that business into Los Angeles largest and most successful used car dealership. During 1973, he came across a cash register manufacturing business, the owner of which was a man named Des Drake, who was on the verge of bankruptcy but in whom Larry nevertheless saw some business utility as Des had some ideas about how business machines could liberate American offices so that by 1974 the wolves of insolvency had been chased away by Larry's money and the business was incorporated as Business Machines International or, as it was known in its first newspaper advertisement, BMI.

Larry's charlatan ways as a secondhand car dealer led to him eventually having to go to court in the fall of 1976 over the rights to the ownership of some of the cars he had for sale in his Toluca Lake car yard. While he was at court, Larry met a woman 14 years his junior, and he took an immediate interest in her. Audrey Stevenson was the pretty young daughter of a poor Nebraska farming family. She came to Los Angeles in December of 1973 hoping to be an actress, but the only problem was she could not act. By the following summer of 1974, a lack of acting work and the need for an income led her to work as a call girl for a discreet madam whose upmarket business catered for the sexual proclivities of both men and women in Los Angeles. Audrey had found the male customers were too rough whereas the women were far gentler with her. She very quickly learnt two facts about herself working as a call girl. The first fact was that she was more sexually attracted to women than men, and she was very skilled to seduce another woman. The second fact was that by the fall of 1975, she was very skilled in utilising her powers of seduction to then extort money from the rich and powerful women who called upon her services for sex. She found the bored and lonely wives of Los Angeles businessmen to be easy targets, and it was because she extorted the wife of a prominent member of the Los Angeles business community that she was now in court. Audrey was fortunate the woman's husband did not want the press publishing the story, so the charges were reduced to a simple soliciting for prostitution misdemeanour.

Despite being within the confines of the Los Angeles County Superior Courthouse, Audrey's services were engaged by Larry for that entire night, which included dining at an exclusive restaurant in Santa Monica. Over dinner, Larry regaled Audrey with tales about his nefarious business activities selling used cars, and he also told her he had established a business machine manufacturing company, which he thought would eventually make him a lot of money. Larry was captivated by the sordid details of Audrey's life as a 'high class' prostitute; her sexual preference for women only appealed to his perverted mind. Subsequently, they formed a strange marital union; her sexual desire for women satisfied his peculiar fetishes; his money ended her career as a prostitute so that she might one day find Ms Right. They were the American dream gone wrong.

During the late 1970s, BMI had become an established and successful manufacturer of all types of business machines including a microprocessor, which was starting to gain popularity in the workplace. Des had died in 1979, and through the unscrupulous actions of lawyers, Larry had acquired the rights to the deceased man's shares held in BMI. By the beginning of 1982, BMI's microprocessor had gained popularity in offices throughout America, the United Kingdom and Australia, but by the end of winter of that year, Naylor became embroiled in litigation as a big multinational company from New York named Business Machines America Inc tried to restrain BMI's trade. Larry eventually won that litigation, which meant Business Machines America owed BMI $50,000,000.00 in damages and court costs. Being the conniving snake that he was, Larry made an offer to waive the damages and costs order, but his opponents would have to obey his every command as he became the controlling shareholder of the merger of BMI and Business Machines America to become now known as BMI, a right of place as the founder to sit in on board meeting of BMI and his lawyers would now be the company's lawyers. Naylor's reputation as a charlatan used car dealer from Los Angeles meant he was not welcome within the business culture of the financial institutions of Wall Street, so he instead found a respected Wall Street executive named Anthony Westaway to be appointed as BMI's chief financial executive and Naylor's man in New York. BMI had already been returning a decent profit for its shareholders during the 1980's but then along came Louis with his business formula which assisted BMI to become the dominant office computer manufacturer and supplier throughout most of the developed world.

So over the month of July of 1991, Naylor had been examining the personnel list of BMI worldwide to find his right-hand man around the globe to expand the business dealings of BMI, and that person definitely could not be a member of the tawdry board of directors of BMI in Manhattan nor could it be Anthony Westaway in whom Naylor sought legitimacy in on Wall Street. There was one employee in BMI's personnel list whom Naylor wished to reward with the benefits of being his trusted offsider, namely Louis Montgomery. Louis' business plan had returned significant profits for BMI, and he was intelligent, hardworking, and creative. Naylor put in a call to the managing director of the Australian division of the company.

Richard Stephens was a traditional company executive, impeccably dressed, university-educated, and well-connected in Sydney's bourgeois business community. Naylor had met Stephens once and found him to be a snivelling fawner. When Stephens heard the domineering tone of Naylor at the other end of the line his submissive side immediately came to the fore. "Larry, nice to hear your voice; I have been waiting to talk to you and to find out when...." Naylor's sharp and derisive tone cut Stephens off mid-sentence and immediately shot pangs of fear into his heart. "Don't you ever fucking kiss my ass like that you weak little pissant!" Naylor's booming voice drilled a hole in Stephens' ear. "You are the head of the Australian division, don't be so fucking pleasant, or I will give you something not to be so pleasant about." Stephens was speechless and he remained silent. After a pause of ten seconds Naylor bellowed down the telephone. "What the fucking hell is wrong with you? Why are you becoming quiet on the other end of the telephone? Is there something wrong with you, Stephens?" If ever Richard Stephens wished he had not picked up the telephone, this was the day. "What can I do for you, Larry?" Without any hesitation, Naylor again bellowed down the telephone line, and his voice was shooting barbs into Stephens' nervous system. "I will tell you what I want. I want a guy who seems to have more balls than you. I want a guy who makes business happen, not one who watches it drift by. I want Louis Montgomery on a plane to Los Angeles in the next twelve hours as I need him to work with me here for the next two weeks, and, Stephens, if this guy isn't on a plane in the next twelve hours, consider yourself fired." The telephone call ended; that was how Larry Naylor treated non-board member management. Stephens then took some time to regain his composure before he dialled his secretary to arrange for Louis to come to his office.

Ten minutes after Richard Stephens had endured the abrupt telephone call from Naylor, Louis walked into his office. Immediately, Louis could detect that Stephens' thoughts were preoccupied with some company news. "What is up, Richard?" Stephens did indeed have some news. "How do you like Los Angeles?" Louis' response was candid within the confines of his continuing to protect his real identity. "I cannot say, as I have never been there, I am only an East Coast boy." Stephens looked at Louis and spoke in the most earnest tone. "Louis, it is most important that you immediately fly to Los Angeles. The founder of the company wants you in Los Angeles for two weeks. That is all I know. My secretary will make all of the arrangements." Louis was intrigued and puzzled at the same moment in time. "Hang on for a moment, what do you mean immediately fly? Do you mean you want me to drop everything at this moment and fly now?" Stephens forthrightly nodded his head, for any delay would attract the brutality of Naylor. "Are you mad, Richard? I have a conference later today with some bankers about how we can expand our market share here, not to mention the fact that my wife, the doctor, has been on shift at the hospital for the past three days, and she wanted to see me tonight." Stephens shrugged his shoulders and looked up from his desk at Louis' ever-increasing tense face. "It is not my call, mate; our founder in America has called for you personally. I guess it may well be your lucky day." Louis momentarily stared at Stephens as he processed his unexpected work directive, and then he reluctantly became resigned to the fact that he had to fly out to Los Angeles that day. He telephoned Victoria, and she was surprised to hear the unexpected news, but he promised to visit her at the hospital before he left.

Louis was able to briefly see Victoria at the Prince of Wales Hospital. Since the evening of his confession, Victoria had not revisited those facts with anyone, including Louis. She was concerned that her husband seemed to be spending more time at work, but she remained committed to him and his career. He had not and would not tell her his work concomitantly addressed the demons of his mind. His total income continued to increase rapidly each month, but his Pleonexia could not be satisfied. This day, like so many before, Victoria presented herself beautifully while at work; most other men would not be able to bear being taken away from such an exquisite specimen of womanhood. Louis had to apologetically explain himself. "I am so, so sorry, but I don't know why it's so urgent, other than the founder of BMI has demanded he wants me in LA immediately honey. It's my career, and I gather it can only be a positive step forward for me."

Victoria did not like the 'me' reference, but she remained calm and gently smiled at him to reluctantly accept the circumstances her husband would not challenge. "That is fine, my ambitious man; life does not slow down for you but why so sudden? What is it for? Who again has summoned you? Why does it have to be for two weeks?" Louis shrugged his shoulders. "The what I cannot answer, babe. The who, well, it is the founder of BMI, the top dog or as they say in America, the big cheese. Why me? Why two weeks? Well, I cannot answer those questions either, other than I believe this is an opportunity for me to step up to the next corporate level. My Uncle Philip told me I had noble blood and now I will show you." Victoria nodded her head, although her concerns had not been properly answered, but then in her very English manner a wicked grin came over her face. She took a step forward, so she was almost chin to chin with him, and after quickly checking over her shoulder that nobody else was present, she surreptitiously placed her hand on his groin area. "Well, my darling, keep your little man in your pants, and don't go changing on me because I think you are already noble." Even with clothing separating their flesh, her touch could still stir his sense of eroticism, and Louis smiled back at Victoria as his now partially stimulated little man responded to her sweet goodbye. Later that afternoon, Louis boarded a flight at Sydney International Airport to fly to Los Angeles International Airport, and it all of a sudden dawned upon him as the jumbo jet commenced accelerating down the runway to take off that he was returning to a country he fled from with a fake identity.

When Louis disembarked from his plane at Los Angeles International Airport, he had been without sleep for approximately 26 hours. Louis could not sleep on an aeroplane; the turbulence was too much of a distraction to allow his mind to rest, and he had also been quietly concerned about whether or not his false identity would be discovered upon him presenting his documents to the immigration officers at Los Angeles International Airport. It was an unnecessary concern; his permanent Australian residency and urgent visa documents were stamped by the immigration officer without him even bothering to check them properly. He had not stood on American soil since that fateful evening when he escaped from Manhattan in 1978 and he had never been to Los Angeles before now. As he entered the arrival terminal to collect his hastily packed bag, he wondered where on earth he was meant to go because even those details had not been provided to him by Stephens, but after a few short moments, these thoughts disappeared as a driver could be seen holding up a placard bearing Louis' name. Louis walked over to the driver to announce his presence. "I am Louis Montgomery. Just give me a moment, please, as I need to collect my bag." The driver was a tall man of humble white origins, and his grin revealed his impoverishment as he was missing his two front teeth. "Hello sir, my name is George, and I will take you to your car. Don't worry about your bag as it is already taken care of."

Louis was escorted to the car by George. His bag was delivered to the car by the airline staff moments after they arrived at the car. The car was big and luxurious. It was a stretch Cadillac that appealed to Louis' mind that he was now a member of the corporate elite class. Sitting in that car, Louis could also smell the money in the air.

The Cadillac drove along Lincoln Boulevard before it eventually connected with the 10 Freeway West. Louis was totally focused on the surroundings of Los Angeles. As a child, he watched programs on Ms Fitzgerald's television about the opposite side of his former country, but he had never been there. The Cadillac turned onto the Pacific Coast Highway at Santa Monica and Louis' eyes lit up at the sparkling beauty of the Pacific Ocean. Eventually, the Cadillac made its way along the Pacific Highway into Malibu, where Louis was enthralled by the large houses, which also commanded breathtaking views of the ocean. Extreme amounts of wealth were being selfishly displayed, and Louis was in his element.

Eventually, the Cadillac made its way to 26880 Pacific Highway and slowed down to turn into a driveway, and a sign on the gate recorded the name of the property as "La Villa Contenta". The car waited at the gate for a few minutes, and then eventually, the gates opened to reveal the magnificently landscaped gardens that lay behind the high walls that separated La Villa Contenta from the outside world of the Pacific Highway. The Cadillac made its way down a long cobblestone driveway, and it eventually turned into a circular entranceway outside of the front of the sprawling villa where the vehicle stopped. Louis was in awe at the sight of such extreme wealth and luxury.

As he was alighting from the Cadillac, a man in his early fifties walked out of the main doors of the mansion, and his booming voice announced his presence. "So, you are the wonder kid from down under? Well, wonder kid, welcome to my house." Immediately, Louis realised this must be Larry Naylor; his arrogance immediately caught Louis' attention. Naylor walked towards Louis who was still standing at the door of the Cadillac, and he extended his right hand to the younger employee in a sign of welcoming friendship. Louis responded kindly. "Pleased to meet you, sir." Naylor looked Louis up and down, appraising him like he was a piece of meat rather than a fellow human being. "You're one of us; no wonder you're good, as you're not an Aussie at all. They tell me you are strong; they tell me you are good. I understand we have you to thank for the plan which has delivered a lot of profit to this company in recent years." Louis humbly nodded his head. "I am going to take you to the next level, kid, but in the meantime, welcome to my home. Now come on, stop standing there like a little schoolgirl and come on in." Naylor then grabbed Louis by his shoulder to usher him into the palatial home, a physical act by Naylor that Louis found just as uncomfortable as being called a 'schoolgirl'. As the front doors of the mansion shut behind Louis, a shadow from a cloud passing above cast a dark and gloomy image over the villa.

CHAPTER 28

Naylor's home was beyond being palatial and lush inside. The extravagance of the decoration was vulgar and indicative of the fact that he was from the ever-growing class of people in the United States who came from new wealth and were lacking in good taste. An abundance of gold trim and red carpets and curtains seemed to be repeated. Statues, which were gaudy reproductions of Roman sculpture, were deposited repeatedly in each room as Louis was shown through the villa by Naylor. Even the artwork hanging on the walls was disjointed. There were masterpieces by great contemporary artists, but there was no theme in any one room; rather, it appeared to be a haphazard display. One thought became prominent in Louis' mind as he was taken on a guided tour, "Victoria would hate this place."

Louis was shown to the pool area by Naylor, and there, lying beside the pool, was Audrey. She appeared to Louis to be much younger than Naylor, but her presentation was as vulgar as the interior of the villa. Naylor held out his hand in pride to introduce his putative trophy wife. "Louis Montgomery, meet my wife, Audrey. Honey, meet Louis; this is the wonder kid from Australia, but it is okay; he is one of us." Audrey got up off the sun lounge next to the swimming pool; her figure was very shapely for a woman in her late thirties, but it was apparent that plastic surgery had intervened from the face down because her oversized fake breasts were almost as big as her fillers in her lips. Audrey looked down her nose through her large and expensive sunglasses at Louis, who could not believe her bathing suit barely covered the top or the bottom of her body. "Pleased to meet you, ma'am." Louis stood there holding out his hand. Audrey looked down her nose at him even more so than she had before, and then, after an uncomfortable pause, she held out her fingertips for the greeting. "Welcome to our home." Audrey quickly withdrew her fingertips from Louis' hand, and her behaviour was anything but welcoming. Without any further interaction with the two men, Audrey turned her back and returned to the sun lounge, revealing as she walked the G-string design to the bottom of her swimsuit, which then crisscrossed up her back to become the straps for the breast cups of this very revealing swimming outfit.

Naylor took Louis by the arm and ushered him back inside the villa, and the words he muttered under his breath were even more vulgar than the decorations. "Don't worry, kid, she is a bitch, but she fucks me and brings other women into our bed, so she is okay." Louis realised he had walked into the den of evil, and it was apparent to Louis from this short exposure to Naylor that he was a man consumed by hedonism. Naylor led Louis to the guest room of the villa, and it was a house within a house. "Have a shower kid, have a sleep and make yourself at home. We are having a dinner party tonight, and it should be a blast." A dinner party? Louis thought he had been urgently summoned to Los Angeles for business, but he remained silent for a moment, and then he decided it was best to just allow events to unfold rather than provoking the man's propensity for volatility. "That is great, Larry, thanks. May I ask one favour?" Naylor looked surprised that a favour was being asked for. "What in the hell is a favour? Tell me what you want. What is it?" It did not require any inflammatory speech or acts for Naylor to become volatile or even mercurial. Louis gestured to the telephone on the bedside table. "Well, I need to call my wife to tell her I arrived safely. May I please use your telephone to call her in Sydney?" Naylor laughed an overly forceful laugh. "Fuck, kid, you're on company business in my house. Call Mars for all I fucking care." Louis nodded his head to acknowledge these words as Naylor withdrew from the guest room.

Louis then sat down on the bed and scratched his head. "What have I got myself into here?" An apposite thought. Louis looked around the room, and it was decorated in a vulgar style, just like the rest of the villa, but in the guest room, it was perhaps worse. There was a ghastly painting on the wall of a boa constrictor python with one human leg from the knee down protruding from its mouth. That painting was not just vulgar, but it was also chilling to the senses. He was tired from the flight, but he wanted to hear Victoria's voice before he rested. It was 1.00pm in Los Angeles, which meant it was 6.00am in Sydney the next day. Louis dialled his home number, and the telephone eventually rang after the international dial tone. Within two rings Victoria answered the telephone. "Hello?" The sound of her sweet English accent was uplifting after having put up with the vulgarity of Larry Naylor's world. "Hi honey, I am safe and sound here in LA." There was a short pause as Victoria tried to decipher the mood her husband was in. "Oh, sweetheart, thank you for calling. I should not worry, but I do. How was the trip?" Louis could not help but be factual. He wanted to say he was terrified but could not do so in this house. "Long and uncomfortable, business class is just a slightly bigger bus seat in the sky." Victoria laughed; her husband's dry wit and honesty after flying in an aeroplane were so appealing to her, but she did not know how this form of transport affected him. "So, what did you say yesterday? Oh yes, that is it. What is the big cheese's house like?" Louis cautiously checked over his shoulder; the walls did not have ears. "It is different, but he obviously likes it."

Victoria could read between the lines of her husband's response straight away; she could tell by his voice something was wrong. "Oh, are you okay, sweetheart?" His usual defence mechanisms kicked in: never display your weakness, not even to your wife. "Yes, I am just tired, babe. Heh, I need to get some sleep, so is it okay if I call you at 5.00pm today your time? Then we can talk when I am not so tired." Despite being concerned, Victoria nevertheless wanted her husband to rest. "That is fine my beautiful man. You get your beauty sleep. I love you." Louis smiled; these words were so comforting. "I love you too." Louis then ended the call, but he wished his wife were with him now and he began to feel isolated and vulnerable. Louis then lay down on the bed and went to sleep, and it only took him a matter of seconds to fall into a deep sleep.

About three hours later, Louis woke up out of his sleep because his dream was confronting. He had dreamt of that night at Newark Bay and watching the shoot-out between Joseph and Philip. His dream was so vivid, as he dreamt about the bullet tearing through the flesh of Philip. It seemed as though time in the dream had slowed down as he dreamt of Philip dying before his eyes, and it was Philip's final words that particularly haunted him. "Louis! Louis help me. I don't want to die, Louis." Those words scared Louis to such an extent that he had awoken to now be alone in a dark and foreign room. Philip's last words of that dream continued to play over within his thoughts, 'I don't want to die Louis'. He did not want to die. Russell's death entered his mind, and he wondered how scared his late friend must have been as he felt his heart attack taking his life away. "Everybody I meet ends up dying. Death is the end." His thoughts then contemplated the syllogism regarding the certainty of death, and it entrenched fear in his mind. "All living things die; I'm a living thing; therefore, I shall die!" His mind had barely recovered from the anxiety he experienced regarding Russell's sudden death, and now Louis' inner demon of death anxiety suddenly became all-consuming. Fear of his mortality promptly overwhelmed his mind. The more Louis tried to turn his mind away from these thoughts, the more he became consumed by them again. "Why? Why? Why?" Louis' thoughts screamed in his mind as he sat on the bed, holding his head in despair.

Louis forced himself to get ready, but he did not know how he would be able to participate in the dinner event. He left the guest room when all he wanted to do was to curl up in a ball on the bed and made his way through the villa towards where the formal dining room was located. As he made his way closer to the dining room, he could hear the coarse voices of Naylor and his guests. Eventually, Louis made his way to the dining room and living room area of the villa, and the sight of Audrey's dinner clothes initially caught his eye as she was dressed in a stunning white jumpsuit that tightly hugged her buttocks and revealed her more than ample fake breasts. Standing on either side of Audrey were two younger women. Both young women were dressed in short, revealing dresses; one had blonde hair and the other red.

Next to Audrey was another small group of people who were a mixture of older men and women with a group of younger men interspersed amongst them. Further around the living room area were other groups of people; some were groups of only men, and other groups were men and women. Then Louis laid eyes on Naylor, who was surrounded by two other men, all of whom were about Naylor's age and perhaps a little older. Louis walked towards Naylor, and as he did so, out of the corner of his eye, he watched Audrey as she fondled the bodies of the two young women who stood on either side of her. Nobody else in the room seemed to care. Naylor made a spectacle of Louis' presence. "Oh, gentlemen, meet our wonder kid from down under, although I do suspect when you hear his voice, you will realise he was once one of us. Louis meet Burt Adams; Burt's company makes adult movies or the king of porn, so he's always welcome in my house." Adams was a balding man whose bright blue velvet jacket otherwise covered up his bloated belly. Louis held out his hand. "Pleasure to meet you, Mr Adams." Adams, for his part, reluctantly held out his hand like he was meeting an inferior human being. "Nice to meet you." Louis did not know what was worse, the inner torment in his mind at this moment or the condescending greeting he received from Adams, the pornographer. Naylor then held out his hand to point towards the other man standing next to him. "And this poser is Chuck Dusted, he is one of our suppliers of computer hardware here on the West Coast." Chuck? Dusted? Louis' inner mirth momentarily relieved his mind. Louis held out his hand to introduce himself, but, once again, rather than receiving a warm welcome, he again was the recipient of a cool response from Dusted. "Hello."

Louis stood there waiting for Dusted to respond but no response was forthcoming. Naylor let out a laugh as he watched Louis standing uncomfortably there. "Come on, kid, don't give into these faggots that easily. They kiss my hairy ass every day." Adams and Dusted immediately let out a hearty laugh. "Yeah, don't worry about me; a few lines more and I will be your best friend." Adams' comment caused Naylor to let out another coarse, forced laugh, and Dusted joined in. "Kid, don't let them put you off, and besides, before you walked in, we had almost agreed on which one of those two sluts my wife was going to screw tonight." Dusted then let out an almighty laugh, and his words were almost choked by his great amusement. "Shit, Larry, I have never known a guy who so casually can make a bet on which woman in the room would screw his wife." With those words being spoken, Naylor, Adams and Dusted all began to laugh even harder out loud. Louis smiled, but for the life of him, he could not understand the source of their merriment as, after all, they were laughing about the sexual antics of Naylor's wife's infidelity. "Hell has no fury than a good-looking wife who wants to fuck every person on the planet other than you." All three men bellowed out loud in laughter. Louis smiled but was not happy. All of the guests resided in California.

Subsequently, everyone sat down for dinner at the dining table set for 24 people. Audrey sat at one end of the table with the two younger women on either side of her. Naylor sat at the opposite end of the table, and he made sure that Louis was sitting immediately to his right. Louis' mind was not concentrating on the cacophony of self-indulgent chatter occurring at the table, and he had to endure Naylor's vulgarity, which seemed to boom into his left ear. Naylor tried to plough wine into his young guest's system, but Louis sipped his glass slowly as he was not in the mood for alcohol. His mind suffered in silence as the theatre of the bizarre played out before him at that dinner table. The dessert was rather surprising for Louis as it was not a treat for people to eat. Each place at the table was served a silver tray that had a line of cocaine in the middle and a $100.00 American note gently laid out next to it. Naylor was triumphant about the arrival of the dessert. "Ladies and gentlemen! It's coke time, and my gift to all of you, 100 dollars!" Louis was not a drug user, so he sat there watching the other guests rolling up their $100.00 bills and then snorting their 'dessert'.

Naylor would not allow Louis to say no to his dessert. "You're a guest in my house kid. Snort the fucking line!" Louis obeyed Naylor's overbearing command, so he reluctantly rolled up the $100.00 bill, and then he paused because he imagined how Victoria would disapprove of him consuming a narcotic. "Just fucking do it kid!" Naylor's tone of voice was threatening, so Louis reluctantly snorted his line of the drug. The cocaine immediately began to take effect, and Louis' mind began to be relieved from its demons as he contemporaneously felt his heart rate increase. He quickly consumed his glass of Pinot Noir as he now felt more inclined to socialise, and within an hour of him ingesting his first line of cocaine, Naylor had his staff bring out a further tray for each guest with another $100.00 bill laid next to the line. "$5,000.00 of fun tonight, folks!" Naylor's gloating personified the nature of the guests in whom hedonism was their religion whilst being bereft of any morality.

The mixture of cocaine and alcohol began to combine, and the effect on Louis' mind and the whole world at the dinner table began to be very strange for him. Naylor talked about money and particularly the software market. Louis could also hear Adams boasting to the wife of another guest about his new 'epic' of an adult movie set in ancient Rome. Another glass of Pinot Noir was placed in front of Louis, and he began to lose count of how many glasses of wine he was consuming. Then Audrey left the dining table with one of the young women on her arm, leaving the other woman sitting on her own as she jealously stared in the direction where Audrey had left the dining room. Dusted was engrossed in deep conversation with a young couple at the table, and his arm was resting around the shoulder of the young male as he talked away. There was a party atmosphere in the air at that dining table as the guests became uninhibited with their behaviour towards each other; partners only swapped with one another; men kissing men and women kissing women. By now, it was after midnight, and Louis was very intoxicated but not so intoxicated as to join in the orgy that was unfolding at that dinner table. As he stumbled away from the table in search of his room, he saw Naylor walking the young woman his wife had left behind in the same direction Audrey had previously departed from the dining room. Louis found his bed, but he was deeply intoxicated and missing his wife. Thoughts about his mortality returned to his mind with even greater ferocity. His last thoughts before he went to sleep were prescient. "I need more cocaine."

At about 6.30am that same morning, Louis was awoken from his intoxicated sleep by the feeling of somebody sitting on the end of his bed. His head was aching as he opened his eyes, and when his focus returned, he was slightly startled to see Naylor sitting at the end of the bed, smiling. "Larry, is everything okay?" Naylor's perverted fetishes knew no shame. "What a night kid, what a night! I watched my wife have sex with those two hookers until, gee, 3.00am and then was allowed to join the fun. Guests were having sex with each other all over our dining room, according to the staff, but not you, Sleeping Beauty; you went to bed early." Naylor then let out a coarse laugh in enjoyment. Louis smiled, but deep down he realised he was caught in a world of hedonism. "Anyway, kid, you have slept enough, and it is time we got to work. We're going to take a little journey." Work? Journey? Louis felt like vomiting, but he submissively nodded. "Have a shower and get changed. I'll see you in half an hour in the driveway. Be there. By the way, look at your bedside table as there's a line there for your head." Naylor then left the guest room.

At first, Louis looked at the cocaine, but after a few moments, he decided that he should not ingest the drug again because of his sore head and nauseous stomach. Nevertheless, as he walked into the bathroom, his mind again began to be consumed by his inner demons, expressing themselves with feelings of fear, despair, guilt and shame. Louis stopped to look in the mirror to stare down his tormentors, but he could not subdue these demons of his mind. Louis thought about the cocaine and the ephemeral relief for his mind. He succumbed to the drug's lure and returned to the bedside table to ingest the long line of cocaine that Naylor had left for him on a tray with another $100.00 bill laid out next to it. The drug began to have the same effect again on Louis' mind; the unwelcome thoughts were displaced by the putative welcome thoughts of his work. Louis showered and changed, but then he remembered he had to call Victoria the previous evening. He called her without any thought of it being 2.00am the next day in Sydney. Victoria answered the call immediately. "Louis, Louis! Is that you?" She was beside herself with concern. "Yes, honey." There was a short moment of silence. "Why didn't you call me? You were going to call me before you went to bed!" Louis knew he had caused his wife an unnecessary level of concern, but he could not say it was intoxication as his wife marvelled at his usual sobriety. "Naylor kept me talking all night, honey, about work; it was 4.00am by the time he let me go to bed. I am sorry I did not call you, but it's a big software deal, and we have to start work on it again soon."

His words had left his lips quicker than bullets being fired from a machine gun. Victoria's momentary silence seemed to be eternal for Louis' intoxicated mind. "That is all right, sweetie, but you made me worried when I did not hear from you. How was the evening other than talking about work?" He had sown his own web of deception in which he was now caught. "Boring. Lots of people were just talking about their money. Typical of us Americans, babe." Victoria laughed as Louis' self-deprecation dispelled her further needs for enquiries. "You may have the accent, my darling man, but you are not a typical American. Indeed, I think you are about to graduate into the realm of being British." Louis continued to sow that web to humour his wife. "Sure, honey, that will be the day. Perhaps your Dad will actually want to meet me when that occurs." Victoria became silent momentarily as she pondered her husband's attempt to indulge her by mentioning her father. "Sweetie, you know that I have told you that until my father acknowledges our marriage, I will not acknowledge him. I love you very much, and as far as I am concerned, we are the Montgomery family. You can trust me. You do know that, don't you, my darling?" Louis realised that in his intoxicated state, he had revealed some of his innermost thoughts about her father and them as a couple. "Heh babe, I was just trying to be funny. Don't fret, honey, as I will always love you." At the opposite end of the line, Victoria smiled as his words of love always made her heart feel warm. "And I love you too, my beautiful, sexy nobleman. Now you concentrate on your work, but please just remember to call me tonight." Louis was relieved as his deception on all fronts had worked; Victoria's tone of voice conveyed her comforted mind. "Sure, honey, I will call you tonight." After the call, there was no time to wait as he had to quickly make his way to the circular entranceway, and when he walked through the front door of the villa, he saw Naylor standing by a stretch Cadillac. Naylor smiled at his young apprentice; work was about to begin.

For the next two weeks, Naylor and Louis did not stop working. Louis ensured he kept in contact with his wife, but the pace of his life with Naylor was never-ending, and Louis had no time whatsoever to indulge in his miserable thoughts. Naylor would start work at 5.00am, and as usual, cocaine was on the table at the start of the day. Louis was flown to San Francisco and Silicon Valley on a regular basis in Naylor's private jet, even though Louis disliked air travel. BMI wanted to dominate the computer software market, and the board of directors had agreed Naylor and his new offsider could turn that plan into reality from the Pacific Rim side of the company's now ubiquitous corporate reach. However, the company's desire to dominate the software market required Wall Street finance, which meant Naylor had to rely upon Anthony Westaway in Manhattan to finance any proposed deals; the financiers on Wall Street liked Westaway, but they despised the 'used car salesman' Naylor.

Even though the head office for BMI was located in Manhattan the company's

Los Angeles office was palatial compared to Sydney. BMI's Los Angeles office was located across two of the upper floors of the US Bank Building in downtown Los Angeles, and the views from the building were panoramic as from one side of the office, Louis could see the Sierra Nevada ranges to the other side of the building from which he could see through the haze the distant sparkling waters of the Pacific Ocean. His mind at night was still under siege from the morbid thoughts of his mortality and the barking memories of Joseph sowing the seeds of Louis' self-doubt, but the frenetic pace of business life and travel maintained by Naylor, distracted Louis' mind, along with the morning dosages of cocaine which Naylor fed to him. Naylor was poisoning the ground from which Louis would shoot towards the sky of corporate dominance, but the young man was oblivious to the dangers of this artificial Garden of Eden; money, success and even cocaine became his religion.

By the end of his second week, Louis had become a clone of Naylor; he was hooked on the business plan of dominating the software market, hooked on Naylor's business philosophy, and regrettably hooked on cocaine. There was just one defining difference between them, though, as Louis had Victoria. Naylor envied Louis' attachment to his wife, but he was also frustrated by it as he wanted his young offsider to totally embrace Larry's same ruthless world of money, greed and sleaze. At the conclusion of those two weeks of tuition, Louis thought he had been tutored more than enough. However, on the day Louis was to leave Los Angeles to return to Sydney, Naylor sat him down to talk at the La Villa Contenta. Naylor discussed everything they had covered regarding BMI dominating the software market they had discussed over the previous two weeks.

Eventually, after 30 minutes of discussion, Naylor turned to the issue that he wanted to impress upon his young apprentice; it was the issue of being totally ferocious and fearless in business. "Kid, you are almost there, but I want you to really toughen up for me." Louis was disappointed as he thought he had proven he was made of metal. "What do you mean, Larry? Have I not proved to you that I am battle-hardened for you?" Naylor nodded his head in the affirmative, but his mind held an opposing point of view. He needed Louis to stay on the hook. "Sure, kid, you have proven to me that you are smart and strong. However, I want you to be ruthless, kid. When you get back to Sydney, I want you to walk up and sack on the spot the first person you see who you do not like. You have my permission; don't worry about the 'board'. Consider it your test." Louis was being asked to 'kill', in the business sense of the word. Louis nevertheless nodded his head like an obedient pet animal. Naylor then gave Louis two lines of cocaine before he left the villa for Los Angeles International Airport.

After he had crossed the International Date Line on the flight home to Sydney, Louis found his mind beginning to come down from the effects of the cocaine haze, and then his fear of flying and his morbid preoccupation with his mortality began to consume his mind again. Then there was Victoria; he felt guilty for indulging in cocaine, but now that he had consumed that drug, he desperately needed it more. When Louis arrived at Mascot Airport in Sydney some 14 hours after leaving Los Angeles, his mind was tearing itself apart in despair. As he walked out into the main lounge of the airport, Louis saw a driver standing near the main entry doors of the terminal carrying a placard with Louis' name written on it. Louis walked over and introduced himself, and the driver then proceeded to take him to a stretched limousine. As Louis entered the back of this car, he saw a gift box with his name on it. Louis undid the bowed ribbon, and he lifted the lid on the box; inside of the box was a vial of cocaine and a small envelope. Louis opened the envelope; it was a typewritten card containing a message from Naylor. "Enjoy the coke, but I want you to sack somebody straight away before you go home to your wife. Larry." Louis snorted the cocaine, and he immediately detected the haze returning to his mind. Louis asked the driver to take him immediately to the BMI office in Sydney's CBD.

When Louis arrived at the Sydney office, he saw Meredith in the lobby of the building. His orders from Naylor were clear: sack the first person you see, but there was a slight feeling of self-doubt creeping into his mind. He had to be short and blunt with his victim. "Meredith, come here!" Meredith was angered to be spoken to like this by someone he thought was junior to him in the company, so he marched over towards Louis with the intention of seeking an immediate apology. Before he could utter a word, Meredith was then struck down with a mortal blow. "Pack up your desk, as you are out of here by midday today, or I will have you thrown out. Larry Naylor has already agreed you must go." Meredith was shocked by how he was being treated, but he would subsequently learn from Stephens that he was dismissed because Louis was now in charge. The cold, fierce and determined capitalist had been created in corporate blood. The warm, loving, and caring person his wife had fallen in love with was gone. The flower of a noxious weed had now bloomed, and it regrettably had shot up from the same callous seed of his father.

After firing Meredith in the lobby, Louis took the elevator up to the floor of his Sydney office. As he walked towards his office, his personal secretary Melanie stood up at her desk to welcome him. "Welcome back, Louis; how was your trip overseas?" Louis stopped and looked at Melanie. She saw with her own eyes he had transformed into a hardened corporate animal. "It was business, and it wasn't a trip. Are there any messages?" Melanie hesitated for a moment as Louis' short and sharp reply unnerved her. "No, there are not any messages. But Mr Naylor had a package delivered for you, and I left it on your desk." Louis looked at Melanie for a short moment of time, and he realised that his demeanour had unnerved her. "Thank you, Melanie. There is no need to stand there like I am a king." Indeed, there was another package in his office; it was more cocaine Naylor had arranged with one of his 'Sydney suppliers' to be delivered to Louis. The small typewritten note explained the dire circumstances Louis was now unwittingly caught in. "Keep up the good work and this will come your way as my little gift."

Later that evening, Louis eventually returned home. Victoria was waiting for him, and even though she had been working at the hospital all day, as usual, she looked beautiful. Victoria was immediately confronted by the sight of him being a tired man, and there was something else, something different and strange about him, particularly the look in his eyes. "Welcome home, my darling." Louis walked into his wife's arms, but the embrace he gave her was initially awkward. Then he relaxed into her arms. "I missed you." Louis' words were sealed by a kiss on his lips from Victoria, but the usual warmth of his lips felt cold to her. "Is everything okay my sweetie?" He blatantly lied to his wife's face. "Yes, I am just a bit jet-lagged. I should not have gone straight to work." Victoria looked into her husband's eyes; something was wrong, but she accepted his explanation, saying it was jet lag. Later that evening, after dinner, Louis and Victoria made love, but once again, something was not right as Louis seemed to be not as tender, and instead, he was rougher in bed. Eventually, Louis fell into a deep sleep, and Victoria looked at her husband, and she was troubled by the noticeable change in his demeanour.

CHAPTER 29

L ife can sometimes speed quickly down the track of time, like a locomotion running out of control; time becomes a distant signpost behind a person as the hands of the clock spin quicker and quicker and quicker.

So did time become the same creature in Louis' life as he became increasingly obsessed with acquiring wealth and power. For the next six years, Louis and Naylor worked closely together from either side of the Pacific Ocean or together when Louis was required in Los Angeles. Sometimes, when he was required to work from the Los Angeles office, Louis would be extended an invitation by Naylor to join him and Audrey for another bizarre dinner party; on some occasions, Audrey would hire prostitutes for her delight; on other occasions, Louis witnessed Audrey walk off with a guest's wife. Louis found Naylor's dinner orgies to be boring, and he would excuse himself early to go back to the guestroom to work while the others played.

Within the context hierarchy of the Los Angeles office, Naylor may have been the founder of BMI, but Louis very efficiently and ruthlessly established himself as the brains. Louis had formulated a business plan so that the manufacturing of the computer hardware could be complemented by including the initial costs of the software; every piece of hardware would be manufactured in China rather than America so the cost per unit of production could be reduced without sacrificing on the quality of the software being produced in Silicon Valley. BMI's computers became affordable for personal household use as well as for businesses, and the manufacturing of the computers could not keep up with consumer demand. Louis even included in his plan the so-called 'affordable' costs of updating each new generation of software. His new plan generated enormous profits, and BMI now became this corporate monster that supposedly could not be slain.

Working in conjunction with the software developers out of Silicon Valley, Louis quickly scaled the heights of BMI's international corporate ladder to become not only Naylor's right-hand man at the international level of the parent company but also the corporate hitman. Sometimes, he would dismiss staff of his own accord. On other occasions, he would dismiss staff at the direction of Naylor or, if requested, by the board. The executives working under Louis worldwide began to fear his voice on the telephone or presence in their office just as much as they feared Naylor. The Los Angeles office may have become the hive of activity as BMI began to dominate both the computer hardware and software markets, but Manhattan remained the company's international head office. Louis did not want to go near the Manhattan office, so this facet of the corporate relationship between the East and West Coasts of America became Naylor's sole responsibility as founder. Larry would tell Louis regarding raising capital when it was needed that it was under control as his man Westaway was looking after the finances on Wall Street.

By the end of the six years, the profitability of BMI had increased by 350% per annum compared to the start of that period, and the corporate benefits were just as plentiful for Louis. Not only was Louis being rewarded with an increased shareholding in BMI's Class A shares, but BMI was also paying Louis a disclosed annual salary of AU$10,000,000.00 per annum to satisfy the Australian Taxation Office's requirements. Secretly, Louis was at least being paid an additional US$10,000,000.00 a year into a secret account he held in his sole name in a trust fund in the Cayman Islands, and annually, he was also receiving millions of dollars of BMI's Class A shares. Once again, Louis would be told by Naylor his man Westaway in Manhattan was looking after the arrangements for these payments to be made to BMI's senior executives.

By the Australian summer of 1997, Louis was personally worth over $100,000,000.00 in clear assets on paper in Australia, and that balance sheet did not include his secret account in a tax haven that held more than that amount in American dollars. He and Victoria had moved out of their luxurious home on Sydney's North Shore and instead had moved into the ultra-wealthy environment of Bellevue Hill, where they had purchased a luxurious nineteenth-century mansion named 'Leura'. The mansion was designed in the Federation style of Queen Anne architecture, a design which was available to the wealthy class of Sydney during the 1890s. It was a beautiful home that was set over a vast 4,600 square metre block of land in one of Sydney's elite southern shore harbour suburbs.

Victoria naturally loved the home; however, she was concerned about her husband's lifestyle, or lack thereof. Louis had become a workaholic. Over the six-year period since Louis had returned from that first fateful trip to Los

Angeles, Victoria noticed that her husband was becoming unhealthily obsessed with making money. She also noticed that his behaviour was becoming obsessive, but she could not find the underlying cause of what was changing her husband's nature. Little did she realise that Naylor was delivering to her husband's office in Sydney a never-ending supply of cocaine. Louis knew he had become a drug addict, but the drug had helped his mind escape his inner demons, and this was particularly so with his morbid preoccupation with his mortality as he counted the clock of mortal time. No matter how hard he worked or how often he consumed the drug of Naylor's choice, Louis' inner demons never went totally away.

Louis and Victoria still shared a sexual desire for one another; however, there were times during their intimacy when Victoria had to stop and bring to Louis' attention that he was becoming a rough lover. He was not violent, but nevertheless, he was not the same tender lovemaker with whom she fell in love. Victoria had put on hold her medical career, as they wanted to have a child. She would question herself whether Louis' decline in his tenderness was a product of the pressure he may have felt to successfully conceive during her cycle, but she would dismiss that thought as it was something else about her husband that was presently an undefinable problem. Annually, she would travel back to England to see her father and friends. Her father was well aware of Louis' good fortune, but he still forbade Louis to set foot on the grounds of the family estate. Amongst her old friends from England, Victoria would express how fortunate life was in Australia, but most of them detected there was something troubling her as each year went by.

As the Australian winter set in and Sydney began to feel the chill of Jack Frost in late June of 1997, Naylor demanded that Louis and Victoria join him and Audrey for a welcoming summer dinner party in Los Angeles. Louis had deliberately kept Victoria away from Naylor's world in Los Angeles for many reasons, but in particular, he did not want his drug-dependent life to be revealed. However, Naylor's commandment was quite specific; the invitation was husband and wife, and no excuses would be permitted as to why Victoria could not attend. Naylor had specifically conveyed to Louis that he and Victoria would be the only couple to stay at the La Villa Contenta.

After it became apparent to Louis that he must expose Victoria to the Naylor's vulgarity, he sat down to dinner that night at the dining table in his home, and he was initially quiet. After a few minutes of silence, it was too much for Victoria to bear. "What is wrong, Louis? You are especially quiet this evening. Please tell me. Have I done something to you?" Louis realised he could not avoid the situation; he would have to reveal that they had been summoned to California. "Larry wants us to travel to Los Angeles for a special party he is planning." Victoria raised her eyebrows in a mocking pleasant surprise. "Well, the famous Larry, I was beginning to think he was like Godot, much talked about but never seen." Louis knew his wife's dry and derisive tone meant that she was not entirely happy about being excluded from the secret world of Louis and Naylor. "Yes, well, his world is different to our world." Victoria became even more intrigued, and she leaned forward in her dining room chair to look inquisitively into her husband's eyes as her patience had been worn thin. "Different? How could it be different, Louis? What do they earn more money? Or do they have more of a life? God knows we have had no life together for the last six years as you do nothing but work, work, and work!" Louis was somewhat shocked by his wife's terse reaction. "Honey, what is wrong? We have a life." Victoria threw her head to the side to look out the window of the dining room, and then she looked back at Louis with tears welling up in her eyes. "No, Louis, no! We do not have a life! We have a lifestyle, but it is no life. You work every day of our lives without even considering a break from your insatiable appetite to make money. You may be married to me, but you are not part of what we started, which is our life, together!"

Louis treated Victoria's plea for help as an imposition, and Joseph's indelible imprint of an obstinate and phlegmatic soul had been reproduced within him. He chose his words carefully. "I am just trying to make sure your life will never go for wanting." Victoria could not believe the words that her husband was speaking. "Louis! Louis!" Her voice was beginning to shriek in frustration. "We have more than enough. I was born into wealth, and I can tell you now that we have more than enough wealth. I don't want any more money. We have more than enough to last us two lifetimes." Louis threw his hands down on the dining room table in frustration as he could not understand the protests of his wife. "So, what do you want? What is so wrong with me wanting to make money for our family?" Victoria's frustration was now transforming into pure bitterness and hostility. "Our family? Our family, Louis?!? What God damn family?!? It is just you and me, and most of the time, there is no you; it is just me!"

With those words, Victoria stood up to leave the dining room table. Louis got up from his chair to try to calm her down, but it was too late. "Hey, honey come back..." Victoria shouted over the top in her commanding English tone.

"No, Louis, no, I will not come back!" Victoria stormed out of the dining room.

It was the first time since they had entered into a relationship that Victoria had acted in this manner, or so Louis thought. The problem with Louis' world over the last six years is that his wife had been subtly revealing her feelings from time to time, but Louis' mind was too distracted. If only she knew what those problems were; however, he had regrettably kept her shut out from their very first date.

Louis sat at the dining room table for two hours. During this time of solitude in his dining room, he could not understand why his world just seemed to crumble earlier tonight, and that was the product of his single-minded pursuit of acquiring wealth, and the state of his marriage was not assisted by his drug-induced state, products to which the blame could be attributed to his inner demons. Eventually, after two hours, Louis' mind had a moment of insight into Victoria's lonely world. Louis walked upstairs to the master bedroom, and when he entered that room, Victoria was lying on their bed, and he thought she was asleep; she was still dressed in the beautiful evening dress she had worn to the dinner table earlier that evening to impress her husband. Louis began to walk on his tiptoes towards the bed as he thought his wife was asleep, but as he neared the end of the bed, Victoria suddenly rolled over and stared at him before sitting up. Louis thought Victoria was still angry with him. "I am sorry, my sweetheart. I did not mean to upset you."

Victoria wiped her eyes; she had been crying for an extended period. "That is alright, and I am sorry that I became so angry." Louis wanted to speak but his wife quickly raised her hand to quieten him. "Don't talk, and just come to bed. I am ovulating Louis, and I want a child. That is why I am wearing this revealing dress on a winter's night. Don't say another word. Just come to bed." Louis did not need any further encouragement as they still had a sexual chemistry that was driven by their like-minded enjoyment of their sexual interaction, even if his tenderness had been missing, but on this occasion, she had an extra sexual desire alluring him. They made love on many occasions that night, and on each occasion, Victoria seemed to be more determined to ensure that Louis would significantly orgasm, including on one of the latter occasions when she manipulated his prostate gland with her finger, which in turn caused him to experience an extreme orgasm the likes of which he had never experienced before.

The next morning, Victoria was the first one to wake. She placed her hands on her lower abdomen, and in her mind, she knew that she must be pregnant as she then showered herself to remove their combined bodily juices from her skin. Twenty minutes later, Louis woke up, and he immediately saw his wife commencing to apply her makeup in the en suite mirror and when she turned to face him, he saw the look in her eyes. Although a pregnancy test would need to be performed in a few weeks' time, Louis could tell by the look in his wife's eyes that she was satisfied they had succeeded in conceiving a child. Victoria was radiant and she was happy because she knew inside her own body that it was likely she was pregnant.

CHAPTER 30

Three weeks later, Louis and Victoria departed from Mascot Airport in Sydney for the first time to travel to Los Angeles together. Louis had made this trip many times over the past six years, indeed, at least once a month, if not twice, but this did not cure his fear of flying. On this trip he happily let his wife have the window seat in first class so that he could concentrate on his latest memorandum in relation to the future international business interests of BMI. However, Victoria was too excited for many reasons about the trip as it was an adventure and she had never been to the West Coast of the United States before, but more importantly, she planned on surprising Louis when the moment was right on this trip with the news her doctor had confirmed two days beforehand that she was definitely pregnant. It was hard not to break the news immediately, but she wanted to tell him at a quiet and romantic location in the northern beaches district of Los Angeles.

Victoria knew that Louis wanted to concentrate on his work, but she wanted to talk. "So, tell me more about this Larry Naylor fellow." It had been only 15 minutes since the 747 had taken off. Louis put down his memorandum and looked quickly at his wife. "What can I tell you? He is a ruthless businessman." Louis then glanced at his work, to convey to Victoria that he had to concentrate on these documents. Then Louis just as quickly went back to his two-hundred-page memorandum. Victoria sat back in her chair, and whatever change in Louis she thought may have occurred after their argument two weeks ago was an ephemeral moment, but she was not going to be deterred because she wanted to find out more. "Louis, you have told me that many times before. I want to know what he looks like, what his wife is like and what she likes. You have been to Los Angeles so many times to work with him; surely you can tell me more." Louis took a deep breath and set down his memorandum. He turned towards his wife and looked into her eyes; it was time to reveal to her a few truths about Naylor. "He is not like you, nor like me. Larry is coarse; Larry is sleazy; Larry has no morals whatsoever, and most importantly, from the moment I met Larry, I realised that I would have to work my way away from Larry to break free of him, and I still am working my way out to be free of him." Victoria raised her left eyebrow, both inquisitively and out of concern. Her husband had not revealed so many facts about Larry Naylor or even his own plans in the past six years, but she had to know more. "Well, what about his wife? Is she at least a decent person?" Louis smiled, but then his next response was even blunter. "She is a closet lesbian. She sleeps with women but keeps Larry entertained by letting him watch, but then she sometimes allows him to participate. Accordingly, she never goes wanting."

Victoria looked away from her husband as she was dismayed to only be informed now about the personal lives of the Naylors and, most importantly, the world of her husband when he was in Los Angeles. After a moment, Victoria turned back towards her husband and the look on her face was quite earnest. "Louis, I trust you, but you have never told me this before, even though every time you come home, I ask, 'How was your trip?'. So, just answer this question for me: what else goes on? What do you get up to when you are gone?" Louis sat back in his chair in disbelief as he was surprised and annoyed his wife would even ask that question. "Honey, honey, honey. How could you possibly ask that question? I am not like that. I am not the unfaithful type, and you should know that." Victoria looked at her husband and examined his reaction. Victoria realised he was telling the truth. "That is fine. I am sorry darling, but just remember this: if you ever did participate in Larry Naylor's sleaze, that would be the death of you and me."

Victoria then remained silent and let Louis get back to his memorandum. A few hours into the flight, Victoria fell asleep, and she did not notice that her husband had quietly left his seat to go to the bathroom. In the first-class bathroom of the 747, Louis removed a vial of cocaine, which was hidden in a secret compartment of his right leather shoe, another gift from Larry. He snorted down two lines of cocaine, and instantly, he began to feel relief.

The 747 landed with an extra thud on the tarmac of Los Angeles International, and the impact of the landing startled most of the passengers, including Victoria. Louis continued to bury himself in his work documents. He had spent the past twelve hours high on cocaine, feverishly working his way through his memorandum. It was just not any memorandum; Louis had drafted a five-year business plan for BMI and its various holdings, which would see it make a transition away from being entirely a multi-national computer hardware and software company. Louis' five-year plan focused on moving the company's business interest to include diversified holdings consisting of Australian mining, Chinese and Indian construction, and related industries. The emphasis on Asia was a bold move as they were emerging countries, and Naylor had said many times over the years how much he hated Asians and Indians. Nevertheless, even though Louis knew Naylor was a bigot, he still knew that the attraction of money was Naylor's only real interest.

As they taxied along the lanes of Los Angeles International heading towards the terminal, Victoria could no longer contain herself, and she had to find out why her husband was working so furiously away on the flight. "So, are you going to share with me the piece of art you have been so occupied with for the past 14 hours?" Louis finally took a break from his paperwork; he closed the 200-page memorandum up like a schoolchild trying to cover up the answers of an examination. "Sure, it is complex." Victoria remained calm but he was testing her patience again. "That is fine, Louis, but for the past six years it has always been complex when it comes to discussing with me your work. However, this is the first time I have been exposed to you close-up working away with such single-minded desire. So please, let me in. What is it that makes you become so focused on your work, rather than me?"

Louis sat back in his plane seat, and once again, within the space of a month, his wife had voiced her soul in protest. After a few brief moments of considering the question, Louis decided that honesty was the best policy. "If BMI continues down the software and hardware path, it will be significantly weakened by what I believe will be a recession in that industry due to a correction of an ever-increasing and over-inflated marketplace in its current economic space. I want to diversify the company into the developing world of construction and the minerals that can be fed to it from Australia. That way, we will, as a company, survive the impending downturn. It is a complicated business and economic theory, and I have to sell it to people whose minds are lost in the bubble of the current greed of the significant growth happening now, happening within my industry, which for some, well, they seem to believe it is an industry to have no ceiling, but I think the opposite is this case." Victoria looked into her husband's eyes; she was a specialist doctor, but even she marvelled at his intellect as he had seemingly assessed the world economy for years to come and had formulated a brilliant business plan to address any economic uncertainty. Victoria's words seemed to imply she may have also been wrong to argue with Louis about his commitment to his work. "If only I had your mind; sorry I asked, darling; no wonder you were working so hard." Louis looked at his wife, and for the first time in many years, he spoke with the same voice when he first married her. "Everything I do is because of you". The words caused Victoria to smile, but they were words that were now spoken too infrequently, and she deep down wondered when her husband would speak like that again.

The limousine drove onto the Pacific Highway to head towards the La Villa Contenta. Louis spoke up as Victoria was otherwise preoccupied with the scenery of the West Coast of America, which she had never seen before. "Larry's house is big." Victoria's attention returned to her husband as Louis still was oblivious to the life Victoria had grown up in, in England and, in particular, the estate manor held by many generations of her family. "Really?" Victoria's contrived surprise was spoken in a disingenuous manner. "However, their décor is vulgar and, in some respects, grotesque." Victoria smiled, and she also sensed Louis was now nervous. "It is alright, Louis; I don't believe they could offend me, so relax, as I can look after myself."

The limousine turned off the Pacific Highway into the driveway of the La Villa Contenta. After a moment, the gates opened. The limousine slowly made its way along the internal driveway, and Victoria was certainly impressed by the gardens, but it was still nothing in comparison with the beautiful tree-lined entryway that led all the way to her family's manor home. However, Victoria made no comment; after all, her father had forbidden her from ever allowing Louis to set foot on the estate. "Very American." They were the bland words that came out of Victoria's mouth as she otherwise was not impressed by the style of the American architecture. Eventually, the limousine pulled into the circular drive of the villa. The driver got out of the vehicle and opened the door to Victoria's side of the back of the vehicle. Louis had already alighted from the limousine and had made his way around to his wife's side to help her out of the back of the vehicle.

As Victoria alighted from the car, Naylor burst open the front doors of the Villa, almost as though he was timing his presence to take command of the situation. Instantly, Victoria was amused because there stood a man well into his fifties, but it was obvious he was trying to feebly hold onto his youth. Naylor had been to a solarium, and his overly tanned skin suggested he had visited a tanning bed. His hair was styled to cover up the march back in time of an ever-growing bald spot, and the paunch of his belly was poking hard through the fabric of his short-sleeved casual shirt. "Welcome to the La Villa Contenta". Victoria smiled at him, but her mind did not entertain warmth for him. Louis walked towards Naylor and grasped his hand. "Larry, good to see you again." Louis then turned towards his wife. "Larry, this is my wife, Victoria. Honey, this is Larry." Larry threw his hands out wide, and as he did so, his belly poked out even further through his shirt. "Of course, Louis has told me so much about you and how beautiful you are."

With those words being spoken, Naylor then kissed Victoria on the cheek, close to her lips. Victoria felt violated; however, she remained outwardly calm for her husband's sake. Louis was stirred and annoyed by Naylor's intrusive behaviour towards his wife, but before he could say anything, Larry triumphantly threw his right hand out towards the front doors of the villa. "Come with me; the driver will look after the bags. Come inside the La Villa Contenta!" Victoria's mind expressed her feelings about Naylor. "Now I realise why Louis was so worried, as this man is really very common." For his part, Louis could detect the look in Victoria's eyes; he knew his wife well, and he could detect that she did not like Naylor. "If she does not like him, wait until she meets his wife," Louis thought to himself as he watched his wife be dragged into the devil's lair.

They walked through the interior of the La Villa Contenta, and Naylor proudly pointed out his artwork and sculptures to Victoria. She smiled as Naylor pointed towards each piece of art, but deep down, she could not believe how revolting the décor and paintings were and, indeed, her husband was right when he described Naylor's world as vulgar. Louis inferred from Victoria's strained politeness that his wife was not impressed with Naylor or his house. He was still not impressed by Larry's conduct in kissing his wife's cheek, but he decided not to express his simmering thoughts now. Naylor then ushered them towards the doors, which led out to the pool, and Louis grimaced as he hoped Audrey was alone and not accompanied by another woman. Naylor walked towards the doors leading out to the pool, his voice proudly boomed out. "Audrey, Louis and his wife are here." As they walked through the doors, Louis' worst nightmare was answered because Audrey Naylor was lying on a daybed next to the pool. Next to her was a younger, voluptuous woman with blond hair, no bikini top, and her leg was lying over the top of Audrey's. He glanced at his wife, and he could see Victoria was visibly disturbed because she had pursed her lips.

Audrey saw Victoria, and her heart began to beat quickly and strongly because Victoria was the woman of her dreams. Audrey promptly composed herself, and as she slowly stood up, she also adopted her best seductive pose.

Gone were the long flowing honey blond locks of previous visits; Audrey now had short, cropped hair, which was bleached white, blonde, almost as though her head had been dipped in a vat of bleach. She was now in her early forties, and she toned her body with repetitive gymnasium workouts. Audrey still knew no shame, and she was wearing a one-piece G-string bikini which barely covered her vagina and her breasts. She walked towards Victoria and held out her hand, and as she did so, Audrey lifted her sunglasses and blatantly cast her eyes up and down to examine Victoria's fine figure. "Nice to meet you". Louis did not even receive a hello when he first met her six years beforehand. Victoria, in her polite English manner, held out her hand. "Nice to meet you too, Audrey." Audrey took Victoria's hand into hers, and then she applied her seductive ways by slowly releasing it so that her fingertips gently slid along Victoria's fingers. Her touch was gentle, alluring and seductive. Audrey's powers of seduction were strong, and even Victoria was slightly aroused by Audrey's gentle touching of her hand.

Louis at once looked towards Naylor, and he instantly detected that Naylor was watching the two women in a depraved manner, almost as though he was hopeful the two women would join him in the confines of his bedroom later that evening. Louis decided to break the silence. "So, Larry, we are pretty tired after the long flight. I don't suppose we can have a shower and get a bit of sleep?" Naylor immediately came to his senses. "Sure. Sure, kid. We have a special dinner planned tonight. Get some rest, and later, Louis, when you wake, call me on the intercom; I have some things I want to show you in my office." Louis knew the 'things' were drugs, and he needed them. Naylor walked Louis and Victoria towards the guest quarters. "Make yourself at home. We have added a bar and a fully stocked fridge." Victoria smiled, and her strained politeness was evident in her voice. "Thank you, Larry, thank you very much." Naylor then withdrew from their presence as Louis and Victoria entered the guest quarters.

Louis closed the doors behind him, and then he turned to face his wife. Initially, Victoria had a blank face, then after an uneasy pregnant pause, she began to laugh. Louis walked towards Victoria to quieten her down as he was concerned that her voice may carry through the doors. "Oh Louis, they are more than vulgar; they are a circus within a show wrapped up in a cheap movie! Now I understand why you were so reluctant for me to meet these people; they have to be the most coarse and vulgar crew I have ever seen. And that wife! Why didn't she just cut straight to the chase and say, 'want to bonk', or whatever her kind says to another woman." Victoria highly disapproved of Louis' boss and his wife.

"Well, honey, I tried to warn you, but I am not like them." With those words Victoria smiled to reassure her husband; however, she wondered what had been going on around her husband.

They were both tired from the flight, and after they had a shower, Louis lowered the blackout curtains so that they could rest. Victoria fell asleep immediately. Louis lay in the bed, but he could not fall asleep immediately like his wife had done. He was now experiencing withdrawal symptoms because it was many, many hours since he surreptitiously consumed cocaine on the flight, and as his mind became depressed by those withdrawal symptoms, it then also became consumed with thoughts of his mortality. It was so many years ago now, but it was like the first occasion he lay on this bed, and that was the final trigger; the counting clock he pictured in his mind then seemed to speed up in his mind about the future. Time ticking away so quickly, and he thought it may not be too long before he too was old with one foot in the grave. Eventually, after an hour, Louis fell asleep.

Two hours after he fell asleep, Louis sat bolt upright in bed. His dream state was just as challenging as his conscious world. On this occasion, he dreamt that he was about to die in his childhood home in Manhattan; in his dream, it was an empty apartment with nobody around him. He could hear his father's menacing voice outside of his window shouting vitriolic and threatening words at him from the front entrance; an ominous moment like a wild animal would feel when its hunter finally corners it, and there is nowhere else to hide. The voice of his father seemed to become louder in this chaotic nightmare terror, and behind his shoulder, the voice of the ghoulish reaper whispered in his ear, "It's time". It was from this terrifying and fateful moment of his nightmare that he awoke, and his heart was pounding from the fear his nightmare had generated. Two menacing figures in his dream of his father and the Grim Reaper had tormented his subconscious mind.

Louis initially took some moments to come to terms with his surroundings, as the room was dark, and he was initially unsure whether he was awake. Eventually, Louis' senses came to him, and he was awake, but the dream he had disturbed him. There was just enough dim light coming from the bathroom for Louis to be able to see his wife. Victoria was sound asleep. Louis slowly got out of bed, and put on a t-shirt, and he then walked over to his bag to retrieve his laptop computer. Louis walked over to the lounge area of the guest room and sat down with his laptop, and then he worked furiously away reading his emails for an hour, and he did not notice that Victoria had quietly woken up 30 minutes after he had commenced work. Victoria quietly looked on in concern as to how obsessed her husband was with his work, and she remembered the times when her husband was just obsessed with her. "Larry wants me. Why doesn't my husband?"

Victoria sat up, and Louis stopped working on his laptop. He stood up and walked over to the bed. "Hey, babe, how did you sleep?" Victoria rubbed her eyes and then looked at Louis. "Fine, but to my disbelief, when I woke up, I realised I was still here. Louis, I know he is your 'boss', if truly you could have a boss after all of these years, but my darling, I really don't like these people." Louis put his finger up to his mouth to quieten his wife. "Quiet honey, these walls may well have ears. Look, it is only for a couple of nights." Victoria looked at her husband; she accepted to endure these grotesque people just for Louis' business's sake. "Alright, for you, I shall put up with them." Louis then walked over and sat on the bed, and he put his arms around his wife and cuddled her. Victoria welcomed this tender moment. "Ok, honey, we had better get ready for the dinner party; you are about to be exposed to the rest of the freak show, so please just be patient."

After Louis showered and dressed for dinner, he returned to his laptop. He was so consumed with his work he did not pay any attention to his wife getting ready. Eventually, after an hour of doing her hair and makeup, Victoria came out of the guest bathroom dressed in a beautiful dress. Her appearance, like always, was mesmerising, and Louis proudly looked at his beautiful wife. Victoria put on her stiletto heels and then turned towards her husband. "So, what do you think?" Louis could only be honest. "Like always, you will be the most beautiful woman in the room." Victoria smiled, and despite her education, she nevertheless liked the way her husband stroked her ego. However, much to her frustration and within almost an instant, Louis returned to his laptop. Victoria could not hide her disappointment. "Perhaps I should have dressed in a computer bag! That would seem to attract more attention than this dress." Louis looked up from his laptop, and he knew his wife's voice was displeased. "What is wrong?" Had she met Joseph she would have known the source of this cold heart. "Nothing, don't worry, I'm still just a little bit tired." With those words, Victoria sat down in one of the armchairs near where Louis was working. There was a magazine on the table next to the chair and Victoria picked it up to read it. After 30 minutes, Louis abruptly closed the screen on his laptop. "Okay, we had better go out and meet the crowd; brace yourself." Victoria looked at her husband, she could not understand why he was being so melodramatic.

Louis ushered his wife into the main living room of the villa and standing within the room were approximately another twenty people, including Naylor, his wife, and the young blond woman from the pool earlier that day. The first thought that struck Victoria was just how vulgarly the rest of the people were dressed. Naylor was dressed in white shoes, white trousers, and a bright red shirt. Audrey was dressed in a long dress that was split in a revealing way in the front, and the top of the dress barely covered her breasts. The young woman from the pool was even more scantily dressed in a tight leather dress that barely came down past her crutch and hardly covered her breasts. The rest of the dinner guests were also an odd mix as the older men were accompanied by either young women or young men. The standard of dress of these guests was generally garish and indicative of new and vulgar wealth. Louis and Victoria were the odd couple out, stylishly dressed and with not a hint of garish taste.

Louis made some of the introductions around the room to old faces he recognised. Dusted was the first person to be introduced to Victoria. Dusted had come to terms with his sexuality, and he was accompanied by a much younger, good-looking man. Next to them was Adams, accompanied by his wife, who was just as cold as Audrey, but at least she came across as being straight. Naylor came over in his usual over-the-top manner. "Look at this beautiful woman, Louis; please, let me introduce her to some of the other guests." Louis reluctantly agreed because he still was simmering over Naylor kissing his wife's cheek. "Sure, Larry, go on honey, meet the rest of the guests." Louis resumed talking to Adams and Dusted. Naylor took Victoria around the room introducing her to the other guests as the beautiful wife of his genius from Down Under. Victoria was repulsed by the lack of recognition on Naylor's behalf for the fact that she was a specialist doctor. It appeared to Victoria that Naylor could not care for what she did, he was only interested in how she looked.

Then, a man entered the room with a woman on his arm, and Louis' heart almost stopped beating. It may have been almost a quarter of a century, but the familiarity of a face is always impressed upon a young mind. Antonio! Tony, as Naylor now referred to him is Antonio! Antonio, the young man in whom Louis and Jack held nothing but abject fear because of his menacing demeanour, was Anthony Westaway, Naylor's man in Manhattan and a reliable source of raising of venture capital. Antonio, or now Tony, had escaped detection by the authorities long before the mayor was brought down for corruption, crime and murder. Tony had used his intelligence to transform himself and was now a respectable Manhattan senior executive. After leaving the world of his uncle the mayor's corrupt ways, Tony had changed his name from Antonio Mancini to Anthony Westaway, or Tony to those who knew him. He had put his mind to use to obtain a business and commerce degree from Northeastern University in Boston, a Tier 3 institution which he had paid for himself from his previous ill-gotten ways. Tony could not hide his obvious Mediterranean looks, but he explained to people he had met that his father had met an Italian girl while serving in the army in Europe after World War 2. After obtaining his degree, Tony then secured a junior associate's position under Donald Harding at the established Manhattan investment banking firm of Wolff, Adams and Harding. Donald Harding was the fourth generation of Harding to preside over the firm as a partner. Harding took a liking to Anthony, and within a year, he introduced him to his prim and proper, but also very plain-looking, daughter Tiffany, or Tiff to those who knew her. Within two years, Tony had married Tiff, and the young early twenties thug Antonio Mancini was well and truly buried in the sands of time. He was the respectable side of BMI in the commercial heart of the East Coast of America.

Louis and Tony looked at each other across the room as Naylor spoke into the latter's ears; Tony did not recognise him, but Louis recognised him because his facial features could never be forgotten. Louis' mind was presently lost in a state of terror for fear of his past being exposed; two nightmares in the same day. "Louis, get your ass over here and come and meet Tony". Naylor's coarse voice awoke Louis from his mental quandary, and he had no other option than to go and meet the person Naylor had mentioned for many years as Tony Westaway, "my man in New York." He walked over, thoughts racing through his mind, but he otherwise maintained his composure. "Louis, this is our money man in New York, Tony, and Tony, this is the wonder kid from Australia I have told you about for so many years, but don't worry, he used to be one of us". Naylor's voice could usually pierce lead, but on this occasion, Louis' mind was consumed with the thoughts of being recognised from his previous life.

Tony's hand extended outwards without any hesitation as he had not recognised the child within the man before him, but as they shook hands, the contact stirred something in Tony's mind, something familiar. "Have we met before?" His question was like an arrow striking the bullseye of Louis' inner terror.

Improvisation was urgently required; however, he hesitated before responding. "No, I don't believe so, unless you grew up in New Bedford". The impoverished town of New Bedford in Massachusetts was indeed an area Tony was unfamiliar with. Tony looked at him for a brief moment without saying a word because Louis' hesitation before nominating New Bedford as his original home aroused slight suspicion in Tony's educated but also street-wise mind. He was about to ask him a question regarding New Bedford, but before he could do so, his wife then spoke. "Forgive my rude husband; my name is Tiffany, but please call me Tiff". The interruption immediately severed the fragment of thought that had stirred briefly inside his mind, and a smile came over Tony's face. "So you're the guy that keeps my money men happy in New York; I am glad to finally meet you". An uncomfortable smile came across Louis' face, as his mind relaxed, but he remained on guard. "Nice to meet you too, Tony".

Before the three men could indulge in any further talk, Victoria came over and introduced herself, and she was relieved after meeting Tiff that she had found someone of culture within the jumble of Americans she had been previously enduring the company of. Indeed, the feeling was mutual for Tiff as well because she quite frankly found Larry and Audrey vulgar. The small group broke off from one another, and the mingling of the guests continued with its artificial spirit of friendship. Nevertheless, Louis was on his guard with Tony in the same room, and the corner of his eye constantly observed what he was doing; living a lie can do that to a person. After thirty meaningless minutes of small talk, a man walked into the room. He was obviously hired to help, and he announced in a loud voice, "Dinner is ready." Louis and Victoria resumed company with each other, and he showed her the way to the large dining room table. Louis sat Victoria at the dinner table set for thirty or so people, and he then took a seat next to her; one part of his mind was watching the opposite end of the table, where Tony and Tiff were now taking their seats at the table. Louis then looked back to Victoria's face, and as he did so, he could detect that his wife was not comfortable with this crowd of people. Victoria was trying hard to be nice, but this was not a gathering of people she had time for.

Dinner dragged on for almost two hours, and meaningless talk was being spoken at the table. Occasionally, Naylor would say something at the table that was shallow and inappropriate, and the other guests would laugh, but Victoria only smiled politely. Louis was his usual self in this company, and he would smile when Naylor made the boorish comments, but otherwise, Louis did not react like the rest of the guests. Nevertheless, Louis had come to a reckoning in his mind that Tony was real, that he was a reminder life can come back to revisit you, but unlike his wife, Louis wanted something out of this meeting; what he wanted was the opportunity to continue forging his business relationships in California so that he could make more money. After dinner, Naylor stood up and said in a commanding voice, "Adams, Dusted and Louis, come with me for a moment to my office; there is something I need to discuss."

It was strange Tony's name was not mentioned, but then he realised that despite the vulgarity of Naylor's world here in California, there was a side to BMI's hierarchical business structure Naylor could not go near to: Wall Street money. Tony was that side of BMI, the respectable commercial world of Manhattan in which ghouls like Naylor would never be accepted. Tony was also living a lie as he had escaped his past, and in marrying Tiff, he had entered the sophisticated and polished East Coast high society set in whom the bourgeois belief of their own entitled world had been engendered within their veins, centuries beforehand so that they, as the descendants of those settlers, thought of themselves as a landed gentry of the New World. Tony did not stray into Naylor's world. Louis turned to look at Victoria, almost like a young child would look at a parent for permission to go somewhere with another child. She looked at him. "Well, Louis, you do not need my permission, go." Her voice was pleasant, but the edge of her tone was enough to convey to him she was patient, but for how long? Louis got up and left the table. As he left the room he looked towards his beautiful wife.

The rest of the guests sat at the table, talking for another hour after Louis had been taken away. Victoria spoke for a lengthy period to Dusted's young male partner, Rick. He had moved to California after growing up in Wyoming. Rick told Victoria he had moved to California to be an actor, but he could not get a break. He explained to her that he was only 18 when he first arrived, and very quickly the predatory nature of Hollywood's gay executives sought him out. Victoria could not understand why he had not succeeded as an actor, because Rick was pretty to look at, with blond hair and the All-American farm boy look. He was pleasant, nice, and his demeanour was not one of a viper. He was a nice young man in whom love was found with a fellow man, but he had the demeanour of a woman. They were in the middle of a deep and meaningful discussion when Audrey Naylor stood up from her chair at the dinner table and walked around towards Victoria, and the young woman from the pool had already walked towards the entryway of the dining hall in anticipation of leaving with Audrey.

Audrey walked up towards Victoria and placed her hand on her shoulder, and her gentle touch slightly startled Victoria, who was not expecting her space to be invaded. "Oh, sorry to startle you. Do you want to come with us?" Her words did not expressly suggest what 'coming with them entailed', but she knew they meant to promiscuously romp in acts of sexual depravity with Audrey and her young prey. Victoria sat back in surprise; she inquisitively lifted an eyebrow and spoke in her well-bred English voice of superiority. "Go where?" Audrey turned towards her young female companion and then looked back at Victoria, displaying her lack of intuition. She misunderstood the rhetorical question and leaned in closely to softly whisper into Victoria's ear. "Come upstairs with us to my bed. I think you are incredibly beautiful, and erotic, and I really want to taste every inch of that beautiful, noble and gorgeous pure-blood skin of yours." Audrey knew how to seduce another woman, and those words she spoke were specifically chosen to appeal to Victoria's noble veins and her vanity. Victoria was very briefly aroused because Audrey's words touched a tender chord long missing in her marriage to Louis. However, it was an ephemeral moment of arousal and her mind very quickly determined for itself it was a risible suggestion she should indulge in infidelity with two other women.

She had enough of this vulgar world, and Audrey's behaviour was the final limit. She sat back in her chair even more as she looked into Audrey's infatuated eyes, and then, after a few moments, she began to smile, which very quickly broke into a hearty laugh that she could not contain. "Goodness me no. Oh dear, sorry, but I have never heard of anything more ridiculous. Sleep with you and your whore? Not in any universe!" The room froze momentarily, as only the command of centuries of gentrified English breeding could stop a person in their tracks. The guests at the table watched, but with those words being spoken, Audrey had been publicly shamed. She turned away in anger. "Bitch!" Her words seemed to echo down the hall as she stormed out of the dining room, grabbing the arm of her young female friend to drag her away with her. The rest of the table sat there quietly; save for Tony and Tiff, some of the other guests looked at Victoria as though she had said something offensive to Audrey when that could not have been even further from the truth. Victoria got up and excused herself from the table. She was amazed how the rest of the guests could have looked at her as though she was to blame for Audrey's outburst. She left the dining room area to return to the guest room, but in doing so, she became lost and instead wandered down a hallway of the villa she walked through earlier that evening.

Victoria then heard the familiar sounds of her husband's voice coming from a room where the door was partially open. She walked to the door and listened, and sure enough, she heard Naylor's distinctive nasal voice. Victoria opened the door to the room, and she saw her husband sitting at an office desk. He had a straw up his nose as he was in the middle of snorting a line of white powder. She did not need any explanation, and she now realised what had been the change in her husband's behaviour for many years now; Louis had become a cocaine addict. Victoria looked at Louis and shook her head. She knew that she was pregnant, and yet here was a man taking drugs who was also meant to be a father to their child. She turned around and left the room as Louis put down the straw. He was intoxicated on cocaine, and the sight of his wife catching him in the act of taking the drug only intensified the effects of it. Add to that toxic mixture his concern his childhood life had returned as a reality with Tony slithering back into the picture, his blood pumping through his body in the most insalubrious way, like crude oil trying to pump its way through an old and dirty pipe.

She managed to find her way back to the guest quarters, and about ten minutes later, Louis entered the room. By that time, Victoria was in bed, and Louis sat on the bed next to her. "Honey, I'm..." his words were immediately cut off by her sharp tone. "Louis, do not talk to me now. I have experienced what can only be described as an unusual day, topped off by discovering my husband has a drug problem! So please, shut up and let me sleep." She rolled over to display her displeasure in the most physical manner. Louis sat on the edge of the bed; he was startled by his wife's harsh tone, so he did not say anything further. Eventually, after an hour, he lay down on the bed. Victoria was asleep. Louis lay there for an hour; his mind was spinning with thoughts of his wife's anger, intermingled with the unsettling reentry into his life of Antonio and all the traumatic thoughts associated with Louis' former life. After about two hours of the thoughts spinning around his mind, he fell asleep. Two worlds had been torn apart that evening; like bulldozers opening heavy wounds in a beautiful garden, life would no longer be the same for Louis and Victoria. A seed was growing in a woman's womb, totally innocuous to the world outside. Can a flower blossom in this excavated mess of a garden?

A few hours later, the telephone on the table next to Louis' side of the bed rang. He picked up the phone, and in a half-asleep voice, he said, "Yes." It was

Naylor. "Kid, your wife has pissed off my wife. You must go. I have booked the penthouse apartment at the Montage in Beverly Hills. Sorry, kid, but it looks like our wives cannot be one big happy family." He did not need any further explanation, and he surmised that Audrey and Victoria had clashed. "What is going on?" Victoria had been awoken from an unsettled slumber by the sound of Louis' voice. "We have to leave. Naylor has booked us into the Montage Hotel." Victoria rolled her eyes, sighed and then got out of bed quickly. "Thank goodness, but don't think I am happy with you. I can't wait to leave this nightmare of a country." In the master bedroom of La Villa Contenta a storm was still erupting in the form of Audrey's anger. She had been humiliated by Victoria in front of the other guests, but what had really angered her was that she really desired her, indeed wanted an ongoing relationship with her because when she first saw Victoria, her heart almost stopped with love.

Early that morning at the Montage Hotel the scene was tense between them. Not a word was spoken until one hour after checking into the room. Louis walked up to the king-size bed where his wife lay with her back turned towards him in disapproval. Louis laid his hand on his wife's back and immediately felt her skin pull away from his; she had never done this to him before, and he knew he was to blame. "So, what is the problem? We have left that place." Victoria turned violently around in the bed and sat up; her eyes were burning with anger, but the words that came out of her mouth were as cold as ice. "So, this is what you get up to, Louis, when you go away? Is this what you have turned into? A drugged man, snorting up rubbish and more importantly, who are these awful people you are mixed up with? That woman, Larry's wife, wanted to have sex with me and another woman! Is that what you want us to be involved in, Louis? Do you want me to be a promiscuous tart?!" The fire that erupted from Victoria's final sentence woke Louis up out of his drugged state, and he had never heard his wife speak with such venom. Louis stood there silent for a few moments as he was trying to say something sensible, but he was still intoxicated, so his mind could not grasp the right words for him. Victoria spoke Louis' next sentence; the mocking nature of her voice displayed her discontent. "Sorry, honey? Are those words you are searching for, Louis? Look, I am tired and still reeling in shock about your deception and the nature of the people you are doing business with here in California. I just want to get some sleep and maybe tomorrow enjoy a little bit of a part of the world I have not seen before. As for you, Louis, wake up! I thought we had something good between us, yet you seem to be living in your own little secret world. Well, here is a little secret for you which I was hoping to celebrate with you, I am carrying your child."

This news about Victoria's pregnancy changed the mood of the room, and Louis immediately stood up from where he sat on the bed because the words Victoria spoke both shocked but also delighted him. "Honey, which is great..." Victoria immediately shot up her hand to silence Louis, and her disdain for him was blatantly obvious. "I don't want to hear it, Louis; your words are meaningless as it is obvious you have been living a lie with me for a long time." Louis threw his hands up in the air in frustration, and in his intoxicated state, it was as if he was back in the schoolyard under attack from Jose. His patience broke, and for the first time in his relationship with his wife, Louis raised his voice in anger. "Okay!! What do you want me to say? Sorry!! Well, I am not sorry, Victoria; I am not sorry because I have nothing to be sorry about. You live in the sweet little life I have made for you in Sydney oblivious to the stresses and pressure I live under every day of my life. So, I am sorry if in your mind I have let you down, but I have not let anybody down in this relationship; I have not screwed another person, and if all I do is have a little bit of cocaine, then Victoria, I am not such a bad person."

Victoria could not believe how self-righteous her husband was, and she looked at him for almost a minute, hoping he would reveal the old Louis, the Louis she fell in love with. The silence was deafening, but in the end, all Victoria saw before her was the stubborn demeanour of a drug-addicted man looking back at her, and the Louis she fell in love with had been replaced by a greedy and drug-addicted man. "Okay, Louis, I understand. This is the way we are to live our lives. But I am carrying your child, and I shall continue to live in this fake world your uncle created for you and, yes, I will not tell a soul. I just hope, no, no, no, I wish that someday you will wake to yourself. Otherwise, now I just want to be left alone; please just leave me alone." With those words, Victoria rolled back into bed. Louis looked at his wife for minutes, and he could hear her crying, but he did not go over to comfort her. Instead, Louis lay on the luxurious lounge in their hotel suite, his mind stewing on the events of the last four hours. "I'm going to be a dad! Why didn't she tell me the news sooner than now." With that final self-righteous thought, he then drifted off to sleep.

With Louis and Victoria unceremoniously ejected from the Naylor household, it would be just Tony and Tiff remaining at the villa. Because of Tony's work commitments, they had flown in late to Los Angeles the previous afternoon to then be confronted by an administrative error in their room at the Los Angeles Airport Marriott was booked by another guest that same evening. Tony had spoken to Naylor and he had offered one of his other spare bedrooms for them to sleep in. Tiff had not wanted to originally stay at the La Villa Contenta, but she reluctantly agreed to do so as premium hotel suites seemed to be fully booked. After experiencing the vulgarity of the Naylor household, both of them wished to leave as early as possible that morning to return to New York at a reasonable time of day. Their limousine arrived at 6.30am and only Larry came to bid them farewell. As the limousine turned onto the Pacific Highway, Tiff immediately broke the silence, and her tone of voice was clear and forthright. "We are not going back to that house for their dinner and orgy ever again, Tony. I have never felt so uncomfortable at a social gathering as I did at that one. Tony, promise me, please, we do not have to ever return to face another freak show."

Tony held his hand up to placate his wife with an affirmative response. He wished to keep his relationship with Naylor on a civil footing, particularly as he and Naylor had been surreptitiously moving some of the offshore income generated from Louis' software plan into their own respective tax haven bank accounts. However, Tony had other matters on his mind for most of that morning. He was thinking about Louis because he was uncertain about him, and he was thinking about where he said he originally came from before moving to Australia. Louis' noticeable inability to promptly recall where he grew up as a child particularly troubled Tony. He could not contain his curiosity. "Do you think Louis was a bit strange?" Tiff looked at him inquisitively because she thought Louis had acted appropriately. "No. Why Would you say such a thing? I thought he was polite, and that wife; wow, born into English nobility, beautiful, intelligent and yes, feisty; that was the best retort to Audrey I have ever witnessed. I think they are both wonderful, Tony. It's Larry and Audrey I am upset with, along with their depraved Californian friends."

Tiff had expressed pure East Coast snobbery but with good reasons about the Naylor household. Tony remained silent as he looked out the Limousine window; he was still pondering, wondering and genuinely concerned about Louis. Tiff could see with her eyes that her husband's mind was preoccupied. "What on earth is wrong, Tony? Do you not like Louis because he is a threat to you?" For Tony, that would be an affirmative, but he did not want to reveal his concerns to his wife. "No, my precious diamond, I am not threatened. I am just thinking about who the right person is to work on deals potentially worth billions of dollars." Tiff looked at Tony for a moment to ensure he was bona fide about his mindset, and then she raised her eyebrows. "You're not trying to suggest that drug smashed conman Naylor would be appropriate? I mean, well, seriously, could you sit him down at lunch in Manhattan, where the table is full of my father's professional colleagues? BMI would be bankrupt in a heartbeat. He relies upon your good name on Wall Street to hold a place of power in that company, and don't you forget that fact, Tony. As for Louis, well, I have only just met him, but he seems respectable to me." Tony mulled over Tiff's words. He nodded his head in agreement and then stared back out the car window. His mind had one question which would not go away. "Who is this Louis Montgomery?"

That same day, Victoria and Louis did not speak. Victoria left the hotel to go shopping and see the sights of Los Angeles. As soon as Victoria left, Louis called Naylor. The telephone discussion was short. "Is there a problem because of your wife?" Louis was immediately angered as it was Naylor's wife who had caused the problem. "My wife Larry? My wife? I think we know whose wife caused the problem here! All my wife did was endure an unsolicited kiss from you, Larry." Naylor snarled like a vicious dog. "Heh! Just remember who the fucking boss around here is! You may be a hot shot, but I am the boss." The telephone conversation went dead; it was as though either person waited for the other to speak; strangely, Naylor gave in and spoke first. "Okay, okay. I don't want to fight with you kid. So here is how it will be. My wife hates your wife and naturally, she now hates you. So, you and I will keep our wives away from us, you don't come near my wife, and I don't want to come near that stuck-up English bitch you are married to." Louis' voice displayed nothing but violent hostility in response. "Heh! Heh! I am not the one married to a lesbian Larry. Just remember that. But, ok, in the circumstances we agree to just work together, no close, happy family." There was a short pause, and then Naylor spoke. "Sure, kid, no happy family, but don't you fuck with me because I would hate to think what the tax office in Australia would say if they received an anonymous tip that a wealthy young upstart was being paid money offshore and not paying his taxes. That would upset your stuck-up wife while you're rotting away in prison." The threat silenced Louis. "Enjoy the next 24 hours in Los Angeles, kid, and I will call you when you are back in Sydney."

The phone hung up, and Louis stood there, silent, still pondering what had occurred; he had not been threatened to that degree since he escaped from

Manhattan. He had been threatened by Naylor, which would now be the fact of his future working life with BMI. Louis had too many real property assets in Australia to lose by fighting Naylor now. He came to a place of reckoning regarding his shareholdings in BMI and, indeed, his long-term future in that company. He had lived by the sword in that company, and he now had to protect his future interests as a father.

Later that evening, Louis and Victoria sat in the business lounge of Los Angeles International, waiting for their flight to take them back to Sydney. Victoria's disposition towards Louis had not changed, and Louis' mind was now working overtime trying to find a way to free himself from Naylor's clutches. He wanted to develop another business plan, one that was so profitable his legacy would always be remembered in the corporate world, and he could sever his ties with Naylor and BMI on his terms. In the meantime, he needed to slowly divest his ownership of his BMI shares just in case Naylor turned on him. He used the private telephone facilities of the business lounge and called his fund manager in the Cayman Islands. Louis gave the order to secretly and slowly divest his shareholding in BMI. He told the fund manager it may take two or three years, but he was determined to divest himself of his shareholding. But then, after this call, Louis' mind began to fixate upon the notion that his intentions to subsequently finalise his career with BMI would be like death for him; his corporate life with BMI had become his life force, and to end it would be akin to him dying. Death. That damn word troubled him as he sat back on the lounge opposite where Victoria was now sitting. An announcement came over the speaker in the business lounge that the flight to Sydney would be delayed by an hour.

The delay added an element of frustration to Louis' mind, and he picked up off the small table in front of him the latest issue of Popular Science to try to distract his thoughts from the present moment. He aimlessly flicked his way through the pages of the Popular Science magazine, but then he stopped when he saw the headline of an article halfway in. 'Immortality' was the headline, and the subject matter immediately seized Louis' attention. The article then proceeded to report the Singapore Government had acquired the services of eminent medical science academics from universities around the planet to now work in a facility in Singapore to commence leading stem cell research, which the scientists believed, with the current financial circumstances available to them may lead to a breakthrough of making a human being immortal in 50 years' time. Immortality! The words rang as a small beacon of hope as Louis' mind tried to quell one of his inner demons. Louis' thoughts embraced the virtues of his corporate life extending beyond BMI. "I can make enough money at BMI to acquire these scientists and to expedite the research so that I shall be immortal." Such a corporate succession plan required Louis to at least double the amount of his current asset holdings or perhaps treble them. Louis would remain committed to BMI, and he now had to devise a future business plan for BMI that would enrich the company and himself. He tore the article out of the magazine; he wanted to become involved in stem cell research.

Later that week, after he and Victoria had returned from Los Angeles, Louis telephoned the scientist in charge of the Singaporean stem cell laboratory, Professor Javier Chandra. During their telephone discussion, Louis asked Professor Chandra, how much money would be required for them to accelerate their scientific research, so that stem cell science could make him immortal within the next decade. Professor Chandra initially thought Louis was joking, but when he realised Louis was serious, he estimated an additional sum of US$150,000,000.00 being invested in their programme over the next few years could achieve the milestone Louis had nominated. Louis then told Professor Chandra he would invest US$200,000,000.00; however, to acquire that sum in cash, he would need a few years to do so, but his investment would be made on the condition, that he would be the first person to be made immortal. Professor Chandra then explained to Louis it would take several years for the Singapore Government to agree to such an investment. They would need to complete their due diligence because it is not that often a millionaire walks into your laboratory and starts donating sums of money.

CHAPTER 31

For the next eight months, life at home for Louis was a roller coaster ride of emotions. Victoria's disappointment with him did not initially subside when they returned to Sydney, but soon, her emotions changed with the hormonal tides of her being in labour. The days varied between his wife being mildly warm towards him and other days of Victoria having nothing but sheer disdain for Louis.

He continued to consume cocaine anywhere save for Leura, but Victoria was too intelligent to be fooled as she could detect the telltale signs of her husband's intoxication. If she had not fallen pregnant, she might have left Louis after the débâcle, which was Los Angeles, but the ignominy of a marriage failure now that she was pregnant and personal embarrassment militated against her taking such a step of separation and divorce. Victoria maintained her composure around friends, but behind closed doors, she would argue bitterly with her husband when she was exasperated with his selfish behaviour. They were sleeping in separate rooms; it appeared to Victoria she was isolated in a cold world.

By late March 1998, Victoria was at her wits end with her life, and she telephoned her father. They had not spoken much since she got married. The Earl had been addressing at that time his emerging difficulties in his life, but he initially spoke in his usual pompous manner even though the butler had told him it was Victoria when he transferred the call to him in his drawing room. "Victoria, it has been a while. How are you?" Victoria did not initially respond to her father, which caused the Earl to become concerned. "Victoria, how are you, my child? Is everything all right down there in the Antipodes?" Victoria paused for a moment to gather her thoughts; she did not wish to reveal her misery about her marriage, but instead, she decided to break the news she should have broken many months beforehand. "Daddy, I am pregnant." The Earl had expected her next words would deliver some form of bad news, but it was to the contrary as this was delightful news. "A grandchild! You clever little girl, you do not know how happy that makes me." Victoria was about to speak, but then she heard the distinct and strange sound of her father sobbing. "Oh, my child, I am so proud of you, but I fear you will not be so proud of me. Firstly, my darling, I am sorry I have been a stranger but..." the Earl's voice broke down again into tears; his daughter's wonderful news had facilitated his mixed emotions to express themselves in anything but an English manner. "Daddy, what is it? What is wrong?"

She was alarmed to hear her father was in such distress. "Speak to me, Daddy." The Earl regained his composure. "I am tremendously in debt to Her Majesty's Revenue Office, my darling, and we may end up losing the estate." Her married life may have some problems, but this was indeed alarming news for Victoria. "How much do you owe, Daddy?" The Earl was trying to maintain his composure. "10 million pounds, and I don't have that money in cash." Victoria was puzzled by the news as her father had always been fiscally responsible. "Daddy, how did this happen?" The folly of his ways was underscored by his shame. "Racehorses, sweetheart. I am afraid my one true weakness has eventually come home to roost." This was not the man she was brought up by, but his finances must be in dire shape for him to express himself so candidly. She had the answer, which she hoped would soothe his mind. "It will be fine, Daddy. Louis and I have plenty of money. The estate does not have to be sold; we shall look after you."

The Earl's dislike for Louis could not be contained, even though his daughter was throwing a life buoy his way. "The Yank, of course, would have plenty of money. Receiving a loan from him? I would not think of it." Victoria and Louis may have been experiencing marital problems, but somewhere in her heart, there was still love. "Be polite, Daddy. Louis is my husband, and he may well be your saviour." There must be a way to circumnavigate her father's pride. "I have an idea, Daddy. How about if we purchased the estate on the basis that we are coming home to live with our child now, but as far as the public was concerned, you would remain the master of the house during your lifetime? Would that solve the problem?" Victoria was just as clever as her husband. "Oh, my little girl, you make me feel so humble, but the estate must be your property, not his. I shall now have a whiskey to toast the imminent arrival of my grandchild to live in our estate." His pride could never be conquered. "Yes, Daddy, I know that. Now relax; I have this all under control." What had started as an exercise to rinse her soul transpired to instead be her duty to save her father's soul; Victoria now bore the burden of further stress she needed to resolve. She then took the necessary steps that day to engage legal representatives.

Louis came home from work late that night, but he had to see Victoria in her bedroom as she had sent him a text message from her cell phone to inform him he must speak to her tonight, no matter what the time may be. She was sitting in her bed reading a novel to consume her time while she waited for her husband to come home, and when she saw him now at this very late hour, she had restrained her hostility. "We need to move, Louis. I need to go home to England to live." This was surprising news for Louis. "What?" Victoria was not perturbed by her husband's response. "My father is in financial trouble, and I need to use some of our money to help him. In return, I shall hold our beneficial interest in his family home, but for the sake of Daddy's reputation, he must remain as the title holder. We can otherwise sort out how our money shall be secured." Now Louis was intrigued; he had never met the Earl, but he knew the man disapproved of him, and now he was being told to save him financially. He accepted the business proposition as he did not care where they lived because of his work's ubiquity. "Right. Fine. How much?" Victoria maintained her composure. "25 million Australian dollars." Louis almost fell backward. "Don't worry, Louis, it is not a gift. We will have our interests protected by the estate, and it will be in my name protected under my father's Will, so there will not be any stamp duty." Louis nodded to recognise his wife's business acumen.

He was working these events over in his mind. This may be an imposition for his plans to move on from BMI, but if he said no, his wife would end up hating him when they had a child on the way, and then there may be a messy divorce. It was too difficult to say no, so he sarcastically consented by asking her the obvious question. "So, I guess this means your father will be living in the same house as us?" Victoria smiled at her husband for the first time in a long time as his reasonableness comforted her. "Yes, but it is a big house." Victoria got out of bed and walked over to Louis, and she hugged him. "Thank you, Louis, this means so much to me." Her touch was unrestrained, but he was still awkward. "I will call the bank tomorrow." He could have stayed in her bedroom there and then, but he told his wife he must return to his home office, where he now slept, to immediately call Naylor to tell him the news. Victoria was relieved for her father's sake, and she hoped England could bring new life to her marriage.

Louis immediately telephoned Naylor to break the news of him moving to England. Louis knew the board would have to approve his moving to England as he would only stay with BMI if the current head executive of the company's London office were removed. His succession plan to leave the company would remain in place, and the success of his final business plan, his corporate masterpiece and stamp of immortality was not contingent on him still working in the Sydney office. If Naylor said no, Louis would have to go to the board himself, but he knew that such a move was attenuated with risk with Naylor's mercurial and threatening nature. They had remained civil despite what had occurred between their wives, particularly as Louis had informed Naylor he was working on a business plan to return immediate profit with very little expense.

Naylor answered the call on the second ringtone. "Louis, how are you, kid?" Louis wanted to cut to the chase. "I am fine, Larry, but I have some business news for you." Naylor sat forward in his chair in his home office. "What is it, kid? Have you made another billion I am not aware of?" Louis smiled to himself. "No, Larry, it is very hard to hide a billion from a billionaire. I have to move to England, Larry; it is a long story, but the short version is that my wife wants to move back home after we have the baby so that she can be near family and old friends." Naylor could infer from Louis' adamant tone of voice that he would lose his biggest asset within the company if he said no. He searched for an answer to remain in control of his human pot of gold.

Then, a moment of inspiration entered Naylor's conniving mind. "No worries, kid. I can sell this to the board because there will not be any change to your income, and we need you in our Manhattan office to look after the company's interest on the East Coast and in Europe while also reducing our costs. That will remove the blood-sucking million pounds a year limey we have in the London office and the welching Spaniard in Manhattan to save us some money. Think you can handle that, kid?" Manhattan was unexpected. "Manhattan?" Naylor was adamant. "Yes, kid, cheesesteak, big skyscrapers, the big fucking Apple. Manhattan. Have you got something against Manhattan?" Louis was quiet for a moment, lost in his thoughts. "Kid?" Louis came to his senses. "Larry, I am moving to England, not to America. How am I meant to be the head of the East of America and Europe if I am living in England but working in the Manhattan office? How can I look after Europe if I am working in Manhattan? How could the board accept such a proposal? How could my wife accept it?" Louis was right, and Naylor knew it. "Okay, kid, I hear you. I will tell you how we can make this work. How about you do two days a week in Manhattan and two days in London? If I need you in Los Angeles, you can fly over from Manhattan and then spend more time in London the following week?"

Louis thought about the compromise for a moment. He hated aeroplanes, but cocaine helped him cope with flights. Victoria would probably accept any proposal as long as her father's reputation was maintained. He knew that he, too, had to compromise his position because his final business proposal would likely require the company's vast wealth. "That may work, Larry. Tell me, how are we going to manage the travel time? That will work out to be an extra two or perhaps three days I am missing from Manhattan if I have to work in Los Angeles?" Naylor laughed out loud down the line. "Oh, kid, you are so bright but have you ever heard of the fucking Concorde? Three hours from London to New York. Some people spend their entire working day travelling to work and back home in their cars for that amount of time. So, what do you say, kid? If you want to leave Australia and live in England, then there will have to be some compromise from you."

Louis knew Naylor was right. He could keep Victoria happy in the meantime and deliver his business masterpiece. "Okay, Larry, we have a deal. You can tell the board." There was one last command from Naylor. "Ring Tony in New York before midday, his time, today, and let him know you are coming to work out of the Manhattan office. I'm speaking to him at 3.00pm his time, but it's better if he hears from you first to reassure him his position as the top finance or money man will remain in place. You're going to have to work around him more often, kid, and I tell you, he is a precious little mother; if he weren't considered to be a god on Wall Street, I would have thrown him out of the office long ago." Naylor then hung up the telephone.

Louis sat still for a moment as his head began to race. He had not considered Tony's presence in the Manhattan office, but that might be fine as long as Louis did not say anything to alert his suspicion. He suspected Victoria may grow tired of him travelling to New York each week with a young child to care for, and it would also deprive him of his time with his newborn child. Manhattan troubled him now as all of the memories of his life in that city were being played out in his mind. His mind was also consumed with his strategy after he had left BMI, to start his new business enterprise of seeking to expedite the process of stem cell medical research to prolong human life. All of these conflicting issues became too much for him, and he needed some cocaine. He did not disturb Victoria. Louis drove as fast as he could back to his Sydney office. When he walked into his office, he retrieved his cocaine box, which was hidden in his office safe, before his mind decompensated. He snorted down a line of cocaine and reclined back in his chair. He closed his eyes as its intoxicating effects worked on his troubled mind, and he now rapidly processed in his mind how he would make this complicated life of his work, notwithstanding his concerns about Manhattan. By midnight, he had fallen asleep in his office chair because he was too tired to stay awake, even though it was now 7.00am in Manhattan.

When he subsequently awoke in his office chair, it was 4.00am in Sydney, and he had told Naylor he would call Tony before midday in New York. He had to call Tony because his ability to raise funds was needed for Louis' business plan, and it was Louis who would have to assuage the man's ego. He picked up his mobile telephone and called Tony's direct line in the Manhattan office. After three rings, it was answered. "Hello, Tony speaking." Louis thought being upbeat and playful was the order of the day, so that Tony could feel at ease. "Tony, it's Louis. How are you doing today?" Tony did not find comfort in confected positivity. "I'm fine." His salutation in response to Louis emanated from Tony's uncertainty about him. "How are you?" Louis was not perturbed by Tony's tone of voice. "I'm fine, Tony. I have some wonderful news." Louis waited, to see if the fish had taken the bait. "What's that?" Tony was not in the mood for trivial telephone conversations. "I am being transferred from Sydney to Manhattan. I will be working with you. Isn't that great? Manhattan! The people back in my old stamping ground of New Adams would not believe me if I told them."

Tony was immediately silent, but Louis had not comprehended his error. "Didn't you say at Larry's party you grew up in New Bedford?" Louis' heart started pounding in fear of Tony and he was also angry at himself as his mind scrambled to provide a cogent explanation for his error. "I was born in New Adams, but my folks moved to New Bedford so that my Dad could find work." It was almost convincing, and he was spared from further interrogation by Tony because his interrogator had to take another telephone call he was waiting on. "I have to take another call, Louis; this is an important call coming." Louis thought he covered his mistake well as he drifted back off to sleep in his office chair for another three hours. Thousands of kilometres away in Manhattan, Tony looked at the telephone, before taking the call his personal assistant had held for him; he was suspicious about Louis' explanation, but the exigencies of business thereafter had greater priority in his life. Tony's suspicion of any person was fed by his fear; a fear that one day his carefully crafted world of living a lie would be exposed. Ironically, he did not realise Louis was a pea in Tony's same pod. Later that afternoon in Manhattan, a quorum of the board members of BMI acquiesced to Naylor's demand, and Louis' new work arrangements were agreed to even though Tony was hesitant about Louis overseeing such a vast area of corporate territory.

That night, Victoria was not happy to hear Louis' news about him travelling to Manhattan each week. She asked him to leave BMI because they had more than enough money. But Louis could not agree to that. He had not and would not tell his wife about Naylor's threat, which accompanied Louis' further act of deception in his failure to tell her about the Caymans Island bank account. He was also now invested in his final business plan for BMI, which would free him from the company and allow Naylor to pursue his own business needs while concomitantly subduing his inner demons. Louis' stubbornness prevailed over his wife's plea for him to reconsider his agreement with Naylor. Victoria was very unhappy with Louis. She kept her word and never revealed his past. She had been patient with long work hours. She had even endured the thought of him returning to Los Angeles after witnessing the drugs and other depravity. Victoria had hope last night, but tonight, she walked away from him to go to bed, believing she had lost the man she had fallen in love with.

CHAPTER 32

On the 16th of April 1998, Louis sat in his office in Sydney, looking out over the harbour, pondering how to best achieve the outcome of his final business plan he could take to Naylor and the board of BMI. He had informed Naylor that his plan was to take advantage of the crude oil suppliers who were suffering as the price per barrel had declined since January 1997 by $17.00, or almost 35% of its January 1997 price. Still, Louis believed the price per barrel would not see the price floor until June or July of 1998 after experiencing what he forecasted should be a further 25% drop in price. It was after the barrel reached the floor that opportunities would open up for BMI to take advantage of the less fiscally secure well owners who had suffered 17 months of rapidly diminishing gross income.

Naylor would say to Louis that this is all fine, but where is the quick and low-expense profit? His civil business interaction with Naylor had not changed, but he was still on guard for his mercurial change of heart, and because he did not trust Naylor, Louis still maintained the steady, slow, and secretive divestment of his BMI shares. Louis looked at the world globe in his office, searching for inspiration for a plan in the oil space, so he spun it around and around so that he could look down upon the Middle East region of the globe. Louis looked at the globe longer and longer, and then, like a bolt of lightning in his mind, he sat back and realised how he could deliver his masterpiece. "Arabian oil." They were words that shot through Louis' mind like a thunderbolt.

Louis had some people he could talk to who were high up in the ranks of the US Department of State, so he was not concerned about being granted access to any one of those countries save for Iran. His telephone rang, and he pressed the answer button, believing the call had been screened by his personal assistant. "Yes." It was Victoria calling him. "Louis? Oh, Louis, thank goodness it is you. I am in labour, and I have called an ambulance. Please come quickly." Louis did not respond for many seconds as his child was not expected to be born for another week; Victoria broke the silence. "Louis, did you hear me? I am in labour. I need you now!" The last crack of Victoria's voice down the line of

Louis' cell phone woke him up because it was a cry of desperation. "Of course, honey. I will leave now." Victoria's voice responded with a genuine plea. "Please do, Louis; I want you to be present for the birth of our child. I have called an ambulance, as my contractions are running very close together. I am going to St Vincent's maternity ward, Louis. Come quickly." Louis paused slightly; he had taken cocaine that day in his office since he arrived at 3.00am, but he worked that out of his system in the past eight hours. "Yes, honey, I will be there."

Louis hung up the telephone. His heart was pumping blood very hard as his mind tried to find clarity. "One more line, one more line before I go." Louis went to his office safe, and took out his cocaine box. He laid out one line of the drug and snorted it clinically down. He fell back into his chair in a comatose state, and he went off into a drugged sleep.

The telephone in Louis' office rang and rang. Like a thunderbolt through his head, the sound woke up Louis from his drug-induced unconscious slumber. Louis wiped his eyes and picked up the receiver. "Yes." Then, his ears were filled with the panicking voice of his young personal assistant. "Louis, the doctors have asked that you get to the hospital immediately at the request of your wife. She is giving birth as we speak." Louis' heart almost stopped beating as his last memory was that he had to be at St Vincent's post haste, and now it seemed as though he had missed the window of opportunity to witness the birth of his child. Without hesitation, he then raced down to the car park and jumped into his Porsche 911. Louis roared out of the driveway and turned onto Miller Street. He turned onto the Warringah Freeway, and pushed his foot hard into the accelerator pedal, and, as his car entered the tunnel the speedometer hit 200kmh an hour. As he drove at this furious speed, deep down, Louis knew that he had missed his window, and by virtue of that failure, he would have disappointed his wife. He was weaving through the traffic and causing alarm for the other motorists as he sped through the highway under Sydney Harbour. As he came out onto the South Shore end of the tunnel, Louis hoped that he had beaten the clock. A voice inside his head broke this illusion. "Not likely, you idiot." The drive to St Vincent's only took Louis another ten minutes until he had parked his car. As Louis alighted from his vehicle, he took a deep breath; he was about to meet his child, but at the same time, he would be met by the eyes of his disappointed wife.

Louis entered St Vincent's and walked to the main reception. His eyes were on fire, and his heart was beating at a very fast rate. Even though it was April, sweat was dripping from his body. Louis walked to the reception desk. He gained the attention of the young lady working at the desk. "Excuse me, ma'am, my wife has been admitted here today." The young girl held up her hand in protest. "Excuse me, sir, I am serving other people; wait your turn." Louis had to get to his wife for the sake of his marriage, let alone see his newborn child. "Excuse me, ma'am, you don't understand..." The young lady's shrill tone interrupted Louis midsentence. "Excuse me, sir, you do not understand. I am serving other people." Like the snap of a stick in his mind, Louis exploded with energy. "No! You don't understand!! My wife is either giving birth to my child or has given birth. I need to know where she is now! Now, sorry, but get onto that computer and tell me where my goddamn wife is! Please!" Louis' final words seemed to echo around the reception and out into the hallways of the entrance of the hospital. The young lady was startled, but she regained herself and quickly focused on the computer screen. "Excuse me." The woman who was being served gave Louis a dirty look and then looked back towards the young receptionist. "That is fine; some of us have manners." The young girl obtained Louis' details and looked up where Victoria was in the hospital. "Maternity ward, 2b, walk down the foyer and take the first lifts on your right. Your daughter is in the nursery." Daughter! Louis and Victoria had not even tried to find out the sex of their child, yet here he was, finding out from the receptionist about the sex of his child.

Louis raced out of the lift and walked briskly down the hallway of ward 2b. He found a nurse casually strolling the hallway, and he grabbed her by the arm, startling the young lady. "Excuse me, ma'am, but my wife is in this ward, Victoria Montgomery. She has just given birth to our child." Almost as though the young nurse was expecting Louis, she pulled her arm free from his grip. "Sir, your wife is in room 19, just another ten metres down from us. However, Mr Montgomery, did you say she just gave birth? Your daughter was born two hours ago." Louis' heart froze; he had been in such a drug-induced sleep that he had not only missed the birth of his child, but he had also missed her first few hours of life. He walked down towards room 19, and Louis' heart sank deep into the cavity of his chest, disappointed in himself and his sorrow.

As he entered the room, Louis immediately caught sight of Victoria, and she was glowing in the radiance of the beauty of being a new mother, but his presence changed her demeanour immediately to sorrow. An old maternity matron was tending to Victoria, but her presence did not matter to this new mother. Victoria looked at Louis, and more tears welled up in her eyes. "Louis? Where were you? This was meant to be our special moment. Why are you late?" The disappointment and simmering anger in his wife's voice could not be contained. The old matron gave Louis a half-disapproving glance. "I am sorry. I got detained." Louis' response was a feeble explanation. "Detained? Detained?!" Victoria looked into her husband's eyes. She did not need to look for too long because his eyeballs were red and indicative of intoxication. "Detained! I understand, Louis, that you were detained by your goddamn drugs!" The old matron left the bedside and quickly glanced at Louis with disdain. "Wait here, sir. I will bring in your daughter." Louis tried to walk towards his wife. Victoria held up her hand to halt him in his path, "No, Louis! I am so angry and disappointed in you. I can't believe you have done this!" Tears began to flow down Victoria's cheeks. Louis once again commenced walking towards Victoria, but she once again held her hand up. "No, Louis, don't. Don't! This was meant to be a special moment, and instead, you have spoilt it because you are nothing but a self-centred, intoxicated and selfish man!" Louis stood still.

What seemed like an eternal pause in time by Louis trying to speak some words, "I'm sorry honey, I am and ..." was interrupted by the doors to the room swinging wide open as the matron wheeled into the hospital crib. Louis immediately felt weak in the knees. There lying before him, sound asleep, was his daughter. She looked so innocent and beautiful. Vulnerable, but at the same time healthy and strong. Louis' heart warmed with delight; his eyes filled with tears, but then his mind turned back towards his wife. Victoria's hostility towards Louis had not subsided. "So, this is your daughter Louis. I only wish you had been here two hours ago." Victoria's words almost matched the words Louis had been thinking. Victoria's next words sealed the disappointment that Louis had in himself. "So, I could not allow our child to live her first few hours without a name. So, I have named her. Meet your daughter, Anastasia Felicia Montgomery." Louis loved the sound of the names. "I so wanted you to be present, Louis, not just for the birth but also for the naming of our child. I know you are caught up in the world of BMI, Naylor and all the indulgences that go with that world. But Louis, for the love of God, this is our family, and you could not get your nose off your table to make it here in time to see your daughter."

Louis watched his wife break down into tears; he walked over and placed his hand on her shoulder. "Don't!" Louis immediately took his hand off her. He stood watching his wife for a minute as she lay there with her back to him. Then, suddenly and violently, Victoria turned towards Louis, and her eyes were still filled with tears. "Do you love me, Louis?" Louis could not believe the words he heard. He walked over towards his wife and grabbed her shoulders with his hands. Louis looked deeply into his wife's eyes; tears welled up in his own eyes as well. "Of course, honey. Of course. I am sorry..." but once again, Victoria interrupted him. "Then you need to get off that rubbish you are inhaling into your body. It is killing you, and more importantly, it is killing us." Louis' honest character took over the conversation. "I wish I could, honey, but, you see, I am an addict. I am an addict both physically and emotionally." Louis' candour shocked his wife. He had not spoken like this before. "What? What is it, Louis?" Victoria detected there was a deeper ingrained pathology in Louis' psyche that was desperately waiting to break out. Louis looked at his wife, wiped his eyes and then covered up the pain in his heart. "Nothing. Nothing, honey."

Louis then got up and walked over to the crib. He leant over and kissed the head of his little daughter. Her little eyes remained closed. "I love you, Anastasia Felicia Montgomery." His whisper did not awaken his infant daughter, but perhaps a seed of love was planted by those tender words. He then looked back towards Victoria. "Give me a moment, honey, and I just need to go outside and think." Louis walked out the door. Victoria started to blame herself. At that moment, the old matron walked in again; her words broke the silence in Victoria's heart. "Don't worry, dear. There are plenty of new mothers here today who have had to put up with selfish men just like him. Welcome to the next stage of marriage." Victoria's head fell back against the pillow. She should have been happy, but an eerie dark cloud was consuming her heart, and, more importantly, anger and abject fear had enveloped her heart.

Louis subsequently brought his wife and newborn daughter home from the hospital three days later. The Mercedes motor vehicle had already been fitted with all the necessary equipment to safely bring Anastasia home. "Home," thought Louis, "but not for long." In about four weeks, they would be moving to England. As the car pulled into the driveway of Leura both Louis and Victoria looked at each other. This home meant so much to them when they purchased it; for Louis, he felt as though he climbed to the top of Australia's business elite. For Victoria, this was a dream home, a little bit of English charm and a place she thought she would raise a child in. As the vehicle pulled up out in front of Leura, two au pairs Louis had hired to assist Victoria came out to assist the couple with the newborn baby. The two au pairs assisted Victoria into the house and took her to the nursery, which had been set up for little Anastasia. The butler assisted Louis with the bags. It should have been a happy occasion, but Louis spent most of the day in his home office while Victoria stayed in the nursery, watching over her child. Few words were spoken between Louis and Victoria that day.

A month after Anastasia was born, the time had come for the journey over to England. They were flying first class on British Airways, so Victoria and Anastasia would be comfortable. Marjorie McCartney had thrown a farewell party for both Victoria and Louis at her home in Vaucluse, and all the people who attended the party were Victoria's friends. Louis was still a very solitary individual. Leura would, in the meantime, remain in Louis' property portfolio as it was his opinion that Australian property prices would significantly increase over the next ten years, and he would wait for the appropriate moment in time to sell the home. As their car approached Sydney Airport, Victoria once again hoped that this change would also bring about a change in her husband. She so wanted back the man she fell in love with all those years beforehand. Louis was not thrilled by the thought of meeting Victoria's father, but he was keen on seeing the family estate, which he had heard so much about and now paid for. The manor house in Lincolnshire would now become Louis' new home.

CHAPTER 33

The British Airways 747 landed smoothly at Heathrow Airport. It had been a long thirty-hour journey with a baby, but as the plane was coming into land Victoria felt a great sense of relief in her heart to be back in her home country. Although they had flown First Class the flight had been a difficult one with a small baby. During the flight Anastasia did not sleep well and she would cry when Victoria wanted to sleep. The cabin crew would check on Victoria to make sure that she was coping. Louis tried to assist his wife during the flight, but he was preoccupied with his work. Victoria did not demand Louis share child minding duties because she knew by the manner in which her husband's head was buried in his work, he probably would not be attentive to his child's needs. Louis had been working on his final business plan for BMI for quite some time, a proposed transaction in the Middle Eastern oil and gas market. He spent a lot of the flight buried in his laptop computer looking at all sides of the transaction. In this rudimentary stage of drafting an initial proposal Louis' preliminary opinion was the transaction may be worth at least $1,000,000,000.00 in profit for BMI of which Louis proposed he should receive 10% of that amount as his commission for his work. As the 747 taxied into Heathrow Airport Louis eventually broke his mind free of the project he had been working on. Victoria looked at her husband as she cuddled Anastasia, and she was sadly resigned to the fact her husband's priorities were his work came first.

Louis had already made arrangements for a car and driver to be waiting for them at Heathrow. He had purchased a Silver Spirit Rolls Royce or, as Louis referred to it at Heathrow the Rolls, for his road journeys in England, a motor vehicle purchase which reflected Louis' inferiority complex. After leaving Heathrow the Rolls drove at a steady pace up the A1 motorway on its way to Lincolnshire. Louis looked out the window to see a landscape which he had never seen before in his life as they passed through Bedford, Cambridgeshire and Peterborough; however, the dull grey skies of England symbolically hung overhead to define the inner dynamics of Louis' mind and the state of his marriage.

Eventually, after a two-hour journey the Rolls turned onto the A607 from Harlaxton Road and made its way towards the Manor. The car then turned into the long driveway and immediately Louis saw the grandeur and sheer magnificence of the manor home. During the time of the arrangements occurring to pay the Earl's debts and Victoria had signed off on the various legal documents, she had shown Louis photos of Harlaxton Manor, but those photos did no justice for just how splendid the stately mansion was as it sat there so proudly in the English countryside. Set in the tranquil surroundings of the rolling hills of woodlands, Harlaxton Manor was a four-story tribute to an era of England when the wealthy-built homes to last through the ages. Constructed of sandstone Harlaxton Manor was a sprawling monument to the finest standards of English architecture and its unique design included several turrets poking up out of the roof of the home like miniature towers. Louis was impressed with the home, but he now wondered what sort of reception he would receive from the 'Lord of the Manor'.

The Rolls pulled up out the front of Harlaxton and it was almost like a rehearsed routine that an elderly man dressed in a suit came out and opened the door. The man was not overly tall and was quite thin and his white hair made him look older although his face was not heavily lined. He looked nothing like Victoria and Louis immediately knew that this was not her father, rather he was the Earl's butler. Victoria swung open the backdoor of the Rolls in excitement. "James! James, Daddy didn't tell me that you were still working for him." Victoria gave James a hug, but he was not disposed to hugging her back because being a butler meant he could be touched but not touch back. "Little Victoria, all grown up now I see." James then turned to the car and laid eyes on the 'American' the Earl had been talking about for many years. Louis was unbuckling Anastasia and James in his natural subservient manner spoke in a respectful manner. "Sir, may I assist you?" Victoria smiled at James' usual polite and professional manner. "James, this is my husband. Louis, this is James. He has looked after Daddy and me since, well since I cannot remember." James nodded at Victoria in appreciation, "Of course Miss Victoria, I was here when your dear late mother walked the halls of this house. Now sir, may I help you with the child?" Louis by this stage had removed Anastasia from the baby seat. He walked over towards James and put out his hand to meet him. "It is fine, I have her. I am Louis, James, you do not have to call me sir." The offer of a handshake took James by surprise, and he was not accustomed to being greeted as an equal. Louis detected James' hesitancy in accepting the handshake and he then pulled his hand away realising that it was not proper protocol to greet the help in this manner. Louis looked up at the fine stone masonry of Harlaxton Manor's glorious front entrance and as he did so in the corner of his eye, he caught sight of a stern looking man looking out the window on the second floor of the manor. "I will get the luggage for both of you, go on now, go inside and see your father. I am sure he will be delighted to see all of you." Louis wondered about that last comment.

Victoria entered the vestibule of Harlaxton like an excited child who was coming home after being away for a long time. Louis followed behind her carrying Anastasia as Victoria walked through the entry to the grand entrance hall of the manor home. Upon entering the entrance hall, the little baby was looking all around her as silverware and mirrors sparkled and artwork tastefully selected over many generations of the Cumberworth family adorned the polished wood lined walls of that grand room. Louis was also captivated by the grandeur of the entrance hall and his eyes feasted on the splendour of the antique furniture, polished wood and fine woven silk rugs upon which some of the furniture sat and as he looked up above the polished wooden stairwell he saw it led up to the first of the other three floors the entrance hall encompassed so that every level of the house could look down onto that grand entrance hall.

Then the Earl appeared for everyone to see as he stood at the top of the first flight of stairs, and he was the same stern looking older man whom Louis had noticed looking out the window only moments earlier. Victoria saw her father and ran up the stairs towards him. "Daddy, Daddy, how I missed you." Victoria raced into the waiting arms of her father. "My little darling, how I missed you too." He hugged his daughter for a good ten seconds while Louis made his way up the stairs holding Anastasia in his arms, which allowed her grandfather to see her little face. Victoria quickly turned towards Louis as he and Anastasia had almost reached the top of the first flight of the staircase. "Oh sorry darling. Daddy this is Louis, and this is your granddaughter, Anastasia." Both the Earl and Louis detected an absence of affection in Victoria's tone when she said the word 'darling.' As Louis stepped onto the landing at the end of the first flight of the stairwell, he extended his right hand out as best he could to greet his father-in-law for the time but almost as though he did not exist the Earl instead reached for Anastasia. "Oh my, she is the spitting image of you and your mother."

Louis still stood there feeling humiliated and angered by the Earl's snubbing of him and Victoria could see the look of anger growing in her husband's eyes;

the Earl had unwittingly engaged one of Louis' inner demons and collateral repercussions were now likely. "Daddy, this is Louis, my husband, please say hello." The Earl half turned his head towards Louis, and he looked at him up and down. "Hello." It was a short, emotionless, and bland salutation that the Earl extended to Louis. The Earl then turned away from Victoria and Louis. He walked down one of the hallways the landing led to triumphantly carrying his infant granddaughter. "Now, you come with your granddad, and I will show you the lovely room James has made up for you my little sweetheart." Victoria turned towards her husband and the look in his eye displayed nothing but sheer contempt for the Earl. "I am sorry, Louis. Please, just be patient, he will come around." Louis half smiled at his wife, but his thoughts were clear. "Why is she protecting that arrogant old son of a bitch?" It was an inauspicious start to the relationship between the two men. The Earl stopped in his tracks and turned back towards Louis. "By the way, some people turned up here yesterday and installed an array of computer equipment in an office for you, just ask James to show you where that room is." Victoria quickly grabbed her husband's arm to try and reassure him that it would be all right, then she turned and hurried down the hall towards her father. "Daddy, come back here with Anastasia please. What do you mean by a room? Daddy, she sleeps in my room." Victoria pursued after her father as he turned a corner of the hallway that led to another wing of the manor home.

Louis turned around to see James struggling up the stairs with three suitcases of various sizes. He walked towards James as he could not accept the master servant culture of an English butler's life because there were elements of that servitude that he endured when he was made to work at O'Malley's Shed. "Here James, let me help you." James was offended as his training was grounded in fawning servility. "You will not be doing anything of the kind sir, this is my job, not yours. Now, give me one moment and I will show you that office the Earl was talking about." James then continued to walk up the stairs and then he disappeared with the suitcases down the hallway Victoria and the Earl had just walked down, leaving Louis alone to feel isolated from the life within those walls. Louis felt like he suffered an Arctic blast of the cold war which was his marriage. About five minutes later James returned to take Louis to his office but Victoria did not follow in the butler's footsteps.

The office was located at the eastern most wing of the manor home, overlooking the grounds of the Italian Garden. James ushered Louis into the room; it was beautifully furnished, and the walls were all lined with built-in bookcases. In the middle of the room was a large wooden desk where a black-coloured desktop computer sat in the middle of it. "The men who installed the computer said they had some materials for you, sir, and they have apparently stored them in the drawers of the desk. Otherwise, they told me you have all the same login details as you did back in Australia. Oh, and by the way sir, they installed that fake bookcase next to the window and it is actually a fold out bed just in case you need to take a daytime nap." James then quickly left the room. Louis felt like his life had led back to his childhood existence of living in a room of another man's house.

Louis sat in his luxurious leather office chair, and he commenced working at his new home office desk made of the finest Mahogany. Louis turned on the computer and typed in his login details to commence perusing the numerous emails he had received while he was in transit. There was a folder on his desktop screen that was labelled 'BMI'. Louis opened that electronic folder and his existing electronic files which he had in Australia were there for him to access but he had left his laptop computer in the Rolls and that device contained his most recent files of the work he was completing for his final business plan. He was about to get out of the chair to retrieve his laptop when he remembered James had said there were work materials stored in the drawers of the desk. Louis opened several empty desk drawers until he eventually found the "work" material James was referring to. Just like back in Sydney, there was a little wooden box. Louis eagerly opened the box to find something he was craving for, a bag of cocaine and a metal straw. A small typewritten card within the box recorded it as another 'gift' from Naylor. Louis quickly consumed a line of cocaine. Like electricity going through his veins, Louis felt the comforting effect of the drug making its way through his body to relieve his mind, to allay his fears and to sharpen his focus.

A few hours after she had unpacked their bags, fed her newborn baby and then put little Anastasia down in her crib for a sleep Victoria walked around the halls of Harlaxton to check on Louis in his office. When she arrived at the door of his office Victoria saw the mad frenetic pace her husband was working at, not realising he was in the middle of analysing almost 100 years of crude oil trade by the price per barrel and how much financial damage seemed to occur as the price goes up again after a fall. Louis' business plan had also been enlarged to include liquefied natural gas or, as some people in the business community referred to the energy source, gas, because it too was a commodity in which Louis saw the potential for BMI to earn a significant profit from the strategy component of his business plan. He then had to examine when it was best to purchase these smaller oil field and gas extraction businesses, including the associated vertically integrated businesses in those sectors of the oil and gas markets, and the pattern, he was noticing was those smaller oil field operations were more vulnerable when the price per barrel improved after a substantial fall, and when it came to the dynamics of the oil and gas businesses in the Middle East, Louis noticed Qatar had the best asset dynamics in the region because of its reasonably liberal economic policy of permitting foreign investors to purchase interests in all the vertically integrated business operations of its energy market, and the additional factor of Qatar's rivalry with Saudi Arabia due to the country's superior gas field holdings. BMI just needed to purchase 30 or so smaller energy businesses and transfer their assets to a joint venture with a Qatar mid-level energy market company that had diversified its asset holdings to be vertically integrated within Qatar's energy market. That was the purchase side of the plan which required greater finesse to move it forward. Then came the first difficult component; when to buy and who should buy. The emails Louis received contained over two years of price data which meant he had to research a lot of corporate, manufacturing, political and even environmental events which may then answer the why and who questions regarding the company BMI should enter into a joint venture with within Qatar. It was into this hurricane of data analysis she walked, and it was also a pivotal moment in their relationship. "Louis." Initially he did not flinch as he pounded down on his computer keyboard in a mad Amadeus moment of brilliance. "Louis." Now he looked, his blank stare hiding his disappointment it took Victoria four hours to come to his office. "What do you want?" She remained calm, even though the telltale indicia of cocaine addiction were blatantly obvious in his eyes. "Hello darling would be a nice way to be greeted."

Victoria then invaded Louis' space by sitting down on his desk, and she leant on her side and subtly exposed her knee and thigh. "I know it's been hard for you but I thought we could walk to the hayshed and..." Louis promptly cut her off. "I'm too busy, Victoria; data has arrived which I shall have to work on until late tonight." He just turned down her offer for eroticism in the hay. Next, matters of the heart. "Well, if you do not want me at least spend time with your daughter." In Louis' mind, he was focused on presenting to the board arguable statistics that should sway them. "Not now, Victoria. I have to work." Victoria got back down from the desk she laid on to seduce her husband, but he had not accepted her advance and now he would not come and say goodnight to his child. Victoria got off the desk, and she was upset. She stopped at the door hoping Louis would catch her eye and the spark would return but Louis remained face down in his data. Victoria walked away tremendously disappointed with the state her marriage had reached and then she openly wept as she walked past the Earl in the entrance hall. "Victoria? What on earth is wrong?" She turned to face her father and her palpable pain and sorrow were etched all over her face. "Ask my husband, Daddy because I don't know what I am meant to have done wrong in our marriage." The Earl would not tolerate his daughter being mistreated.

Later that afternoon the Earl entered Louis' office on his own. The conversation was short, confronting, and impolite. "What did my daughter do to deserve you as a husband?" The insult within the rhetorical question required a response. "Don't try to intimidate me, sir. Without me she could not have kept this roof over your head!" Pistols at dawn. The Earl looked at Louis with disdain and then he left the office. Louis' immediate thoughts were ironic given what had occurred before in his life. "Hell, get me out of here on a damn plane to New York!"

CHAPTER 34

The Concorde sat in the taxi lanes cooling its heels as it waited to take off, like a supermodel waiting to walk the catwalk. Louis sat in his first-class chair, busily working away on his laptop to otherwise distract his mind from flying on this supersonic firecracker for the first time in his life. Over the past nine days Louis had suffered in the confines of Harlaxton at the hands of a father-in-law who considered an enemy was in his midst.

The trip across the antipodes had not thawed the ice which now encircled the once warm glow of his marriage and within the dark and bleak world of Harlaxton Louis' mind began to decompensate rapidly at the end of that first week. At first his feelings of a lack of self-worth rose up with each day that passed when the Earl would cast his imperious and condescending eye towards him. Then that clock he could not conquer would tick away in his mind late at night as he remained a captive in his home office. When the Rolls would drive to him London and back each day it seemed the graveyards centuries old in time beckoned for him until his worst innermost demon rose up to paralyse his mind with a ferocious onset of death anxiety. He had to work on his masterpiece of a business plan but all he wanted to do deep down inside was escape and run away from Harlaxton, run away from the Earl, run away from Victoria and worst of all to run away from the one life which did bring him comfort, Anastasia. But he would ask himself at 1.00am or even 2.00am how could I leave my newborn child? He couldn't and it was Anastasia that held him by the scruff of the neck so that he did not escape this world.

Louis sat in his first-class seat working furiously away. It was not until the engine of the Concorde fully opened on the runaway that Louis was distracted from his laptop. The sheer force of the acceleration was simultaneously a novelty for Louis, but it also terrified him they would crash, burn and die. After the Concorde had taken off Louis returned to working away on his laptop. In his seat Louis single-mindedly remained focused on the Middle Eastern oil transaction and gas business plan he was trying to draft in a simplified manner for the board to understand as this was a corporate raid in a foreign land that was not particularly receptive to American companies. Louis had to prepare a persuasive business plan for the board members of BMI to buy a mid-tier oil and gas company, accumulate the rights to own interests in oil and gas businesses in Qatar and then offload everything to the highest bidder which Louis was banking on being the Qatar Royal Family. Many local owners of the various vertically integrated oil and gas business interests in Qatar were either on the verge of insolvency or were imminently likely to become insolvent, so Louis' business plan contended BMI needed to promptly undertake the strategy he proposed. Nevertheless, some of those mid-tier families were wealthy and ambitious but were also dangerous people and their feelings regarding Western influences in the Middle East were anything but hospitable.

After considering all the potential options, Louis decided that Zogby Oil would be the appropriate Qatar company to include in his business plan. His research into Zogby Oil was extensive and he discovered Amir Zogby's name given to him by his own people was "the Devil." That was just the type of person Louis wanted to approach in Qatar because the energy market needed to see BMI were ruthless, for the Royal Family of Qatar to feel threatened and intimidated to then pay the money to buy BMI out of Qatar.

While he was working away in the first-class cabin Louis' mind would occasionally turn to his wife and daughter. In his heart, he was missing his infant daughter, and, to a lesser extent, his wife. Since moving to England both Louis and Victoria had moved further apart rather than mending their bridges; he was ignorant about his intractable nature, a corollary of which was she started displaying the worst side of her personality. Notwithstanding the state his marriage was in, Louis believed in the institution of marriage, and they had a daughter to raise until death do they part. Death! There was that demon again within his mind. Then his father's attributes entered his mind, and he pugnaciously blamed his wife for the latest onset of his demons. "She was responsible for me now living a life in which her father could emasculate me. She is the reason why I am now suffering in my mind like this." He had become lost, lost in a world of money and drugs, and the two worlds seemed to be incompatible with one another.

His cocaine addiction was now affecting his mind as the stressful Concorde flight completed its fourth hour. The effects of the line of cocaine he consumed at Harlaxton before he left to travel to Heathrow was now wearing off and his mind now desperately sought another cocaine high which would relieve it from its inner demons. "When I take it my world is free from all these thoughts to just work; I need another line or I am going to go crazy." It was this exact justification for the use of the drug that Louis confirmed in his mind again as the flight captain of the Concorde announced they would soon land at John F. Kennedy International Airport.

It was not possible for Louis to smuggle the drug on board at Heathrow because security at that airport was far too strict. His mind needed relief from this dreaded death anxiety that had returned, relief from his inferiority complex his father caused but which the Earl now manipulated, relief from the frustration he felt about the state of his marriage and life at Harlaxton. In his tortured state his mind thought about the flight captain's announcement and now a further worry entered his mind as it began to focus on the fact he was returning to the city of his tormented childhood. He thought before departing Heathrow that after over 20 years he had moved on from that torment, but Louis was wrong. As the Concorde landed images flashed through his mind from his childhood of his cruel father, the wharf, the shed, and the deaths of so many people including most importantly his uncle. "Why am I doing this? I need cocaine." With that misguided thought about the medicinal powers of cocaine curing his mind Louis finally disembarked from the Concorde onto the skybridge.

As he walked down the skybridge he became wary of his environment. He was living a lie, and his nerves were now boiling away inside of him for fear of his fake passport being discovered, and the fear of someone from his Midtown West life recognising him. The former was an unnecessary drug induced fear because he had travelled through immigration many times in Los Angeles without his documentation causing him problems, but the latter, yes, the latter, may be an issue at any time while he works in Manhattan. Externally he displayed an iron will as he walked down into the immigration area of John F. Kennedy International; however; with the further deleterious effects of his cocaine withdrawal working within his mind his nerves were going to melt down if he had to remain in the public view of New York like this. Fortunately, Louis was still an American citizen but a permanent Australian resident and that meant he would be processed quickly through immigration. Then the decisive moment; he handed over his passport and other documents to the United States Immigration Officer who was a large African American woman with what seemed to be a permanently imprinted scowl on her face. She looked at Louis' documents, then looked at him then she looked at the documents again. She then stamped his passport and ushered Louis through to American soil; part of his anxiety regarding his real identity being revealed dissipated.

He hoped that when he eventually arrived at the Manhattan office Naylor would have supplied him with some cocaine as he was desperate for it. As he walked out into the arrival terminal Louis looked around to try to find his bearings because he was lost. Although he had spent his childhood in Manhattan Louis had never been to John F. Kennedy International before. As his eyes scanned around the terminal, he caught sight of a rotund Caucasian man dressed in a driver's outfit and he held a sign that had Louis' name written on it. Another environmental anxiety for Louis was cured and he walked over to that driver to introduce himself but there was still his desperate need for cocaine eating away at him. He did not know if he could cope with the environment of the Manhattan office without the putative medicinal benefits of cocaine. The driver showed Louis the way outside of the terminal to the car parked in the pickup zone, a black stretch Limousine. Louis entered the back of the car and there sitting on the seat was a small wooden box; Naylor always looked after Louis' addiction because he believed it bought him loyalty. All of Louis' cravings, all his pain and torment were now temporarily gone as he consumed a line of cocaine in the back of that Limousine. His mental focus on his work returned.

Some 40 minutes later Louis had arrived at the Manhattan office of BMI which was located within the heart of the commercial and finance district of Manhattan. The BMI Manhattan office took up floors 75 to 82 of the 100-floor building named $$$, a building name that was an unapologetic celebration of capitalism. $$$ was an elaborate and impressive building that was the international home for major corporations since the 1930s and the name itself, $$$, was illuminated on the very top of the building at night by three individual $ symbols which were lit up in gold light, as a symbol of America's dollar being stabilised by the US Treasury. There was a world of Pleonexia within that building that exuded the 'members only' mantra that people like Tony had created their world around to be part of it and it was also a world that only tolerated Naylor's new money persona in small doses.

When he was a child Louis would look on from a distance and marvel at the sight of the golden glow and now years later, he would work in that building. BMI's presence in this building was more of a credit to Tony than Naylor; he had the East Coast business connections when Larry Naylor approached him years beforehand about raising venture capital to support Louis' first business proposal; Tony had the old money connections when he joined BMI to raise significant venture capital and shareholder investment, and it was Tony who was able to secure the strata title in $$$. As much as Manhattan's 'business high society' found Larry Naylor distasteful it otherwise unequivocally trusted Tony. It was evident to Louis when he walked into $$$ for the first time in his life that it was a tower of power with a ubiquitous corporate reach around the planet.

When the lift doors opened at the reception of BMI on level 75 he could smell the money he had generated to create this corporate empire. The extremely pretty 20 something Latin American receptionist did not even need an introduction, as she had got up out of her chair upon seeing Louis alight from the lift 40 feet away. "Hello, Mr Montgomery, I am Jennifer and we have been waiting for you to arrive." The luxuriously appointed office and the extremely pretty Jennifer left Louis unusually lost for words. He could only nod in response. "Come with me in the lift and I will take you to the board members' level." When they entered the lift Jennifer entered a code on the panel which permitted access to floors 76 and 82, and when they alighted from the lift on level 82 Louis saw just how opulent the offices were for the senior executives like him and the members of the board. Jennifer ushered him into the boardroom and there sitting at the head of the boardroom table like a lizard in the sun was Naylor. "Kid!" That damn name was now wearing thin on Louis. "Welcome to Manhattan, kid. Did you like Jennifer? What a great ass." Louis looked at Naylor and his thoughts expressed his mixed emotions to be back in Manhattan. "Welcome? I wonder how many people in this dirty old town will welcome me."

On this trip to Manhattan, and, indeed his subsequent trips, Louis would keep to known places to try to eliminate the prospects of him encountering any person he knew during his former life in Midtown West. He was also now coming to terms with the fact he had to work with Tony in Manhattan and Louis would lecture his own mind to be careful not to say anything which may arouse Tony's suspicion. Manhattan was a house of cards ready to fall over but he had to persevere because of his greed. The first night of his working life in Manhattan he laid on the hotel bed looking at the brilliant golden lights on the roof of $$$, wondering whether working in Manhattan was the right thing to do. He had consumed another line of cocaine that evening as he had a busy night ahead of him to stay abreast of two significant regions of BMI's corporate interests, and he had to also finalise his initial pitch to the board members regarding his Zogby Oil business plan. Before he opened his laptop computer for the evening Louis spoke briefly to his wife; on this occasion they were civil to one another, but their discussion was mainly about Anastasia. When the call concluded, there were no expressions of affection or missing one another.

The following day the time had come. Louis had to have a face-to-face meeting with Tony that morning before the board of BMI met to listen to Louis' Zogby Oil business plan. He was also having his first face-to-face meeting with Tony since his previous blunder in saying he grew up in New Adams and that blunder troubled him. Louis' prior blunder was still troubling Tony, but he had not as yet made the connection between his past and Louis. Two men living a lie; one knew the real identity of the other, but the other was suspicious in return. It was not an auspicious way for Louis to start such an important meeting with the chief financial officer of BMI. Tony was his usual civil but business savvy self as he listened carefully to Louis about the Zogby Oil business proposal, and he could see there was a path to a fortune by raising the right sources of capital. Tony, in return, then raised leveraging debt for the acquisition of some of the oil and gas assets rather than equity raising by issuing new shares because the board and existing shareholders would not like to dilute their shares. The more they talked about the proposal the more familiarity bred contempt of Louis' better judgment; their interaction was like some of the occasions of dropping off the bags many years beforehand as Tony began to display a less cautious demeanour.

Then Tony raised another angle to acquire some of the oil and gas assets by acquiring the interest in the delinquent debt of some of the lenders to the struggling oil and gas asset holders in Qatar and then foreclosing on the debt. Louis' excitement over the utility of purchasing the debt got the better of his judgment because those insolvent local businesses were the main targets of his plan. Tony was looking out of his office window, his hands were behind his back as he finished explaining how they would use the debt of some of the struggling local businesses to acquire their assets. "Just like a boy from the Bronx." As he finished his final word even Louis realised there was no coming back from his impetuousness. Tony's hands noticeably gripped each other harder behind his back as he restrained himself to not let his fear and anger break the shell around his lie. The ten seconds of silence were excruciating for Louis as he berated himself within his mind. "I am not from the Bronx. Whoever said I was from the Bronx?" Tony began to turn on his heels to face Louis but at that moment Naylor walked into Tony's office to gather them up for the imminent board meeting, his coarse manner cutting the tension that filled the air. Subsequently in the boardroom of BMI Louis displayed his corporate magic as he sold the interim proposal of Zogby Oil to the board. While he was speaking, he could see by the look in Tony's eyes their relationship was extremely strained and it appeared to Louis his impulsive words had made Tony leery. The board liked the proposal and agreed it was a project that warranted further BMI resources being devoted to it. It was time to work up the Zogby Oil proposal into a tangible financial opportunity document to sell to the man himself, Amir Zogby.

After the board meeting Tony's immediate priority was to commence investigating who this person Louis Montgomery really was. Now he needed a favour. Now he needed old Dominico or, 'Dom' as he was known back when they first met in the early 1970s, to do some digging into Louis' life. Dom was the former Deville driver turned private detective who like Antonio had escaped the clutches of prosecution investigations and the hitjobs the henchmen ruthlessly undertook against one another. Tony made a call on his cellphone and his Wall Street voice gave way to his original Bronx accent. "Dom, it's Antonio. Yes, I know it has been a while, but I work Dom. I have a bit of paid work for you, a research job." Dom liked the paid work. "Paid? That is music to my ears." Now the real music for Dom's ears, the amount of paid work involved. "This little job is going to take you a while, Dom, but I think the arrows will eventually point back to our days together in the Bronx. That is what my gut is telling me. The guy I want you to investigate claims he was born in New Bedford, but he subsequently told me he grew up in New Adams. He started in BMI's Sydney office but now he is working here, and in London. He's younger than me, but how much younger I don't really know because I think his identity is made up and before you say it Dom, just like me. How much will this cost?" Dom knew it would take up a lot of his time to do a background check on an Australian come former American, probably a year. "$100,000.00 cash, Tony, and that doesn't include the cost of making him disappear if you also want me to do that for you." $100,000.00 was a lot of money but for Tony the price did not matter when it came to protecting his identity. "Okay, Dom let's do it. I will let you know when I have the cash and be careful, I do not want any of your shit blowing back into my face." That night in his Upper East Side home Tony could only have a half an ear for Tiff's words because of his paranoia about his true self of being just a guinea from the Bronx being exposed to the world. Meanwhile on the other side of Manhattan Louis was melting down with anger at himself in his suite because of an even more serious blunder his drug effected mind had made about Tony. Louis had gained some insight that night to understand that perhaps it was the cocaine that caused his mind to stumble when he met with Tony, but he was afraid that in giving the drug up his mind's inner demons would conquer him.

CHAPTER 35

Time went by quickly for Louis over the next twelve months, as he worked between his home in England, the London Office, the Manhattan office and then Los Angeles. He visited Sydney only once in that time. When he was not managing BMI's affairs in Europe and the East Coast of America Louis had otherwise spent most of the twelve months, developing the business plan, which he believed he could sell to Amir Zogby. BMI had not even approached Zogby Oil in those twelve months and the board were content with the idea that Louis would draft a business plan to introduce them to a world that was wary of American influences becoming involved with their business regime. Louis tried to initially abstain from using cocaine but just as he had feared that night in his hotel room in Manhattan his inner demons consumed his thoughts when they were triggered.

Anastasia was now a toddler walking around the halls of Harlaxton, which was a never-ending playground of new adventures for her to become involved in. The Earl revelled in the presence of his granddaughter because she looked like Victoria's late mother. When her father was home Anastasia's little eyes would light up around him, but Louis' mind was so preoccupied with his work, and there was insufficient time being dedicated by him to his daughter's life. Victoria was not coping with her husband's even more frenetic devotion to his work. She had noticed a change in his demeanour in the first few months that indicated to her trained medical eye he was not under the influence of a drug, but then the indicia of his drug addiction reappeared and Victoria's desperate hope he would become the man she fell in love faded away again. When he was at home Louis would retreat to his office where his work and drugs were always on tap. There was no sexual relationship between Louis and Victoria anymore, and she progressively lost her vain streak regarding her physical presentation. Louis was not eating properly, and his body weight had dropped to a lowly 70 kilograms; he was skin and bone but the desire to make a fortune in the Middle East drove Louis' compromised body.

It was on one of Louis' trips away that Victoria finally vented her spleen to her best friend since childhood, Elizabeth Drysdale. Victoria had remained a stranger to Elizabeth for the first six months of her return to England; however, over the last six months they had rekindled their childhood friendship. Elizabeth knew something was up with her old friend, but it was on this spring morning in 2000 that Victoria finally opened her heart after Elizabeth had travelled to Harlaxton at Victoria's request. The Earl walked Elizabeth to the drawing room, and his words about the state of the marriage between Victoria and Louis concerned Elizabeth as she walked through the vast hallways of Harlaxton. What troubled and saddened Elizabeth the most was that she remembered back to many years beforehand when Louis and Victoria seemed so happy, and how Victoria could not understand completely why the Earl did not want to be part of the wedding.

Elizabeth walked into the drawing room and Victoria's physical presentation alarmed her. The beautiful, striking, and confident woman was replaced by a tense and withdrawn looking person. Gone was the long flowing hair; instead, Victoria wore her hair up in a bun and there was not even a hint of make up to be seen. Anastasia was playing with her toys; she had not even noticed that Elizabeth had entered the drawing room. Victoria stood up when she saw Elizabeth enter the room, they looked at each other for a moment and then Victoria virtually jumped into the arms of her friend for a long overdue friendly and comforting embrace. As they hugged Victoria began to sob. Elizabeth turned her head slightly towards the Earl in deep concern; the Earl nodded back in recognition of the fact that Elizabeth needed to talk to her friend. Anastasia stopped playing with her toys and she began to cry out loud at the sight of her mother being so upset.

Victoria strolled through the Italian Garden with Elizabeth. She had still not previously revealed to Elizabeth the sad state of her marriage, nor did she dare reveal to her the truth regarding who Louis really was. In relation to Louis' past Victoria's word was her word. Deep down there was still a love that she held for Louis, and, of course, she could never allow the Earl to be right. During their stroll she did not even reveal her reason for returning to England was to save Harlaxton from being sold.

She did reveal to Elizabeth how she missed Sydney, particularly the medical community of friends she had left behind. Victoria then told Elizabeth they should sit as she was tired. They sat down on a bench that overlooked a small pond in the gardens and Elizabeth knew her friend was ready to talk, candidly, about the state of her life but needed her reassurance. "So, Vic, I would not be a good friend if I did not say I am worried. If you do not wish to discuss what I am about to ask you that is fine but if you wish to talk, I promise I will not tell a soul." Victoria contemplated Elizabeth's promise and then she nodded to confirm her willingness to talk. "What is going on between you and Louis?" Victoria looked away into a small Magnolia shrub that was in bloom, but the beautiful flowers did not bring any joy to her eyes. Eventually Victoria turned back and looked into her friend's eyes. "Lizzy, my husband is in love with something else." Elizabeth held up her hand to her mouth. "No Lizzy, not a person, a thing." Elizabeth's facial expression changed from shock to confusion. "A thing?" Victoria nodded to affirm her statement. "Yes, a thing. My husband is in love with making money. It is all he thinks about, it is all that he has had time for over the last few years of our marriage. And there is something else".

Victoria could not talk anymore; she turned her head to hide the tears that were welling up in her eyes. Elizabeth pulled her friend's head into her shoulder and rubbed her back for a minute while Victoria sobbed deeply. After half a minute, Victoria lifted her head away from Elizabeth's shoulder. "He is a drug addict Lizzy. He snorts down cocaine fed to him on a tap by his company." Elizabeth could not believe her ears. "What?" Victoria's eyes revealed the torture in her heart, but Elizabeth's desire to discover facts persisted. "Cocaine. Oh, my goodness Vic, how long has this been going on for?" Victoria once again looked at the Magnolia shrub for some moments, as revealing this secret was hard for her, but she then looked back to her friend's now concerned gaze. "Long enough. Long enough to change the man I married. Long enough to drive me into a state of never-ending concern that one day I may walk into a room to find him dead from an overdose." Elizabeth was truly shocked to hear this news about Louis. "That bad?" Victoria nodded her head. "Yes Lizzy, that bad." Elizabeth decided to empower her friend. "Why don't you leave him Vic?" Victoria shook off the question as though it was an inappropriate suggestion. "Leave him Lizzy? How can I leave him? I have had a child to him. Anastasia loves her father. And, and, and I still love him." Elizabeth nodded to confirm she accepted her friends' reasons for staying in the marriage but she was still deeply concerned about Victoria's mental state.

Victoria and Elizabeth continued to talk in earnest that afternoon. They walked through the woodland of the Harlaxton estate with Anastasia, both taking turns from time to time to pick her up as she complained about the distance, they all had walked. It was only a five-hundred-metre walk but for a small child it was as though she was walking ten miles. When they came to the end of the woodland an open plain of grass lay ahead of them for the next 100 metres before the woodland again became a feature of the landscape. Just at the foot of the distant woodland there was an unusual aberration in the landscape; a plot of flowers of various types and that plot was approximately 20 metres in length. Elizabeth had never seen this part of Harlaxton estate before but the sight of it was quite breathtaking in the afternoon light. A hint of a smile appeared on Victoria's face as she gazed out towards those flowers. "My family has kept this flower bed for generations. My mother's ashes are spread here. My grandparents' ashes are spread here. Eventually my ashes will be spread here." Elizabeth was surprised to hear her friend being so fatalistic. "Well, Vic, that will not be for quite some time. You have this beautiful little girl to rear." Victoria stopped gazing at the flowers and returned her gaze towards her friend. "Of course, Lizzy, of course".

Later that afternoon the pair bid each other farewell. The Earl looked out of the window of his bedroom on the second floor of the manor home, and he noticed that his daughter seemed to be unwilling to let her friend leave. As Victoria turned around and looked back at the striking display of Harlaxton, she felt nothing but the sorrow of the empty void of her heart. The Earl could see from looking out the window that his daughter was depressed.

CHAPTER 36

During the northern summer of the year 2000 Louis had finalised the formal proposal for the board of BMI to approve the Zogby Oil proposal. Tony had made some contributions to the formal proposal regarding the machinations of capital raising to leverage debt as opposed to asset manipulation by purchasing debt. He and Louis maintained an artificial demeanour of civility towards one another, but neither one of them trusted the other. Dom continued to assure Tony he was making progress with his inquiries, but it was a difficult job for him because he had to work backwards from Louis' time in Australia.

His formal written plan had been submitted to the board members a fortnight before the scheduled board meeting at BMI's head office in $$$. Louis' plan was simple; Qatar had implemented a transformative vertically integrated economic regime regarding the extraction of its oil and gas reserves, right through to refinement and liquefaction which was ripe for exploitation for a large multinational like BMI, particularly all the non-royal offshore gas interests in its offshore gas reserves. Louis believed exploiting gas businesses was a certainty because Qatar has the world's largest supply of natural gas, and its growth in output of natural gas was anticipated to boom over the next twenty years. When BMI acquired $100,000,000.00 in oil and gas interests it would then acquire Zogby Oil, which was a wealthy, but non-royal, player within the vertically integrated Qatar oil and gas industry. The sudden drop in the international price for a barrel of oil in 1998 left many oil and gas interests in Qatar struggling to pay their debts and taxes, so BMI would be able to manipulate the purchase price or buy debt and threaten the owners with insolvency action.

As long as any overdue taxes and rents were paid, the Qatar Royal Family would not otherwise blink an eye about a multinational company taking over failing companies or buying them out. A new company would be incorporated, in Delaware, and with the ongoing involvement of Amir Zogby the new company would accelerate purchasing larger joint venture interests in Qatar's offshore oil and gas reserves industry, so that the book of assets would be US$1,000,000,000.00. Then the final act, BMI would indirectly threaten the supremacy of the Qatar Royal Family by publicly making enquiries with the Saudi Arabian Royal Family about them purchasing the BMI and Zogby interests which should in turn cause the Qatar royals to offer a premium, of at least US$2,000,000,000.00 to save them from regional embarrassment. Since gaining independence from Britain in 1971, the Qatar Royal Family had permitted a vast number of joint ventures and sub-units in oil and gas extraction through to refinement, and there was immense rivalry between Saudi Arabia and Qatar.

Zogby Oil was the company to use as the bait because the Qatar Royal Family despised Amir Zogby. He was despised because Amir had been selling much of his crude oil at a reduced price to the Saudi Arabian Royal Family in return for a guarantee of purchase, and as a consequence of this arrangement, the Qatar Royal Family received far less revenue. Zogby was protected by the Saudi Arabian Royal Family and the Qatar Royal Family did not have the military resources to fight Saudi Arabia. The worst outcome for BMI in this transaction, if the Qatar Royal Family did not buy out the new company, would be owning a significant interest in an ever-expanding energy industry. Such a daring raid had never been tried before, but Louis had devised a plan the board could accept, as all of them saw the potential for a very good profit. However, then came the bombshell Louis had wrapped up within his own salary and financial interests; he would contribute some of his own financial resources for BMI to immediately commence purchasing these interests in Qatar, in return for an upfront commission of 10% of the more than likely final profit margin of US$1,000,000,000.00, as well as him being reimbursed at that same time the total amount of his contribution of funds to acquire the oil and gas business interests, upon Zogby Oil signing over all of its rights and interests to BMI. To sweeten this offer Louis also offered to forego his rights to his usual corporate salary until the Qatar Royal Family bought out the new company, saving BMI US$10,000,000.00 gross per annum. Louis explained to the board members his proposed offer about using some of his own money and foregoing his rights to a corporate salary was a bona fide statement of his confidence in successfully engineering this audacious deal. Louis' offer surprised everyone in the meeting at first; however, then Naylor shrewdly agreed but only on the basis that he and Louis both worked on this business venture together.

The board members then agreed to both Louis' and Naylor's proposals. Tony objected about him not being involved in the transaction and the whole notion of paying an upfront commission, but the board members did not accept Tony's advice. Ed Fisher, who was the Vice-President for Mergers and Acquisitions on the board, intervened. "Tony, this kid is smarter than all of us. He is smart enough to talk the talk to these people. He should be the main guy in the room over there. Sorry, Tony, it is nothing personal, but Louis has always delivered for this company, and he is backing this deal by using his own money. As for Larry, well he is the founder and our largest shareholder so he should oversee and manage this project. We need you to oversee our usual global financial interests. As I said, sorry, it's not personal." Tony reluctantly acquiesced to the will of the board but deep within him, his suspicion of Louis was now accompanied by jealousy and hate for him. The board of BMI were unanimous in agreeing Louis would be the main negotiator of the Zogby Oil transaction, but Naylor would oversee the project in BMI's 'best interests'. With that resolution being made Tony stormed out of the boardroom.

Immediately after the board meeting, Naylor came into Louis' office. Naylor stared at Louis for a short while without saying a word, which was then followed by a sly grin. "Okay, kid, it seems it will be just you and me. I don't know what you are up to by personally backing this deal, but I am backing you because I stand to make a lot of money as a shareholder. Don't fuck this up or I will fuck you up." With those words being spoken, Naylor turned on his heels and left the room to once again return to his sanctuary in Los Angeles. Louis wondered about Naylor's easy acceptance of his terms, and he was equally mystified about Naylor's motivation for agreeing because of any dividends being distributed to him as BMI's largest shareholder. There was also Tony and Louis was constantly on his guard around him. As for Louis personally contributing some of his own funds, those resources would be accessed from the sale of his remaining BMI shares, as well as some of the funds held in his secret Cayman Island bank account, so Victoria would not need to know.

Later that evening, Louis continued his arduous work duties which now included the Zogby Oil transaction. He took a break to look out the window of his Manhattan office. The full moon was hanging in the sky outside of the office window like a lantern, but due to the extra pollution, it was more red than white as an ominous warning of the dangers which his future may bring him. At that moment, a striking looking woman in her early thirties walked into his office while simultaneously reading a folder of documents. She had long auburn hair and a face that displayed pure East Coast class and beauty. She had meant to walk into the office next to Louis' office, a space that was intermittently used by visiting BMI management staff stationed in other offices around the globe, but in her distracted state she had made a mistake and walked into Louis' office.

Upon realising her mistake, she was apologetic without sacrificing any fibre of natural self-confidence. "Oh, I am sorry. I have walked into the office. That will serve me right for being multifarious." Louis sat up in his chair as he had not been so taken by a woman's presence since he had first laid eyes on Victoria. "That is fine, I was just using the time to relax." The woman smiled; it was a natural, friendly and inviting smile. "Excuse me, I am Annabelle Jones, I work in the Japanese business development team. I am visiting from Tokyo. I arrived earlier today but I have been in a meeting down on level 77 until now." Louis got up out of his chair and walked towards Annabelle. "I am Louis, Louis Montgomery". He held out his hand to shake her hand but instead Annabelle held her right hand up to her mouth in awe. "Oh, my goodness, I know who you are. All of us know who you are. They call you the wonder kid. It is my pleasure to meet you." Louis stood there silent for a moment, the sexual tension between the pair of them was so evident.

Any concerns he may have had about Larry or Tony had disappeared into this strange and enticing sexual lure he found in Annabelle. Eventually Louis spoke, after he had contained himself. "So, are you still working?" Annabelle nodded her head and her movement of it was smooth as she continued to gaze into his eyes. "Yes, I need to link into Japan in a moment for a telephone conference. It will be a very late evening for me tonight." Louis smiled; every word spoken by this lady excited him. "Sure, go ahead. I am going to go back to my hotel room in a moment to continue working, so you will be alone." As she left the room his eyes remained focused on Annabelle and in return she looked back into his eyes and smiled. Louis' heart felt faint, and he had not felt like this for many years. After she left the room Annabelle took some five minutes to come to terms with her encounter with the great man. She too had felt faint in her heart.

Later that night Louis looked out the window of his penthouse hotel room in Manhattan. He had still not ventured anywhere near Midtown West but his view from the hotel looked out onto the distant world of his tortured childhood. He thought about Annabelle for a while and then his mind returned to his wife and child back in England. Louis shook his head to bring himself back to his senses. "What are you thinking, man? You are married and have a child." These guilty thoughts about Annabelle accompanied him as he retired to his bed for the evening. Nevertheless, as Louis lay in bed he could not stop thinking about Annabelle, her beautiful face and slim body were etched in his mind. Louis laid in bed thinking for an hour about Qatar, Lincolnshire, Victoria, Naylor, Annabelle and then eventually briefly before he went off to sleep his dead uncle. How he wished his Uncle Phillip were still alive for him to speak to; as Louis went to sleep, he never felt so lonely in all his life.

The following afternoon Louis returned to England on the Concorde. While he was travelling he started recording with a fountain pen in a notepad his succession plan after he had pulled off the corporate deal of the century. He was going to go out on his own and commence purchasing stem cell research centres around the world. With the investment of his money, Louis was determined to accelerate stem-cell science so he could live forever, and he would sell the opportunities for immortality to other wealthy people. Then for the 97% he would not offer immortality, but instead offer longer lives, in return for increased work hours and productivity for the companies these people worked for, and the payments for their medical enhancement would be derived from funds they may have received as extra salary in return for the increased productivity. There was a business method in this idea, there also was a tremendous exploitation of primal fear.

When he arrived at Harlaxton Manor that evening, it was almost as though it was a ghost town. Initially nobody came out to greet him. Certainly, his wife and daughter were nowhere to be seen. Eventually, James came quickly out through the main entrance, as though he had been caught unawares of Louis' return. "I am sorry, sir. Ms Victoria did not tell me that you are returning today". Louis held up his hand to allay James' fears. "It is okay, James; I was going to return tomorrow but I had nothing left to do in Manhattan. Where is my wife?" James looked up towards the second floor of Harlaxton and his eyes revealed that perhaps all was not well within the house. "She and your daughter are with her father in the upstairs drawing room sir." Louis knew from James' eyes that he had obviously heard words being spoken about him. Louis smiled. "Okay, James, I understand, the in-house constabulary are waiting for me. That is fine, I will deal with them, but do me a favour please?"

James was surprised to hear the word favour being used in relation to his services. "Yes sir?" said James in a pleasantly surprised response. "James, just take me through to my office and let me sleep for the next few hours. If they ask you if I am home just say yes and that I need to sleep. I have had a very busy few days and I need some rest." James nodded his head, although he himself doubted Louis intended to sleep. "Yes, sir." Louis nodded back, then spoke one last time. "James, do me one more favour. Please do not call me sir again. I am a Yank as his lordship so kindly describes me. Call me Louis, you and I are no different." James was initially surprised but then he realised Louis was being quite true to his words. Slowly he responded, the words felt foreign to his servant trained voice. "Yes Louis, thank you, thank you very much." Louis then left and walked towards his office in Harlaxton.

When he entered his office, he closed the door behind him and walked over to his desk. Louis retrieved his little wooden box from the locked drawer of the desk. He lined up two lines of cocaine and snorted them down in quick succession. After ten minutes of coming to terms with the high, Louis then pulled out the day bed in his office. He lay on the day bed thinking about the previous 24 hours. In particular, Louis thought about Annabelle before he fell into an exhausted, drug induced sleep. Early the next morning, Louis gave the order to the Cayman Island trustee to sell down every A class share, at the highest price offered for those shares, and then with the proceeds of the sale of his shares, along with some of the funds held in his existing Cayman Island bank account, transfer the sum of US$50,000,000.00 into a new Cayman Island bank account, to be opened on trust for him, and that new bank account was to be named, 'Louis Montgomery Qatar.'

After speaking to the Cayman Island trustee, Louis then made a telephone call to Professor Chandra, and that government man remembered him, although he thought that initial telephone call was strange. Louis confirmed that he still wished to invest US$200,000,000.00 in the laboratory, but he would not have those funds for perhaps another year. Professor Chandra told Louis to contact him when he had the money, because then the Singapore Government would have to perform a rigorous due diligence on Louis' background.

Tony was finally meeting with Domenico at Coney Island to see what by now was $150,000.00 had bought him. It was a result, but that result did not settle Tony's paranoia, it only entrenched it deeper within him. Domenico handed over a thick file as he sipped an espresso. His next words drove the fear deeper into Tony's heart. "Louis Montgomery is Louis O'Brien. His dead father Joseph O'Brien worked for your uncle. You probably remember him as the kid picking up and dropping off those bags." Tony remained speechless and when he did speak, his surprise was interwoven with his dismay of potentially being exposed at any moment, emotions which were palpable and visibly expressed in every crinkle of his worried forehead. "For $200,000.00 I could have him whacked, never to be seen again. That includes the price to silence the whackers if you are curious." Tony contemplated the idea of a hit job in his head for a moment, but then he shook the idea off for the immediate future because he had no choice, he had to work with Louis until the Qatar deal was done. "I will come back to you if I need you. Thank you, Dom."

Little did either Tony or Dom know that Dom's clumsy stumbling for access to public but restricted documentation came up as a red flag within the alert system of the FBI. The private investigator was now having his tracks investigated by the public investigators. What a mess Manhattan still was.

CHAPTER 37

For the next nine months, Louis' world revolved around the oil and gas fields interests of Qatar which also meant he had to placate the financial concerns of Tony. He knew his comment about the Bronx had heightened Tony's suspicion of him; however, Tony being ever the strategist down to his bootlaces did not reveal the information Dom had provided to him. Neither Louis nor Tony realised Dom's clumsy snooping had caused the FBI to set up a special investigation team that slowly but surely was putting pieces together about everyone; BMI, Naylor, Louis and Tony. Louis still had his general duties to attend to, overseeing the operations of BMI in Europe and the East Coast of the United States. Occasionally he would travel back to Sydney to meet with the directors of BMI Australia.

On one of the occasions when he travelled to Sydney, Louis took his wife and daughter with him. They had sold their final Australian property interest of Leura, not because they needed the money; money was not a problem for them. Leura was sold as the Australian property market was buoyant in Sydney. Leura had been purchased by a Chinese company for twice the price Louis and Victoria had paid for it. Accordingly, Louis and Victoria decided that they would go to Sydney for four nights to stay at Leura for one last time. It was the start of winter in Australia, which for both Louis and Victoria meant the temperature was virtually the same as England. On the plane trip over to Australia, Victoria spent most of her time keeping Anastasia occupied. Louis, on the other hand, remained focused on his laptop. He had spent the previous three weeks in lengthy communications with Amir Zogby. He was now finalising his sales pitch for Amir, the big plan, the business case that would take BMI into the world of Middle East oil money and for Louis, it meant a windfall of a lot of money if it came off.

Victoria had hoped the trip to Sydney would rekindle some fire in their marriage, but she was to be sorely disappointed. Louis spent most of the trip at the Sydney office of BMI. Victoria was left for most days on her own with Anastasia. She would entertain her friends from her time in Sydney, like Victoria, they too were rearing young families and had to put up with their husbands working long hours. There was a difference between her friends' lives and Victoria's life, namely her friends were not having to put up with a drug addict whose sole interest was making as much money as he could in his business life. As Victoria listened to her Australian friends' stories about their family lives, she became angry and resentful towards Louis. Notwithstanding their hours these women's husbands would spend as much time as they possibly had left devoting themselves to their family lives. "Why doesn't my husband spend time with his family like these men do? Is it me? Does he even love his daughter?" All these questions ate away in her mind the more Victoria listened to her friends discuss their lives.

Louis had promised Victoria that he would spend half of the final day in Sydney with her and Anastasia. He promised Victoria he would only spend a few hours in the morning at the Sydney office. Louis was keeping to his promise, he had addressed everything he needed to attend to with the Australian directors. He was just about to step into the lift when he heard the sweet tone of a female voice which he instantly recognised. "Louis Montgomery, fancy you being here in Sydney." Louis turned around on his heels and there before him stood Annabelle Jones. She looked as enchanting as her voice; Annabelle was dressed in a figure-hugging white suit, her blouse was opened to just above her cleavage and her long auburn hair seemed to fall perfectly positioned over her shoulders. Even the fringe of her hair was turned slightly outwards to lure and welcome her male companions. "Hi, what are you doing here?" His delight could not be hidden behind his query. "I am here for the next week for a joint Japan-Australia training conference. And I guess if I may dare, I could ask you the same question." Louis did not know what to say. His heart told him to remain quiet about having his family here with him. His head told him to be honest, with everyone concerned. His heart won out. "Work and personal business. So, what are you doing now?"

She was slightly flattered that he had asked her this question, as she immediately sensed she was being asked to do something other than work. "Well, nothing for the next hour. Then I have another meeting for a few hours." Louis smiled, he knew he had to spend the afternoon with Victoria and Anastasia, but this liaison with Annabelle was only to be for a short while. "Great, how about you come downstairs and have a coffee with me?" Coffee. Annabelle knew that it was more than just coffee, it was an opportunity for her to get to know the hero of the company. "Sure, why not." For the next hour Louis and Annabelle talked over coffee. Louis spent most of the time finding out about her. Annabelle told him that she grew up in the Mid-West of the USA, but went to university at Princeton. She regaled Louis about her life travelling after university. After hanging onto to her every word for over an hour, Louis looked at his watch. He realised he was late for his wife and child, and he had to politely, but quickly, excuse himself. As he walked away from the table of the café he turned and looked at Annabelle; she gave him a warm smile, and it made Louis' heart skip a beat. He drove as quickly as he could back to Leura but the midday traffic in Sydney was busy.

Eventually, after 30 minutes he arrived. Victoria and Anastasia were waiting out the front of the house. Anastasia was excited when she saw her father get out of the car. However, Victoria's eyes displayed the anger which was oozing out of her. "Sorry, work took longer than I expected." A lame explanation. "Work is always taking longer. Work is always first!" Her raised voice made Louis stand still, it even shocked Anastasia. During that afternoon, and into the evening, Victoria eventually calmed down, but she did not have too many words to say to Louis. Instead, she focused on spending time with Anastasia and at least having her husband around their daughter for half a day from work was a privilege. Nevertheless, deep down, she was even more disturbed as it seemed her husband may no longer love her. When they left Australia the next morning, Victoria found herself in a state of complete inner despair, she did not know who this person was who was meant to be her husband.

When they landed at Heathrow it was almost as though for both Louis and Victoria, they had been granted parole from one another. They had hardly talked to each other since leaving Sydney. During the journey back to England they both concentrated on Anastasia's needs. Louis would sleep while Victoria tended to their daughter. Similarly, Victoria would sleep when it was his turn to tend to Anastasia. If they did talk on the flight, it would be about their daughter. Louis had hidden some cocaine inside capsules of a small container that bore a label marked penicillin. His so-called medication satisfied his drug craving for the duration of the flight. Victoria suspected her husband was snorting cocaine when he went to the toilet, she was both concerned and angered by Louis' addiction.

Louis turned on his cellphone as the 747 taxied towards the bay at Heathrow Airport. He saw an SMS that Naylor had sent, which informed him that including the sum of US$50,000,000.00 that Louis had contributed to BMI's reserves the company had just completed stage 1 of the deal by purchasing all up US$100,000,000.00. in oil and gas interests in Qatar. Louis read the words of the second part of the message twice as he could not believe the good news. Naylor's message was simple. "Kid, great news. Zogby Oil has taken the bait. You must fly to Qatar immediately. I will meet you there. Great work kid." Louis knew Victoria would not be happy, he had to immediately leave. He tried to explain the important nature of the business trip. She could not hold back her frustration. "You love your work more than me. You love making money more than you love your family. Go, go because you don't want to be with us." Anastasia started crying out loud as her father was leaving. "Daddy!" Her scream echoed in the terminal as Louis quickly headed to a British Airways counter to book a flight to Doha. Anastasia continued to scream out for her father as he walked towards the escalators, he looked over his shoulder to see his wife looking at him with eyes which displayed sorrow and his daughter crying, holding her little hands towards her father in desperation wishing for him to return. Louis stopped in his tracks, for a brief moment in his head he almost came to his senses to go back to his family, to forget about Qatar. However, Louis' desire to finish this deal, this commercial masterpiece which he had started, to make even more money, all had a greater pull on his destiny than that of his family. He turned and walked onto the escalator, leaving his wife to contend with their extremely upset daughter. Two hours later Louis departed Heathrow on his way to Doha. He worked on his laptop for the first two hours of the flight, but then he fell asleep.

The Rolls Royce pulled into the main drive of Harlaxton. As the car slowly drove up to the main entrance Victoria felt relief, she more than ever needed to see her father. The Earl was waiting at the main entrance door of Harlaxton, he had already been contacted by his daughter from Heathrow to be told the disturbing news about how her husband had left them at the airport. Victoria bounded out of the back seat into her father's arms, sobbing before she had even felt her father's touch. Anastasia saw her mother crying which caused her to break down into uncontrollable crying. The Earl's words were simple. "I gather Australia was not the success you hoped it would be?"

CHAPTER 38

When Louis arrived at Doha Airport, he was suffering withdrawal symptoms. He was now in a Middle Eastern country where a person would be jailed, perhaps even executed, for possessing cocaine. He was sweating and he was nauseous. Even the personnel at immigration were concerned when they saw him, such was his state. Despite his physical presentation Louis otherwise passed through immigration at Doha Airport. As he entered the main terminal, he saw a familiar face as Naylor had arrived some two hours beforehand.

Naylor was concerned by the sight of Louis. "Shit, kid, what happened to you?" He knew because he had caused the problem. "I need some coke, Larry. Please tell me you have some." Naylor put his hand over Louis' mouth. "Quiet, kid, we will have every guard in Qatar all over us if you keep talking like that. Yes, I have got some but shit, kid, look at you! You're a junky!" Naylor was speaking under his breath, but his words conveyed an intense concern about the health of his business colleague. "Come on kid, walk with me to the car, I have some medicine in my bag which will help you". Louis was relieved to hear these words. As their chauffeur driven Limousine slowly drove out of the airport Naylor lined up a line of cocaine for Louis. Naylor had a medical container marked antibiotics which contained capsules of cocaine. They arrived at the entrance of the Sheraton Hotel. Louis made his way to his room; he was sick and tired. Louis knew that he should try to call his wife, but instead he fell asleep on his bed. Back in England Victoria was so hoping the telephone would ring but it did not; her disappointment with Louis could not be contained once again.

About 24 hours later Louis and Naylor met with Amir Zogby at his palatial home in Doha. Tony had sent by email to Louis an electronic dossier of documents to explain how capital for the deal would be raised; Tony had given his imprimatur for the deal and wallets had opened up on Wall Street. Louis had encountered some hard people, but Amir was at a totally different level. He did not trust Americans. They talked about the international oil industry in general for the first 30 minutes with Amir doing most of the talking but then Amir's tone became quite earnest and grave. "So, I have read your proposal, I understand it, but I need you to step me through it. Why do you say you can make my family a lot of money?" Louis looked at Naylor and smiled and he then turned back to look at the hard stare of Amir but there was not the slightest hint of warmth in Amir's eyes. Louis would explain. "Okay, it is simple, the Qatar Royal Family and its 'state' owned Qatar Petroleum control the major oil and gas fields but good people like yourself can still make a lot more money than you presently are by rapid growth within a transformative economic policy agenda which has allowed for too many joint venture partner and sub-unit operators to enter this country's economic system. The sheiks will not like that. By rapid expansion you, us, will own something the royal families of this region will pay a premium to take off us because we're going to offer it for sale to the Saudi Arabian Royal Family, and that will cause the Qatar Royal Family severe panic they are about to be embarrassed in the region. The Qatar Royal Family to save face will offer us a premium to purchase all these interests we have and will acquire."

Amir looked coldly into Louis' eyes. "If I wanted a salesman, I would have gone to fucking Amway. Tell me how we will make money so quickly, I don't want your fucking sales talk!" Amir's final words were full of venom, and it was obvious that he was a man with a zero-tolerance level for sales pitches. "Well, Amir, you have the family ties in this part of the world. You also hold the protection of an agreement with Saudi Arabia they will purchase your crude oil at a reduced price. We have a lot of money. There are many joint venture operators and small business units working in oil fields and gas reserves, and they're still struggling from the large drop in the price per barrel of oil in 1998. There are a lot of oil and gas business interests we can acquire dirt cheap and, together, we can offer a joint venture interest two royal families will pay a premium for. We will buy financially compromised businesses out or throw them out by buying their debt; we will use your family company as the vehicle and our money as the capital. Once we have acquired enough of these smaller operators, we will have an oil and gas field holding to rival or at least concern the Qatar Royal Family. BMI has already purchased $100,000,000.00 in these vertically integrated petroleum and gas interests. Not only does nobody at the top want to watch a competitor to perhaps outgrow them, but also the Qatar Royal Family will not be able to help themselves; they will buy us out for a premium just to maintain the status quo. We can turn your $100,000,000 business into a $500,000,000 profit within a few short months".

Amir still looked at Louis without displaying any emotion in his eyes. "Why? Why do you say we will make so much money?" Louis' face remained unchanged, but inside he was beginning to smile as he knew Amir was just like any other person with money, he was interested in making more. "Because, Amir, there is not a single royal family in the Middle East that wants to see its oil and gas interests sold to a rival, particularly when your rival is the Royal Family of Saudi Arabia, and that's where you come in Amir. You have the business relationship with the Saudi Arabian Royal Family to provide legitimacy to the early discussions about them purchasing BMI's interests. As soon as the Qatar Royal Family hear about the potential for a rival to buy, they will pay twice the book value of our acquisitions to save face." Amir's gaze diverted between looking into Louis' eyes and Naylor's; Amir saw honesty in Louis' eyes whereas Naylor's eyes displayed his snake within.

Amir's gaze fixed again on Louis. "So, you are asking me to gamble? What about the contracts, overheads, taxes, rents and costs? You are asking me to take on all the risk?" Louis' stare did not depart from Amir's eyes, after ten seconds he nodded his head. "Yes, but it is not a hunch. For two years I have been examining the conduct of the royal family in this country. They have billions of dollars Amir, and they are happy to buy out a competitor the moment they start becoming too big for their boots. You mentioned it being a gamble; would you like to know how confident I am in this so-called gamble? $50,000,000.00 of my own money is being invested in this country. As a sign of good faith, I am not drawing my big, fat and lucrative salary of $10,000,000.00 until we have the Qatar Royal Family's pen dropping ink on the agreement. This is what occurred only eighteen months ago with the Hakimi family, and it will happen again. Well, imagine, just imagine how much they will spend if Zogby Oil rapidly grows from its current six oil and gas fields extractions to say fifteen in a very short period? One mention of you, a successful non-royal trading crude oil with Saudi Arabia, the Qatar Royal Family will sell their clothes just to make sure that transaction does not happen."

Amir continued to look at Louis for at least thirty seconds, then he nodded his head in agreement. "Alright, I agree, I am in. But gentlemen, pay attention, if you fuck this up or fuck me over, I will cut your throats! I will blow you out of the skies in that false church you call $$$." The three men talked some more for fifteen minutes and then Naylor and Louis left. In the car on the way back to the Sheraton Naylor let out a massive roar of jubilation. "You are a genius kid; I have never seen such a sales pitch". Louis looked back at Naylor with a grin, but he wondered why Naylor was even here and why Naylor was so comfortable with an obvious succession plan for Louis. Amir's mind was also occupied after that meeting by the manner in which he could surreptitiously mitigate or respond to his risk.

Subsequently, over the next two months, Louis and Naylor visited Doha to monitor how the transition was occurring regarding their $100,000,000.00 purchases for BMI oil and gas interests. The Qatar Royal Family permitted the purchases in return for them receiving any overdue taxes or rents. During this period of BMI acquiring oil and gas interests in Qatar, Louis and Naylor would also occasionally be invited to the Zogby mansion, and Amir during these meetings would be briefed about each interest BMI had acquired.

In April 2001, Amir met with Louis and Naylor to make a proposal of his own. Amir was ready for the formal merger of BMI and Zogby Oil, and then take the final steps which he agreed would result in the Qatar Royal Family paying a premium to buy out their interests. Naylor immediately informed Amir he would have his lawyers draft the written agreement, and Amir's eyes immediately turned to look into Naylor's eyes, to determine if any deception awaited him from Naylor utilising 'his' lawyers for the documentation to be drawn. Louis swiftly interjected to assure Amir they were the company's lawyers, and he was free to engage his own lawyer to consider the agreement. Amir trusted Louis, whereas he had formed the opinion Naylor was a stupid leech in whom good fortune had favoured him by locking his fangs around corporate warriors such as Louis. Then Amir made the announcement neither of the two men were expecting. He wanted the written agreement to be signed here, at his house, and to celebrate the merger he wanted Louis' and Naylor's families to come to Doha to stay at his palatial home for dinner that night with his family. Louis had to agree as he knew that Naylor and his wife would be there, but Louis was not confident that he could persuade his wife to come.

Over the past two months, their marriage had sunk to new low depths. Victoria would not leave the bedroom they were meant to share and any communication between them was conducted via James. There was also another issue that Louis had not revealed to anyone, let alone Naylor. That issue was Annabelle and the ever-growing relationship between her and Louis. Louis would regularly chat with Annabelle electronically over the internet, using their work emails or private chat rooms. By withdrawing into an uncontactable world

Victoria was obviously not privy to the relationship, which was flourishing online between Louis and Annabelle, but she nevertheless suspected something was up. James kept on telling her how upbeat her husband was, and for Victoria this was a sign that something was wrong. For his part Louis went through his usual highs and lows. Louis knew his behaviour in relation to Annabelle was wrong, but in his drugged state he was increasingly losing his grasp on what was wrong and right in his world. He had arranged to meet up with Annabelle in New York on 10 September, that had been arranged on the pretence she would be in that city for a conference at BMI. It was a date that coincidentally would also eventually live in infamy for business reasons.

Tony was subsequently informed by Naylor he was not being invited to the Zogby dinner, and this news enraged Tony, as he felt Louis had further betrayed him by taking all the glory for Tony's hard work raising the capital. Along with his underlying fear of having his past exposed by Louis, this news about his apparent exclusion from the dinner was the final limit. Tony's electronic calendar on his computer also recorded Louis' schedule, and after examining that calendar he telephoned Dom to arrange a hit job on Louis when he was scheduled to return to Manhattan on September 10. They discussed the cost of the hit job, which included how Dom's people would bury Louis in concrete, just like Tony and Dom did with many others back in their days in the Bronx. The FBI had been monitoring Dom's telephone call for his illegal activities accessing government records; now as they listened in on this telephone call, they had a conspiracy to commit murder and perhaps answers for cold case missing persons.

Having hardly spoken to his wife for two months, Louis walked into the bedroom at Harlaxton early one morning after returning from New York. His entrance into the room startled Victoria as she did not expect to see this stranger being her husband. Anastasia was playing on the bed that morning, she had come into the room early from her room across the hall. Victoria did not look well, she had cut her hair short, and she was pale in colour. She still had a beautiful face, but the state of her mind had taken the glow out of her. Anastasia bound off the bed when she saw the stranger who was her father. "Daddy!" Victoria looked at her husband; she still had feelings somewhere in her heart for him, but her mental state was deteriorating, and she displayed a cold exterior. "What do you want?" Louis was initially surprised by Victoria's reaction, but he knew there was a problem in their relationship. "I need you to come to Doha. Our Middle East business partner wants to have a family function, which means our families". Victoria raised an eyebrow. "Our families?" Louis nodded. "Yes, us and the Naylors." Victoria raised her eyes to the ceiling of the bedroom. "Great, I have to put up with that lesbian again, do I? What will it be this time, Louis? Sleeping with her?" Louis was mortified. "Look, I know you do not have a lot of time for me, but I have never behaved in that manner, and I have never asked you to behave in that manner". Victoria smirked; her facial expression portrayed disdain rather than warmth. "So why Doha? What are you and Naylor up to in that part of the world?" The allegation of impropriety had an immediate incendiary effect on Louis. "What is your problem? I am working myself into an early grave for you and Anastasia, so why am I being spoken to in this manner? Why?"

Victoria sat upright in bed; her husband's defiance angered her. "Why? Why, Louis? First, an early grave, well, perhaps if you stopped snorting that garbage the early 'grave' may not be an issue. Secondly, you treat me and Anastasia like strangers, you are hardly ever here, and you ask me why I am so hostile? What is enough for you Louis? You love money more than your family and it seems your greed has an insatiable appetite in your heart. But what about my heart Louis? I kept the secret, so why can't my heart be loved?" Anastasia started crying, the raised voices of her parents had scared her. Louis knew what Victoria was referring to by the secret, namely protecting his fake identity, but he was angered that his wife even broached the subject. "Why are you criticising me, Victoria? I am doing this for my family." Victoria's face curled up in a derisive ball as she looked upon her husband. "Your family? You would not even know what that meant. Alright, I will go to Doha, but if that bitch your friend Naylor is married to tries to come onto me again, I will punch her lights out." With those words being spoken Victoria took Anastasia into her arms and cuddled her.

CHAPTER 39

The Boeing 747 landed at Doha international airport on a Tuesday morning. In first class there were a collection of different and odd people. Nevertheless, there was nothing odder than the one couple in first class on this flight being Victoria and Louis. They had hardly talked to one another during the entire journey. Louis wanted to try and tell his wife that he was confused, that he loved her, but he had met another woman, a woman who talked to him. Victoria wanted to tell her husband that he was a drug addict, that she wanted the man whom she had married to appear again, but she was now afraid of this other man, and more importantly, she was afraid of the influence this new Louis would have on their daughter.

Anastasia had been left behind in England with the Earl and the au pair staff. The little girl had cried incessantly as she watched her mother leave in the car and this was an image that Victoria was still trying to forget, but she could not cut the metaphorical umbilical cord from her daughter. `Later that day the Earl received a telephone call from Marjorie Grace in MI5. When the Earl had been told by Victoria that she was required to go to Doha to meet the Zogby family he could not help himself, he had to check up on who the Zogby family were. Much to his alarm Marjorie informed him the Zogby family were not a nice family at all; yes, they owned oil and gas interests, but the Qatar Royal Family believed the Zogby's had been long involved in international criminal activity. Marjorie then informed the Earl that MI5 could find no evidence, from any sources, that proved this underworld criminal activity extended to BMI's business activities. The news was still alarming for him and the Earl was most insistent. "I must get an urgent but secure message to my daughter! She is en route to Doha as we speak. Please, I need your help." It was not a usual routine matter for MI5 to attend to, but Marjorie believed an exception could be made for a member of the English nobility. "We can assist with that. Which airline is she travelling on and what flight number is it?" The Earl briefly searched his diary note of these details Victoria informed of. "British Airways, flight number B for Brian, A for Albert 8, 1, 2."

As she alighted from the plane onto the skybridge of the airport gate one of the first-class airline stewards took Victoria aside, much to her husband's surprise. "Mrs Montgomery, I have a telegram for you." She was also surprised. "For me? A telegram?" She took the envelope from the steward's hand. Victoria looked at Louis and he shrugged his shoulders to indicate to her to open it. She opened the telegram and commenced to read it; it only took a few seconds for her to become alarmed. The telegram was from her father and its message was blunt. "*My darling daughter, be careful. Your husband whether he knows it or not is mixed up with Middle Eastern criminals. The Zogby family cannot be trusted. The sheik of Qatar has confirmed as much through the secret service channels in this country. Your husband is lost in making money, he may not even know the danger he is in, but I ask that you be careful and return home as soon as you can.*" She was shocked by what she had read but Louis was lost in making money and he did not realise the danger he was in. "Everything okay?" Victoria forced a relaxed smile. "Sure, just a nanny overreacting over our daughter coming down with a cold. I'm sure it is fine." Louis looked at his wife for a moment, then he shrugged his shoulders, turned around and walked towards the main terminal. Victoria walked with him; she remained outwardly calm, but within she was nervous because she knew her father had connections within MI5. She should have told her husband, but she was afraid it may further alienate him to do so.

The Zogby family Rolls Royce was waiting outside of Doha International for Victoria and Louis. Victoria was surprised by the development, which was underway in Doha, buildings were commencing to come out of the ground, buildings of different heights and shapes. There was a sense of excitement in the air, as oil rich families throughout Qatar, whether Royal or not, were beginning to become very wealthy as the price of the barrel of oil continued to appreciate in value.

Eventually, after driving for about 30 minutes, the car pulled into the drive of the Zogby mansion. Victoria was impressed by the tasteful presentation of the exterior of the home. The Rolls Royce pulled up outside the main entrance of the home, and a number of staff came out to open the doors and to attend to the luggage. Walking out behind the staff was a middle aged Middle Eastern man; he had a handsome face, but his eyes displayed nothing but cool, hard evil. Victoria could see this evil within him; she immediately knew who this was, and her thoughts confirmed the contents of her father's telegram. "Amir Zogby, he looks like the devil himself". Behind him was a person Victoria had not seen for several years; he had aged and was a little bit fatter, but he still looked like the same snake she remembered him to be. Her sotto voce remark revealed her disdain. "Oh, my goodness, Larry Naylor".

Louis alighted from the vehicle. "Kid!" Naylor's American accent irritated Zogby and he turned around to glare at him. "Amir, Larry." Louis must have walked six paces before realising he should display some gallantry towards his wife to introduce her to Amir Zogby. Too late, he saw Victoria had already made her way out of the car, so he turned to face Amir as he was Louis' primary focus on this trip. "Amir, meet my wife, Victoria. Victoria, meet Amir." Amir walked over towards Victoria. Despite the fact she had cut her hair, and she did not shine like she had done so many years beforehand, she nevertheless displayed her English upper-class style and Amir was already smitten with her because of her visible class. "Pleasure to meet you." Even though she had her father's telegram ringing alarm bells in her mind, Victoria remained composed as Amir walked towards her, and she held out her hand in the manner which etiquette demanded. Zogby took Victoria's hand and to everyone's surprise, he brought her hand up to his mouth to kiss it without an invitation to do so. Victoria felt a cold chill go up her spine, as though the angel of death had just touched her skin. "Come in, come into my home!" Amir spoke most triumphantly because he knew he was hosting English nobility in his family home.

Victoria walked into the Zogby mansion and Amir eventually ushered Victoria and Louis into his spacious drawing room. There before their eyes was Audrey; it was the first time Victoria and Audrey had been in the same room since that fateful night at the Naylor's dinner party. Audrey was now looking quite thin, old, bronzed and even butch. Her hair was now a tight, short, permed blond crop which made her look more like a male than a female. She stared at Victoria with cold eyes; however, deep down she still had a tremendous sexual desire for her. Standing next to Audrey was a fifty something Middle Eastern woman in whom nature had blessed with a nice face, but her eyes displayed the pain of being married to Zogby. The tone of Amir's voice was more of a command than welcoming. "Meet my wife, Delia. Delia, meet Victoria and Louis". Delia walked towards Victoria and bowed just slightly; her submission surprised Victoria. Delia then turned towards Louis and displayed the same respectful greeting. She did not have the spirit of her husband, then again, none of the visitors knew the torture she had gone through over the years being married to Amir Zogby.

Audrey continued to stare daggers at Victoria while simultaneously desiring her. Victoria displayed her class. "Audrey, so lovely to see you again". Audrey was initially shocked by Victoria's charm, but she remained insincere and cold to hide her lust. "Victoria, fancy meeting up with you in Doha. You have put on a little weight since I last saw you." Victoria raised her eyebrows in disdain. "Audrey, you seem to be looking even more masculine than your husband these days. How are the girls going?" Delia Zogby was surprised as she had never seen two women openly display their apparent hostility like this before. Louis interrupted the standoff between Victoria and Audrey, because he feared the Zogby family would be offended by this type of behaviour. "Good to see you two ladies rekindling your old friendship, now, how about we focus on our guests?" Both Victoria and Audrey looked at Louis with quizzical looks of disbelief on their faces, because they were both being told to essentially shut up. Audrey broke the ice in her usual manner of walking out of the room in disgust, but as she did, she briefly stopped and looked into the eyes of a pretty young servant girl who was bringing refreshments for the guests. Nobody else noticed but there was a spark between Audrey and the servant girl, which also meant Victoria would not be subjected to Audrey's sexual frustration. The rest of the group stood silent for at least half a minute before Naylor broke the silence with an uncharacteristic diplomatic and lighthearted comment. "Good to see the BMI women being themselves". Louis turned and looked at Naylor; he wondered to himself why Naylor was being so diplomatic. Delia commanded the pretty young servant to promptly serve their guests. "Noora, quickly; our guests are waiting!"

After he and his wife were shown to their guest room by Noora, Louis sought the privacy of the en suite. Victoria lay on the bed as she was tired from the flight, as well as being also annoyed with Naylor and his wife. Before she rested, she sent a text message to her father to confirm they were fine and to ask how Anastasia was coping with her being gone. The Earle's short response allayed her concern about her daughter. Louis opened his carry-on toiletry bag from the flight, and he retrieved from it a bottle of Bayer aspirin. It was a made-up bottle of tablets that contained cocaine inside each of the capsules. Drug importation was a capital offence in Qatar, but an addict will risk the danger to feed the habit. He broke open a capsule and snorted it. Louis' mind ran out of control initially with the cocaine rush, but soon after his mind began to focus. This was the meeting that mattered; in two hours he, Naylor and Zogby would meet and sign off on the oil and gas deal he had been working on for the past two years.

Louis' greed for accumulating wealth would also be satisfied as he would now increase his own personal wealth to in excess of US$750,000,000.00 thanks to the healthy commission the board of BMI agreed he should be paid upon Amir Zogby signing the agreement today. Louis would not see any money at the backend of the deal when the Qatar Royal Family hopefully bought out BMI and Zogby, nor did he want to be there as he was now planning to get out of BMI. Louis had not only made enough money out of BMI, but there was also the 'Tony' factor he had to escape from, as his repeated drug induced blunders must have led to that man discovering his true identity. Then there was Annabelle as he had mixed emotions about her because he was a married man. He just could not reveal any of these matters to anyone, especially his wife.

An hour later Louis watched Zogby and Naylor sign the written agreement. The document had been drafted by Naylor's personal lawyers. Zogby had read the document, but he had failed to appreciate the consequences of the clause which allowed all of the funds to be deposited into Naylor's Cayman Island bank account, to then be distributed from that account at the discretion of the account holder or authorised representative. Naylor was the named account holder and Tony was nominated as the authorised representative. Amir Zogby and Larry Naylor signed the agreement on behalf of their respective companies. The agreement had been finalised, and upon Naylor confirming this in an email sent to Tony, the commission would now be paid to Louis. He thought he was now free, but little did Louis realise how much trouble that piece of paper would be. As the agreement was being signed, Amir's secret army of hired killers whom he had previously sent over to Manhattan, had commenced to take care of any 'risk' at $$$, after they had fooled Jennifer into permitting them to access the air conditioning ducts located in the ceilings of BMI's offices for the purpose of 'maintenance'.

Back in Manhattan, Tony ruminated in fury about the extent of Louis' upfront gain; in what would prove to be a decisive fact, Tony then electronically transferred to his account from that same BMI account the hit job funds of a lump sum amount of $200,000.00 he had to subsequently pay in cash to Dom. Had he been thinking clearly, he would have transferred the sum to himself incrementally, but his fear and jealousy of Louis were driving his irrational behaviour. Tony too was a beneficiary of the Zogby Oil deal, but his benefits were far less than Louis' and he had to wait at the backend of the deal.

After Louis received Tony's confirmation the money had been transferred to

Louis' Cayman Island, he called Professor Chandra. The discussion was simple. Louis told the professor he now held in cash the sum of US$200,000,000.00 to invest in Singapore's stem cell research laboratory. Professor Chandra informed Louis the Singapore Government would take at least three to four months to perform their due diligence on Louis, then there would be a further wait until the statute was amended to permit his investment and involvement in the program. Perhaps six months. It was a long wait, but Louis had no other choice than to wait.

Dinner that night at the Zogby mansion was initially a cool tempered affair. Naylor, Zogby, and Louis talked about the oil industry. Delia remained quiet, as she did not dare to join with the men discussing business matters, such was the misogyny she had to endure in that home. Victoria and Audrey continued their cold war of hostile stares and mutual silence; Audrey's somewhat earlier bizarre desire for Victoria quickly turned to frustration which in turn fuelled her hostility. Audrey's sexual appetite had in any event focused on a new, scrumptious dish. During the entire dinner service of entrée, main and dessert Noora discharged her obligatory acts of servitude, and as she did so she would fleetingly see Audrey's eyes looking directly into her eyes, a secret stare of passion she deciphered and found to be seductive to her innocent 21-year-old soul.

After the dessert course had been cleared from the table by Noora, and the men became engrossed with 'business' talk, Delia then explained to Audrey and Victoria that Noora was the daughter of Amir's secretary, and she was a virgin who had been in waiting for marriage, but her husband to be had died in Afghanistan six months ago when he was fighting for a rebel army. Now she was redundant and could only be a servant. A virgin! That information compelled Audrey to leave the table, without excusing herself, as she was now on a mission to find her now irresistible sexual prey. Her departure was not in keeping with custom and Naylor once again proffered an uncharacteristic bit of feeble diplomacy. "Well, I guess my wife has had enough to eat." Amir Zogby looked at Naylor, his eyes displayed their displeasure. "Women do not display such defiance in my household." Victoria's blood pressure immediately rose, but Louis quickly put his hand on his wife's knee to keep her quiet because the back end of the deal had to be completed. This was the first moment of any form of physical contact between them for a long time, but it was not welcome in the circumstances of its submissive intent. Victoria removed her husband's hand from her knee and stood up. She made a point of excusing herself to Delia, who nodded back in approval for her to depart from the table, and with that formality behind her, Victoria made her way to the guestroom to sleep off this misery. Amir's eyes squinted in disapproval because he should have been the member of the table to excuse a guest. "Westerners!"

Audrey had followed her prey into a room far away from the dining room, and she initially stood at the entry to the room looking her in the eye with the same seductive stare. Whilst Noora was appearing to perform a rudimentary act of dusting the shelves in the soft light of this room, inside of herself she was nervous, but also excited, by what Audrey's eyes were offering up to her. Then Audrey performed the final act of seduction by slowly walking up behind Noora as she was pretending to work by dusting a table and Audrey touched her slightly exposed neck with her fingertips; her gentle touch causing that young woman to lose all her inhibitions. She turned her head slowly around and tilted it so that her full lips gently met with Audrey's heavily made-up set. As they softly kissed their lips together, Audrey felt a spark in her heart she had never experienced before; this passion was love. That tender kiss very quickly turned into a passionate open-mouthed frenzy of kissing. They quickly disrobed within the next two minutes and then their mouths started roaming over the other's body while their respective hands squeezed breasts or buttocks. Their passion for one another was intense and Noora's immaculate body became intertwined with Audrey's.

After half an hour of listening to boring stories about her husband's oil and gas industry exploits, even Delia found that she needed to be excused from the table. She was also worried as Noora had not returned to offer tea or coffee to the guests. Although she was a servant to her, the very proper Delia was nevertheless responsible for her welfare. She was not in the kitchen, so Delia had to explore the 50-room mansion to find her. Eventually, on the opposite side of the house to where men were discussing oil, Delia heard the muffled groans of what seemed like pleasure emanating from a rarely used small drawing room. She quietly walked towards the door of the room and as she was about to step into it, she froze in her tracks in shock and then she just as quickly withdrew to a position where she could see, without being easily detected. There before her in the soft light of that room were the naked bodies of Audrey and young Noora, who were both now perspiring because of the frenetic pace of their sexual interaction. Delia felt like screaming out to her husband, but she feared what the repercussions of this would be if he saw this forbidden act. Should she surreptitiously terminate this act of passion and lust to forever protect Noora's reputation? However, as she pondered in her quandary, Delia found herself succumbing to her own feelings of unrequited eroticism. Her heart began to race as she watched Noora positioned on top of Audrey kissing her neck, as their bodies moved in unison together bringing repeated waves of delight. This was a sensual dance a man could never achieve; the two women were uninhibited with each other's bodies but also, they were gentle. Delia's heart raced faster as she suddenly allowed her imagination to place herself in the mix of the lust playing out before her eyes, and she allowed her own touch to satisfy her while she lived in this fantasy. She climaxed in silence, but then she immediately felt immense shame because she had allowed those erotic feelings to flourish, because she had also satisfied herself, an act which she was also forbidden from performing by custom. She quietly closed the door of the room leaving Audrey and Noora to continue in their secret act of lust, which would not conclude for another two hours. Delia raced to the prayer room at the other end of the corridor where she had just sinned. "I will have to tell Amir, but when? How? Will he hit me again?" She had to tell her husband, but this could only occur after she had dismissed Noora from her service, for the young woman's own safety.

In the early hours of the next morning Louis sat on the end of the bed, shaking his head, he looked at the ceiling of the bedroom and fell backwards onto the mattress. Louis' mind was so overtired and slightly intoxicated by the fine single malt he had sipped while listening to Amir's droning voice. He quickly fell asleep and did not take off his trousers and shirt. Victoria awoke shortly after he had fallen asleep, and she looked at her husband; his treatment of her had mortally injured her self-esteem but there was a still chance, what modicum of love remained may blossom again. She could not understand why Louis had displayed such an indifferent state of mind towards her for so many years. Victoria could not sleep, and she wanted some warm milk to comfort and relax her busy mind. Louis could not assist her at this time, so she decided to go in search of the kitchen, wherever that may be.

It was 2.00am. Victoria was lost in the dark rabbit's warren which was the maze of the Zogby home, but at the end of the corridor, she thought she could see some faint light coming from another corridor which was down the end of the one she was now carefully tiptoeing on in the dark. She thought that at this time of night it may be the lights of the kitchen and continued towards that faint light. As she turned the corner to walk down that next corridor she immediately stopped in her tracks, as further down the corridor she saw Delia walk out of the room to stop Audrey, who appeared to be heading Victoria's way.

Noora had left Audrey in that secluded room at about 1.50am, but not before they had one more passionate kiss. Audrey could not believe it; she had finally found love. She had slept with many women in her life, but this was different. Her heart had raced uncontrollably when she was with Noora and now, when the younger woman had left her, Audrey's heart missed her. Audrey finished dressing herself and as she walked out of the room, she was adamant; Larry would have to be told that she wanted to leave him to live with this sweet flower of her heart. As she walked down the corridor Delia emerged from a room, an unexpected event which startled Audrey. "I saw you with her." Audrey was taken aback, but Delia continued to condemn her. "I saw your illegal sexual act in that room with Noora. Leave Noora alone and I will not tell my husband what you did. If you even look at her before you leave, I will tell Amir and he will kill you and your husband!" Delia's final words were venomous, and she stormed back into the prayer room slamming the door behind her.

Audrey felt humiliated, but then she suddenly realised this was not California and for the first time in her life, she felt the terror of potential punishment for acting upon her sexual desire. It would break her heart, but Audrey realised she could not see Noora ever again. She commenced walking down the corridor to return to the room Naylor was drunkenly snoring away within, but then to her further surprise and dismay, she saw Victoria standing there in the darkness and she had heard every word Delia had spoken. Victoria had that condescending English upper-class look on her face as she slowly turned her head from side to side to also condemn Audrey and then, she lifted her chin and turned around, to leave a now demoralised Audrey standing in the dark seething with pure hatred for her. "I will get that bitch! I want her dead!"

All of the guests left the Zogby mansion by 10.00am that morning. Naylor and Audrey had left before 5.00am because of Delia's threat. After all of the guests departed, Delia walked around to the separate quarters for the servants, where Noora was fast asleep after her physically draining sexual interaction with Audrey. Noora did not believe anyone had witnessed her illegal sexual act, and she had crept into her quarters without disturbing the other servants. She had forgotten to set her alarm, and as a consequence of that omission, she failed to attend for her breakfast duties, leaving the other two older servant women to do more work than they should have performed. Delia summoned her in their native tongue to get up out of bed. Within a short time, Noora walked out into the small living area of the servants' quarters and Delia dismissed her from her service, effective immediately. Later that day, Amir would ask his wife why his personal secretary's daughter had been so promptly dismissed. Delia's response was evasive. "I cannot tell you now because I must pray." Amir shrugged his shoulders.

CHAPTER 40

Over the next three months, Louis and Naylor worked on the oil and gas interest deal with Zogby. They would travel to Doha regularly, to oversee the purchase of these new oil and gas interests under the corporate umbrella of the merger of BMI and Zogby Oil, to now be known as ZOI. Naylor's lawyers had arranged for ZOI to be incorporated in the State of Delaware, and ZOI's trading accounts were offshore in the Cayman Islands. It was a mistake on Amir's behalf to agree ZOI's bank accounts should be held in the Cayman Islands, because he was sacrificing his power to control accounts held in Qatar for the cynical purpose of avoiding paying tax.

The acquisition of oil and gas interests in Qatar was as swift as Louis had promised they would be; Louis had been doing a lot of research for almost three years, so he knew the weaknesses of each owner of these oil and gas interests. The activity was not going unnoticed at the Royal Palace in Doha, a new major player was rapidly growing and the only way the Royal family could address the problem was by the power of contemplating a buyout. The international finance papers took an interest in the new company, and they quickly referred to ZOI as the new 'Mover and Sheiker' in the Middle East, a byline that did not impress the Qatar Royal Family. As each month went by the ZOI project acquired many additional oil and gas interests to its holding. Within three months, ZOI's acquisition of oil and gas interests had a threefold increase in these interests and, as predicted, the Sheik of Qatar was now not only aware of the size of the holding, but he was also keen to acquire it.

During those three months Louis' life was chaotic as he also managed the East Coast and Europe, and what time he did get to spend at Harlaxton was invariably consumed by his work. The wall in his marriage seemed to be immoveable, but Louis' greed dispelled any chance of insight on his behalf regarding his contribution to this problem. He would regularly communicate by email with Annabelle, and it was a confusing time for Louis. He was conscious of the fact that he was married, and somewhere in the dark universe of his deteriorating marriage there may be a chance to revitalise it. Louis also realised that if he left Victoria he would be separated from his daughter. Annabelle was just as addictive to Louis' mind as the cocaine without which he could not live. Louis had arranged many months beforehand to meet with Annabelle in New York. There were occasions when he would compose an email to call off the meeting, such was the guilt he felt in relation to betraying his wife and their wedding vows. Just as he was about to press the button to send the email Louis would change his mind as he would think about Annabelle, his mind becoming overwhelmed with the desire to feel her naked body against his body. At night-time he would torture himself as he pictured the image in his mind of the Earl's imperious face condemning him for his infidelity.

By early August 2001, ZOI had accumulated US$1,000,000,000.00 of oil and gas interests in Qatar. ZOI was now the largest non-royal owner of gas and oil interests in Qatar. The next stage of Louis' masterpiece was then completed by ZOI leaking to the international press they were speaking to the Saudi Arabian Royal Family who were interested in buying them out. There had indeed been discussions facilitated by Amir Zogby, who had spoken to one of his contacts working within the bureaucracy of the Saudi Arabian Royal Family's corporate arm, and ZOI then leaked to the international press the details of those discussions after the first news item was reported. Louis and Naylor were working in Doha when both of these news reports were leaked, and the international business media seemed to be permanently stationed outside of ZOI's Doha office, the media reporters were seeking further information regarding what many business commentators believed to be an embarrassment for the Qatar Royal Family, because their vertically integrated system could now be compromised by Saudi Arabian ownership. The members of the Qatar Royal Family were now speaking to their legal representatives. The catch of the day had taken Louis' bait.

It was during early August 2001 that Naylor caught sight of an email Louis had received on his computer from Annabelle, which Louis had inadvertently left open on his computer screen while he was out of ZOI's Doha office. Naylor couldn't resist the temptation of reading it, and he teased Louis when he returned to the office. "So, kid, you finally have come to your senses and are looking elsewhere for a bit of fun?" Louis turned around like a child who had been caught putting his hand in the cookie jar. "What are you talking about, Larry?" Naylor laughed. "Come on, kid, it is me. A good-looking employee from our Tokyo office writes to you to say she is looking forward to your arranged meeting in New York? Come on, kid, I have lived too long not to see a guy about to nail a younger woman." Louis was uneasy about Naylor having any information at his disposal about his private life. "I don't know what you are talking about Larry. This is business."

That night in his hotel suite in Doha, Louis imagined the lascivious nature of his planned sexual liaison with Annabelle, but then images of his wife and daughter entered his mind. Inexplicably he experienced extreme feelings of guilt which then overwhelmed his mind. Just like with his preoccupation with his mortality, Louis found solace in the cocaine Naylor had arranged to be smuggled into Doha. He consumed a line of cocaine in the bathroom of his hotel suite, the marble surface of the hand basin made it easy for Louis to clean the remnants of cocaine away. This brazen offending of Qatar law reflected the chaos in Louis' life, as he single-mindedly pursued the successful completion of his ZOI business plan. His inner demons were presently held at bay as he believed the successful completion of the ZOI transaction would be the first step to him then pursuing immortality in his next business venture.

His cell phone rang while he was in the bathroom and when he retrieved it from his bedside table the screen on the cell phone suggested the call was coming from his office in New York. Louis answered the call. He was still irritated by his guilt. "Yes!" There was a short pause on the other end of the line, then a timid female voice spoke. "I am sorry to interrupt you Mr Montgomery, it is Daphne from our New York office. A man has called, and he said it was very urgent and that you would want to speak to him. He is waiting on the line." Louis waited for the further information, but Daphne was not forthcoming with it. "Well, Daphne I am not a mind reader. Who is it?!" Once again, the abrupt nature of Louis' reply startled the young assistant, and she took a deep breath and then tried to speak as calmly as possible. "He says his name is Wilbur Childe-Harcourt. He says that he is a lawyer from London. He says he is calling on behalf of the Sheik of Qatar. He says he needs to speak to you urgently." Now Louis felt a butterfly in his stomach. He had planned on receiving a call from the Qatar Royal Family and now the plan was coming into fruition. "Put him through."

There was the brief sound of BMIs on hold music and then the calls were connected. "Louis Montgomery speaking, how may I assist you?" Childe-Harcourt's voice was typical of an English lawyer, pompous and arrogant. "Mr Montgomery, Wilbur Childe-Harcourt is my name. I am a partner of Churchill and Brown; you may have heard of us. We are the largest law firm in the United Kingdom." Louis had not heard of them. "I represent the Sheik of Qatar, or the royal family, Mr Montgomery, and my client wishes to buy out all your company's oil and gas interests it holds in Qatar. Are you interested?" As much as Childe-Harcourt's voice irritated Louis of course he was interested. He remained composed. "Go on". It was only a second, but it seemed like an hour when the solicitor responded. "Well, as I explained, my client wishes to buy you out. I propose that we meet in Qatar in one week to hold a round table discussion, to see if a mutually satisfactory deal can be arranged. Shall we say 12 August 2001 at the Royal Palace?" Louis knew the importance of this moment required an immediate commitment. "Fine, I will arrange for all of our people to be there; send me an email with the details." He then hung up the telephone without entering into any idle chatter.

Louis smiled as he felt the satisfaction of his plan playing out in the manner, he had previously perceived. He rang Zogby who proclaimed Louis' virtues in celebratory delight down the telephone line. Louis then rang Naylor. Their discussion was brief, but Naylor seemed to be happy. After Naylor had finished speaking to Louis, he then dialled a telephone number in the Cayman Islands.

One-week later Naylor, Zogby and Louis met with the Sheik and his lawyers at the Royal Palace in Doha. Tony was once again not invited, and his exclusion further entrenched his ill will for Louis. Wilbur Childe-Harcourt was present for this meeting, and he was just as arrogant in person as he was on the telephone; however, Childe-Harcourt's behaviour was ignored on the ZOI side of the bargaining table. It was hard not to be overwhelmed and even Zogby's behaviour was moderated by the importance of the moment, as he revelled in the notion of the Sheik wanting to do business with him. Naylor had gained the approval of the board of BMI to fly his personal legal team over to Doha to act on behalf of the company, since they had previously drawn the contractual documents for this moment. The negotiations took two days to finalise but in the end the Sheik was willing to pay a premium to acquire all of ZOI's oil and gas interests in Qatar. The agreed price of the buyout would result in a net profit of US$2.2 billion dollars for ZOI and it was double the amount Louis had initially contemplated three years beforehand. The agreement was to be kept secret while the Sheik's lawyers performed their usual due diligence, but the Sheik already knew they were oil and gas interests that were too valuable to fall into the hands of the Saudi Arabian Royal Family. The Sheik had saved face with his people, but he was not impressed that it came at the price of further enriching Zogby.

At dinner that night in Doha Louis, Naylor and Zogby enjoyed a splendid feast as each one of them quietly savoured their own personal thoughts of success. Seven days later, when Louis was in the London office of BMI, he received an email from Childe-Harcourt which had also been sent to Naylor's personal legal team. The email confirmed the due diligence clause of the agreement had been satisfied, by virtue of which their client was ready to proceed to settlement and the settlement funds would be electronically transferred to the nominated Cayman Islands bank account. BMI were to provide the details of a date, time and place for settlement.

Louis smiled after he read this email. He had now achieved a goal in his working life which he knew would be his swan song at BMI, and then he was free to pursue his private business plan, to deliver him even greater wealth and immortality. All that remained now was to sort out his private life. After speaking to Naylor's lawyers Louis was able to arrange for the settlement to occur on the morning of 10 September 2001 at BMI's offices in $$$, an arrangement which suited his personal plans of being in Manhattan on that date, when Annabelle would also be working from that office. Louis' mind now wrestled further with the notion of commencing a personal relationship with Annabelle; there was now a legitimate business reason for him to be in Manhattan on this day, but the additional collateral purpose was an illegitimate reason.

As Louis was driven along the A1 that late summer evening, he could not work out what he would do with his personal life. When the Rolls stopped outside of Harlaxton he looked into the nearest window, and there he saw his wife playing with his daughter. "Could I really do this to them?" He then thought about Annabelle; she excited Louis sexually but she also excited him emotionally, as he seemed to not be surrounded by the pretension that was Victoria's world back in England. To complicate his thought processes, his relentless preoccupation with his mortality now entered his mind, as the next business plan to achieve immortality would soon be commencing. Death, desire, and deceit, the three "d" words consumed his thoughts for at least two hours later that night. There was nobody within the house who he could share his thoughts with. That was the state of Louis' misconceived mindset; there was an ear to speak to within Harlaxton, he just needed to open the door of his mind to her.

Over the next two and half weeks there was much work to be done. Louis worked around the clock, and he flew to Doha to meet with Zogby as well as the Sheik's representatives. He exchanged emails with Tony, and although Tony peculiarly requested a personal meeting to occur in Manhattan on the day of settlement, Louis' sole focus was the actual settlement itself. His inner conflicts regarding his personal life had to be compartmentalised during this time of onerous work obligations, as there was simply too much at stake for Louis to be distracted about the conundrum of leaving Victoria for Annabelle. At night in his lonely hotel room in Doha he would try to resolve this inner conflict. His heart was being torn in two directions; however, Louis could not make a clear decision. His arrangement to meet up with Annabelle in New York remained in place, but as each day grew closer the guilt in his mind would grow stronger.

CHAPTER 41

All the necessary steps had been attended to by all of the parties on the morning of 9 September 2001. Louis was working from home that morning, because the Concorde flight to Manhattan from Heathrow was scheduled to depart late in the afternoon. He started the day by consuming a line of cocaine. He was still no closer to resolving in his mind what he was going to do about his personal life. His head was saying to go with Annabelle, but his heart was telling him to stay with his wife and daughter. Louis was finishing a final email for Naylor's legal team; however, his mind was distracted about whether he should cancel his liaison with Annabelle or take that step to open the next unknown chapter of his life.

He saved the email for the lawyers, which he was still settling, and he instead opened on his desktop screen the email chain he had exchanged with Annabelle, which included an email he sent to her the previous night. Louis read through the emails he and Annabelle had exchanged with each other for the past four months, and it was apparent to him that she really wanted him, and him alone, to be in her life. Some of the emails they exchanged would bring a smile to his face when he read them again, but others would confuse him as he thought about his own family. "Do I really want to leave?" Then he would read another email and the obvious mutual display of subtle affection he and Annabelle had for each other, could easily be read between the lines. "My life could be a lot happier with Annabelle, couldn't it?" Louis asked himself this question in his mind as he grappled with the significance of leaving his family for another woman. "I still have some feelings for Victoria? I don't want to hurt her, but does she love me? Can I live with hurting her as well as the risk of losing my daughter?" So many questions went through his mind and no answer made sense, as in his intoxicated state he was not thinking clearly.

After about 30 minutes he was no closer to resolving his inner conflict about Victoria and Annabelle. Louis minimised the email trail rather than closing it, as he was going to return to reading it again when he finished settling his email to the legal team and, in doing so, he would make the final decision that would impact his future relationship with either Annabelle or his wife and daughter. As Louis returned to his work email, he felt a presence next to him in his office. He turned around to see Anastasia standing near his desk and he noticed his daughter had a troubled look on her face. "What is wrong?" Anastasia looked her father in the eye, like she was an adult. "Daddy, why do you make my mummy cry?" Her words were innocent, but nevertheless contained that degree of inquisition that suggested an adult had spoken to her. "Why do you say that Anastasia? I don't make Mummy cry." Anastasia continued looking into her father's eyes. "Poppy told me Mummy always cries because you hurt her Daddy. Why do you make Mummy cry?"

Louis was infuriated by the Earl's conduct, as in his mind it was one matter to be rude to him personally, but it was another matter altogether to poison his child's mind against him. Louis looked into Anastasia's young eyes. Suddenly, the gentle eyes of his daughter strung a chord in his heart, and he became fatherly with Anastasia for the first time in a long time. "Sweetie don't listen to Poppy, he should not..." Louis' words were interrupted by Victoria bursting into the room. She had not seen where Anastasia had gone, and she had become frantic. "There you are Anastasia. You scared Mummy walking off in the house like that."

The sight of Victoria stirred Louis' passions regarding what her father had been up to in poisoning Anastasia's mind against him. Louis stared coldly at his wife; the anger was directed towards her father, but she just happened to be present in the room at this time. "Why are you looking at me like that Louis?" Victoria's defensive tone could not subdue her husband's anger. "It is one thing for you to speak to your father about me, it is another thing altogether for him to try and influence my daughter about me. Tell that old fool to stop poisoning my daughter's mind about me." Louis' tone was short, crisp, and contained enough elements of hostility to spark similar feelings in response from his wife. "What? What are you saying? Don't try to act so self-righteous Louis, as you have not displayed in this house over the past year anything but contempt for me. If my father is saying anything to our daughter, it is not as though it is being said without just cause!" Victoria's agitated tone only incensed Louis. "Hey! She is my daughter as well and legally I also own this house. Just remember who is feathering the nest here!"

Louis' raised voice caused Anastasia to start crying. Victoria took Anastasia into her arms, and she then proceeded to dress Louis down like a school mistress dressing down a wayward child. "All you ever do in the house Louis is cause pain. We could have a lovely family life, but you don't seem to want a family. When was the last time you spent quality time with your daughter? When was the last time you even told me you loved me?" Louis commenced to try to deny that accusation, but Victoria spoke over him. "No Louis, it is true. It is obvious that you do not love your family. In particular, it is obvious that you do not love me anymore. I try to warn you about the people you are mixing with in the Middle East, and you dismiss me. I have kept our secret out of my love for you. I can't take this anymore Louis, just tell me honestly, do you still love me?" Louis looked into his wife's eyes, but he could not find the answer to that question. "I don't have to answer any questions like that in my own house." His inability to confirm his feelings for Victoria caused her eyes to fill with tears.

Anastasia saw her mother commencing to cry and her little voice shot arrows at the heart of Louis. "Daddy, you made my mummy cry. You make Mummy cry. I don't like you, Daddy." Louis could take no more, and he walked out of the room, but in doing so he neglected to turn off his computer. Victoria called out for him causing Louis to stop and turn back towards her. "You didn't even ask me how I felt about you. I know our marriage has been strained Louis but deep down I still love you, and I still pray every day for the man I fell in love with to reappear. Look at me Louis, look at me, I, we, love you. You are mixing with some deadly people out there in that world of BMI, so just remember, you have a family." Victoria continued to cry and she held her daughter tight in her arms as Anastasia was also crying. Deep down in his heart, Louis knew that he should stay at home, but he was now even more confused than ever. However, his head told him to leave now, because the settlement of the ZOI project was looming large in the window and even if he wanted to stay, he couldn't. Louis looked at his wife for a few more moments and then he walked away without saying a word. He walked out into the Italian Gardens, kicking the ground furiously in a rage that could not be subdued.

Half an hour later, Louis returned to his office after he had asked James to make sure the driver of the Rolls was ready to take him to Heathrow in the next five minutes. Victoria and Anastasia had left Louis' office not long after he stormed out. Louis then quickly packed his work travel bag for the trip to Manhattan. "Get me out of here." The words at the forefront of his mind emanated from the state of confusion he was now in. He then walked out of the house to be driven to Heathrow and in doing so, Louis even neglected to say goodbye to his daughter, such was the terrible state of his mindset. He did not even see that Victoria and Anastasia were looking out of a window on the second floor of Harlaxton. Anastasia broke free of her mother's arms when she saw the back door of the Rolls close and she ran down the second floor hallway of Harlaxton calling out for her daddy, but it was too late as the Rolls had now left, leaving in its wake some dust and leaves.

That evening, as Louis flew to New York he fell asleep in the first-class chair of the Concorde. His mind had been filled with confusion after the events which had transpired at Harlaxton that day. His wife's declaration of love surprised him, because Louis had thought those feelings had long gone from Victoria's heart. The sight of his child being so upset with him deeply troubled Louis. He had realised during the flight that he had hardly seen his daughter grow from a baby to now become this almost three-year-old fountain of wisdom, even if it was wisdom implanted by an interfering father-in-law. As he slept Louis had a dream, a taunting yet enlightening dream. Louis dreamt that he was back at Mrs Smith's house and everything in his dream appeared to be like he was living in the 1980s again. As he walked into the old living room of Mrs Smith's house she was sitting there in her chair, staring blankly at him with lifeless eyes. In his dream Louis raced over to the chair and started shaking Mrs Smith to bring her back to life. He shook her violently in his dream. Then, like an arcade game coming to life, Mrs Smith's eyes opened wide, and she looked at Louis. "I look at her and see someone I want to be with in old age, somebody I want to grow old with." The voice was Louis', but the words emanated from Mrs Smith. Her mouth opened again as she got up out of the chair. "I look at her and see someone I want to be with in old age, somebody I want to grow old with. I look at her and see someone I want to be with in old age, somebody I want to grow old with." Louis commenced to try and run away, but then his own voice followed him through the hall of Mrs Smith's house and once again the same words kept on ringing out loud. "I look at her and see someone I want to be with in old age, somebody I want to grow old with."

As Louis' dream continued, he felt he was trapped inside Mrs Smith's old house as the old woman continued to track him down, and just at the moment of the dream when Louis seemed to be cornered, he was awoken by a steward on the Concorde. Louis was still half asleep. "Where am I?" The steward placed a glass of water on his tray. "Sir, you appeared to be having a terrible dream. Is there anything I may get you?" Louis wiped his eyes, looking around him to gain his senses, he saw the concerned looks on the faces of some of the other passengers in the first-class cabin. "Sir, are you alright?" Louis nodded his head in confirmation to the question. "Yes, it is okay, thank you but I don't need anything." The steward looked at Louis for a moment then nodded his head. "Very well, sir, just let me know if you do require something." The steward walked down the aisle to another passenger.

Louis sat in his first-class seat coming to terms with his vivid dream he had just woken up from. Like he was experiencing an epiphany Louis sat up in his chair. He could not believe he had been so stupid for so many years. "I love my wife; I love my daughter. Why didn't I tell her? Why didn't I stay?" He repeated these words in his mind many times before that flight would be over. He knew that he had to save his marriage. He also knew that he could not enter a relationship with Annabelle. He decided he would tell Annabelle their relationship had to remain a business one. He would tell his wife he loved her, that he would give up the drugs, that he was sorry and that he wanted to grow old with her. He wanted to speak to Victoria now, to make his personal life right again. Notwithstanding the great speed which the Concorde was flying, it still could not fly quickly enough for Louis. "I have to get to a telephone." These thoughts of contacting Victoria remained at the forefront of his mind for the rest of that flight.

A storm blew through Harlaxton and the surrounding areas at 11.30pm that evening. The telephone lines had been blown down and it would take the telephone company most of the night to repair the damaged landlines. Victoria had turned off her cell phone earlier that evening, she was in no mood to speak to anybody and she just sat in her bedroom crying after she had put Anastasia to sleep. The Earl had stood outside of Victoria's door listening to his daughter cry. He mistakenly decided to leave her alone as he believed that if his daughter needed him, she would speak to him.

The time in London was approaching midnight and it was approaching 7.00pm in Manhattan. By the time the Concorde landed it would be 8.00pm in Manhattan and Louis would not be processed through immigration until 9.00pm. He believed it would be 2.00am in England when he eventually made his way through immigration. He needed to tell his wife how he felt as soon as that Concorde landed. The next hour felt like an entire day as Louis waited for the Concorde to land. Eventually, when it did land, he immediately turned on his cell phone and attempted to call Victoria's cell phone. The message was clear, Victoria's cell phone was switched off. Louis then tried calling the landline number for Harlaxton, but that number was unavailable. Louis continued to try and call his wife's cell phone again, but it was still turned off. The steward who had assisted Louis when he had his disturbing dream saw him using his cell phone and he told Louis he could not use his cell phone on the plane. It would be another frustrating 15 minutes before Louis could disembark from the Concorde to then be able to use his cell phone again.

As he made his way through customs and immigration Louis continued to try to call his wife. He had felt so polarised by the Earl, he had never obtained his cell phone number and now he regretted his obstinance in not seeking that detail. Whenever Louis tried to call Victoria that evening, he was met with the same messages; Victoria's cell phone was switched off and the Harlaxton landline was not contactable. Louis continued to try and call his wife from his hotel suite at the Plaza Hotel. At 2.30am Manhattan time Louis gave up trying to call his wife. He was exhausted and needed to get some sleep before the scheduled settlement conference at 11.00am that day. He had not taken any cocaine since he had that dream on the Concorde, and he vowed he would never do so again, but then his withdrawal symptoms began to aggravate his growing anxiety because he could not contact Victoria. He sent a short SMS message to Victoria at 3.30am to say that he would call her in about three hours but he did not realise that the text message could not be transmitted at that time due to a functionality issue with his cell phone; technology was working against him.

When Louis went to sleep at 4.00am that morning in Manhattan, the telephone company had just finished the repair work on the telephone lines in the Harlaxton area. Victoria also switched back on her cell phone only five minutes after Louis had drifted off to sleep but to her immense disappointment, there were no messages from her husband.

It was midnight in Los Angeles and the Naylor house had just finished off one of their usual orgies. This orgy was even more of a celebration because of what was waiting in the wind later that day, when the scheduled settlement conference was convened at $$$. As Naylor lay in bed with his wife and the usual hired female guest, he revealed to Audrey that he had recently read one of Louis' emails, which revealed Louis was having an affair with one of the younger female employees of BMI and he is going to nail her, today. "Great." Audrey's delight was encapsulated in that one word, and she immediately jumped out of her bed to put on a thin negligée to now seek her revenge, as she had been stewing about Victoria's arrogance ever since that infamous night in Doha. Audrey raced into Larry's office. She knew that he still kept a telephone index of telephone numbers recording every contact detail for each BMI senior executive, which also included their spouse's telephone numbers. Sure enough, there it was, right before Audrey's eyes, the cell phone number for Victoria Montgomery. She dialled the cell phone number for Victoria. To Audrey's delight, the number began to ring on the other end of the line. It was 8.00am in England.

Victoria walked around the halls of Harlaxton after she had been disappointed to see Louis had not tried to contact her. She had not decided what she was going to do about her marriage, but she still hoped it could be salvaged. At 8.00am, as she aimlessly wandered the halls of Harlaxton, Victoria's cell phone rang, and she immediately flipped it open without looking at the screen to see who was calling. "Hello?" There was the sound of hope in her voice that it was her husband calling. "Hello, Victoria, guess who?" Victoria did not need to guess; she knew the sound of Audrey's voice. "Audrey! What do you want!" Her crisp tone further fuelled Audrey's malicious intent in calling her. "It is not what I want sweetie, it is what your husband wants." Victoria was puzzled by this comment. "What do you mean Audrey?" Audrey smiled at the other end of the telephone line, and it exhilarated her to deliver this news to Victoria. "Why, don't you know? Oh, Victoria, your husband is having an affair with a younger woman at BMI." Victoria was dismissive of this news. "That is rubbish, Victoria. I have heard some vulgar rubbish come out of your mouth over the years, but this is a new low, even for you." Audrey was stung by the condescending tone of Victoria's voice, and she leapt into action. "Well, Vicky, if you don't believe me then go check out your husband's emails. My husband told me that little Louis has been emailing this young woman to set up a little date in New York today. Check his emails if you do not believe me." There was nothing but silence on the other end of the line and Audrey knew she had hit a raw nerve with Victoria. Audrey smiled as she went for the kill. "Good luck Victoria, oh, and by the way, if you need someone to talk to don't call me because I will not care. I hope you enjoy being disgraced there in England." Audrey then hung up the telephone; laughing out loud she knew that she had sent an arrow into the heart of a foe.

Victoria stood still in disbelief for a minute trying to comprehend the information which had just been conveyed to her by an enemy. She then made her way to Louis' home office. She entered Louis' office and when she pressed the keyboard, she saw the computer had been left on by Louis the previous day. She hoped Audrey was just being a drunken nasty bitch, but she could not be sure as Louis had shown a contumelious disregard to her for such a lengthy period. Victoria sat down to start reading Louis' emails and when she pressed on the email file folder Victoria noticed that one email addressed to 'Annabelle' was open but had been minimised. She clicked on it and started reading the trail of emails her husband had exchanged with this woman. Audrey was not lying; this email recorded the arrangements Louis had made to meet with Annabelle that day. Victoria could read the words being used by her husband as displaying an interest, displaying a flirtatious tone and Annabelle's responses which recorded words of a similar nature clearly displaying her desire. She continued to read over and over again the email trail which contained the plans for Louis to meet up with Annabelle in Manhattan.

Victoria sat in her husband's office chair for 15 minutes in disbelief. Her father had taken Anastasia for a drive into 'town' that morning, so she was alone in this mausoleum of a house feeling heartbroken, isolated and betrayed. Tears rolled down her cheeks and Victoria's heart began to sink into a bottomless void of despair. "I cannot take this any longer." Victoria returned to her bedroom and then penned a note on a notepad which she kept by her bed; the note was addressed to her father. She walked into the en suite bath of her bedroom and opened the cabinet. There in front of her was a container of sleeping tablets she purchased for her insomnia caused by her stress. Victoria opened the jar and poured the entire contents of it into her mouth. She washed down the tablets with water from the tap and then returned to her bedroom. Victoria locked the bedroom door, drew the curtains and then she laid down on the bed. Subsequently, at about 10.00am English time, Victoria died in her sleep. Her father did not come to her bedroom to trouble her during the morning, as he believed his daughter needed rest after her harrowing night. An angel had departed and gone to heaven without anybody realising.

CHAPTER 42

The sound of Louis' cell phone woke him up from what had been a night of restless sleep. He reached over to the bedside table and picked up his cell phone. As he lay on his pillow, he saw he had received on his cell phone a text message from Tony, which requested the personal meeting occur after the settlement conference, at a property development project he and Tiffany had underway in Queens 'because we want to expand the project and believe the Qatar Royal Family may be interested'. It was 5.45am and Louis had hoped the SMS he received was a response from his wife. Louis did not pay much regard to Tony's text message other than sending a short reply. "Sure." Louis placed his cell phone back on the bedside table and he did not pay much thought again to that message. On the Upper East Side of Manhattan, Tony moments later smiled when he received Louis' SMS in reply because he believed his devious plan to dispose of Louis would come to fruition that day. Louis was intending to get up to try to call Victoria again but in his exhausted state he had drifted off to sleep.

Louis' cell phone rang about three hours later and he reached over to the bedside while he was still half asleep to answer it as he hoped it would be Victoria. He wanted to tell her that he had been a fool for far too long, that he was sorry for upsetting her, that he would rehabilitate from his drug addiction and that he loved her and their daughter very much. He looked at the screen of his cell phone and to his disappointment the number calling him was not that of his wife, rather the telephone number calling him was from Annabelle's cell phone. He momentarily paused to decide whether he should take the call. He decided it was best that he speak to Annabelle now and explain to her that he could not go through with their planned liaison. "Hi, Annabelle." She could immediately tell by the sound of Louis' voice he was in a cold and sombre mood. "Hi to you. Is everything okay?" Louis became quiet as he had never been in this position before of having to tell a junior employee he could not enter into a relationship with them. "Louis, is everything Okay?" Annabelle's voice was far more earnest when she posed this question for the second time. Louis realised that now was the time to end this relationship. "Annabelle, I'm sorry. I can't enter into a relationship with you. I think you're great but I'm married. I have been confused about my marriage and I now realise more than ever that I love my wife so, sorry, I just can't be with you." Annabelle was disappointed to hear him say this as she had been looking forward to exploring a personal relationship with Louis, indeed she had even fantasised about sleeping with him. "Well, I am glad you told me now Louis rather than after we commenced seeing each other." Then she paused for a moment before speaking again. "I still have a job at BMI, don't I?" When Louis heard her question, he realised he should have been encouraging her mind rather than playing with her heart. "Annabelle, you are one of our bright and rising young stars. I wouldn't dream of letting BMI lose you. Thank you for being so understanding." The pair of them exchanged their goodbyes down the phone, neither of them realising this would be the last time they would speak to each other.

It was 8.45am when Tony left his home that morning to tie up his loose ends from his past. He had made his arrangements for Dom to meet him at the Queens property development, and he kissed Tiffany on her cheek as he always did each morning, confidently believing his past would not come back to haunt him. Little did he know the FBI had been intercepting his telephone calls, cell phone messages and emails and they knew everything about the proposed hit job on Louis, they knew the ZOI transaction was going to be deposited into an offshore account that day, to then be fed down financial ratholes to eventually make its way into BMI's American bank accounts, and they knew Tony's routine down to the minute of that day. As Tony turned the key in the ignition of his car four local Manhattan police cars and an FBI car pulled up in front of his driveway to his 'Silk Stocking District' home. The wailing of the sirens on the cars startled Tiffany while she was finishing her breakfast and when she came racing out of the house she watched in horror as Tony was arrested, handcuffed and thrown into the back of a police car. His final words were crushing for Tiff. "Call my attorney."

As soon as he had finished his call to Annabelle, Louis then tried calling his wife again. His phone said the time in New York was 9.00am and Louis had to be at BMI's office at 11.00am for the settlement conference. Victoria's cell phone commenced ringing, much to Louis' relief. However, Victoria did not answer her cell phone. Louis tried to call her again, but her cell phone rang out. He then tried calling the landline telephone at Harlaxton but that call also rang out. After another few minutes Louis then rang the landline at Harlaxton again and to his relief that call was answered. "Hello, Harlaxton Manor." It was James. "Oh James, thank goodness, it is good to hear your voice. I need to speak to my wife. Do you know where she is?" James did not know where Victoria was, and he had not seen her all day. "No Louis, I don't know where Ms Victoria is, I have not seen her all day. I believe the Earl told me earlier she was resting after a bad night's sleep." Louis was desperate to speak to his wife. "Well, James, would you please go and wake her up. It is urgent that I speak to her." James obeyed the order. "Yes, hold on the line while I go to her room." Louis heard the receiver being placed down on a hard surface, then he briefly heard James' footsteps as the butler walked off down the hall to go to Victoria's room.

Louis waited patiently and he so wanted to have this discussion many hours beforehand. After what seemed like an eternity, Louis heard another receiver being picked up, it was James again, not Victoria. "I knocked on the door to her bedroom Louis but there was no answer. I then tried to open the door, but it was locked. Is Ms Victoria all right?" Louis was uncertain; however, he knew that his wife was very upset with him and believed the reason there was no response was because of her anger. "No James, I believe my wife is obviously still extremely angry with me. I will try again in a few hours' time. If you do see her would you please tell her I called to say sorry, and that I will call again in about two hours." Even though he knew the marriage was in trouble, James was quite honoured Louis was revealing such personal details to him, including requesting he convey to Victoria his contrition. "Yes, Louis, I would be delighted to convey that message to Ms Victoria on your behalf." Louis ended the call first; he was disappointed he could not speak to his wife, but he now had one hour to get ready and then travel to $$$.

Across the other side of the Atlantic Ocean James on the other hand was troubled that Victoria had not responded to his knocking on her bedroom door. The Earl was out walking in the fields with Anastasia. James decided he would raise what had happened with the Earl as soon as he returned from his walk.

Naylor had only slept two hours after the orgy he and his wife had into the early hours of September 10, 2001. He was eager for the settlement conference to occur in Manhattan as soon as possible. He had decided long before today that he would not be travelling to New York for the settlement conference. It was 6.30am in Los Angeles, and Naylor was sitting in his home office which overlooked the Pacific Ocean; it was the best time of day to look at that ocean. He picked up his landline telephone and dialled the number for the Cayman

National Bank in the Cayman Islands. It was a direct line. "Hello, Godfrey Patterson speaking." Naylor smiled; he was about to deliver a simple message to the recipient which would have significant consequences for BMI and Naylor personally. "Godfrey, it is Larry. That little project is about to pay off today in about one hour. Would your people commence implementing the new protocol I have spoken to you about?" Patterson did not need to be reminded of any express details; he nodded his head. "Yes Larry, consider it done. My fee is still the agreed 1%?" Naylor did not think twice about the fee. "Yes Godfrey, I can't do what is about to be done unless you get your agreed commission, so, just get it fucking done." Naylor hung up the telephone. He got out of his chair and opened a drawer in his desk. Inside the drawer were two folders of documents. One of those folders of documents related to a bank account in Switzerland. The other folder of documents was from American Airlines which contained two first class tickets to Argentina that had been booked in Naylor's and Audrey's names.

The Earl returned from his walk in the fields with Anastasia. They had spent a delightful three hours in the fields walking, and then they had a picnic down by the flower bed where the new shoots of seedlings had not as yet appeared from beneath the soil. After the storm the night before, the clouds had parted mid-morning which made the afternoon pleasant. The only au pair on duty had accompanied them just like she did on their drive that morning, and she was carrying the picnic basket back to the house while enjoying the sight of the Earl playing with Anastasia on the walk back to the manor. As the Earl and Anastasia approached the main entrance of Harlaxton James came out to greet them. He took the Earl to one side so that Anastasia could not hear what he had to say under his breath. "Sir, I am very worried about Ms Victoria. I tried raising her two hours ago when Master Louis telephoned trying to speak to her. She did not respond to my several knocks on her bedroom door. She has not come out of the room since then." The Earl's face changed from delight to extreme concern. "Well, good grief man, you have a key. You should have opened the door!" The Earl turned to the au pair. "Watch my granddaughter. Come on James, quickly, let's go to her room."

Both James and the Earl made their way quickly to Victoria's bedroom, leaving Anastasia in the care of the au pair. James put the key in the lock and opened the bedroom door. As the door swung open it was apparent the curtains had not been drawn and the room was in darkness but the light from the hallway cast just enough of its illumination to reveal Victoria lying on top of the covers of the bed. James switched on the light as the Earl raced over to the bed. The Earl put his head next to his daughter's mouth for a brief moment. Then, with a tear in the corner of his eye he turned towards James and gave him an order in a trembling voice. "Quick, call the doctor, she is not breathing." James quickly left the room to fulfil the order of his master. Although he was distressed, the Earl picked up a note which was placed on the bedside table. He opened the page and commenced reading the note. It was from Victoria, and it had been addressed to him.

Within 20 minutes, Dr Robinson from the nearby town of Harlaxton Village had made his way to Harlaxton Manor. James showed the doctor to the bedroom where Victoria lay. By now the Earl had gone to his parlour with Anastasia and his grief was all too evident for the little girl. The doctor examined Victoria and confirmed on his assessment that she had been dead since mid-morning that day. He delivered the news to the Earl in his parlour and the old man wept like none of his staff had seen him weep before. Anastasia, not quite understanding why her poppy was crying, also commenced crying out loud. It was a clear blue day outside but inside the manor it was as though the dark clouds from the night before still had not left them.

CHAPTER 43

Louis walked into the boardroom of the BMI Manhattan office for the settlement of the sale of ZOI. Sitting at the boardroom table were Naylor's lawyers, and their assisting staff of associates, as well as the plethora of lawyers acting for the Sheik, which included the forever arrogant Childe-Harcourt who was sitting side on to the boardroom table and not directly facing his opponents. He sat with his chair swivelled to the right, his long nose pointing upwards adding to the pompous presentation of the man. Louis was the first to speak. "So, ladies and gentlemen, are we ready to do this deal?" Childe-Harcourt swung on his chair to face Louis. "Indeed, we are ready so time to get this done." BMI's in-house Counsel handed to Louis a folio of bound documents. Every document that was needed to transfer interests in ZOI worldwide had been signed. Louis spent ten minutes looking over the documents one more time, then he signed them where required as the authorised representative of ZOI. After signing all the designated pages Louis then turned to Childe-Harcourt and handed over the folder across the table. Childe-Harcourt then inspected the documents for the next ten minutes.

After inspecting the documents Childe-Harcourt turned to one of his assisting lawyers and nodded. The lawyer handed over a laptop computer to Childe-Harcourt. The laptop was opened by Childe-Harcourt, and it revealed a bank account page for an account held at the Commercial Bank of Qatar. Childe-Harcourt ensured that Louis could see the screen as he typed in an account number held at the Cayman National Bank. Then Childe-Harcourt typed in the figure, 3.2 billion American dollars. He looked at Louis and smiled, pressing the button to process the payment while he spoke. "Don't spend it all at the races, ladies and gentlemen. Nice doing business with all of you. One last message from His Royal Highness, please don't buy up oil and gas interests in Qatar again." The laptop then revealed a message, that the funds had been successfully wired to the Cayman National Bank. One of the BMI in-house legal team looked at the screen for the Cayman National bank account and it had recorded a message of funds in the sum of 3.2 billion American dollars having been deposited electronically into the account from the Commercial Bank of Qatar. Louis saw the screen and nodded at Childe-Harcourt to confirm the transaction was now complete. Now Patterson was getting to work in the Cayman Islands; his stealthy mission was going unnoticed by anyone at BMI as Tony was nowhere to be seen to monitor the distribution of the payment.

Immediately after the settlement, Louis decided he would go for a walk outside for a while, as his withdrawal symptoms from refraining to consume cocaine were now causing him to become agitated. Having to endure Childe-Harcourt's painful behaviour had only exacerbated his agitation, and he needed to clear his mind, before he would try to call his wife. He had successfully completed his exit strategy and he considered that his time with BMI was almost done; however, he could not be completely satisfied at this time as he had not received a response from Professor Chandra about his proposal to invest in their stem cell research program, and this delay was also frustrating him. He thought a walk could help him, but what he really needed was a doctor.

As Louis walked down Vessey Street and onto Broadway he remembered that a quarter of a century ago he was roaming the Lower Manhattan area as a child working for his father's evil crew of criminals. "Has life really changed? Who have I been working for over the last fifteen years?" Louis' intuition during that walk was regrettably 15 years too late. He had returned on many occasions to Manhattan over the last few years, but this was the first time he actually had an opportunity to observe his childhood city. The memories of his life in Midtown West began to depress him. He believed he needed to continue walking to clear his mind.

Louis had walked down Broadway for 100 metres when his cell phone commenced ringing in his pocket. The screen revealed the call was coming from Harlaxton Manor. "Victoria." Louis' tone of voice was simultaneously desperate but also relieved to finally receive a telephone call from his wife. "Hi, I have been trying to call you since..." Louis was very quickly stopped mid speech by the voice of the Earl. "You killed her, you American bastard, you killed her." Louis was startled to hear the Earl speak but then angered by the way the Earl was speaking to him. "Don't you talk to me like that sir...." But the Earl talked over him. "How dare you, you killed her, you killed my daughter." Now the Earl's words were being understood by Louis and he knew that something had occurred in relation to his wife. "What has happened, what has happened to Victoria?" Louis had barked down the phone. The Earl continued, his voice deteriorating the more he spoke. "She left me a suicide note. In it she wrote that she received a call from Larry Naylor's wife, then she checked your emails. She saw that you were arranging an affair with some little American harlot. My daughter killed herself this morning, thanks to you."

He stood on Broadway in shock and his blood seemed to instantly drain from his face. Louis' eyes then began to well up with tears and now he too could not control the trembling of his voice. "My wife is dead? Where is my daughter, where is my daughter?" The Earl continued his disparaging dressing down of Louis. "How could you do this to my daughter? She loved you and you repaid her with betrayal?" Louis shook his head; he had called off the meeting and now he was cursing himself for leaving on his computer at home; he was also cursing Audrey for her act of pure evil. "I did not have an affair. I could not go there. I'm sorry…" Louis could not finish his sentence as he broke down in tears. The Earl had had enough of the conversation, and he hung up the telephone not convinced by Louis' explanation.

Delia had decided that today was the day she would tell Amir why she had dismissed Noora. She had been too afraid for allowing so much time to go by, but her shame compelled her to finally reveal the truth to her husband. She had decided just after lunchtime would be best, as that was when the ZOI transaction would be settled. As Amir finished his final mouthful of lunch Delia spoke, and her apologetic voice explained to Amir what she had witnessed Audrey and Noora doing to one another that evening, the lesbian sex occurring in their house when it was forbidden by law and that she was sorry for not telling him sooner, but she had to protect Noora. When she finished revealing to Amir what she had witnessed that night, he looked into her eyes for about thirty seconds, and then his words were the response she did not expect. "Did you enjoy watching them perform this sexual act? Did you wish you could join them? Did you act in any impure manner?" The answer to each question was yes but poor Delia could only respond with an embarrassed ashen face, which was all Amir needed to know. He rose quickly from his chair and he strode over to where his frightened wife was seated and he then plunged his closed right hand into her face, and the immediate scream of pain rang out from her vocal cords as she toppled over in her chair.

Amir was furious and he was not finished with Delia, as he had grabbed from the centre of the table the large pure silver candelabra that he intended to crush her head in with. Fortuitously for Delia, his cellphone rang before he could deliver these killer blows and he was immediately distracted when he heard his lawyer's voice. Amir's voice was already agitated from his wife's revelation. "What do you want?" His Doha lawyer was used to this tone, so he continued talking in a professional manner. "What?" Amir's voice thundered in rage, and he then kicked the chair which had toppled over when he punched Delia, causing its elegant frame of fine wood to break. "How did this fucking happen? How did this fucking happen?" His scream down the telephone was met by the same professional voice back from his lawyer. "Naylor. I will kill that bastard and his whore of a wife!" Amir slammed his cellphone shut and stormed out of his house to go to his lawyer's office immediately. He put a call into his New York team as he drove out of his driveway; his one command was simple. "Blow the bastards up!" The team had previously installed the remote wiring in the air-conditioning ducts of BMI's offices in $$$ on the day Amir signed the agreement, as his management of any risk; however, they would now return to $$$ to connect high-grade plastic explosives to all of the remote wiring on each floor of BMI's Manhattan office. Amir was the Devil, and he would exact his revenge after these infidels' deception.

Louis stood on Broadway sobbing. The large crowd of passers-by looked at him as though he was some freak in the streets of Manhattan and despite being overwhelmed with grief not one person stopped to check on Louis' welfare. He must have stood there for ten minutes crying and in his mind, Louis could not stop lashing himself in anger. "Why did I send those emails to Annabelle? Why did I even get tempted? Why did Audrey call my wife?" Louis repeatedly asked himself these questions as he grieved openly on Broadway. His heart was broken for his wife was now dead and Louis realised over and over again he knew he only had himself to blame. The ring of the cell phone briefly interrupted his grief.

The number on the screen did not look like it was coming from England but in his grief-stricken state, he took the call. Louis tried to hold back his tears as he spoke. "Hello." The call was not from England. "You fucking little shits, you think you can double-cross me?" It was Zogby, his voice conveyed no other emotion than pure rage. Louis was now being abused for the second time in 20 minutes and he could not contain his anger. "Heh, fuck you, Amir. I have not done any double-crossing!" Amir's core body temperature erupted in his rage. "Fuck me! Fuck me! You bastard, you say fuck me when all of the funds have been taken from the account! Fuck you fucking liar." Louis had now been delivered his second piece of bad news, although this news was more surprising than heartbreaking. "What are you talking about Amir? I saw the Sheik's lawyer transfer the funds to the Cayman Island account." Zogby was unrelenting with his anger. "The funds are fucking gone, you imbecile! My people tell me that not long after the transfer to the Cayman Island account, a further transfer has occurred, and the funds are now held in some secret account in Switzerland. You are not trying to tell me you didn't know because you must. You brought great embarrassment to me and my family name. I will kill you! I will kill your family! I will kill your wife!"

Louis' world was spinning out of control. Naylor had deceived everyone but Amir Zogby's taunts enraged Louis. "Hey! Fuck off, Amir! My wife is dead Amir, thanks to Naylor's wife; Audrey and Larry have double-crossed everyone, and my wife is fucking dead." Amir did not even acknowledge Louis' loss. "Respect! Fucking respect! I do not have my money and you fucking ask me to show fucking respect! BMI is dead, you are dead, Naylor is fucking dead!" Amir ended the call. Louis knew that Amir Zogby wanted blood and he would seek vengeance for this deceit, but in the meantime, Louis had to alert the other directors of BMI about Naylor's act of fraud. He tried to call Tony, but his cell phone rang out; he was supposed to be meeting with him at Queens in about an hour, but that meeting would have to wait. He also knew that he had to alert the Earl about Zogby's threats. He wiped his eyes with a handkerchief which he kept in his jacket pocket and turned around to walk back towards BMI's office while simultaneously using his cell phone to call the Earl.

His discussion with the Earl was brief. He told him about Zogby's threat. The Earl told him that everyone had tried to warn him, and this was just a further issue the Earl used to criticise Louis at this time. He did not respond to the comment, but he told the Earl he would hire security personnel to guard Harlaxton. With those words being said the Earl then shouted back at him. "Well done, Louis, you have caused my daughter to die; now Anastasia and I have to deal with this, prisoners in our home!" Louis immediately realised his little girl must be distraught, as she would know her mummy was dead. "Let me speak to Anastasia please. Now!" Louis' boisterous demand enraged the Earl. "Don't you shout at me Louis Montgomery!" The call was then immediately disconnected by the Earl.

He was angry and upset, but for the Earl this further news was alarming for himself and Anastasia. The Earl made a telephone call to speak to Marjorie

Grace at MI5. The Earl was very emotional as he informed Marjorie about his daughter's death and the fears he now held regarding Zogby seeking revenge. Marjorie did her best to extend her sincere condolences to the Earl regarding his daughter's passing, but she assured him, that MI5 would monitor the situation, and accordingly everyone at Harlaxton was safe. After the call, the Earl was still concerned and angry. "Damn that Louis!" His angry voice echoed down the hallway as he made his way to Anastasia's room. When he walked into the room, the Earl could see Anastasia was being hugged by the au pair and her tears flowed quickly down her cheeks as she cried out loud. "Mummy, I want my mummy!"

Louis had to address the board of directors about Naylor's deceit. He was extremely upset, but he managed to contain his emotions before he dialled his cell phone. He rang Fisher first, and after a few minutes of alarmed discussion Fisher then patched in the rest of the board to the telephone discussion. The board of directors of BMI were outraged when Louis told them what Naylor had done. Some were present in the New York boardroom as Louis spoke on his telephone outside on Broadway and others were listening in on a conference call from their individual offices.

Calls to Naylor's home telephone and cell phone numbers were not being answered; indeed, nobody in Los Angeles knew whether or not Naylor was still in the country. Hundreds of millions of dollars were owed by BMI to its banks to fund the ZOI project and the settlement was meant to repay those funds, as well as deliver a healthier profit to the company's balance sheet. Tony could not be contacted. Every board member was panicking as it appeared Naylor had deceived everyone, including Louis. BMI should have been safe and assured as the funds trickled from the ratholes to hide their profits, an unlawful step Tony had previously used. Instead, the company was now in peril and the banks upon finding out this information would call in the loans and shut down BMI if they could not repay their debt. Louis informed the board of his wife's passing; there was a bare mumble of condolence from some of them, as they were otherwise more concerned about the fraud that Naylor had committed. Regarding Zogby's threat, the board mistakenly expressed the view to Louis that they believed he was not a threat to BMI, rather he would focus his attention on Naylor. Louis tried to convince the board members to think otherwise about Amir, but they did not want to alert the authorities as yet because they believed this would alert the banks and the financial markets. The panic was rife and no senior person working on floors 75 to 82 of $$$ could think straight.

By the time Louis had finished dealing with the board members, it was early in the evening in Manhattan. He had tried to talk to Anastasia during the afternoon, but the Earl had told James not to allow the little girl to talk to her father. Anastasia was distressed by the news that her mother would never see her again. Even though her late mother had previously tried to explain to her what death meant, she did not now understand why her mother had left her for good. James had the difficult task of explaining to Louis that his daughter could not come to the telephone. Louis told James he understood the Earl was preventing him from speaking to his daughter, and he then proceeded to ask James to tell Anastasia he was coming home. James subsequently informed the Earl he had been asked by Louis to tell Anastasia he was coming home, but the Earl told him Anastasia must not be disturbed.

The traffic had been exceedingly busy, so Louis had eventually arrived at the counter of British Airways at JFK International Airport at 7.00pm that same night. He had tried booking a seat to London since 1.00pm that day but all the airlines were pre-booked. After imploring British Airways to find him a seat, Louis was told by the British Airways staff member he could wait at the airport for any last-minute cancellations. Louis walked to the check-in counters of all the international airline carriers, hoping that somebody would have a space open for him to fly home tonight. Instead, the same frustrating news was delivered to him; all the seats were booked, and he would have to wait for any last-minute cancellations.

Louis was the fly caught in two webs, but it was the web of the 'Devil', the cold and ruthless Amir Zogby, who worried him the most. He telephoned the London office to inform them about what had occurred with the bank transfers and to hire trained security personnel because Zogby was known to hire teams of ruthless mercenary killers.

PART 5

"Redemption"

CHAPTER 44

Louis sat in a coffee shop of the departure hall of John F Kennedy International Airport waiting for one of the airlines to call him. One hour went by, then two hours. It was apparent to Louis that he was not going to be able to secure a flight home that evening. As he sat there thinking about his wife Louis did not notice an old familiar face had been staring at him for at least thirty minutes. Omar was now an old man, and he did not look like his former younger self. His hair was now grey, and his face had significantly wrinkled from the years of sun damage. However, Omar recognised Louis, even if he was now an older man. Eventually, Omar got up from his seat and walked over to where Louis was sitting. Louis looked up at Omar, but he did not initially recognise him. Omar spoke to rekindle Louis' memory. "It has obviously been a long time Louis, and maybe my old face is too wrinkled now for you to remember me." The voice sounded familiar, and Louis stood up, "Omar? Omar is that you?" Omar nodded and held out his arms in a friendly embrace. Louis hugged Omar, his grief overwhelmed him again and this display of emotion worried Omar.

Eventually, Louis regained his composure and explained to Omar what had happened that day. During their lengthy discussion, Louis finally received the first sympathetic words from a person all day. Louis repeatedly told Omar that he had been a fool and as a result his wife was dead. He told Omar how he wished he could turn back time to the day that Naylor first offered cocaine to him, because he would have refused to accept it if he knew what he now knew. Omar listened to Louis' story. The pair must have talked for a good hour with Omar assuring Louis that there was still a life ahead of him despite what had occurred. Louis was appreciative of Omar being so patient for the last hour as he poured out his heart. Louis asked Omar about his life, and the old Sudanese man then explained to him he had retired from the merchant navy life, and he was now seeing the world. Like Louis, he was waiting for a flight, but this was how Omar was seeing the world, cheap stand-by airfares and then exploring the interior of a country by any other means. Omar proceeded to explain to Louis all he had done all his adult life was see ports other than occasionally travelling a short distance inland for some momentary sightseeing. Now Omar was seeing the interior of countries, and he was opening his mind to new frontiers.

It was 2.00am in the morning when Louis realised he would not be able to board a flight to London until later that morning. He had paid for a seat on a 10.30am Concorde flight out of JFK International that morning, and after purchasing his Concorde ticket, Louis told Omar that he was tired and needed to get some rest. Omar was an old friend, so Louis offered to pay for a room for him to stay at the airport hotel. Omar was initially reluctant to receive such a generous gesture, but he decided that given what had just occurred in Louis' life he should perhaps once again be his good shepherd and keep an eye on him. When they arrived at the hotel it was 2.30am, and after receiving from reception their respective room keys, the two men said their goodbyes before walking their respective ways towards their rooms. Omar's last words were a prescient reminder for Louis about his parental responsibilities. "Louis, just remember, no matter what happens in life you have a daughter. You must fight for her and be strong. Nothing else matters now and she needs a father." Louis nodded his head. He knew that Anastasia was now his sole focus in life.

During those early hours of the morning, as Louis tried to sleep, two vans bearing signs purporting to be a cleaning company arrived at $$$. There were two men of Middle Eastern background in each van. They were the same group of men who many weeks before had deceived Jennifer on the pretence of them attending at BMI's office for 'maintenance' of the air-conditioning ducts. The security guards took for granted an explanation from the driver of the first van they were coming to clean BMI's offices, and an electronic pass to access was provided to the driver of the first van for him and his colleagues to access floors 75 to 82 of $$$. The guards did not even bother to check what was going into or coming out of the two vans over the next few hours. These 'cleaners' were now making sure Zogby could exact his revenge. By dawn the last of the vans left.

CHAPTER 45

Later that morning Louis woke up at his scheduled time. He opened his eyes and stumbled towards the curtains. Opening the curtains Louis looked around the room to gain his sense of sight. As his eyes came into focus, he noticed a piece of folded paper had been slipped under the door. The paper was standard issue Hilton JFK letterhead. Louis picked up the paper and opened it. Omar had written a short message, but it appeared as though an omen had been written for Louis to digest: *"My old friend. So good to see you and thank you for your generosity in paying for my room. I just want to say that life may get harder for you, my young friend before it gets easier. Do not give up or give in, your child needs you to remain strong. Your friend, Omar."* Louis pondered the message contained within Omar's short note, he was trying to come to terms with the comment life may get harder. "How much harder can get?" Louis thought to himself.

When Louis arrived at the departure gate at 9.30am for his flight to London, he had no idea of the chaos that was simultaneously occurring in Manhattan. Amir Zogby's command to his men in New York was simple; blow every bit of plastic explosive up; kill everyone. As the head office of BMI was forging ahead with a working day at 9.25am an explosion erupted on the 79th floor, then the 80th floor, then there was an explosion on the 81st floor and a room which Annabelle was working out of at the time was located right next to one of the main centres of hidden explosives.

Similar explosive devices then erupted over the next four floors below the 79th level, and finally a device hidden in the ceiling of the 82nd floor exploded just near the boardroom where the board had just sat down to meet again to discuss the financial crisis the company was now addressing. In all seven floors of BMI's offices in $$$ had been ignited at once in a huge display of explosive force. Windows exploded outwards, taking with them human lives who were unfortunately standing too close to the blast, the flames, the shockwaves, and the windows. For the remaining surviving souls within those floors, they were trapped in an incendiary hell of flames which was the aftermath of substantial amounts of explosive material activated at the same time. All the staff of BMI

New York had been killed, including Annabelle who was just unfortunately visiting the East Coast office from Japan for amongst other matters, to see Louis. Three quarters of the BMI board of directors had been killed, and, tragically, many hard-working employees whose only crimes were that they had turned up to work that day. And for $$$? Well, the shock waves caused the three golden $$$ signs on the roof to topple over, and with its toppling so did American society that day as they came to terms with Zogby's act of terrorism.

Louis had expected that he would be boarding a Concorde at 9.45am, but instead a delayed message came up on the departure screen. Rumours spread around the departure lounge that there had been a terrible attack in Manhattan; people did not have any details, but the rumours were a building housing a significant American company had been destroyed and many people were dead. Louis did not need to be told; his instincts told him that Zogby had started seeking revenge. Sure enough the rumours were soon being confirmed by news programs being broadcasted on the airport television screens that the head office of BMI had been attacked. The news media reported on the airport television screens the horrifying details that almost everyone within the seven floors of the BMI office were expected to be dead. Passengers waiting to depart New York on any flight, were being advised by loudspeaker announcements that all flights for that day had been cancelled and for security reasons they must all leave the airport.

He was extremely agitated because his withdrawal symptoms had not improved with his brief sleep, but Louis reluctantly commenced walking away from the departure lounge and, as he did so, he saw several men and women dressed in cheap dark suits walking towards him. Louis did not need to be introduced to them as he knew they were law enforcement officers of some kind, probably FBI officers. A burly male walked towards Louis and greeted him in a serious manner. "Louis Montgomery?" Louis looked the officer in the eyes, despite his personal sorrow he was not one to be submissive to authority figures. "Yes, what do you want?" The burly officer was just as blunt with his reply, "You are coming with us!" Louis protested as he had not done anything wrong. "What for? What have I done?" However, his protestations were all to no avail and Louis was placed in an arm lock by the officer and one of his colleagues. He was escorted out of the airport in full view of the other people who had also attempted to fly out of Manhattan that morning only to now be told they must go home. Louis was physically thrown into the back of a large Ford van by the

FBI officers. After the doors of the Ford van were slammed shut it then sped off.

The back of the van was dark and smelt like urine. Louis' withdrawal symptoms of agitation, frustration and now fear were all consuming in that environment, and he screamed at the FBI officers to let him out but the van kept on moving. The trip in the back of the van would continue for about another seven hours and when it finally stopped, the officers then handcuffed Louis in the back of the van before forcibly marching him into a building. Louis did not know where he had been taken and the FBI officers would not answer his questions. When he commenced screaming at them one of the FBI officers would hit Louis' head with a baton. The first room of the building was a secure reception and a sign hanging above the only other doorway left no doubt for any person who was in charge of that facility; 'Restricted entry for CIA personnel or authorised persons only'. Louis' mind was already suffering from the effects of his withdrawal symptoms, but the involvement of the Central Intelligence Agency in his being detained alarmed him. There were two CIA personnel waiting in this holding area, and they relieved the FBI officers of their duties regarding them holding Louis in custody. He was dragged to the door leading further into the facility by these two CIA agents, and any protestations about his ill health, or his right to a telephone call to a lawyer, which Louis made were ignored. That night after he was fingerprinted, photographed and stripped naked Louis was placed in a cell. He had been walked past a row of the detained people, who were standing behind the half wall of thick Perspex which permitted the agents to see into the cells.

Louis did not take any notice of the person in the cell next to his, but that person saw him being escorted by the CIA agents. It was Tony in that neighbouring cell; his bail had been previously refused to be granted by a judge the bay beforehand. He was allowed to speak to his very upset wife who knew by now he was Antonio Mancini. Their discussion was very brief. "I want a divorce Tony or, Antonio. You have brought shame to my family name." He had been charged with conspiracy to murder, and then he cracked under further police questioning and told them where the cold case bodies had been buried under concrete. The FBI had brought Tony to this CIA facility approximately six hours before Louis had arrived, and he had already endured one bruising interrogation by two burly CIA male agents regarding his knowledge of ZOI, Zogby and what role he had played in the transaction. Tony told the CIA agents the same information he told the FBI officers about how the funds would be drip fed into different American bank accounts, so that only a very minimum sum of tax would be paid but that was the extent of his involvement in the transaction. During the identification process Louis had been informed by the CIA agents about the extent of Tony's confession and therefore he had to cooperate. The CIA agents also told him he was lucky to be alive, as the FBI had thwarted Tony's plan to kill him. Louis continued to demand his right to a telephone but the agents denied him that right, and he was thrown into his inhospitable cell which the CIA had deliberately arranged to be next to Tony's cell.

Each detention cell had a portal in its wall; a portal from it to the neighbouring cell to permit the detainees to talk to one another; however, there was no privacy because hidden microphones were recording each word detainees spoke. Louis had been in his room for barely 15 minutes when he heard Tony's voice emanating from the portal. Louis walked close to the portal and bent slightly down to talk into it. "Is that you in there, Tony?" Initially there was silence for a moment, and then the old Bronx Antonio spoke again. "It's not your fairy godmother." Tony's sarcasm irritated Louis. "Don't be a smartarse, Tony, because I am in no mood for it." There was a moment of silence and then Tony spoke again. "Did they tell you that I had planned to whack you? Indeed you would be dead by now if my plan succeeded." Louis had been told. "Yes, one of the agents told me. I knew that in the back of your mind you must have worked out who I was, I just didn't realise you had engaged Dom to background check me and then pay him for the hit job. Why Tony? Why the hit job? If I exposed you I would be exposing who I really was as well. That was stupid, as was the lump sum payment to yourself to withdraw in one transaction $200,000.00 for Dom's fees. That type of transaction is obviously undertaken for a personal purpose; you were sloppy."

Tony nodded his head in agreement. He had been sloppy. He looked at the floor of his cell in abject disappointment with himself for almost a minute then he decided to change the subject of their discussions. "I spoke to my wife while I was held in the FBI's custody, and she knows who I really am. She is going to divorce me; I always knew that would occur if my real identity was revealed hence my desperation to conceal it. To tell you the truth, Louis I give up trying to be another person and I give up on being myself. I'm going to be spending a long, long time in jail, so I just don't care anymore. I'm done." Tony's personal revelation was then reciprocated by Louis. "My wife committed suicide two nights ago." Tony did not respond to this news, but Louis did not expect there to be any heartfelt condolences coming his way. He then decided to investigate just how much information Tony had been told by the authorities since being detained in custody. "Have you heard BMI's offices at $$$ have been destroyed, and most of the staff, and board members, working there at the time have been killed?" Tony had been told. "Yes, both the FBI and CIA have interrogated me about it. Oh well, it's probably for the best the whole shit show in New York was blown up."

Tony's insensitivity caused further irritation in Louis' suffering mind and his petulance could not be restrained. "Innocent people died Tony. Show some respect for god's sake. Even my wife has died but you don't seem to care about that as well." Tony half laughed when he heard Louis' final comment, and his ironic response was not properly thought through. "Well at least your dead wife can't take you to the cleaners like mine will do to me." Before Louis could respond with words that would have been dripping with acrimony Tony spoke once more. "I'm sorry, Louis, that was uncalled for. I do not give a damn anymore about me, but I cannot face a wife I still love in a courtroom and to see only hatred being expressed on her face. I just can't face it." Tony broke down into tears and as much as Louis tried to reengage in conversation with him Tony resisted it.

During the middle of that evening, when there were no agents monitoring the detention cells, Tony managed to make a noose from his belt. He secured it by tying one end to the bars installed in front of the ventilation shift which was located on the back wall above the filthy steel toilet. He stepped off the edge of the toilet and then he embarked upon his macabre journey to terminally finish his interaction with this world. It took a few minutes for him to lose consciousness and then within the next five minutes Tony had successfully hanged himself. Louis was oblivious to this fact at the time.

Dom had a heart attack that next day when he first appeared in the court on charges of attempted murder and murder, and he was dead before he hit the floor. Save for Louis, it now appeared there were no people remaining on this planet from the days of Joseph and his men and there were also no living souls left of Mayor Sabatini's feared gang of henchmen. Louis did not need to hide his identity anymore; at least that was a positive aspect out of an otherwise maudlin collection of broken lives.

For the next two days in custody Louis suffered in his mind as his severe withdrawal symptoms were expressed through the severe depression which was now entrenched in his mind, and he had not even been interrogated by the CIA as yet. He had been fed, but it was insufficient to satisfy his increased appetite which was caused by his withdrawal symptoms. He craved cocaine, but his mind cursed itself for seeking to consume this drug. He had not been allowed the luxury of a shower, nor could he contact anyone, not even a lawyer. Instead, Louis had been left to fester in the smell of his own stench after three days of detention. Louis' mind was in pain, not only from the poor treatment he was receiving in custody, but also from the symptoms of his severe withdrawal from cocaine. By the fourth day in custody Louis was experiencing severe mental trauma, and even though he continually screamed out in despair the CIA agents did not care about his welfare.

When his fifth day in custody had almost ticked over Louis had not been informed about his wife's funeral. In accordance with her Will a religious ceremony was conducted at the Anglican church in Harlaxton Village. A small group of family and friends from England and Australia attended the ceremony, but there would not be a burial of her remains in the family plot at Harlaxton Manor. Victoria's remains were subsequently cremated and in keeping with her last will and testament her ashes were spread over the flower bed at the edge of the woods, a bed of flowers which she so admired and had taken Anastasia to on many occasions. It was a sombre occasion, one which Louis would have attended but perhaps he would not have been welcome at. The Earl comforted Anastasia as her mother's ashes were poured out of the urn, and although she was of a tender age Anastasia knew that this occasion was to say goodbye to her mother. Her daddy had not returned; accordingly, the poor little child was like an orphan in the field that afternoon with her poppy.

Amir Zogby's next command for his men after destroying BMI's office at $$$ was just as ruthless; track Naylor and Audrey down and cut their throats, particularly the woman's throat. He wanted Audrey's throat cut to soothe his ego, because his wife had found pleasure in watching her and Noora making love to each other. Back in Doha, Amir was settling the matter of his pride with both Delia and Noora. He had taken them to an abandoned workshop he owned in Doha where he had proceeded to thrash both of them with a whip until their backs were just flesh with no skin. He then poured petrol on them and set them alight. The old wooden shed burned brightly and when the fire brigade was eventually able to put out the fire four hours later Delia and Noora had been turned to ash. Amir truly was the Devil.

By the sixth day of Louis' custody, stories were already circulating in the media about a man who had been removed by federal authorities from JFK International on the day of the attacks, who may be an important link to the attack on the BMI offices which had killed so many people. It was also on the sixth day of his incarceration that Louis was finally taken by the CIA agents to an interrogation room within the building in which he was being held as a captive. Within that room there were seated four further CIA agents, a young male and female and two older males. There was also one investigator from MI5 who had flown over from the United Kingdom: Marjorie Grace. An MI5 agent was present because Louis was a permanent resident of the United Kingdom and Ms Grace was already well acquainted with Louis' involvement in the ZOI transaction. The lead interrogator was Bill Marshall, a CIA agent with some 35 years of service. Marshall by name and nature, as he considered himself to be a tough proposition for any person whereas his colleagues considered him to be an overweight fool, kept in employment by the CIA because they were too afraid to get rid of their driftwood.

Louis was forcibly seated in a metal chair and his hands were cuffed behind his back and the backrest of the chair. Louis was the first one to talk, the sight of Marshall and his similarly overweight senior colleague being all too much for a now irate and depressed person. "So, Captain Cholesterol and Barney Beach-ball, I presume." Marshall reached across the desk separating them and punched Louis in the mouth. "Shut your mouth." Marshall's voice boomed as his hand retracted back to his side of the desk. Louis initially shook his head; the taste of blood was in his mouth, but he was not going to remain silent. "At least you could buy me some flowers before you kissed me." Louis' retort again earned further punishment and Marshall again reached across the desk and punched Louis in the mouth; the force of the punch caused his head to fly backwards. Blood began to trickle from Louis' mouth, but he was not going to be subdued by the CIA, nor was he going to be subdued by an old hatchet job like Marshall. "Thank you, believe it or not you just dislodged a piece of meat I've had stuck in my teeth for the past two days." Louis' quick repertoire was making an impact on the younger agents. The young female agent could not hide her smile.

Marjorie Grace remained silent as she witnessed Marshall's brutality; she had witnessed many violent interrogations during her years of service in MI5. Marshall persisted with his inelegant interrogation. "So, I want to know why you sold your shares in BMI before the attack occurred?" Louis replied instantly, without a second thought. "I started selling my shares two years before the attack, there is no connection between the two events." Marshall clumsily continued. "Well, I don't know about that." Louis delivered the knockout blow; he had had enough of this fool. "Based on your powers of investigation you still haven't worked out who your father is after all of these years." That comment was too much for the young female agent, as she could not hold back her laughter and she had to flee from the room to try to regain her composure, Marshall watching her departure with anything but an approving eye.

Marshall turned back towards Louis; his inane interrogation ploughed on. "So, tell me about Zogby." Louis was candid. "Zogby is an asshole, but he was done over by a bigger asshole being the former head of BMI, Larry Naylor. I was also fucked over by Naylor, so I guess I am wondering why a couple of cowboys like you pair are interrogating me, why the CIA is holding me like this, when Naylor is the bad guy in this story?" Marshall stared long and hard at Louis, then he revealed some news that Louis was not aware of. "Larry Naylor and his wife were found dead yesterday in Buenos Aires with their throats cut and, in particular, Mrs Naylor's throat was savagely cut open several times." Louis pondered over this news, then he spoke. "Zogby?" Marshall responded in his usual derisive tone. "Well, you tell us. You seem to know so much about this terrorist." Louis glared in spite at Marshall because every question he asked was pure supposition. Marshall did not recoil back in his chair. Louis wanted to scream abuse at the man, but he realised such behaviour would only encourage this mindless brute. "Look, all I can tell you is that Larry Naylor conned all of us, including me. Zogby is obviously a bad guy, something I did not appreciate until after Naylor had conned everyone. I did not know any of this would happen, and, if I did, I would not have allowed it to have happened. So, all I want to do is to go home, say goodbye to my dead wife and to hold my daughter, if that is all right with you?" Louis' condescending tone of voice did not go unnoticed by Marshall or anybody else in the room.

Marshall looked at Louis for a moment, then he rolled backwards in his chair laughing loudly before returning his gaze to him again. "Go hold your cock you half smart little lord. By the way, we are the CIA, and we know who you really are. Montgomery! Hello to you Louis O'Brien." Marshall turned to Marjorie Grace; Louis followed his eyes over to her. He did not know who she was or why she was there, but she nodded to confirm she was also aware of

Louis' true identity. Louis' life had been the subject of scrutinised investigations by police departments and spy agencies in three separate countries for the past week, and the investigators were left with no doubt that the Louis O'Brien who was charged and convicted of assault during the 1970s was the same Louis that now sat before Marshall, Grace and the other agents. He may be known as Montgomery, but everyone in that room was certain he was indeed the believed to be dead person, Louis O'Brien.

Louis was initially discomforted by his true identity being revealed, but he began to realise that even this line of investigation would not lead to a too harsh punishment in a court of law. "So, what! I was a kid escaping from people trying to kill me. I would not be sentenced to imprisonment by an American court in those circumstances. So, knock yourselves out." Marshall smiled a smug smile only a seasoned CIA investigator could smile. "Oh yes, perhaps you are right from a legal aspect in this country. But the newspapers have already been provided all the sordid details by me. So, you little half smart prick, my friends in the press are already assassinating your character worldwide. A District-Attorney here may not even end up charging you with any offence Louis Montgomery, sorry, O'Brien, but the whole world will find out your real background; Louis O'Brien! How do you think your little daughter will react to this news?"

The reference to Anastasia enraged Louis and he wanted to scream his heart out about being deprived of seeing his daughter when she must be so traumatised. However, he still had one last Midtown West jive left within him. "Better than you because when you get home tonight you will see your usual homecoming sight of your wife getting a good one from all of your colleagues." Louis' knockout blow had worked; Marshall was defeated and frustrated by Louis' sharp tongue. He quickly got up out of the chair and left the room, leaving his corroborating officers to eventually release Louis from this cruel restraint and torture.

Before he left the interrogation room, Marjorie Grace made sure she delivered some further bad news to Louis. "Louis, my name is Marjorie Grace, and I am here on behalf of MI5. I thought you should know some of these facts for you to think about back in your cell. Victoria's funeral has already occurred, and her ashes have been spread in accordance with her Will." Her cold delivery of this devastating news drew unrestrained spite from Louis. "Fuck you, you fucking cold hearted bitch!" Marjorie Grace remained composed; there was one more string in her bow. "Now, now Louis, be nice. You should also be aware the Australian government has revoked your university degree and removed from the university's records that you were a recipient of the University Medal. They will not tolerate academic fraud." Louis raised an eyebrow in anger. "What do you mean fraud? I studied hard and passed every test without cheating!" Grace nodded her head in agreement. "Yes, we know how hard you must have worked to receive that degree while at university, the only problem is you should never have been accepted to study at Sydney University in the first place. In any person's language you were accepted into that university because of fraudulent academic records. And don't worry, MI5 has already spoken to the government authorities in Singapore."

Louis felt depressed and defeated by Marjorie Grace's cold news. Victoria's funeral, Sydney University and his plans for Singapore had all been thrown back into his face. Grace was about to leave the room when she stopped in her tracks and turned back towards Louis. The narrowing of her eyes and the smirk on her face revealed her cruel intent. "Oh, by the way, I know your father-in-law. He wanted me to tell you he is disgusted with your antics, as is your daughter." Louis tried to jump to his feet, but his restraints would not permit this movement. "My daughter. You bitch, don't you dare do my father-in-law's dirty work. Let me out of here. I'm a UK resident!" Grace did not respond to Louis' abusive language, rather she turned around without blinking an eye and left the room. After being uncuffed by the remaining agents in the interrogation room Louis was subsequently taken to another cell within the building; there were no windows in that cell, there was no light, he did not have a bed to sleep on and he only had a bucket to use for his bodily excretions. The torture began as the spy agencies continued their investigations.

In the darkness of his cell Louis continued to experience varying degrees of mental torment. His intense withdrawal symptoms manifested in his depression which in turn manifested themselves in his inner demons. He thought about what the media would be reporting about him, not only in America but also in Britain and Australia. He wondered about the trauma his little daughter was suffering at this time, as she had coped with her mother being dead, and her father now locked up like a criminal. In his dreams Louis would be taunted by his subconscious interactions with Joseph. "I told you many times boy, you are no damn good. You are nothing but the son of a dead whore!" The words Joseph would say in those dreams were like poison arrows striking Louis in his heart in his subconscious world. He would think regularly about Victoria and most of the time he cried because she was gone. He would scream to be let out, but nobody responded to his call. He starved himself of food until his death anxiety told him to eat.

Days became weeks, torment became torture as Louis remained in dark isolation, putting up with his own stench and his guilty conscience. Then it dawned upon him; his masterpiece that he worked so hard on to achieve, corporate immortality, laid in a burning heap, and his succession plans to take over stem cell research and expedite the science, so that he would be immortal and never die, were also lost forever. Combined with the torment of not being able to see Anastasia it all became too much for Louis, and he then commenced a downward slide into the darkest valleys of his mind where his inner demons were waiting for him.

CHAPTER 46

During those many weeks when Louis was held by the CIA in solitary confinement, he tried to come to terms with how he treated Victoria. His heart bled for the loss of his wife; he would do anything to turn back the clock so that she could be alive again. There were times while he was being held in his pitch-black cell that he would scream out his wife's name; but such calls were all in vain. He experienced moments of utter despair in which he believed the only way he could ameliorate the pain he suffered for causing Victoria's death was to take his own life. At the height of his suicide ideation, when he was adamant in his own mind taking his own life was the only option, Louis' death anxiety would prevail upon his mind again in what was the paradoxical circumstances of yearning for no life while his covetousness for immortality lived on.

On other occasions when he was suffering in the darkness of solitary confinement the faces of the dead people Louis had seen in his life haunted him, as the images of all of them repeatedly appeared in his mind. He longed for his mother's return, just like when he was a child, but then his Uncle Philip's words about her murder by Joseph would fuel his feelings of hatred for his father to only then be replaced by his feelings of guilt that perhaps he had grown into adulthood to be just like that monstrous man. Uncle Philip; how his sorrow and guilt weighed heavily on his mind that he had an ephemeral familial relationship with him, to only then be the reason for the man's untimely demise. Each face of the departed he recalled would be contemporaneously accompanied by the pangs of fear of his death anxiety, and all these functions of his tortured mind were further exacerbated by his severe withdrawal symptoms.

His demons within his mind were feasting upon his suffering in the dark, but it was his death anxiety that flourished the most in this environment because Marjorie Grace's comment that MI5 were in contact with the Singapore Government meant any hope, he had of buying himself the chance of immortality via stem cell technology were now surely lost. On every occasion his mind contemplated what he may have achieved in Singapore his worst inner demon would roar triumphantly within his mind that eventually it would prevail and extinguish his life.

Within that dark universe of solitary confinement, he would also long for the embrace of Anastasia and he considered she was his only positive contribution to this world. Louis would then become alarmed by his thoughts that the Earl must be turning Anastasia increasingly against him. He would scream at the top of his lungs that his captors should release him because he feared for his daughter's wellbeing, but then he would collapse into a state of hopelessness when he realised there was nothing he could do while he was held in that cell.

Finally, there was Annabelle. The guilt Louis was experiencing for her death was also quite profound. Had he been sensible and told her months beforehand they could have only ever been friends she would not have been in Manhattan on that fateful day, and she would still be alive.

In the dark environment of his cell Louis' heart broke, his fears ravaged his mind, his guilt consumed him, his mind shattered and what Joseph could not destroy during his childhood the investigating authorities succeeded in his place. Uncle Philip had told him his matriarchal bloodlines were noble but, in his mind, he believed he had been the antithesis of nobility. Louis was broken. All he had to fight for in life now was his daughter's love, but he believed he was now fighting a losing battle against the Earl in that regard.

The CIA and MI5 could not uncover a shred of evidence that even suggested Louis had been involved in any form of international terrorism, and about five weeks after his mind had totally decompensated, he was eventually released from the CIA's secret facility and transferred into the custody of the Federal Prison Authority, while the FBI and the Department of Justice investigated federal offences Louis may have contravened during his tenure of being one of the most senior executives employed by BMI. Each transaction was examined, every email was read, and every document was reviewed by the FBI and Department of Justice. Upon him being detained in a federal prison, Louis was immediately examined by a doctor, and as a consequence of that examination he was admitted to the United States Medical Centre for Federal Prisoners in Missouri, to be treated for severe depression and malnutrition.

The FBI and Department of Justice were also obliged to contact a public legal defence attorney for Louis, and in turn that attorney then contacted a private legal defence firm. While he was still receiving medical care in Missouri Louis finally had an opportunity to speak to a lawyer, and after he transferred

$200,000.00 to the law firm's bank account his legal team then commenced work trying to secure his release from custody. His lawyers' task became more difficult when the United Kingdom Department of Immigration deemed he would not be entitled to reenter England, and therefore preventing Louis from seeing Anastasia. These legal issues Louis had to address only caused him further mental torment.

Despite all the joint investigations conducted by police departments in America, Australia and the United Kingdom, none of the investigating bodies could charge Louis with one single offence. Phillip had legally changed Louis' name, even if he did pay some extra money to obtain this new identity for his nephew. Strangely, Coonan's statement provided to the police back in 1978 effectively cleared Louis from any wrongdoing. The offshore payments he received from BMI were held on trust by an unnamed corporate trustee in the Cayman Islands, thereby shielding Louis from any tax liabilities in America, Australia and the United Kingdom. Try as the investigators might to find any evidence of offending on Louis' behalf, the facts proved otherwise. His late wife was right; he was brilliant. However, the mental health damage was done; Louis had been tortured and he was now severely depressed.

The worldwide media revelled in the information about Louis which the CIA, MI5 or other investigative bodies had leaked to them. Repeatedly in America, the United Kingdom and Australia the news outlets and tabloid magazines would refer to Louis as the 'Prince of Charlatans' or the son of a notorious New York thug who then went on to deceive the world. The business journals changed their reference to him from the 'Wonder Kid' to the 'Blunder Kid'. This news spread around the world and the Earl was a recipient of it. Much of that news he was aware of long before the media had reported it. Marjorie Grace maintained close contact with the Earl, and she ensured that each new piece of investigation material regarding Louis' background was being reported back to the Earl. On each occasion of being informed about a new revelation, the Earl shook his head in disbelief about the level of deceit that he believed Louis had committed against him, his deceased daughter, and his granddaughter. The Earl's heart continued to break about the loss of Victoria and that sorrow would then fan the flames of his discontent about Louis.

Eventually, after four months of being incarcerated in America without charge, Louis was finally released from custody because a decree of habeas corpus had been granted to him for his release by the United States Supreme Court. His lawyers then had to argue before the House of Lords for his permanent visa to be reinstated, so that Louis could return to England to be with his daughter. By now Louis was very frail and sick, and his medical condition almost prevented him boarding the 747 flight from New York to London. Everywhere Louis travelled in public after his release from custody, and his eventual return to Harlaxton, he detected the same manner of disapproving eyes of him, whether they be the eyes of Americans, the English or any other person acquainted with his story. This silent but very noticeable public condemnation further militated against any prospect of Louis' mental health improving. Just like his escape from New York during the late 1970's, Louis was once again leaving America with a very troubled mind.

Louis had left Harlaxton on September 9, 2001, and now he finally returned to the manor home on March 1, 2002. It had been six months since he had last seen his daughter, and it would be with great trepidation that he took the first step to finally enter Harlaxton again to determine how he would be received by Anastasia. James had faithfully welcomed him back, but he also warned him the Earl was waiting for him in the grand entrance hall and he was not pleased about his return. Louis was very ill, and it took a while for him to gain his strength to walk into the stately manor home. He had not been charged with any offence, but he was apparently being treated like a criminal by the Earl. The Earl could not prevent Louis from entering the manor home because Victoria had bequeathed in her Will her entire legal interest in Harlaxton to Louis, in recognition of his payment of all the Earl's debts.

The Earl stood at the bottom of the staircase in the entrance hall, and Louis immediately noticed the old man's eyes narrow as Louis took his first step into that room. "You may have a legal interest which prevents me from throwing you out onto the streets where you belong, but this is my house and it was to be my daughter's house, so do not feel as though you are at liberty to march anywhere within these walls." The Earl displayed no mercy for him, which was not an unexpected event for Louis, but he did not want to fight as all he sought in life now was his daughter's love. "I know you hate me, and I accept your reasons for that but this is also my daughter's house and I am her only parent now. Where is Anastasia?" His conciliatory response had not been anticipated by the Earl, but the old man was unrelenting in his position as to how Louis should be received within these walls. "Anastasia does not want to see you, because she blames you, for her mother's death, as do I!" Louis' worst fears while he was incarcerated were now becoming a reality. "Anastasia, it's Daddy, sweetheart. Daddy is home Anastasia. Please come down."

Louis' loud voice echoed within the entrance hall and travelled down the hallways attached thereto, but his daughter did not come to him. He began to try to call out again, but the Earl interrupted him before he could speak a word. "You are wasting vital oxygen I am afraid. My granddaughter does not want to see you and I am not going to force her to do so. Now, begone with you this instant; go to that room your flesh festered in for the past few years." Louis could not bear the thought of having to enter that office as it held too many skeletons within it for him. "Please don't make me stay in that room. There are too many memories for me in that room and it will kill me to have to return it. Please, please let me sleep in another room. Okay, I will try to avoid you having to endure my presence, but please do not make me sleep in that room!"

The Earl stood there, examining every detail of Louis' face and he could see the terror in the man's eyes. "Very well then. James!" The old butler quickly entered from the vestibule where he stopped in his tracks after Louis had entered the entrance hall. "Yes, Master?" The Earle's right hand reached out and pointed to the third level of the house. "Take this man please to the guest room on the third floor and make up that room for him." The butler nodded and he turned towards Louis to assist him up the stairwell as the Earl marched back up the stairs, and he then disappeared down the hallway where the au pair was entertaining Anastasia in her bedroom and out of earshot from her father's return home. "Come with me Louis, I shall assist you up these stairs." For once Louis did impose his burden upon the butler as he was frail and did need assistance up those stairs. It was evident to James that Louis was not well and after he made up the room he too took it upon himself to call the doctor in the village to request an urgent home appointment.

Dr Robinson was an elderly general practitioner in whom the local community members in Harlaxton Village and its surrounding areas placed their trust in. When he walked into that bedroom that afternoon and immediately saw Louis' very noticeable poor health, he knew this visit would not be his last. Louis was lying down in bed and although he tried to get up out of bed, the doctor quickly assured him he must remain lying down. Dr Robinson thoroughly examined Louis from head to toe and then he called for James, who had been waiting in the hallway outside of the bedroom. "This man is gravely ill. He needs around the clock medical care in a hospital. I recommend he be taken to the hospital in Grantham to receive urgent hospital care." Louis would not accept that recommendation. "No, please don't send me to a hospital. I was kept in a cage for four months and I could not bear the thought now of leaving this house when I have only just returned. Please doctor, I beg you."

Dr Robinson acknowledged there was a psychological element to Louis' medical condition which militated against his being admitted into hospital care. "All right then, well in these circumstances you are going to require around the clock medical attention here at Harlaxton. You must have nursing care 24 hours a day until I consider you are well enough to go without it. There is a telephone number for a private nursing service which I shall call now. I am also going to call the hospital immediately for them to deliver the necessary equipment for me to restore your health. You will need an intravenous drip to replenish your body, as well as administering antibiotics, because your feverish temperature is being caused by a respiratory infection, which by observing the state of your ears and mouth you must have had for weeks. For the next week I shall visit you every afternoon at 4.00pm to monitor your health and if the nurses require me urgently, I shall attend upon you at any time. But, and this is a big but Mr Montgomery, if I consider at any moment you need to be admitted to hospital that shall be done." Dr Robinson turned to the now gravely concerned old butler who naturally worried about the arrangements for hospital care to be put in place. "James. Would you please take me to the nearest telephone in this house so that I may make the necessary arrangements for Mr Montgomery's care?" James nodded his head. "Of course, doctor." Dr Robinson and James then disappeared from view as Louis lay there in his bed suffering from his compromised physical and mental conditions. He had only one thought. "Please come and see me, Anastasia."

Dr Robinson made the necessary urgent medical arrangements for Louis to be treated at home. The doctor visited Louis every day for the next two weeks as his physical health slowly but surely improved with treatment. By the end of the third week, Louis did not need nursing care anymore, but Dr Robinson continued to visit him at home each afternoon for another week to monitor his health. He was now able to walk up and down the stairwell at Harlaxton without requiring James' assistance.

It was during one of his strength exercises walking up and down the stairs in that fourth week that Louis finally saw Anastasia. He was about to walk up the staircase from the ground floor when he heard the sound of his daughter's laugh as she entered the vestibule of Harlaxton, after the au pair had collected her from kindergarten in the village. He turned around to see Anastasia run into the grand entrance hall from the vestibule and, upon seeing her father, the little girl immediately stopped in her tracks and just stared at him. Louis held out his arms to invite his daughter for a long overdue cuddle. "It's all right my little sweetheart, come over here and give Daddy a hug." Anastasia did not move so Louis persisted. "Don't be afraid Anastasia, I'm fine now and I will never leave you again." Louis proceeded to try to walk over to his daughter as he now saw her little eyes becoming wet with tears, but he then stopped in his tracks as an arrow was shot into his bleeding heart. "Mummy died because of you, Daddy. I don't want you, Daddy. Leave me alone Daddy." With those final words being spoken Anastasia ran up the staircase to go to her room with the au pair following close behind her. Louis' heart had shattered into a thousand tiny pieces, and he slowly walked back up to his bedroom to lock his broken heart away for the evening.

At the conclusion of that fourth week of his treatment the doctor was satisfied Louis' physical condition no longer required his daily attention, but his patient's psychological condition worried him. He asked Louis to see a psychologist for counselling, but Louis would not agree to that. He did not want Anastasia to find out from any person her father was mentally ill. James had already privately mentioned to Dr Robinson before the start of this home appointment that Louis was not faring well at all mentally since his daughter had rebuffed him in the grand entrance hall about a week beforehand. After the appointment, the doctor told James he was very concerned Louis was going to decompensate and slip into major depression, so if James saw any signs that suggested the possibility of Louis committing suicide, he must call his practice number immediately.

Subsequently, in the time that followed thereafter there would be many occasions when Anastasia would come across her father around Harlaxton, but she would not speak to him or even touch him, rather the ongoing disappointment for Louis occurred as his daughter would turn around and walk away from him. Anastasia had not received enough paternal care from Louis prior to her mother's passing and since that time she continued to blame Louis for Victoria's death. Louis could not speak to the Earl and any mention by James of him seeing a psychologist, as recommended by Dr Robinson, was resisted by Louis. He would fight his demons and disappointment on his own as he believed his little girl would eventually love him again.

CHAPTER 47

Five years ticked by for Louis without any change in the manner in which he was treated by his daughter. Anastasia would not talk to him. Indeed, when Louis would try to approach her, she would continue to turn her back on him or scream out for her poppy. The world's reaction to the BMI and Zogby affair was harsh and in Louis' case, profoundly unfair as he was being blamed by reporters and columnists for the economic instability arising from BMI collapsing due to its insolvency. Some of the children at Anastasia's kindergarten would tell her that her father was a bad man, and a criminal, which in turn entrenched the little girl's animosity towards her father. The condemnation of her father followed her into Anastasia's early years of primary schooling. The Earl had no choice but to arrange a change of schools for early in her second year of primary school as the playground teasing was affecting her emotionally.

Louis had slipped into a deep depression over Victoria's death as well as the uncompromising presence of his inner demons in his thoughts after he had returned to England. The torture he endured during the time of his incarceration in solitary confinement had caused him substantial trauma, and it further militated against his prospects of returning to some form of functional life in the community. For those first two years after he returned to England Louis resisted Dr Robinson's ongoing recommendations, that he be treated for his mental health illnesses.

Louis would try to avoid reading newspapers or watching television news, because he could not tolerate the misreporting about him allegedly being to blame for Zogby's terrorist attack on $$$. However, one bleak winter's morning in late February 2004 James had to urgently call Dr Robinson, after Louis had commenced breaking items in his bedroom in a fit of despair and rage. The Fleet Street Press had printed articles that claimed he and Victoria had been involved in the fraudulent activities of Naylor and Audrey, because they had all visited the Zogby household together in 2001. There was no substance to the claims of collusion by Louis or Victoria in the subsequent fraud Naylor perpetrated against BMI, but the press ran with the story as it sold newspapers. James had inadvertently left one of the Earl's newspapers in the kitchen one morning, and Louis saw the headline when he walked in there for his morning coffee and upon reading the allegation that his wife had been colluding in criminal activity, Louis' mind exploded with anger and sorrow that his late wife's name was being sullied. Dr Robinson had no other option than to agree to sign a mental health directive that permitted Louis to be physically removed from Harlaxton by the police and ambulance.

Fortuitously for Louis his daughter was not home at the time of his being taken away from the manor home in this state. The Earl was home, and he accompanied James as they followed behind the stretcher the ambulance officers had wheeled him out on and they watched the ambulance depart to urgently whisk Louis away to hospital. The Earl's hostility for Louis began to wane from that day onwards, as he felt some small twangs of pity for him suffering like he was. Louis was treated in the hospital for almost two months before being allowed to return home after his treating psychiatrist, Dr Geoffrey Millard, opined he could be discharged from mandatory hospital care, but the proviso was for Louis to attend such counselling sessions as he saw fit to require him to attend.

During these sessions Dr Millard would explore the dark universe of Louis' psyche arising from the concomitant trauma of Victoria's death and the torture he endured while he was incarcerated in America. Like the universe itself there seemed to be no end to Louis' pain and suffering but he would not disclose or admit to the genesis of his mental suffering which had been his inner demons that tormented him since he lived in Midtown West. Whether it was him feeling shame for his mind entertaining these demons or his fear of being hospitalised again, Louis could not open this door of his mind to Dr Millard. After two years of counselling and drug treatment, Dr Millard opined that Louis was permanently mentally disabled because of his depression. Louis would also never be able to work again in the corporate world because of the BMI controversy, and because of his fragile mental health he rarely left Harlaxton Manor during the first five years of his returning from Manhattan. Despite Louis' obvious suffering, the Earl still shielded Anastasia from him.

Dr Robinson would also attend Harlaxton Manor on subsequent occasions to treat Louis after James became concerned about Louis' physical condition. During that five-year period Louis was admitted to hospital on two further occasions due to malnutrition. Because of his mental health he rarely ate food and seemed to just survive on his daily vice of drinking coffee. His body would suffer the deleterious effects of malnutrition and then Louis would become afraid he would die, and he would call upon James to contact Dr Robinson. On the final occasion that Louis was admitted to hospital the Earl watched from his parlour window as the ambulance officers took Louis on a stretcher and placed him in the ambulance. The Earl's anger about the death of Victoria had not totally subsided, but he could not bear the thought of Louis' ongoing suffering and there was a further issue, which concerned him, as he watched the ambulance take Louis to Grantham Hospital again.

The Earl was now very old, and he knew that he would not be around for much longer to care for his granddaughter. "I had better speak to this fellow when he is brought back, my granddaughter needs him," the Earl said to himself as the ambulance drove away. The Earl then rubbed his chest because there was a niggling pain that he had to endure over the past six months, which he had attributed to being stress as he too still suffered from the heartbreak of Victoria's death.

During that five-year period of Louis' varying degrees of health, the American military eventually tracked down and killed Zogby. After his act of terrorism at $$$ Zogby fled Qatar as he knew the Sheik would hand him over to the American government to maintain relations with that country. Zogby fled to Northern Algeria, taking refuge in the Atlas Mountains with local villagers. However, the might of the American military eventually tracked him down to one of those villages one evening. Special Forces troops surrounded the house Zogby was held up in. The orders from the American Military commanders to the Special Forces troops were clear; Zogby was not going to be taken alive and do whatever was necessary to kill him. When Zogby saw he was surrounded he opened fire on the Special Forces troops with his machine gun, wounding one of them. The return blast from the Special Forces squad was ferocious; there were grenades and return machine gun fire from all angles of the house. After ten minutes of incendiary tactics the commander of the squad ordered a ceasefire. The troops entered the house and looking around the Special Forces troops identified Zogby as he lay dead on the floor of a bedroom after he had been killed by multiple bullet wounds and shrapnel from the grenades.

The news of the raid in Northern Algeria was broadcast back in the United States. People celebrated on the streets in relation to Zogby's death as American pride had been restored after the devastation people suffered because of the attack on $$$. That building had been restored after the attack but it would not see the likes of BMI within its walls again.

By 2006 the corporate empire of BMI had finally collapsed. Although there had been a tracing exercise and account undertaken in numerous court jurisdictions around the world to recover the defrauded sums of the settlement funds stolen by Naylor, it was the lawyers who ended up being significant recipients of any of the funds recovered. The banking institutions could not recover the total sum lent to BMI to undertake the purchase of the oil and gas interests.

Some of Naylor's money had been recovered by BMI but he had established an elaborate web of transferring money from the Cayman Islands to Switzerland and then further transfers to any other corporate safe havens. Each transfer entailed a fee for the banker involved. The funds deposited in South American banks were seized by those countries and never returned because the jurisdiction of the American and European courts was not recognised in those countries. The legal expenses became too much and given the damage to its reputation its revenue significantly declined so that BMI could not repay its debts. The world market had rejected BMI and the share prices of all the BMI entities throughout the world had plummeted to being worthless stock. Divesting his ownership of BMI stocks before September 10, 2001, had ensured Louis' fortune was protected.

Louis' second admission to hospital for his malnutrition had been longer than expected. His body had deteriorated significantly due to many years of drug abuse followed by his depression and consequential starvation. Gone was the immaculate presentation of a young man with the world at his feet and in its place was the presentation of a severely depressed man. Louis' hair was longer, and he had grown a beard. His clothes were simple rather than displaying sartorial elegance. Louis' medical team at the hospital were all concerned about his ongoing depression. Dr Millard was once again brought in to treat Louis. A treatment regime of anti-depressants was implemented while Louis was in hospital.

Eventually, after two months of intense treatment, Louis was diagnosed as being fit to be discharged from the hospital. Dr Robinson as the local treating general practitioner still had to regularly check on Louis but the specialist doctor believed the treatment in the hospital, and the ongoing home treatment would prevent any chance of suicide. Dr Robinson had informed Dr Millard that in his view the main reason Louis did not eat food was due to his daughter having no contact with him. On one of his home visits Dr Robinson raised this issue with the Earl. The good doctor was told by the Earl that his opinions about the personal matters of Anastasia's relationship with her father would be dealt with by the Earl, and to kindly stay out of those personal affairs. Dr Robinson raised his eyes to the sky; he knew the Earl was an arrogant old man, but he had to try intervening. Dr Robinson did not realise the Earl had already decided to try and restore the relationship between Louis and Anastasia.

Louis had been home from the hospital for a week. He was sitting on a chair admiring the Italian Gardens section of the grounds of Harlaxton on what was one of the rare occasions that he came out of his room. Anastasia still had not spoken to her father properly since he returned to England, although Louis would catch sight of her running around the grounds of Harlaxton. Despite everything which had initially occurred during the first six years of her life the little girl appeared to be happy, and this fact pleased Louis. As Louis sat on a bench seat admiring the Italian Gardens that Autumn Day the Earl approached him. Louis was initially guarded and ready for some form of argument. The Earl held up his hands as a sign of a truce. "I am not here to abuse you, Louis. I am here to talk to you and to make peace between you and Anastasia. My granddaughter, your daughter, she needs you." Louis was pleasantly surprised by the offering of the olive branch from the Earl, as he had only ever known the man to be hostile towards him. "Well, thank you but I think my daughter hates me because of you." The Earl shook his head in disagreement. "No Louis, she doesn't hate you, she just never got to know you and then she lost her mother. I admit I have said some things over the years to Anastasia, and I am truly sorry I said those words."

Louis looked deep into the Earl's eyes; his remorse was genuine. Louis extended his intentions of goodwill back to the Earl. "I am so sorry about..." Louis was initially unable to speak because, in his depressed state, he found that he could become tearful quickly and he was unable to contain these emotions. After two minutes of gathering his composure, he spoke again. "I am sorry for Victoria's death. If I could turn back time and change my actions I would. Greed got the better of me Earl. Greed for money, greed for drugs, greed for a world in which I could relieve my troubled mind." Once again, the Earl held up his hand, as if to reassure Louis that he did not have to be subservient to the old man. "My name is Henry, please call me Henry." Henry then sat down on the bench seat with Louis in what was a physical display of this truce. He then fixed his gaze upon Louis in whom he earnestly sought the truth. "I must be honest; I may never forgive you for the way that you treated Victoria, but I have to accept that she placed those pills in her mouth. Please, please tell me this, did you sleep with that young American woman?"

The Earl's earnest stare was rewarded by the truth. "No, Henry, I didn't. I couldn't go through with it but yes, I did want to for a long time. However, for a long time that desire for another woman was checked by the realisation that I was married to your daughter, and perhaps our troubled marriage would restore itself to the way it was when we were first married. Had I not been so addicted to drugs that would not have been a question for me to consider, had I not been so drug addicted my marriage would still have been the same as when Victoria and I first got married. I was a drug addict, Henry; I now realise that fact. I just was not strong enough to give up those drugs."

Henry was now experiencing mixed emotions as Louis confessed to his drug addiction, but he knew he had to heal all the wounds so that his granddaughter could have a family life and so that she could have a father. "So why did you still travel to Manhattan if you did not want to sleep with the young woman?" Henry's piercing eyes did not waiver from staring deep into Louis' eyes. "Well of course I had still wanted to meet up with Annabelle when I left here that day Henry, even though I was in two minds before I left. We may well have ended up still getting together; however, the night I flew to Manhattan I came to my senses halfway across the Atlantic Ocean as I realised that I loved my wife and wanted to be with her. Had technology not been working against me that night I could have told Victoria how I felt, and the fact that she died because of my actions is something that I have to live with, my sorrow and regret about that fact is something I will take to my grave."

Henry nodded his head in accepting Louis' candour. After he continued to look into Louis' eyes for an eternity, Henry then decided he should broach the next topic. "So, tell me who you are Louis. Obviously, the newspapers have said a lot about you for a while there but let me understand who you actually are." Louis knew that he had to reveal all his past life to Henry, and it was now time for an explanation to be provided. For the next two hours Louis revealed all to Henry about his childhood and about how his father treated him. No stone was left unturned, the years at the shed in Manhattan were discussed, the murder of his mother, meeting his uncle who revealed to him his French nobility bloodline, the night of the death of his uncle and the life in Australia prior to meeting Victoria. The only matter that Louis did not touch upon was the mental torment he went through regarding his inner demons.

After the Earl had digested all this information he stood up and looked into the fields for a moment, then he turned back to Louis. "You should have told Victoria about this life of yours, old boy, it explains so much and she would have helped you heal from it." Louis was somewhat filled with admiration for his dead wife, because despite how much their relationship had soured, she had not revealed to her father prior to her death the truth about Louis. "Anyway, we must now move forward into the future so let me help you heal your relationship with your daughter. She needs you, Louis, she needs a father." Henry then held out his hand seeking a handshake in return from Louis, an ancient ritual between men but an important symbol that they were no longer at war.

CHAPTER 48

Two weeks after his discussion with the Earl it was time for Louis to once again sit in his favourite spot of the Italian Gardens of Harlaxton Manor. Anastasia had not yet resiled from her position of ignoring her father and this was despite Henry encouraging the young girl to do so. Eventually, Henry had enough of the soft approach and that Autumn afternoon he spoke in a commanding voice to Anastasia, demanding that she go and speak to her father. Initially, Anastasia ran away from her poppy and fled to her bedroom crying. After 30 minutes, she came out of the bedroom and approached Henry in his parlour. "I am sorry, Poppy. I will speak to Daddy if you want me to." Henry smiled at his granddaughter, her innocence was sweet, and it was because of her love for him that she was now willing to interact with her father. "No Anastasia, you are not doing this because of me, you are doing it for yourself. Your father loves you very much and he wants to be a father for you. I know what that feeling is like, and I still wish that I could be a father for your mother, but sometimes life does not work out the way we want it to." Henry then took his granddaughter by the hand and commenced the long walk through the manor to go to the gardens.

Louis sat in the Italian Gardens, a cool breeze was blowing that afternoon, but the beauty of the gardens seemed to be hypnotic, and the cooler conditions could not break Louis' concentration. As Louis pondered the chapters of his torrid life, he was oblivious to the fact that Henry and Anastasia were walking over towards the chair he was sitting in. The Earl broke the silence and Louis' concentration. "Louis, somebody wishes to speak to you." Louis turned to face Henry and to his great joy, and surprise, there standing beside him was Anastasia. She had grown into a pretty little girl; she had the looks of her mother which at that moment made it even harder for Louis to remain calm. A tear drop rolled down Louis' cheek and he got off his chair. Louis initially was frozen in his movement; he was fearful that Anastasia would run away if he tried to approach her. Then he took a deep breath and walked over to his daughter. Louis pulled up right in front of his daughter, her eyes were welling up with tears. Louis got down on one knee and hugged her tightly for 30 seconds. Louis then held the little girl between his hands. "I am sorry about your mummy darling. I too wish she were here with us. I, no, just..." Louis was finding it hard to express the words he wanted to say.

Henry could see Louis was struggling to speak so he reached over and gave Louis a reassuring pat on the back. Louis looked into his daughter's eyes again and it was as though he was looking at Victoria. "I love you, Anastasia, I love you very much. From here on in I am going to make my life all about being your daddy as best I can; no more work; no more making money; my life will only be just about you." Anastasia smiled and then hugged her father. It was the first time that she had shown her youthful feelings of love for her father in this manner for a very long time and his heart lapped up his daughter's affection. Anastasia then looked at her father in excitement. "Can we go and say hello to Mummy, Daddy? Poppy told me we could. I want to tell you all about the flowers." Louis smiled at his daughter; he had hoped for so long there would be a day like this one. "Of course, sweetheart, of course." The pair of them then walked off through the fields to go see the flower bed. The Earl did not go, it was still too difficult for him to come to terms with Victoria's death and the flowers where her ashes were spread would be too discomforting for him.

Although it was the middle of autumn, there were still some flowers to which abscission's hand had not as yet taken them from the flower bed. Dahlias, Little Carlows and Gold Strum were all in bloom and the mixture of violet and gold made the flower bed take on a regal appearance. Louis had never been to the spot where his wife's ashes had been strewn. He was somewhat uneasy about going to the site, particularly as he still bore the burden in his mind as being the cause of his wife's death. Anastasia ran up to flowers, as she had done on many occasions beforehand. She would regularly go to the flower bed to speak to her mother. Her mother's friend, Elizabeth, had told Anastasia on the day of the ceremony to spread her mother's ashes that if she "ever needed to speak to her mother she could always come here and talk, the flowers would listen to her words because this is where her mummy now lives." Over the past five years Anastasia would do that; she would go to flowers, and speak to her mother. She would tell her mother about all the events that were happening in her life. Now she was here with her daddy, and, as Louis wondered what to expect from visiting this sight.

It did not take long as he then witnessed his daughter's world reveal itself to him. "Hello Mummy, I have brought Daddy today to speak to you. Daddy has become nice again Mummy and he has promised he will always be nice to me." Anastasia looked at him and she gestured as though there was something he should be doing. "Come on Daddy, speak to Mummy, she is listening to us." Louis looked at his daughter, as at first, he thought it was strange that she wanted him to speak to the flowers, but then he realised this behaviour was no different to the behaviour of people who grieve over a gravesite, and speak to a relative many years after they have been buried. Louis looked at the flowers for a moment as he tried to think of what words were appropriate for him to say. "Hello, my darling wife. I wish you were here in the flesh for me to say these words. I am sorry Victoria; I am sorry for every shred of pain I caused. If I could turn back the clock I would, because I now realise I let greed get in the way of our relationship. I am sorry I did not listen to you about Naylor, BMI and well..." He contemplated his next words as he did not wish to reveal all his secrets in Anastasia's presence. "My guilt, and shame, will never leave me about your light fading before its time, which has denied Anastasia of the time she should have spent with you. I have changed, changed for the better."

The inner demon of his fear of his mortality challenged his mind to dispute he had changed, and its immutable presence caused him to experience another pang of shame. "I guess my change for the better will ultimately be decided by Anastasia but what I meant to say is I will always look after our little girl, she looks just like you sweetheart, which is even more heartbreaking for me every day." Tears flowed down his cheeks. Anastasia held her father's hand to comfort him. "Don't cry Daddy, it is okay now. Just like me Mummy forgives you Daddy." If ever the words from an innocent child could cure a broken heart they did so on this day, and for just a moment the clouds slightly parted in Louis' mind that afternoon at the flower bed as the afternoon sun warmed their backs. As they walked back towards Harlaxton Manor from the flower bed Louis' temporary moment of solace was interrupted by Anastasia. "Daddy, one day I will join Mummy in the flowers and then she and I will be together again." Louis stopped, knelt, and turned Anastasia to face him. "My little girl, why would say that? You are going to be with Daddy for a long, long time." His fear would have been palpable to the mature eye, but it was beyond the comprehension of Anastasia as she nodded and then smiled. "I know Daddy, but one day I would like to be able to be with Mummy again. Poppy told me so." Louis looked at his daughter and his inferiority complex challenged him for being so weak about fearing his mortality compared to the courage just displayed by his daughter. She was her mother's daughter and this further motivated Louis to be the parent he should have been.

CHAPTER 49

For the next 18 months life was normal, as it could be, at Harlaxton Manor. The resolution of their differences meant that Louis and Henry could share a whiskey together in honour of Victoria on the sixth anniversary of her death on 10 September 2007. It was a solemn occasion, but it represented the extent of the relationship which Louis had now developed with the Earl. Anastasia seemed to be very happy in her life, and her schoolteachers had commented upon her improvements at school after she and Louis had talked to one another the year beforehand. The protesters were now gone for good from outside of Harlaxton as there were other fish for them to fry. Christmas 2007 was a joyous occasion, and the Earl even invited some old friends and family to join the three of them for lunch.

As the calendar turned over to the Spring of 2008, Louis felt as though life was now comfortable. One morning in late March 2008, Louis was sitting in his former study which he had now converted into a sunroom, a place where he could read quietly, and he no longer felt disturbed by it. Anastasia was at school, and apart from the sounds of James and the other servants walking the halls cleaning, Harlaxton Manor was otherwise in a state of peaceful bliss. Louis had not seen Henry leave to go into Harlaxton Village that morning. It was about 11.00am, when Henry entered the sunroom and broke the peace and quiet that Louis was otherwise enjoying. Louis looked up from his chair and the face of the old man looked troubled, as if he had seen a ghost. "What is it, Henry? What is wrong?" He had never seen Henry looking so vulnerable. The Earl remained quiet, and he just stood in the sunroom looking blankly at no particular object or thing. Louis was now concerned, "Henry, what is wrong?" Henry's ruminating was disturbed, and he looked at Louis, his eyes were almost lifeless and lacking the usual authority they possessed. "I am afraid I have some bad news for me, for you and for Anastasia. I have just returned from Dr Robinson's surgery and the prognosis is not good. I have advanced breast cancer, which is terminal, and I only have three to six months to live."

Louis could not quite fathom what he was being told by Henry and at first, he thought the old man may be playing a trick on him but the more he stared at the Earl's listless eyes, the more he realised it was only the plain truth. "Henry, that is terrible news. Have you obtained a second opinion? Have you seen a specialist? How about I arrange something? I know of this clinic in Europe, money is no object Henry as I will pay for the treatment." The Earl shook his head before he then faintly smiled and held up his hand to stop Louis from speaking any further. "I have seen many specialists over these past few months Louis, it is too late for me. I should have picked up on the warning signs quite some time ago, but like most men I didn't take any notice of the symptoms. Anyway, old boy, I am done for so don't you go wasting money on treatments because the cancer is too far advanced."

Louis could not comprehend how Henry felt right now and his vulnerability about his ultimate death was the genesis of his next inquiry. "Aren't you afraid?" Henry's next words would only cause Louis' shame to become further entrenched. "I was old enough to watch my father courageously walk out these doors to serve for the Royal Air Force during World War 2, only for him to be shot down and killed by the Hun; no braver officer and gentleman I have ever known. You learn so much about life and death when you have lived through such acts of courage. Afraid?" There was a moment of silence as Henry pondered his question; then he displayed his father's courage which lived proudly in his soul. "No, where there is life there is also death. I have had a good life and I am ready to face my god." Louis could not comprehend how Henry could be so courageous but then his mind swiftly focused on how his daughter would feel when she heard this news. "Anastasia is going to be devastated by this news. She adores you Henry." He nodded his head in agreement with Louis; Henry too was concerned about how his granddaughter would receive this news. It became apparent to Louis he must break this news to his little girl. "Well, I will break the news, Henry. I'm her father and she needs to hear it from me. Is that fine by you?" Henry once again nodded his head in agreement with Louis as this was a parent's duty.

Although she was only weeks away from celebrating her tenth birthday, Louis could still see a vulnerable little child inside of Anastasia. As James brought her inside of Harlaxton Manor from picking her up at school Louis looked at Anastasia and he knew that what he was about to tell her would upset her very much. Anastasia saw her father standing at the main entry of Harlaxton Manor, and she was like a cat chasing a bird as she exploded off the mark into her father's arms. "Daddy." She was full to the brim with an enormous amount of glee. "Daddy, I had such a fun day at school, and guess what Daddy?" Louis tried to act as surprised as possible, the thought of having to deliver the news to his daughter about her grandfather was extremely confronting for him. "What sweetie, what is the news?" Anastasia stepped away from the embrace with her father and proudly placed her hands on her hips. "Well, I have been chosen to star in the school musical. I am going to play Yum-Yum in *The Mikado*. Daddy I am so excited, you and Poppy can come and watch me sing and dance."

Life could not have chosen a more difficult moment for Louis to deliver the news he was about to deliver to his daughter and now he would shatter her happy world. He believed he had to tell her now, but he should have allowed her to enjoy this moment. "That is great news sweetie, I am so proud of you, I really am. However, Daddy needs to talk to you about something so come with me to the sunroom." James looked at Louis and nodded, having taken the Earl to Dr Robinson's surgery that morning he knew this would be grim news. Anastasia could not wait for the news, and she importunately pressed her father to reveal his news. "No, Daddy, tell me now. I don't want to go to the sunroom." James took this moment of defiance as an indication he should leave the area.

As James walked down the hall out of earshot Louis knelt on one knee to speak to Anastasia and he had to use every bit of his strength to gather up the courage to deliver the terrible news to his daughter. When he felt he was right to speak Louis delivered the news. "Anastasia, Poppy is not well sweetie. He has cancer. The doctor has told him that he only has a short time to live and there is nothing the doctor can do to save him." Anastasia froze, it was as though ice had instantly taken over her body. Then she began to cry, quickly followed by a loud scream as she spoke. "No Daddy, no Poppy is not going to die. Why would you say that Daddy, why would you say that to me?" Anastasia was hysterical and Louis tried to calm her. "Hush sweetie, I know it is upsetting but you have to be brave for Poppy." Louis' words only aggravated Anastasia's distress. "No, Daddy, I won't hush. It's all your fault. You caused Mummy to die and now Poppy is dying because of you." Anastasia ran away from Louis, screaming out loud it was his fault, and she ran up the staircase to then lock herself in her room.

Louis could not move. He was hurt by Anastasia's words, but he realised the words were spoken in a moment of trauma; his little girl was being told her grandfather was dying. His guilt for causing his daughter's sorrow ate away at his heart as he then made his way to the Earl's living room. When he entered that room, the old man was staring out the window. "Well, that did not go so well." Henry nodded in agreement. "I heard her, Louis. I will go and speak to her in a moment, she should never speak to a parent like that." Henry then sat down in his chair, he stared at Louis, and he could observe from his son-in-law's demeanour he was blaming himself for his daughter's reaction. "Come in Louis and sit down. You don't need to suffer there in silence. I have something to share with you."

Louis then sat down on the sofa opposite the Earl's grand armchair, but he was still lost in his world of guilt. Henry cleared his throat to make sure he had Louis' attention. "My wife died when Victoria was only seven years of age. Heart attack, way too young and very upsetting. Anyway, Louis, I had to break the news to Victoria about her mother's death. Her reaction was not too dissimilar to the reaction I just heard Anastasia scream down these halls. Victoria blamed me on that occasion. I don't know why I reacted the way I did, but I belted her for the manner in which she spoke to me. I have regretted doing that for the rest of my life." Henry's regret could be seen in his eyes. Then he refocused his attention on the reason why he was sharing this memory. "You're a good father, Louis. Many men just like me would have reacted angrily to be spoken in that manner. You didn't react in that manner. You're a good man, and a good father. I just wanted to let you know that."

Louis was moved by Henry's words; he had never spoken to Louis in that manner before. "Now, let me go and sort out that granddaughter of mine." Henry got up out of his chair and it was noticeable he was in immense physical pain. Louis thought about Henry's kind words, before his mind returned to the courage he had just displayed about his imminent passing. Thoughts of shame entered Louis' mind about his long-term demon of death anxiety. Then that ferocious demon itself, death, entered Louis' mind with spine chilling force. There were no drugs for him nor was there a business project for Louis to bury himself in to pursue his chase for immortality. Like he had done on many occasions since he returned from being incarcerated in America, he suffered in silence during this egocentric period of morbidity.

Henry knocked on Anastasia's bedroom door and when she did not respond, he then commanded her to open her door. Moments later his granddaughter opened her bedroom door, and she was still visibly upset. Henry hugged Anastasia, and then he took her by the hand so they could sit down on her bed, where he then spoke to Anastasia for about an hour. There were tears between them and Henry told his granddaughter how much he loved her and how much she reminded him of his own daughter. She told him she was sorry for her behaviour. Henry told her that he knew she was upset but she could never speak to her father like that again, because he was her father, and he was all that she would have in a few short months. Anastasia was too upset to tell her poppy her news about her being selected for the role of Yum-Yum in *The Mikado*.

Louis was now sitting in the formal lounge room of Harlaxton Manor while Henry was speaking to Anastasia. He was lost in his self-centred thoughts about his mortality, so much so he had not noticed Henry walk into the room with Anastasia. Henry announced their presence. "Louis, I have someone here who wishes to say something." Anastasia walked into the large room and her grandfather then left them to talk to each other. Anastasia walked up to Louis with her head bowed as she knew she had said some hurtful words. Anastasia looked into her father's eyes; she was oblivious to the torment he was now suffering. Her eyes welled up with tears and Anastasia spoke through those tears as she threw herself into her father's arms. "I am sorry Daddy; I didn't mean to hurt you." Louis hugged his daughter close to him. He had to fight through his inner fears for Anastasia's sake as this was a day when she needed comfort. "That is okay my sweetie, Daddy still loves you the same."

Subsequently, the sickle of the Grim Reaper began its reach into the lives of Henry, Louis and Anastasia. Although Henry was reluctant for any money to be spent on him, he nevertheless acquiesced in the face of Louis' insistent request and his living room was converted into an upmarket hospital room for him. Henry's treating doctors felt it would be best if he was admitted to a hospital in the last month of his life, but neither he nor Louis would accept that. Instead, the living room had every item a hospital would have to treat a man dying of cancer and no expense was spared by Louis. Henry was embarrassed, as there was no means by which the money could ever be repaid by him, because he had limited funds as most of his family money was now gone. Even the household staff, including James, in the past few years had their wages paid for by Louis. Money did not matter to Louis anymore; family was all that mattered, and he was once again saying goodbye to a member of his family.

Henry's health deteriorated quickly and that only militated against Louis being able to come to terms with his most dreaded inner demon. It was just like he was reliving Eunice Smith's ignominious passing as Henry was quickly stripped of his dignity. His weight dropped off him and Henry could no longer walk. He had so wanted to live to see his granddaughter play Yum-Yum in *The Mikado*, but death's cold hand would not let that happen. One week before the scheduled opening night of Anastasia's school musical, Henry slipped into a coma and he then passed away the next day with Louis and Anastasia by his side. Henry's passing was peaceful, and as his last breath was exhaled the sun's gentle rays shone on his proud head. Anastasia cried and cried as she said goodbye to her grandfather, but then her courage would be evident later that day, when she told her father her poppy was now hugging her mummy, which made her happy. Louis on the other hand laboured under the crushing thoughts about his mortality.

In keeping with his testamentary wishes, Henry was buried in the family plot on the grounds of Harlaxton Manor. He did not believe in being cremated and then having his ashes being spread over the flower bed, like Victoria's Will so requested to occur. The day of Henry's funeral was overcast and wet and the inclement weather was one of the factors which aggravated Louis' inner demons. Henry's testamentary request was that a funeral service be held at the Harlaxton Village Anglican Church he had loyally attended since he was a small child. The religious service attracted many members of the English gentry and nobility, all of whom turned their noses up at Louis while subsequently extending their condolences to Anastasia who was sitting next to her father. Even Victoria's old friend Elizabeth paid very little regard to him, as opposed to her overbearing condolences being extended to Anastasia.

The deliberate snubbing and snobbery ate away within Louis' mind. In addition, he could not understand how these people could be so vicious towards him when he had noble blood within his veins. These insults also consolidated the feelings of isolation Louis had felt for most of his life. The gloomy nature of a funeral ceremony within a church amplified the howls within Louis' mind regarding death as the minister preached about hell, heaven and salvation. Louis was also intrigued to watch Anastasia sing hymns and pray, because he was unaware for all those years, when she would not speak to him, that every Sunday morning was spent attending church with her late poppy. The ordeal for Louis' mind this day had not concluded with the funeral ceremony, as Henry's Will required a private burial service of his coffin attended by only his immediate family. As Louis watched Henry's coffin lowered into the grave, he thought about his own corpse being one day confined within a box six feet underground and the sensation of terror ran down his spine as his most feared demon roared within his mind.

During his state of melancholy that day Louis swore he would never reveal his condition to Anastasia, because he was so ashamed as he watched his daughter courageously standing there in silence watching her beloved poppy being lowered into his grave. Five nights later Louis then watched his daughter bravely perform the role of Yum-Yum on the opening night of the school musical while he sat there in shame fighting his inner demons. The crowd gave her a standing ovation when the curtains were drawn at the end of the musical. Louis clapped the loudest and he had tears in his eyes as he watched his brave little daughter curtsy to the crowd. "I wish I could be so brave." As he walked out of the school hall with Anastasia after the concert, he heard a woman behind him say to her husband 'he is that corporate cretin from BMI'. The humiliation and shame Louis felt at that moment was palpable, and it was made worse for him because his daughter was present to witness this ignominious moment of his life.

CHAPTER 50

Achild's teen years can be hard for any father, but for Louis, they were made even more difficult by the fact that he was on his own, and significantly housebound due to his mental state. Being a single parent with a pubescent daughter is hard enough; however, Anastasia was a strong-willed young lady and that strong will kept on growing the older she became. Save for the fact that Anastasia knew her father should always be obeyed, she otherwise had developed into a young lady who was not going to be dominated by her peers. She was brilliant in her academic prowess. She was also now socially adept within the context of a girls' private school environment at holding her ground with her peers, and, more importantly, winning them over.

By the age of 14 Anastasia was attending her secondary schooling at the Kesteven and Grantham Girls School in Lincolnshire. Louis had thought about sending Anastasia to a girls' private school in London, but when he considered she had been previously teased by other students about him, he thought it best she attended school in Lincolnshire County. The choice of school seemed to be paying dividends, and, as far as Louis could ascertain, his daughter appeared to be happy there. Or so it seemed. Just prior to the summer break Louis was summoned to the school by the headmistress, because Anastasia was in trouble for hitting another girl. Going outside of Harlaxton Manor was usually a struggle for Louis, but when it came to his daughter, he knew he had no choice, he had to leave the grounds of the home. James drove Louis to the school, and during that challenging trip Louis hoped he would not be chastised by any person at the school for his widely reported history. As Louis approached the headmistress' office, he saw Anastasia sitting on the sofa outside; she had her mother's determined look in her eye. Louis approached his daughter, and he was naturally concerned that she was in trouble. His childhood memories at this moment were vividly flowing back to him of his fight with Jose and how that encounter had forever changed his life.

He kissed his daughter on her head and then sat down on the sofa next to her. "What did you do Anastasia?" Anastasia's eyes flashed up at her father as quick as Louis' words had departed his lips. "Defending your honour my father, that is what I was doing." He feared the worst, but he needed an explanation. "What do you mean, defending my honour?" Anastasia's eyes displayed her displeasure. "Well, Dad, there is this girl in my class, Charlotte Fontaine, and she keeps on telling me that you are the son of a thug, and you are a criminal. Today she told me all the newspapers had once upon a time called you a liar, a fraud and that Mummy was also a fraud. Well, that was it, I had enough, and I hit her, I hit her as hard as I could in the nose. I don't think she is going to say anything to me again."

He was mortified to hear her story. Louis closed his eyes and shook his head; his past would never escape him. He looked at Anastasia, she was seeking approval for her actions, but he could not condone her violence. "I understand, my darling why you reacted the way you did but you cannot go around hitting people." Anastasia remained defiant and self-righteous. "Daddy, she was telling lies about you." Louis very quickly dismissed the discussion. "We will talk about that tonight but first of all, let me deal with the headmistress." Therese Bell was a lady who had risen through the ranks of the private education system. She did not attend a prestigious private school, accordingly, she made sure that she was a stentorian educator in all respects. Ms Bell asked Louis to come into her room without his daughter. Anastasia sat outside listening to their conversation. After a while she could hear her father raising his voice in defence of her and Anastasia smiled as she heard her father speak. In particular, she heard her father tell Ms Bell that Charlotte had been bullying Anastasia about him as well as his dead wife, and, while it did not matter whether what she was saying was true or not, she should not be bullying his daughter. Unlike when he was a child, justice prevailed, Ms Bell decided that she would not take any further disciplinary action against Anastasia, but she was warned never to hit another student again.

Later that night after they had returned from school Louis walked into Anastasia's bedroom. She was studying at her desk like she did every night, and her mind was totally focused on the textbook in front of her. He interrupted her, which startled her as she was so engrossed with her homework. Just like the afternoon when he revealed to the Earl the full details of his past Louis explained to Anastasia every detail about his childhood and escape to Australia. It was a difficult discussion as Anastasia was being told by Louis that he was not a Montgomery, that a large part of his life had been a lie in relation to his background, but nevertheless he had noble blood. When Anastasia heard the mention of noble blood she questioned her father, so then he explained to her how he came to meet his Uncle Philip and how he and Joseph died. It also took Louis quite a while to explain to his daughter the complete history and all the facts about Naylor, Zogby and the demise of BMI, and that her mother was not involved in any fraudulent business activity, nor had he acted dishonestly. It was a difficult discussion which no parent should ever need to have with their child; however, eventually, Anastasia understood the reasons why her father changed his name, and why he had been living that lie. Once again, Louis would not tell his daughter about his inner demons. In what turned out to be one of life's great ironies, Charlotte and Anastasia then became friends a few months later. Louis could never understand the way in which women thought; one-minute enemies and now friends.

Louis had hoped the difficult years were behind him after the fight between his daughter and her now new friend Charlotte, but he was surely mistaken. With the advancing teen years of his teenage daughter came her interest in the opposite sex, and being accepted by all of her peers. Although Anastasia was the top student at the school, she nevertheless was overwhelmed with exploring the invasion of boys into her young world. When Anastasia was about 15 years of age, Louis had been requested by Ms Bell to meet with her again at the school about his daughter's behaviour, and on this occasion the headmistress told Louis his daughter and Charlotte were seen in school uniform in Harlaxton Village kissing boys from Stamford College. Ms Bell told him it was inappropriate behaviour for a young female student. Once again, she warned Anastasia but did not further punish her, nor did the headmistress subsequently punish Charlotte.

Being a parent continued to cause him undue concern, because when Anastasia was 16 years of age Louis received a telephone call one Saturday evening from the Harlaxton police which every parent dreads. Anastasia had been involved in a car accident. This call was even more troubling for Louis as Anastasia was driving his car, and she did not have a license. The police officer told Louis that Anastasia was being treated for minor injuries at the Grantham Hospital. During their brief telephone conversation, the officer wanted to know why a 16-year-old child was driving a Rolls Royce. Louis advised the officer that he could not understand that either, as his Rolls Royce was meant to be parked in the garage, or at least it should be. After speaking to the police officer Louis checked the garage and sure enough the Rolls Royce was missing.

Louis had to drive Henry's old Land Rover to the hospital, on his own, to collect Anastasia because James was not working that evening, and despite his fear of leaving Harlaxton Manor on his own, his love for his daughter gave him the courage to overcome his fears. Louis entered the emergency ward of the hospital and he was informed by a nurse Anastasia was being treated by a doctor, for a cut to the side of her skull. The injury had been caused during the crash, but apart from requiring a couple of stitches it was otherwise not serious.

The police officer Louis had spoken to over the telephone was an older man who was easily in his mid-fifties. He introduced himself to Louis as Constable Ernestine, and he allowed Louis to speak privately to his daughter first, as Anastasia had now finished receiving treatment from the doctor. Louis found it difficult to contain his anger, because this behaviour was inconsistent with Anastasia's usual conduct of being an intelligent young woman. Nevertheless, he did not become angry and he remained calm, because he wanted to find out why she had stolen his car. "Well, I didn't expect to spend a Saturday night like this. Would you mind explaining to me why I am spending my Saturday evening like this?"

Anastasia knew that she could not charm her father on this occasion, she had to tell him straight up what she was up to. "Well, Dad, Charlotte some weeks ago was invited to a party by some boys from Carre's Grammar School. She had no way of getting there so I told her I could drive if she paid me five pounds. She agreed and two Saturdays ago I drove her to the party. Well, she then told the other kids that I could give them lifts in exchange for money. So, for the past few weeks, I have been driving kids around in exchange for a few pounds each trip." Louis was surprised his car had been used by Anastasia on so many occasions. After processing all this surprising information, he was more curious than angry. "So how much money have you made?" Anastasia's grin foreshadowed the next bombshell. "Two hundred pounds." Louis was further surprised by his daughter's commercial instincts; his daughter was making a healthy little fortune out of stealing his car each Saturday night. Louis' curiosity changed to laughter, an emotion he could not contain. He laughed openly in front of his daughter and then Anastasia laughed with him. Eventually, when Louis stopped laughing, he looked at his daughter and delivered to her the bad news. "Well, you are grounded." Anastasia was now perturbed as she thought because of his laughter she had got away with this incident. "But Dad, you were just laughing!" Louis nodded his head. "Yes, my dear girl, it is damn funny how much money you have made, but you still stole my car and crashed it. So, you're grounded, and don't argue anymore with me as I may get angry. Now, let me go outside and see if I can make the police go away." Louis then went outside and spoke to Constable Ernestine. Initially, the officer was reluctant to let the matter go, but after Louis explained that his daughter was otherwise a good girl doing well at school the police officer reluctantly agreed not to charge her with unlicensed driving.

On the drive home, Louis held out his hand and only said eight words. "Two hundred pounds please when we get home." There was a smile on his face. Anastasia was safe and well; however, in addition to being grounded she could also pay for the costs of the repairs to his car.

CHAPTER 51

In the summer of 2016 Anastasia graduated from secondary school as the dux of her class. Her marks were exemplary, and she had applied to Oxford University to study medicine. Time seemed to drag on as Anastasia waited for the outcome of her application. Her friends from school were not in Anastasia's realm of academic achievement to apply to study medicine at either Oxford or Cambridge, which meant if her application to Oxford was accepted she would not know any of the other 'freshers' commencing their undergraduate studies of medicine at that medical school. Anastasia was not concerned about the notion of having to make new friends at university; like her mother before her, Anastasia was a free spirit who would not be afraid to explore a new academic environment. On 11 January 2017 Anastasia and Louis were sitting in the informal meals room of Harlaxton; he was drinking his black coffee while his daughter was eating some lunch. James, who was now becoming quite elderly, entered the room. "I am sorry to disturb both off you, but I have some mail. I thought Miss Anastasia may be interested in it." Anastasia burst out of her chair; she had been waiting on a response regarding her application to go to Oxford Medical School and sure enough, contained within the mail was an envelope addressed to her from Oxford University.

Anastasia held the envelope in her hand, she was too afraid to open it. Louis, on the other hand, could not wait and like an eager child on Christmas morning wanting to open a present he wanted to know immediately whether his daughter had been accepted into the prestigious university. "Well, don't wait. Open it." Anastasia nervously opened the envelope and pulled out the letter. She read it and saw that she had been accepted into the medical school. A smile beamed all over Anastasia's face and she let out a huge cry of delight. "I got in Daddy, I got in." Louis was overjoyed and he hugged his daughter, telling her how proud he was of her.

Later that afternoon, when he was on his own, Louis went for a walk to the flower bed. It was winter and prior to this afternoon he had not previously seen the flower bed during that season of the year, but he had been informed by Anastasia several days before that day there were some flowers in bloom. On the walk to the flower bed, Louis recalled from his childhood how happy he was when he thought that he had a chance to escape his father by being selected for the gifted student class. Life was different for Anastasia compared to Louis' life, but he could not help to live vicariously through her at this moment. Louis stopped short of the flower bed, and much to his surprise the flowers were in bloom. Winter roses, paper daisies, and fairy primrose. Louis looked at the flowers for a moment. Then he needed to verbally express his thoughts. "Well, my beautiful wife, I wish you were here today to witness our little girl being accepted into the Oxford University School of Medicine. Just like her Mummy, she is going to be a doctor. You would have been so proud..." Louis had other words to say but he could not go on, his emotions overcame him. Louis wiped his eyes and then proceeded to walk back to Harlaxton Manor. He was almost 56 years of age and his mental health for the present moment was stable.

The remaining weeks that Louis shared with Anastasia at Harlaxton before she went to university were the best moments of their father-daughter relationship. Louis could not hide his pride in his daughter, and he decided to spoil her as much as he could. They travelled to London for several days, just so Louis could buy her an entire wardrobe for her new life living on campus at the university. Travelling away from Harlaxton Manor was always a major undertaking for Louis because he had become so housebound since Victoria's death that travelling outside the gates of the manor home was an ordeal for him. However, London was large, London was apparently safe and in London Louis knew it was highly unlikely he would be recognised and finally, well, he had no choice, he believed he had to take his daughter on this shopping trip. Fine pens were purchased, indeed all the items Anastasia required for her studies were purchased at the best stores London had to offer.

They stayed in a 2-bedroom suite at the Ritz Hotel under the name of Cumberworth; it was not a false identity as Henry had previously established an account at the Ritz Hotel many decades ago. Over lunch on the second day of this shopping trip, the pair of them were discussing generally about the life that Anastasia had ahead of her. Then he turned to the more important matters to talk to his daughter about. "So, I know it is a long time away, but have you given some thought to where you would like to set up your medical practice?" Anastasia almost choked on her mouthful. "That is a long way away Daddy, I have to pass this course first." Louis nodded his head, he realised it was perhaps somewhat premature of him to ask this question, but he wanted to know whether his daughter had any plans with her medical career. "I know, but seriously good early planning always makes a difference in professional life. Look, I have been giving it a lot of thought sweetie, and, once you have finished your medical degree and you are a doctor, I would be happy to buy a medical practice near home for you, so that you can work near where you like to live."

With these words being spoken by her father, Anastasia's mood changed, and her face became serious. "Daddy, my whole life has been spent being so sheltered at Harlaxton Manor. I am grateful for everything you have done for me, including this spending spree, but Dad I want to see the world. I want to work in a foreign land, I want to make a difference." These were words that Louis was not expecting as he had always thought his daughter would remain at Harlaxton Manor, now she was indicating that she wanted to move away from the United Kingdom. "But you are happy here? Why move when you can have everything at your disposal which so many of your classmates will have to work so hard for?" Anastasia closed her eyes and shook her head; her father was simply not listening to her. "Daddy, that is the problem, I have too much. I need to experience my own life, doing what I want to do. Can't you understand that?" Louis nodded his head as though he did understand, but deep down he did not. "I understand, Anastasia, but those feelings may well pass..." Anastasia interrupted her father, she had heard enough. "They won't pass. I want to see the world; I want to make a life for myself." Louis did not say another word about this issue as he did not dare argue further with his daughter. She had her mother's strong will in her.

The day Anastasia left to go to university she did so by travelling on the train. This was what she wanted to do. As they waited at the train station for the train to arrive the pair of them stood there silently, one not knowing what the other should or would say. As the train approached the station, eventually Anastasia broke the silence between them. "Look, Daddy, I know you are always worried about me but don't, please. I will be fine. Be happy for me, I am about to start my amazing journey."

The train pulled up, its bell signifying it was time for the passengers to either disembark or for new passengers to get on board. Louis smiled at his daughter and he did not want to interfere with her life, but he did worry about her, he did not want something to happen to her like had happened to many others in his life. He spoke simple words at this time, although in his mind he wished to express his deeper thoughts. "I know you are excited; I am excited for you.

Just be safe, that is all I ask of you." Anastasia laughed, not a mocking laugh, but rather a laugh of genuine affection. "Oh Daddy, I will be fine. Don't worry about me. Worry about yourself. Now, I must go. I will miss you Dad." With those words Anastasia gave her father a hug; their embrace was for a good 30 seconds before the train's conductor rang the bell to indicate the new passengers better get on board as it was about to depart. Anastasia walked up the short flight of stairs to enter her carriage, and, as she did so she quickly looked back at her father. Louis watched his daughter enter the train for a brief moment to disappear out of sight and a short moment later her face then appeared again in the window of her carriage. They waved at one another as the train departed. Louis watched the train depart the station, he watched it disappear out of sight around the first bend, he watched his little girl leave his life and he knew that she would never be the same person again.

CHAPTER 52

It was a lonely existence for Louis at Harlaxton Manor. Anastasia was residing at Oxford University and save for the Trinity end of term break, which also heralded the end of the university year, she would otherwise remain on campus to continue studying. During those lonely times when Anastasia was residing at Oxford Louis would experience lengthy periods of mental illness. That tick-tocking clock he counted while it counted the time became the dominant thought of his mind for the first six months of Anastasia being away at university. He counted the ticking once too often and then his mind slipped quickly back to the dark recesses of his mind where his innermost demons were waiting for him. He stopped eating and began to lose weight in an almost rhythmic manner to the declinature of his appetite. He did not watch the television because the news reports depicting bloodshed in the ever-escalating crisis of combat in the Middle East aggravated his death anxiety, and apart from reading the emails he received from Anastasia he otherwise became a hermit who had lost contact with the outside world.

Those years of Anastasia being away studying at university seemed to melt into one another for Louis on each occasion his daughter returned to Harlaxton Manor at the end of the Trinity term. Louis had aged very quickly. His hair was now completely grey. His body was frail as Louis' appetite had been significantly disrupted by his lengthy periods of extreme depression. James had retired from service some two years after Anastasia had started university and, in his place, there was now Andrew, but he was not like James. Andrew did not know about the complete history regarding Louis' health, nor did he know about the telltale signs of Louis' mental health deteriorating.

Before Anastasia left Harlaxton Manor to commence her third year of studying medicine at Oxford, she decided to speak to Andrew to determine why her father looked so frail. Her discussions with the butler revealed he knew very little about Louis' antecedents, so Anastasia stepped the butler through the telltale signs of her father's mental health deteriorating by virtue of which his physical health would decline. Her final riding order was for Andrew to call Dr Robinson when he believed medical help was required with either Louis' mental or physical health. She was extremely concerned about her father; however, like her mother Anastasia was determined to be the best medical student in her class so she returned to university. After three months of Anastasia commencing her third year of university, Andrew had cause to call Dr Robinson as he was so worried about Louis not eating any food for three days running.

Dr Robinson held one view alone about Louis' physical state, he needed to venture away from Harlaxton Manor, he needed to find a life again. Dr Robinson suggested to Louis that he become involved in village life. "Harlaxton Village needs a person to take an interest in it, Louis they need a Lord of the Manor." Louis did not accept his doctor's recommendation. "You must be joking; I would rather be locked up again by the CIA than face those people." Dr Robinson persisted. "Louis, we are talking about an event that happened almost two decades ago. A lot has happened in Harlaxton Village. There are a lot of people who have moved here and they either know nothing about you, BMI or the events of 2001 or, they do not care." Louis knew Dr Robinson was right, but Harlaxton Village worried him. "I know there has been a change in the demographics of this village doctor, but there has also been a lot of history here for me of being verbally abused by passersby. I just don't know if I can become involved in the local community."

Dr Robinson was intrigued by Louis' paranoia. "Louis, you have managed to travel back to London over the last five years." Louis nodded his head; however, his mind was still fragile, and he felt he could not achieve anonymity within the village as opposed to the large population of London. Being verbally excoriated or physically attacked by an unknown member of the public worried him. "I know doctor; however, in London I can be anonymous. Harlaxton Village reminds me a lot of Midtown West; everybody seems to know you." Then Dr Robinson had an idea. He knew from speaking to Louis previously he had an interest in Anastasia returning to practice medicine in Harlaxton Village. "Louis, why don't you come down and assist me at my practice. How does that sound?" Louis was curious about the proposition, a doctor needing assistance from him did not seem right. "How? How can I assist you doctor?" Dr Robinson leant forward in his chair. "I know you would like Anastasia to practice medicine here in the Village, to be close to you. I don't want to work forever Louis, so why don't you become acquainted with my practise, get to know the people and then one day, if

Anastasia wishes to return to Harlaxton Manor, the three of us can discuss how she may take over my practice."

The prospect of Anastasia practising medicine in the Village appealed to Louis, but he could not see how his involvement in Dr Robinson's practice would make any difference to that. "I don't understand doctor, how will I make a difference by assisting you to, in turn, make it possible for Anastasia to practice medicine here, but more importantly, what will I do?" Dr Robinson considered the question for a moment; it was a fair question. He looked out of his surgery window where he saw Louis' beloved Rolls parked in the car park where Andrew could also be found smoking a cigarette next to it, and then the doctor had a further idea. "Some of the elderly people need assistance to travel to my surgery, so you could assist them with that travel. You still have a driver's licence, don't you?" Louis nervously nodded his head to confirm that he did. "Medications may need to also be picked up from the pharmacy and delivered to very sick people. There are occasions when I need a second person Louis, even just to drive me. With you working with me, by my side, I am sure the good folk of this village and the surrounding area would really admire you doing that."

Work! Louis had not been able to do any work for almost two decades because of his mental health and now he had an opportunity to work. The idea of the public admiring his benevolence appealed to him but his fear of the opposite reaction was a hard thought for Louis to dispel from his mind. "Doctor, we have a deal. I am happy to do this but on one condition." It was now Dr Robinson's turn to be intrigued. "What is it, Louis?" Louis sat down in front of the doctor again, he looked him in the eye like a parishioner would look into the eyes of the parish minister at confession time. "Please help me get my little girl back to Harlaxton Manor. Please help me to convince her to come home. She is all I have in this life, and if she goes away for good, I have nothing else to live for." Dr Robinson nodded his head. He was concerned just how emotionally dependent Louis had become on his daughter, but he also knew he was now a shell of a man.

Louis would spend his time around Harlaxton Village assisting Dr Robinson as agreed. Much to Louis' relief many of those people who had been critical of him after the BMI controversy had either moved on or died or forgiven him. The elderly people who did remember him were generally so poor and sick they did not care whether he was once one of the most hated people in the area. As Louis assisted the people of Harlaxton Village, so too did Dr Robinson be proven correct as the people of the village accepted Louis. However, Dr Robinson also believed Louis needed to perform an unselfish act of substantial contribution. He decided one afternoon to raise it in his surgery. "Now Louis if what I am about to say upsets you let me know, and I will not say anything further." Louis became slightly nervous, and he sat down in the patients' chair. "Yes, take a seat. My apologies as I should have told you, take the weight of your feet. Louis, I have been thinking about how I can assist you in restorng your confidence. The work you have been doing for me is appreciated in the community, but I believe you would engender even more widespread goodwill if you could donate a larger sum to health services in the county. What do you think?" Louis was not expecting this question, but it was for a charitable cause. "I spent some time at the Grantham Hospital. Would 20 million pounds help them?" Dr Robinson's eyes could have fallen out of his head. How much money does Louis have? The doctor could only agree. Louis donated 20 million pounds to be used for redeveloping the Grantham Hospital. His standing in society was not just improved in the district or even the county; his standing improved around the country.

Dr Robinson kept his promise to Louis. Once a month the doctor would correspond with Anastasia by email, and he would inform her about Louis' benevolent work in the community and how it seemed to be improving his mental disposition. Dr Robinson would also remind Anastasia that one day the Village would need a good young doctor like her when he was ready to retire. Anastasia would initially respond to Dr Robinson, who unequivocally informed him she would never return, but Dr Robinson did not share these responses with Louis for fear it would result in only dire consequences for his mind. However, as the years went by, and Anastasia read more about the benevolent work her father was performing around the Village the more Dr Robinson saw a softening in her attitude as she approached her graduation day from the Oxford University Medical School. Dr Robinson even accompanied Louis to watch Anastasia be awarded her degree in medicine with first-class honours, and subsequently, when the doctor quietly mentioned to Anastasia after the ceremony, he thought he would probably in about five years' time retire she subtly winked at him.

Notwithstanding the peace and tranquillity of life in Harlaxton Village, the world was otherwise in chaos. War in the Middle East had been raging out of control for many years. Just when it seemed one hostile tribe had been subdued by foreign fighters another group would rise up and commence taking hostile action against whomever they felt was responsible for their grievances in life. The Western nations were not listening to the commonsense advice being provided to them by people well apprised of the philosophy of these tribes. That advice was for the Western nations to refrain from attacking these groups as it was only causing more hatred, more anger, and more war. Millions of people had been displaced from their homelands because of the never-ending warfare.

Economic conditions worldwide were poor. The rich were getting richer, and the poor were becoming poorer. Louis had protected his wealth many years beforehand; his investments were safe, but he felt for the people of Harlaxton Village and its surrounding area as the economic conditions militated against their standards of living. Each year Louis donated a large sum of money to local charities in a bid to try and improve the lives of the not so fortunate members in the district. Because of his work with Dr Robinson, and now his two separate acts of charitable generosity, Louis was now considered by many people in the United Kingdom to be a philanthropist who now used money for charitable reasons. Louis even resumed reading newspapers to be informed about what was happening in the world, but he was always troubled by the reports of the ongoing hostilities in the Middle East to which he considered BMI were partially to blame for it commencing. Dr Robinson's idea had paid dividends in quelling Louis' inner demons of inferiority and lack of self-esteem, but he continued to suffer in silence with the inner demon he was too ashamed to fully reveal the details of to any person.

After graduating from Oxford University Anastasia had a veritable smorgasbord of leading hospitals and medical institutions offering her an opportunity to embark upon specialist medical training, but she had decided to adopt her own field of benevolent work by joining the World Health Organization to specifically train for providing medical treatment for the people injured in combat by the now uncontrollable outbreak of hostilities in the Middle East. Dr Robinson agreed with Anastasia's motivations to work in such a hazardous environment, but he recommended she immediately tell Louis. She had briefly returned to Harlaxton Manor to delicately break this news to her father.

They were sitting in the comfort of the lounge room of Harlaxton Manor enjoying their morning coffee and tea. "Daddy, I want to thank you for your support over the years, particularly your support of me during my time at university." Louis smiled in appreciation. "Thank you, sweetie, but you are after

all my child so of course I will always support you." Anastasia smiled back at her
father; she did not know how he would react to the news she was about to tell
him. "Dad, I am going to work overseas as a medical intern. I know you wanted
me to return home immediately to practice medicine here in Harlaxton Village,
but I have been accepted by the World Health Organization to work for them as
an intern on the battlefields of the conflict in the Middle East. My first posting
will be Afghanistan."

Louis almost choked on his coffee when he heard this news. "Anastasia. Are
you kidding me?" Anastasia remained calm. "No, Daddy, it is the truth. I want
to make a difference in this world by providing help where it is currently most
needed. There are thousands of people in need who are being injured each day
because of this never-ending war. I want to help them, Dad; I want to make
a difference." Louis was not convinced his daughter was thinking clearly.
"Anastasia, you are going to work in an extremely hostile and dangerous part
of the world. I know you want to make a difference, but you don't have to put
yourself in harm's way to do so." Unfortunately for Louis there was too much
of him in his daughter. 'No, Daddy. I am doing it. You are always writing to me
expressing your discontent with the way these people are being neglected so I am
going to do something about it. You went overseas when you were young."

Louis continued to try and change his daughter's mind. "Anastasia, I went to
Australia, not Afghanistan. It is dangerous and you could be killed." Anastasia
would not yield to her father. "I know it is dangerous Daddy, but I could be
killed here as well driving on a road. Who knows what the future has in store
for any of us? Look, this is something for me to look back on with pride, doing
something of a humanitarian nature. So, I am going, and I am not changing
my mind." Louis looked at Anastasia for a moment and realised his daughter's
heart had already left on the plane for Afghanistan and there was nothing he
could say to change her mind. Eventually, he nodded his head to acknowledge
his daughter's wishes. They changed the subject of their discussions, but Louis
now had a new beast emerging within his mind, Anastasia's safety.

One week later Louis travelled with Anastasia to Heathrow Airport. It had
been well over 20 years since Louis had been to this airport and so much had
changed. Security was even stricter than it had been in 2002 when he returned
from New York. Anastasia told her father that he did not have to wait to watch
her leave, but Louis was not going to miss out on one minute with his daughter,
he did not know when she would return or return at all. Louis held his little

girl tight to his chest to say goodbye; he did not want her to leave but he knew she would not stay. "Bye my little darling, please, please stay safe. I love you." Anastasia saw her father had tears in his eyes. Her eyes were also welling up with tears. "Bye, Daddy, I will miss you. But please, don't worry, I will be fine." She turned to walk away but then stopped and turned back around. "You thought I may not say it, but I love you too. I just want you to know that despite everything that has occurred, you are a good father." With those words being spoken Anastasia walked through the doors of the main terminal to be processed before eventually departing on her flight. She was gone and Louis would now not relax until she returned.

CHAPTER 53

For the next three years, Louis followed the news religiously to be informed about the war in the Middle East. Whether it be the news reports on the television, articles in a newspaper or news disseminated on the internet, it did not matter, he had to be informed about every detail of the hostilities that may affect Anastasia. Any news about any violence in Afghanistan or any other country in the Middle East which Anastasia was subsequently deployed to work in by the World Health Organization was obsessively examined by Louis.

On one occasion he was alarmed to read on the internet about a bombing of a World Health Organization medical facility in Iraq. Medical personnel had been killed. Louis quickly searched his computer for the most recent email he had received from his daughter. Fortunately, Anastasia was not in Iraq now as she had been redeployed to Syria. Louis felt relieved on this occasion.

He and Anastasia would regularly communicate by email, and she would tell Louis how appalling the loss of life was in the combat zones she was working in, and how sad it was to also see the destruction of ancient buildings, temples and homes. Anastasia's emails asserted the Western nations were just as much to blame for the death and destruction as the rebellious tribes they were fighting. On one occasion Anastasia sent Louis a photo of a school that had been destroyed by a missile fired by the Western armed forces. The school had been full of children who were still trying to gain an education despite the chaos around them. Out of 200 children only ten survived although they were suffering from severe injuries. The photo Anastasia sent to Louis depicted a young girl who was about ten years of age; she had lost her right arm as a result of the missile striking that school, and Anastasia had been treating her for many weeks. The little girl's right arm was the arm she wrote with, and Anastasia told her father her injured patient was now trying to teach herself how to write with her left hand. Louis shook his head in shame at what the world had become. He was mortified to read this barbaric loss of life at a school was caused by the Western forces who were relentlessly bombing and attacking this region of the world, and the rebel tribal groups who seemed to also display no hesitancy in killing their own people. As his death anxiety became increasingly triggered by each reported event of loss of innocent life Louis' thoughts embraced his entrenched rejection of mysticism. "The world is truly now a soulless place, if ever a soul even existed."

It was on the afternoon of 17 May 2027 that Louis finally could feel relieved about his daughter. When he turned on his computer and opened his email account Louis saw there was an email he had received from Anastasia several hours beforehand. Louis clicked on the message and started reading. The opening lines said everything he needed to know:

Dear Daddy,
After three years working on the battlefields of this ghastly war, I am proud to say that I believe I have done my share. I am coming home Daddy! You will be pleased to know that I am away from the danger zone. I am sending this email from Dubai. It is an interesting city to say the least but be rest assured I am safe. Oh, by the way, there was no way for me to break this news other than to be simple. I met a man and have fallen in love. He worked with me in Syria and Iraq. We are engaged to be married. I hope you like him.
I should be home in one month. I cannot wait to see you, Daddy.
Love always,
Anastasia.

Louis was delighted to read that his daughter was safe and that she was coming home. He was, however, surprised to read that she was engaged to be married. Not once in any of her previous emails had she even conveyed to him that she had met someone, let alone fallen in love.

One month seemed to drag on for an eternity for Louis. During that long period of waiting, he had come down with a bout of influenza, which he was still recovering from when his daughter and husband to be finally arrived at Heathrow Airport. He did not feel up to the trip to London, so Louis asked Andrew to drive down to the airport and to then bring home his daughter and her fiancé.

Even though he was unwell Louis was excited about the return of his daughter. He made sure that the servants had polished up Harlaxton Manor for the grand return. Approximately five hours after he had left for Heathrow Andrew returned in the Rolls. Louis was looking out of the living room window, and he could see Anastasia sitting in the back left passenger seat, but he could not see the face of her fiancé. Louis had asked Anastasia in an email for her to provide more information about the man she intended to marry but she had replied to him that it would be a surprise for him when they eventually returned to England, but Louis should not worry as her fiancé is also a doctor. Louis commenced to make his way to the main stairwell so that he could go down and greet his daughter and her mystery man. Louis was still weak because of his recent bout of the flu and the walk down the long flight of stairs was difficult.

As Louis approached the main entry door to the manor home, he heard the delightful tone of Anastasia's voice. Then, like an angel from heaven, she appeared in the doorway, a big smile grew all over her face as she saw her father now standing before her. Anastasia raced towards Louis in delight. "Daddy. Oh, Daddy, I am so glad to see you." Louis embraced his daughter and held her tight. "My darling little girl, you're home, thank goodness you're home." Louis stared at Anastasia's pretty face. She certainly had her mother's good looks and she had grown into a beautiful looking woman. He then detected that there was another person in the background but due to the daylight coming in through the main doors he could not see this person properly, other than it was a male. Anastasia very quickly turned her attention to her fiancé. "Walid don't be shy. Come on in and say hello to my father." Dr Walid Lari was a graduate of Princeton University in America. He was born in Pakistan, but his family had subsequently immigrated to the United States when he was 13 years of age. His family were not wealthy, but Walid had received a scholarship to study medicine at the prestigious Princeton University Medical School.

After graduating from Princeton University Walid had joined the World Health Organization to assist in providing medical treatment for those poor persons injured in the war zones of the Middle East. Walid had a nice face, his nose was fine, and his skin was not particularly dark, in keeping with his family's origins being from Northern Pakistan. Louis was initially surprised; he was not dismayed about Walid's Pakistani heritage, that was not the genesis of his surprise. The genesis of his surprise was the kindness of Walid's heart which found its expression in his eyes. Louis reached out with his hands and embraced Walid, taking the young man slightly by surprise. "Welcome Walid, welcome to the family." He then let go of Walid with his left arm to also include Anastasia in his impulsive embrace. The lingering symptoms of his bout of influenza were disturbingly evident to the two young doctors. "Don't mind me, I had a bad cold but with both of you being doctors I should be fine soon." Walid smiled at

Louis' pleasant little joke to welcome him as he politely removed himself from the loving embrace. "Thank you, sir, thank you for making me welcome in your home."

Louis was mortified to hear the word 'sir' being mentioned and he immediately dispelled any notion Walid may hold that he had to be subservient to him. "Sir? Walid, it is Louis. Call me Louis. Sir makes me feel like I am a schoolteacher." Walid was relieved to hear these words being spoken by his future father-in-law as he did not know how the man would react to him. "Thank you, Louis, thank you for saying that to me. Anastasia told me not to worry about meeting you, but I felt obliged to honour you as her father." Louis' main concern had been satisfied; his little daughter was going to marry a kindhearted man.

That evening Louis made sure the staff prepared a wonderful coming home dinner for Anastasia and to welcome Walid into the family. Anastasia loved duck chassis, so Louis made sure this dish was on the menu. Fortunately for him, Walid ate all types of meat, and over dinner Anastasia told Louis she and Walid were going to search for a house in the district to purchase and live in. Louis would not hear of it. "Why live in another house? This house is so big we could go a month without seeing each other." Anastasia queried her father's position. "Are you sure, Daddy? Walid and I do not want to get in your way." Louis was adamant. "Get in my way? Nonsense, it would be my delight for the pair of you to live here. Besides, this will all be yours one day so you both may as well start living here." In being so gracious Louis had also now triggered his death anxiety by mentioning his daughter's right of succession to Harlaxton Manor, which then caused him to become subdued in his mood for the rest of that evening. Anastasia subsequently asked Walid whether he detected her father's sudden change in his mood, but Walid had not detected it, and he told his fiancé' if there was such a change in her father's mood it was probably the effects of his lingering cold.

CHAPTER 54

In June 2028 Walid and Anastasia were married on the grounds of Harlaxton Manor. They had spent the past year obtaining the necessary licenses to practise medicine in England, and much to Louis' relief, they had also decided to set up a medical practice at nearby Grantham which would be solely to provide medical services to the poor. Dr Robinson had offered for them to both take over his medical practice in Harlaxton Village; however, Walid and Anastasia turned his offer down as they wanted to start something new, something of their own and most importantly, be close to a hospital where they could provide their services if a medical emergency arose.

The wedding was a very special occasion. Walid's family were flown out from Boston by Louis and at his insistence they stayed at the manor home, much to their pleasant surprise. Walid's father had passed away, but his mother and two sisters were now present for the proudest day of his life. His sisters dressed in modern attire despite their Islamic faith, but Walid's mother still wore her traditional ceremonial clothing which included a veil. Louis invited Anastasia's matriarchal second cousins, as well as Her's and Walid's former World Health Organization medical colleagues to whom the couple were so thankful for introducing them to one another. Even Charlotte, Anastasia's closest friend from school, attended the wedding. Once again, Louis did not spare any expense. He had a magnificent marquee set up on the lawn with tables covered in all the usual fine dinner settings of linen, silver, and crystal. A chef from one of London's finest restaurants catered for the wedding reception which would also be held on the grounds of the manor home that evening. To appease Walid's mother the marriage ceremony was jointly officiated over by an Anglican priest and an Islamic cleric; it was the juxtaposition of two different religious faiths which was otherwise missing in a very divided world. Anastasia wore a beautiful wedding dress, and, in keeping with the Muslim ceremony it was the traditional attire of a Pakistani woman when she married, save for one feature, Anastasia would not wear the veil over her face. She looked beautiful and Louis proudly watched his little girl marry Walid.

Subsequently, at their wedding reception both Walid and Anastasia spoke together, welcoming their guests to their special day. Then it came time for Louis' speech. Louis felt a strange nervous feeling in his stomach as he made his way to the microphone to speak; he had not spoken to many people since his regrettable days of working for BMI. He took a deep breath as he looked at the various faces of the guests, and then Louis found comfort when he saw his daughter's happy face. "My darling little girl. I am the proudest father in the world today. I only wish your mother were here in the flesh today as she too would be so proud of you. While I am not a particularly religious man, I do believe your mother is here in spirit today, watching on proudly as her daughter now embarks upon married life. May I also unreservedly welcome Walid to my family as my son. It gives me great pride that my daughter has married you Walid. I also welcome your family and look forward to many occasions meeting with them again. Ladies and gentlemen, I am also relieved that Walid has taken my little girl off my hands, as goodness knows there have been some occasions, she has made me worry. Not many of you may know that my daughter on one occasion became the local taxi driving service in this district and Anastasia I still don't know how you managed to drive my Rolls into a pond."

The crowd laughed as they watched Anastasia blush. Louis' demeanour then changed from that of glee to sober reflection. "All I can say about marriage is that you need to listen to one another. If you listen to each other your marriage will be fine. Observing the pair of you together as I have over the past year, I do believe that you listen intently to each other, and I do sincerely believe you will both enjoy a long and happy life together." Louis found he was becoming overwhelmed with emotion as his mind wandered back in time to the day he married Victoria in Sydney all of those years ago. He had to finish the speech quickly, for fear of breaking down in tears in public. "I wish you both a happy life together. To the bride and groom." Louis held up his champagne glass to the crowd who all joined in unison toasting the bride and groom. Anastasia's eyes were filled with tears of joy, as were Walid's. The rest of the evening was one of joy, music, and dancing. Later that night Louis sat in his room as he recalled the day's events. His little girl was married. Life was good. Perhaps now there would be peace in his life.

CHAPTER 55

Walid and Anastasia had their first child on the 31st of March 2029. It was a little girl and in honour of Louis' mother and her own mother, Anastasia decided to name her Adele Victoria Lari. Louis was overjoyed to have a granddaughter in his life. Unlike the early years with Anastasia, Louis was going to make sure that he would always be involved in the little girl's life. He watched with delight as little Adele turned one year of age. He was present when she took her first steps at the age of fifteen months in the ballroom of Harlaxton Manor. When Walid and Anastasia were working at the medical practice Louis would look after his little granddaughter. Adele had blond hair, unusual considering her father had dark hair but nature is a curious thing.

The morning of 1 December 2030 was cold and grey and the skies that day seemed to be more inhospitable than usual as Louis was sitting in his living room reading the local newspaper. He was deeply engrossed in a story about a proposed bypass road that may double the amount of traffic in the district, a proposal which concerned him regarding the splendour of the environment in which he lived. The story occupied Louis' mind to such a degree he did not notice Anastasia and Walid had both entered the room. Eventually, Anastasia made a noise to gain Louis' attention. Louis looked up from the paper to see both of them standing there. "Well, what do I ask gives me the honour of both of you coming to see me this morning?" Walid eyes appeared to be swollen, as though he had been crying for quite some time. Anastasia's face also gave away there was a problem. Louis was immediately concerned. "What is it? Is it Adele?"

Anastasia shook her head and then she sat next to her father on the sofa. She took Louis' left hand in her hands. Louis could see that Anastasia's eyes were beginning to fill with tears. "What is it sweetie, what is wrong?" Anastasia then took a tissue out from the pocket of her pants and wiped her eyes. She took a moment to think and then she spoke. "Daddy, there is no way to say this gently other than getting to the point. I'm dying Daddy. I have seen an oncologist, and he has confirmed that I have an aggressive form of breast cancer which cannot be cured. At best I will live to see Adele's 3rd birthday, but I cannot be saved."

Anastasia's tears began to flow freely down her cheeks. Walid sat next to his wife and commenced comforting her.

It was like a supernova had simultaneously exploded in Louis' mind and heart, and the most dreaded inner demon of his mind reared up to cause a cold shiver to go down his spine. He could not believe the horror of what he had just been told, his darling little girl was dying! "What? It can't be true, Anastasia? I won't let it be true. Are you sure Anastasia? I will pay for the world's finest doctors to treat you. You cannot die." Anastasia held up her hand to stop her father from speaking. "That was the second opinion, Daddy. Nothing can be done. It is same strain of breast cancer which killed Poppy." Louis shook his head and then he held his daughter close to him. "Oh Anastasia, please don't leave me. It can't be true. It can't be true."

With those words, Louis broke down in tears. He kissed his daughter on the head and then walked out the doors that led out to the Italian Gardens. He stared into the distance in disbelief. "Cancer, bloody stinking god damn cancer!" Louis' scream startled one of Adele's au pairs and Adele herself who were picking vegetables in a nearby garden. "Why, why, Anastasia?" Louis' screaming to the heavens would not deliver any just answer in his mind. His life in old age appeared to be relaxed, happy and normal as could be given all of the deficiencies of his mind. Now Louis was going to have to experience an event no parent should ever have to suffer, outliving their child. The skies became darker as the clouds closed in. A cold breeze blew across the Italian Gardens followed by freezing rain. Louis did not move, despite the au pair trying to encourage him to come inside as she quickly removed little Adele from the wind and rain. Adele's innocent eyes were troubled by the sight of her grandfather standing in the rain. He stood in the gardens with his head bowed, sobbing as he tried to come to terms with the harrowing fact that his daughter was dying.

Over the next 18 months Louis and Walid did everything possible to make Anastasia's life comfortable. She continued to work at the medical practice for twelve of those months, but then as the cancer started to take its deadly final course Anastasia gave up practising medicine. Once again, a room of Harlaxton Manor was converted into a hospital ward by Louis; he was not going to allow his little girl to be admitted into a hospital. On 31 March 2032, Adele turned three years of age. Although she was very weak and ill, Anastasia nevertheless made sure her daughter had a memorable birthday party. Over the next week her friends and family came to visit Anastasia to say their goodbyes to her. Walid hardly left his wife's side and right there beside him was Louis who had now slipped into the grips of the foulest depression of his mind as he watched this dreaded beast called death eat away at his daughter's once bright light of life.

It had been over one week since Adele's third birthday party. The entire household at Harlaxton Manor, including the staff, had been trying to get on with life as though it was 'business as usual', but realistically everyone knew that was not the case. The skies in early April were cold and grey, and the exterior colour and temperature of the world outside matched the sombre mood inside the manor home. Both Walid and Louis tried to maintain a positive and light atmosphere around little Adele, but the presence of impending death was in the air. Anastasia became bedridden by 7 April 2032; she was now totally reliant on others to clean her bodily waste, to bathe her and to dress her. On some occasions she would scream out in the middle of the night in distress from the ignominy of not being able to control her bodily motions. Both Walid and Louis assured her it was not an issue but deep down both men, in their respective roles as husband and father, were internally distressed to witness the cruelty of Anastasia's fast deteriorating body causing her such pain, so much sorrow and so much embarrassment.

On the evening of 12 April, it was all too much for Walid. The stress of watching his wife wrestle with her pain overwhelmed him and he had not slept properly for three days. Louis told Walid to go to bed as he could look after Anastasia for the rest of the evening. Although Walid initially resisted the offer, it did not take too much gentle persuasion from Louis for him to decide to seek some rest for the night. After Walid had left the room to go to bed Louis attended to assisting the nurse to turn Anastasia in her bed. After turning his daughter Louis asked the nurse to leave the room, so that he could be alone with his daughter. Louis' mind was labouring under the exigencies of his inner torment as he maintained his vigil with his daughter lying in her bed with her eyes closed, and just for a moment Louis thought that she had passed away, but to his relief Anastasia opened her eyes and looking over towards her father she immediately detected the concern on his face. "Dad, what is wrong? You look like you have seen a ghost." Louis looked into the eyes of his daughter, his relief that she was not dead now became quite visible on his face. "Nothing is wrong sweetie; I just did not want to wake you up." Anastasia knew he was lying, and she also knew from her medical training that in observing him for such an extended period of time he appeared to be wrestling with his mind. Anastasia with great effort lifted her right hand and ushered for her father to come over closer to the bed, so that she did not have to project her voice.

Louis brought his chair closer to the bed and his despair was clearly etched in his now substantially wrinkled forehead. Anastasia looked into her father's eyes, she only wished to speak to him about one matter, an issue she had wished to speak to him about since she was a little girl. As she knew she only had a limited time to live it was now more than ever that she wished to discuss this concern. Her eyes opened quite wide as she looked into her father's eyes, the question which passed her lips had remained unresolved from her childhood. "Why did you treat my Mummy like you did Daddy? Why did you make her cry?" Louis was mortified, as he did not in his wildest dreams believe that after all of these years his daughter would ask him this question. "What do you mean, Anastasia?" His disingenuousness did not fool her and Anastasia's eyes did not depart from looking directly into her father's eyes; her determination to explore this question could not be quelled by any form of disingenuousness. "Why did you shut her out of your life?"

Louis knew his daughter needed an answer to her question after all these years; it was like the hands of the clock had turned back in time to 9 September 2001. Louis pondered this question for a while. "Why did you, Louis?" The question he asked himself now unravelled a lifetime of fear of shame. After approximately 30 seconds of deliberating Louis was unable to completely open his mind. "Because my little darling, I was nothing more than a self-centred fool back then." Anastasia acknowledged the limited candour displayed by her father, but she still wanted a more in-depth explanation to be provided by him. "That may be so Dad, but why? Why did you act in that manner?" Louis realised that he would have to reveal more details about his inner self to his dying daughter than he had ever revealed to any person in his family before in his life. "Well Anastasia, you recall what I told all of those years ago about my upbringing?" She nodded her head, confirming that she recalled that conversation. "Well, you see, my little girl, my mind went on me at quite a young age. Sure, I could perform well academically and then in business, but everything that I had witnessed in my young life caused me to become extremely obsessive, extremely depressed." Anastasia nodded her head soaking up the conversation as her father finally spilt his heart out to any person. "Everything I went through, everything I saw, Anastasia, for some reason it resulted in me becoming morbidly preoccupied with my mortality, to the point whereby I was so terrified about it I would even contemplate, and, indeed once tried, to commit suicide. I was too ashamed to admit these fears and I cannot believe I am expressing them now. I also felt so inadequate and inferior to other people because of the way my father treated me that I felt I had to conquer the world financially, to be the richest person. My endless pursuit of money also partially assisted my fear of death, and I even considered at one stage using my wealth to try to facilitate medical science to make me immortal. But it is my death anxiety which I blame for making your mother cry."

Anastasia was facing her imminent death, she had gone through her own rollercoaster of emotions as she had come to terms with it, and now here was her father finally opening a door to his mind. "I understand Daddy, but why did you shut Mummy out? Why didn't you reveal this mental torment to her?" Louis knew there was no answer to the question, other than admitting to his daughter a further truthful fact to which he held great shame. "Because I turned to drugs to try and address the problem Anastasia, rather than turning to the one person who loved me so much that she may well have been able to have helped me through this mental torment." Louis thought for a moment about his misconceived use of cocaine as an escape mechanism for his mind and then he shook his head as he now was struggling to understand why he did not turn to his own wife for help. "Then again, I don't know, maybe nobody could have helped me. My fear of death was so profound, so intense, and so constant, that perhaps nobody could have helped me. I really don't know Anastasia, I was young, I was a fool."

Anastasia began to understand the extent of her father's suffering. "I now understand Daddy. Your mental torment must be excruciating, and also terrifying." Louis smiled at his daughter's undeniable wisdom. "You said 'was' so profound Daddy, do you no longer fear death?" Louis looked deep into his daughter's eyes. "After everything that has happened my little darling, you don't wish for a life like this one, but death? No darling, it still terrorises me." Louis' revelation had worn him down, but now he too had a question for his daughter. "Anastasia, I wish I could be brave like you. How do you manage to be so brave?" Anastasia was annoyed by her father's question. "Brave? Dad, you must be kidding! I don't want to die; I want to live! I want to live and watch my daughter grow up. I wish to live until an old age with my husband. Daddy, I am terrified. You don't have an imminent end date in front of you! I do!" Anastasia's eyes welled up with tears and she needed to be comforted. Louis could not but help to then take his daughter in his arms and hold her tight. Louis gently rubbed her back and stroked her head as he attempted to console his distraught daughter. Anastasia had always been such a headstrong and confident girl and woman, but tonight she was vulnerable, and in need of comfort.

She regained her composure, and she wriggled out of her father's embrace to once more look into his eyes. "I am sorry about my behaviour tonight, Dad." Louis tried to speak to tell her she was entitled to be upset but Anastasia held up her hand to stop any words from leaving his lips. "Why didn't you see a psychiatrist or psychologist about your psychiatric condition?" Louis was intrigued to hear her say he had a psychiatric condition. "What do you mean by psychiatric condition?" Anastasia's faint smile belied any serious acceptance of another disingenuous response from her father. "Don't tell me you didn't think it was, Daddy?"

He stubbornly shook his head when he knew his daughter's assessment was right. "Dad, Dad, Dad. You know you are mentally ill; don't try to bluff your way out. You could have been treated long ago; you did not need to suffer in silence like this. The starting place for such a fear is to understand it is an innate survival instinct of your subconscious mind. The philosophical treatment for that condition I learned while I was studying for my Bachelor of Medicine. Ask yourself the question, why do people worry more about what happens when they die but they don't seem to worry about what occurred before they were born?'"

That philosophical insight tore open the caverns of Louis' mind and finally let some faint light in, but his daughter had more to teach him that night as she saw her father's mind was still processing her first philosophical proposition. "Death is a part of life, but you can always extend that life by living a healthier one. You could live until you were 100 years old with the fortune you have acquired and who knows? Perhaps by the time you turn 100 years old medical science may have opened the doors to immortality for wealthy people like you. But don't build your hopes up Daddy for that medical breakthrough may be even a more remote proposition than religion's afterlife. However, you believe in science don't you Daddy?"

He cautiously nodded his head to confirm he did as he wondered where his daughter was taking his mind to. "Then there was something Mummy once told me when I was a very young girl while we were visiting the flower bed here where her ashes are now scattered. I don't know why her words have survived in my memories from such a young age but thank goodness they did as they assisted me during the most terrifying moments of working within a combat zone when my religious beliefs otherwise deserted me." Anastasia had to catch her breath for a moment. "Yes, so I must have heard this question being asked on television because I do not know why it came to my young mind at the time, but I asked Mummy at the flower bed 'What happens to us when we die?' She looked at me with that warm smile of Her's and proceeded to explain death to me in this manner, 'There is no such thing as death my darling, all of us live in our children, grandchildren and great-grandchildren. I will live forever in you, just like you and me will live on in your children one day. The best thing sweetheart is that with you both Daddy and I will live on in you. Just like these flowers, a new and maybe stronger person grows inside their children and grandchildren.' Later on, when I was studying science at school I learnt about how our bodies pass on our immortal chromosomes; they are an immortal imprint of our ancestors which then become the immortal imprint we pass on to our descendants. That was the message my Mummy told me when I was a child. That is why I have been so brave Daddy but thank you for letting me purge my mind of its trifling fear. Your supposed fear of death has otherwise been your safety mechanism Daddy to guide you safely to this moment of our lives, and it is your friend; it's not your foe now nor has it ever been. But I need you to keep on living Daddy so that you can assist me to keep on living within Adele. Would you do that for me, please?"

Louis nodded his head. His daughter's words not only took him on a philosophical journey that perhaps may turn the worst demon of his mind into a friend, but she also took him on a journey back in time to her young life, a time which he missed out on experiencing because of his greed to acquire great wealth. Victoria's words had equipped Anastasia's mind to conquer such primeval fear and now his wife was speaking to him all these years later through the memories of their daughter. Victoria's wisdom was now soothing his mind. Anastasia started crying again because she missed her mother, but her father would now cuddle her like when she was young a child and his embrace was comforting for her soul. She eventually fell asleep in Louis' arms, but he dared not to move for at least another hour. He held his daughter in his arms and looking down at her he remembered the face of the little baby he held in his arms so long ago. She was helpless then; she was once again helpless now. Looking at her sleeping face he only wished that she had more time on this earth to be with her family and to watch Adele grow. Louis only wished he had spent more time with Anastasia like this when she was a little child. A little flower perhaps had lost its petals too early, but now her father had to help a new flower grow.

At 7.00pm on 16 April 2032 Anastasia took her final breath; it was her 34th birthday but no candles would glow. Standing by her sides, holding her hands were Louis and Walid. The passing of Anastasia was too much for Walid; he broke down in tears and became inconsolable. Louis too was upset, but he was able to at least kiss his now deceased daughter's forehead and whisper in her ear. "Goodbye, my little sweetheart, goodbye. Your mummy is with you now." With those words being spoken Louis took Walid by the shoulders and helped him leave the room so that the medical staff could attend to dealing with Anastasia's remains. Louis and Walid then had to go and break the news to Adele that her mummy was now with the angels. Louis just hoped if that was true then Victoria was there to greet their daughter in the afterlife. Anastasia was a powerful force in Louis' heart from the moment she was born until the moment she had died. Louis returned to her room after the nurse told him she attended to ensuring his daughter's dignity was maintained in her eternal sleep and he noticed the hint of a little smile in her now lifeless lips, a symbol of peace in her heart and now her father's.

His emotions overwhelmed him as he stood to leave the room. When he reached her bedroom door to leave Louis stopped and turned around to look at his precious daughter one last time and in doing so his tears ran down his cheeks. "Goodbye, Anastasia. I will never stop loving you." Louis then left the room to let his baby rest in peace.

Three days later a simple funeral ceremony was conducted at the Anglican Church where Anastasia had accompanied her grandfather during her early life. Anastasia's remains were cremated and in keeping with her testamentary wishes her ashes were spread over the flower bed to join with her mother in bringing new life to that soil. The colours of the flowers of spring were vibrant this day but the mood was anything but colourful.

PART 6

"Flowers"

CHAPTER 56

The little girl asked her question again because the old man was lost in his thoughts. "What is wrong Grandpa?" Old age had not helped Louis heal any of his wounds and all his pain was trapped inside of a mind and body which had endured far too much for one person alone. He persevered to honour his promise to Anastasia to watch her grow within Adele.

Louis then wiped a tear from his eye and regathered his thoughts. It had been one year since Anastasia had passed away. He and Adele had gone to the flower bed to speak to Anastasia. He did not mean to yell at Adele when she was running towards the flowers, but he did not want her to accidentally tread on them because after all, this was the resting place for his wife and his daughter. He stood at the edge of the flower bed in silence and little Adele patiently stood by his side holding his right hand. Then Louis spoke carefully making sure that every word mattered. "My darling wife and daughter. How I miss both of you so much. I only wish that life's little vicissitudes had not taken you both so early from me, Walid and Adele. My darling Victoria, I tried my hardest to be a good father for our daughter, and you would have been so proud of her. You don't know how sorry I am for the pain I caused you. Anastasia, how we miss your glow around this house. Your beautiful little girl is growing up way too quickly and you should know that Walid is a very good daddy, but then again, you probably already knew that. The flowers are so beautiful today. They remind me of both of you so, so much and I love you both."

They stood in place looking at the flowers, and Louis' mind revolved around like the wheels of a poker machine as he contemplated his life; Manhattan's austere environment of his life with his father which he managed to escape the clutches of when others had not; the deceitfulness of the life he then lived trying to be anything but his father to only then ending up becoming a gentrified version of him; the years of his marriage he lost because of the dark shadows of his mind and the consequences of which was Victoria's demise; the heartbreak no parent should ever experience of watching their child die. Death. Everything about the word could still grip Louis' mind but Anastasia's words of wisdom would soften its blow.

Louis then knelt down in front of his granddaughter, and he looked in her eyes as he opened up his mind. "Your mother had a soul I always lacked Adele. I could be greedy whereas your mummy always wanted to share her kindness with the world; your mummy always made other people happy, but I could not make anyone happy. From the moment she was born your mummy was like these flowers; she was beautiful, bright, happy and brought joy to this world. She was always kind. Be like your mummy, but be better Adele, be a better person because nobody can stop you from making people even happier than your mummy could."

He paused for a moment because his emotions were getting the better of him, and he needed to wipe away more tears that were now flowing down his cheeks and into his mouth. "Don't waste your privilege my little sweetheart, make people be happy, make this a better world for everyone. Do you understand what I am saying, Adele?" She nodded and a warm smile spread over her face. Adele then threw her arms around her grandfather's shoulders and cuddled him, bringing warmth to his old, wounded heart. The warmth of her innocent embrace helped to stop the flow of his tears, but even such a loving embrace cannot ameliorate a lifetime of pain as those brush marks are an indelible dark stain on the canvas of his existence. Louis then took Adele by the hand and commenced walking back through the field towards Harlaxton Manor. As Louis walked through that field, he thought some more about the sorrow of what had been his life; his sorrow had been more than any person should ever have to endure. Perhaps, just perhaps, the demons of Louis' mind may now be his friends as he fulfilled his promise to watch Adele grow.

The last flower standing in that flower bed would eventually lose its petals and wither away, but perhaps emerging from its legacy a stronger new shoot would one day rise towards the sun in its place.